THE MOSAIC ARTIST

JANE WARD

Copyright © 2010 Jane Ward
All rights reserved.

ISBN: 1453860045
ISBN-13: 9781453860045

For my father

Acknowledgments

A phone call from Tiffany Sedaris on Mother's Day 2002 turned into a conversation about her idea for building and furnishing a house from scavenged materials. The concept rattled around in my mind for a while until it found an outlet in the character of Mark. Like Mark, Tiffany is an accomplished mosaicist and glass artist (*www.tiffanysedaris.com*), and her work offered me visual inspiration as I wrote Mark's story.

Even with such inspiration, this was a tough book to finish. So I was elated in 2004 when I printed off what I thought was the last clean, corrected page. Something nagged at me, though, and when an early reader had the same impression and suggested Shelley's story wasn't quite right, it was back to the manuscript for rewrites for me. Fortunately I never had to face any part of the process – from the very start to the book's real finish – completely alone:

Robin Yanucci, Pat Crawford and Pat Easterly, excellent friends, got me out of the house when I needed socializing and made me laugh with their own stories. Oldest (and most aptly named) friend Faith Van Dusen bucked me up when the work threatened to get me down. Bobi Crump, the abovementioned reader who offered up criticism of Shelley early on, opened my eyes to the story's real possibilities. Emma Ward proofread diligently.

My deepest thanks go to all of the other advance readers as well, the many book lovers who graciously accepted a copy of the manuscript and read it with an eye toward making a better story.

Love to my family who provide the beacon lights that help me out of my own mind at the end of every writing day.

I have taken liberties with the Cape Ann landscape and created houses and gravel roads where none exist, all for the sake of fiction. But Halibut Point State Park does exist and begs a visit for its granite quarrying history and rugged coastal beauty.

Funeral

Jack

The walls of the guest room are a rosy taupe. When Sylvie chose it I told her that the paint in the can looked like women's face makeup, an unnaturally pink flesh tone I felt would make the room too feminine. She laughed at my criticism, saying, "Don't make me angry and you'll never have to spend a single night in here." That was a challenge I happily accepted, and the memory of my success in that area makes me smile. The guest room was left to our overnight guests and, unless one of us was traveling, in twenty-three years of marriage Sylvie and I never slept apart.

Until now.

Sylvie visits me many times throughout the day, before she leaves for work; and for a few hours after work, if I am not too tired, she will sit with me and stroke the back of my hand. Or my face. But for the past three months she has slept alone upstairs.

This morning there is no one in the house but me. I am not often left alone like this, but Sylvie had an early meeting that she couldn't get out of, and the home nurse couldn't come any earlier than usual. Thirsty, I try to sit up, try to reach for the carafe of water on my nightstand, but I make it only as far as propping myself on my left elbow before I am overcome with such dizziness that I see stars. I drop back down to my pillow, resigned to wait for the nurse to come and spring me from the trap that my own body has become.

The room too is a trap. The curtains are heavy and dark, the blinds are down, the windows shut tight. When the nurse comes, after she pours the glass of water I crave, I'll ask her to crack open the blinds and let some sun in.

Not that the light will matter much to me by then. My effort to pour a drink has exhausted me and my eyelids flutter and close. The doctors had explained that there would be fatigue that would get worse and worse with time. The room is kept dark for me so that I may fall in and out of my naps. Naps! I am so tired all the time now that it feels like every minute could be a nap if I allowed. Three months ago I was moved from the master bedroom upstairs to this first floor guest room. The nurse told me, "It's getting too hard for you to manage the stairs," and she was right. My decline, once it started, came on with a vengeance. Then she told me her plan to make "a hospice room in the guest room." But I misheard. Whether because she mumbled or my hearing had failed, the words reached my ears distorted. I heard, "a hospice room in the *death* room" instead. I've thought of this room that way ever since, the Death Room. I suppose the words should have frightened me, or at least sobered me. But they didn't. I was resigned.

Resigned then, resigned now to my body failing me. Even after I was brought to my new bed and realized my mistake, death room seemed entirely appropriate, for I will die here.

There is light on the back of my eyelids. Is it sunlight? Or the final, beckoning white light, the end? For a moment I fear my time is up, until I feel the race of my heart – panic, surely a good sign. I had only dozed; for how long, though, I couldn't say. I open my eyes and see that the light is only the sun finally coming out from behind the morning clouds, light creeping in through the narrow gaps in the blinds. They are not as tightly closed as I had imagined. With even this littlest bit of light I can see bubbles collecting along the sides of the carafe of water on my bedside table, the dark outline of a dead moth trapped in the milky glass globe of the overhead light. I'm still alive. Alive enough to come to terms with the fact that I am dying a deeply flawed man. Alive enough to regret the harm my flaws have caused. But also alive enough to appreciate the irony of my life: that these personal flaws allowed me to enjoy a great happiness.

I committed the sin of falling in love with Sylvie while I was married to another woman. Sylvie and I married in a private civil ceremony one month after my acrimonious divorce was finalized. No haste. Present on our wedding day were two friends whom we asked to be our witnesses, Sylvie's solemn-faced parents, and the Justice of the Peace. That's it. Few people at work even knew we were marrying, although by the day of the wedding they surely knew we had long been a couple.

I wore a dark blue suit. Sylvie's dress was ivory, knee length, very simple. The Justice of the Peace stood in front of the desk in his small office, and we stood before him. When we contacted him to perform the ceremony, he had invited us to embellish the standard marriage text by writing some or all of our vows in the true spirit of the decade. Together Sylvie and I scanned a sample of the text he would use. Some phrases were familiar from religious ceremonies, but mostly the language was businesslike, overwhelmingly legal. In the end we decided we didn't mind.

"Legal is good," I said, laughing.

We agreed that anything personal we wished to say to each other had been or would be said in private. High on happiness, I chose not to fight with Kay about her decision to keep the children away from the wedding. A good friend had generously offered his Rockport house, the vacation home Sylvie and I had long been using for our getaways, for an entire week of honeymooning, and Sylvie and I thought at first that the children might even join us there. In the face of Kay's protests, we quickly saw that would never happen. We agreed instead that we would see Mark and Shelley in Rockport at some later date. We had stayed in this house already many times, and planned to stay there as often as we could manage in the future. There would be time for the children to join us. To keep my mind off the children's absence, I suggested a complete change of scenery, a honeymoon trip to New York City, something completely different than what we had originally planned, but Sylvie held out for the beloved cottage. "Rockport it is," I agreed. Only the two of us.

On our wedding day, after the Justice of the Peace finished and we comprehended that the Commonwealth of Massachusetts had recognized our union, I leaned in to kiss Sylvie, then stopped. I looked deep into her eyes, she into mine. "One thing," I said so softly that only Sylvie heard. "One more thing. Forsaking all others," I promised.

"Absolutely," she agreed, and repeated my words, "forsaking all others."

We kept our promise. For the next twenty-three years we successfully kept everyone just outside the inner circle that is Sylvie and Jack, Jack and Sylvie.

No longer limited to my lungs, the cancer roams everywhere inside me. I imagine the disease finding new breeding ground as I lie here, moving fast and without discretion. My doctors also warned me that I may have unbearable pain, but as yet I have nothing like the pain I was promised. Yet. When that time comes doctors will recommend at the very least morphine drips, but I don't want these either. Awareness up to the very end is an issue; my active mind – for thinking, talking, remembering – is all I have left. I don't want to cloud my memories. Sylvie understands. She vowed she would let me live these last days on my own terms.

She spoke the promise once out of the doctors' hearing as, stunned, we made our way to the car. Sylvie had driven that day and I can't forget her hands clenching the steering wheel as she fought against the hopelessness of my diagnosis. Six months. To a year. Maybe. To be fair, no one actually spoke the "maybe," but I saw the doubt in their eyes. The oncologist broke the news in a voice that balanced confidence with professional regret.

"How can you know?" Sylvie had demanded. "You don't know my husband!"

"No," he acknowledged. "But I know cancer."

"Arrogance, arrogance," Sylvie had muttered angrily once we were safe within our car, banging the steering wheel with the flat open palms of both hands.

In a rage she tried to start the car but couldn't, couldn't turn the key, couldn't remember how to drive. "What am I doing?" she asked me in despair.

I took her hands from the wheel and held them in mine. Instead of driving, we sat in the parked car without a word. In time I said to her, "I'm scared." I held out my hands, appealing. "I don't want to die."

"I'm scared too," Sylvie said. "Of life without you."

Sylvie

Jack looks deep into my eyes and I look into his. "One thing," he says so softly that only I can hear. "One more thing." And then his eyes close, he takes one shallow breath, and he dies.

"What?" I whisper, then louder, "What one more thing?"

A kiss, a profession of love, a change of plans, a secret, a revelation? (*I forgot to tell you* ...) A plea for another minute, second, or nanosecond? (*I'm not ready* ...) I feel like shaking Jack's corpse, I feel like screaming, "Not one more thing; many. There should be *many* more things." Walks, drives into the office, work, discussions. Breakfasts, lunches, dinners. Making love, sex, fucking. So many things.

I lie down and rest my head alongside his one last time and look at his profile, the sharp nose, the hollows under his cheekbones. I press my face into Jack's pillow. There, under the Tide fresh scent of the recently laundered pillowcase, I find it: Jack's smell. That is what is left for me, I think, the rank and sour odor of decay. The smell of death lingers, a smell that no amount of the nurse's disinfectant nor my orange oil or wood polish or laundry detergent could obscure. As he weakened, as he physically slipped farther away from me, this smell was practically all I had left. That, and my memories.

Maybe some of Jack has sloughed off in this very bed. I won't change the sheets. Perhaps some of his cells had splashed with shower water, only to stick to the sides of our tub. Never again clean the tub. Maybe pieces of Jack have joined dust particles suspended in the air, settled, filling in around every piece of furniture, all the nooks and crannies and surfaces bound by walls and ceiling.

I find I don't feel so alone when I think of myself doing something as natural as breathing, helping pieces of Jack enter my lungs.

Shelley

Mark and I stand graveside holding hands, our fingers linked like best friends, like children. Today we bury our father, and with our father now dead, our mother long dead, we stand here as each other's only close blood relative in a strange new parentless world. We've been inseparable since childhood; our link is as solid and real as our tightly joined fingers. The bond courses on beneath our skins too, unseen but felt. Bonds visible and invisible, both are persistent and intermingled, as codependent as flesh and blood.

Although we are grown – I will be forty in this new end-of-a-decade year – this death makes us feel young again, and powerless, and we cling like some unsettled but plucky orphans in a Victorian novel, determined not to be separated. Today it feels like Mark and Shelley against the world.

My stepmother, Sylvie, had called me in my classroom at the end of Thursday's school day. My father's death was not unexpected. When I last visited, his breathing was labored, his speech difficult, his skin gray and waxy. The news rattled me anyway. I barely remember replacing the phone receiver in its dock on the wall, or taking the few steps and dropping into the chair at my desk.

"Dead," I said out loud, the words rudely breaking the stillness around me.

"Mrs. Bennett?"

I looked up and blinked my eyes into focus, only then remembering I wasn't alone in the classroom.

"Oh. Asya."

In the wake of the phone call, I had forgotten my student was in the classroom with me, doing her homework under my supervision as she did a few afternoons a week while she waited for her father, Ian, to come and collect her. Asya Samuelson: blonde and pale to the point of looking anemic, which, I considered time and again, she probably had been when she first transferred to my class. Even her eyes were washed-out looking, a watered down green. These eyes were now trained on me.

"Asya, I'm sorry. I had some news," I told her. "Some sad news."

She nodded. She never spoke much in school, even to me, and I believed she felt more comfortable with me than she did with almost anyone here.

Asya had joined my class in December when her mother surprised Ian, from whom she had been divorced, first by giving him full custody of their child, then by splitting almost immediately for the lure of Big Sky and a new boyfriend living there. By moving in with her dad, Asya had changed towns and homes and, of course, schools. Ian was able to spend a lot of time helping his daughter adjust to her new living situation. He is a potter and his studio is in his home. But when it came to Asya's education, there were significant gaps in her knowledge because of the change in schools, and she couldn't concentrate well enough to get up to speed on her own because she missed her mother. Missing a parent was something I knew more than a little about.

I had been eager to help for other reasons too. In many ways helping Asya reminded me of helping my brother when we were younger. Asya was a lot like the younger Mark: extremely sensitive and solitary, dreamy instead of focused. She was shy and uncomfortable with new people and I also hoped to help her overcome that shyness.

Her pale green eyes stayed trained on me, and in them I could see all sorts of questions: *What bad news? Are you all right?* These were questions I couldn't bring myself to answer. Living in her father's home was still too new, being abandoned by her mother too recent. Given all the uncertainty in her life, I didn't want to even suggest that parents might die.

"Everything's all right," I told her instead. "I'll be fine.

"You know," I continued with a quick glance at the clock, "your dad will be here any moment. Why don't you go to your locker and get your coat and all your other homework together? That way, you'll be ready to go home when he arrives."

Standing, Asya closed her book and the notebook she was using for her homework and slid both into her backpack. When she reached the classroom door she turned and said, "I'm sorry, Mrs. Bennett. I'm sorry you're sad."

"Thank you, Asya. I'll be fine, I promise. Now, scoot."

When Asya left, I dropped my face into my hands. For the second time in my life my father had left me and this time he wasn't coming back.

"Dead," I said again, on the heels of a large exhale. I uttered the word and then I fell silent, trying to recall my father as he used to look. His ever-present smile in these recent years, the thick and dark but graying hair, and the robust good looks I remember from my childhood, my teens, even a year ago. But the only pictures I can call to mind are those of my father on his deathbed, in the last few weeks of his illness: the tight lines of pain around his mouth, the gauntness of his cheeks, the angles of bones and ridges of veins protruding through his skin as he wasted away.

"Shelley?"

I looked up from my hands to see Ian standing in the doorway, here sooner than I even predicted. Shelley. We had long since dispensed with titles and last names. Mr.? Mrs.? Out the window. At some point in the past few months we had become friends, allies united to help Asya. But more than that, we were comfortable with each other. Improbable, maybe even inexplicable, but true.

"Ian," I said, and I stood. "I'm sorry. I just– " I began then paused, taking a minute to compose myself. "Asya's out at her locker. I told her to get ready for you."

"What's wrong?" he asked, ignoring me. He took a few steps into the room and the closer he got I could see that his eyes, like his daughter's had been, were full of concern.

Our friendship took root from the start with common experience – I could relate to abandonment and divorce – as its fertile ground. I had confided in Ian about my father's illness during a conference not long after Asya arrived in my classroom, only a couple of months after I learned the news about the cancer. I felt I had to. I had been distracted at the parent-teacher meeting from the get go; my father's decline post-diagnosis had been swift. My intent that day had been to concentrate on Asya – there had been some setbacks, she had begun to neglect her homework – thinking that I could use work as a focus as I always did, a way to keep my mind from obsessing over the inevitability of my father's death. Instead I had found myself apologizing for my distraction and then explaining it. More than explaining, I had confessed my fears. This was unusual for me, sharing burdens.

But there was something about Ian, the way he paid close attention when I spoke perhaps, or perhaps the fact that he didn't know me well enough for me to hide behind assumed strength. Or perhaps because he too had been left. Whatever the reason,

I spilled and Ian was sympathetic and comforting. Consequently he knew more than anyone, even more than my husband, about how distressed I was over the prospect of losing my father yet again.

"It's my father," I told him. "My father died today."

With two more broad steps he stood right in front of me. He opened his arms wide enough to draw me in. I had never been embraced by a student's parent and it should have felt awkward, but it didn't.

"My father is dead," I said and, finally, feeling safer than I had in months, I cried.

Our father is dead.

I squeeze Mark's fingers in mine.

It is late April, cold and wet; the ground is mushy underfoot, finally thawed after a lingering winter. Any earlier in the month and the ground would have been frozen solid and hard to break, resistant to accepting the coffin. I wear a sensibly warm black wool dress, black stockings, and unattractive flat-heeled black shoes, trouser shoes, chosen at the last minute for the muddy ground. My wool coat is loden green, dark enough for a funeral without being black.

Mark's rough hands are bare. I keep one of his hands warm by holding it in my own; the other Mark shoves into his pants pocket. He wears jeans and work boots that he neglected to tie at the top. The laces dip in the mud each time he shifts on his feet. His sweater is the same color as my coat, as if on purpose. In the damp cold, Mark's cheeks and the tip of his nose are red, but the short, rather thick and ropy scar running along his chin blanches, stands out silvery white, as if no blood flows there.

Earlier in the day I had tried unsuccessfully to convince Mark to put on a coat. He did, however, pull on a black knit cap just before leaving the house for the chapel. As he passed through the front door, I stopped him and attempted to neaten him by turning up the cap's unraveling edge. Mark pushed my hand aside.

"You look like a thug," I told him as he breathed in his first gulp of cold morning air on the front step. And yet I smiled with the indulgence I always feel toward my baby brother, showing that I really didn't mean the reproach. My husband, Steven, looked at me and rolled his eyes; I could only shrug in reply.

"I am a thug," Mark in turn admitted, "and a slob. What would Dad say? Oops! Forgot. Dad's dead. He now has the ultimate excuse for not giving a shit. Good for him." Mark then smiled and showed me his white but imperfectly aligned teeth.

"Mark." I spoke his name in a cross between a whisper and a plea.

My older daughter, Margaret, had been standing between us at the door, and her eyes widened in amazement. I knew she hoped for a moment that she would get to witness her mother flipping out. Knowing Margaret, she would have committed his sarcastic tone to memory, rolled the sound of sarcasm around her brain, enjoyed its zing, promised herself to test its power sometime soon, and silently she would have congratulated him. *Cool, Uncle Mark.*

But Margaret stood to be disappointed; I wouldn't be tested today. Instead of upbraiding him for his lack of respect, I had pulled Mark closer to me, embraced him.. I lifted a hand to the back of his head and gently drew his face down to my shoulder then to my lips. I kissed his cheek. When he straightened up, even Margaret could see that his eyes were wet.

"Let's just get this over with, Shell," Mark had said, pulling the knit cap further down on his forehead, obscuring his eyebrows, shadowing his dark eyes.

Mark and I now stand hand in hand in front of our father's coffin. My husband, Steven, stands behind us; our two daughters flank either side of him; he has a protective arm around each girl. This funeral for their grandfather is their first. Before we all left for the chapel, Steven told me he felt that Margaret, at fourteen, would probably be old enough to attend, but he worried for nine-year-old Libby, whose vivid imagination hardly needs populating with more ghosts. I take my attention away from the service and Mark for a moment and turn to see Steven pull both girls closer, to see that both girls let him.

Mark and I lost our mother ten years earlier so now, even in light of our advanced ages, we are orphans, real orphans. We had a dress rehearsal for this feeling of abandonment many years ago, first when Jack moved out and married Sylvie, and then, shortly after, when our mother stopped leaving the house, stopped caring for herself, stopped taking care of us. Jack's death is simply a formality.

Despite the cold and damp, Jack has a grand turnout for his funeral. Such a large gathering is what he would have wanted and what we all could have expected. Together with his second wife, Jack Manoli cultivated friendships and business relationships with care, and within this world of work and friends he was well liked. Jack understood the power of personality in running his business. As did Sylvie. In 1976, after working for years in a big, well-established advertising agency, Jack split to form his own upstart boutique firm. Sylvie drove their success through her aggressive marketing of their personalities — Jack's geniality and her own special brand of allure — as much as the work product.

Today's attendance boasts scores of truly grieving friends and supportive business associates. But there is one person who does not like Jack, who cannot forgive Jack his human failings, or Sylvie

The Mosaic Artist 17

for taking our father from us, and he stands firmly at my side. Mark and I belong to Jack's first life, the life he took on after finishing college, the one he ultimately rejected for Sylvie.

Sylvie now stands on the other side of the grave among all the floral arrangements that traveled from the chapel with the coffin, and I see Mark sneak a look at the woman standing directly across from him, her sleek blonde head, her red-rimmed eyes. Wife Number Two, he calls her when talking to me, pointing out how absurd "Stepmother" would be. Sylvie is, after all, only eight years my senior, in age and attitude more like an older sister than a parent. Mark persists in thinking that Wife Number Two took the best parts of our father – his time, his attention, his physical presence – until Jack had nothing left to give his children. Sylvie had shed copious tears last night at the wake, and after, still weepy, she had tried to pull Mark and me aside. Mark strained away as if Sylvie were a heat he couldn't bear or a smell he couldn't stomach. Sylvie then had pressed something into my hand and closed my fingers into a tight fist around the object. She held onto my balled fist for a moment, met my eyes with her own. "It's for the cottage," Sylvie said as I withdrew my hand, opened it flat, and looked down at the key that had been cutting into my palm. "The cottage is yours," Sylvie continued. "He wanted you and Mark to have it. Use it. Or sell it. It's what your father wanted."

Over the past several years, after the death of my mother and the birth of my second child, I had reached a fragile but growing peace with my father and his second wife. Unlike Mark, I chose simply to call her Sylvie. Yes, once I had been as hurt as Mark, but I was older and had responsibilities that left me little time to stay upset. As I entered my father's home and life with more frequency over the last few years, I came to appreciate Sylvie's feelings for Jack, how strongly she loved him and cared for him. I felt for Mark too, and his pain begged my allegiance, but I couldn't ignore that my father was a happier man in his second marriage. Recalling last night's wake – Sylvie's proximity, the intimacy of her words and her grief, the unexpected gift of a house – I look again at my brother. He has dropped his gaze to his own feet. His hand in mine feels cold; I should have insisted he wear a jacket.

For the twenty-three years following our parents' divorce, Mark has remained estranged from our father. When Jack left us, Mark felt bitter at being set aside until, finally, he rebuffed all attempts to be drawn in to Jack's rebuilt life. Mark couldn't forgive. He begrudgingly drove out from Somerville to the western suburbs of Boston only after I telephoned and begged him to come. At first, Mark refused, "no" being by now a reflex. I asked again. As I waited on the phone for Mark's answer, I heard the voice of his live-in girlfriend, Jen, in the background telling Mark he would live to regret such a rash decision. Mark laughed at her.

With patience I repeated my request. I asked my brother one last time to come for me, to help me, and eventually he relented and came to me because this is what we have always done for each other. He drove out to the wake last night, and to the funeral this morning. He made both trips alone. When I asked about Jen, Mark told me that she had offered to come with him, but he had insisted she stay home.

Next to me, Mark shifts on his feet in his loosened boots. I imagine he wishes he were at home right now, not sitting quietly with Jen but rather in his art studio smashing the glass he needs for one of his mosaics, for the feel, the sound, and the satisfaction of doing something destructive.

Mark's restlessness only feeds the anxiety I feel for him, have always felt for my brother's well-being, and makes it grow and swell until I feel pressure building inside my chest. The pressure of this untimely death, coming just as I was beginning to feel at ease with my father after years of uneasy relations, and coming long before Mark was ready to reach any kind of peace. The pressure I feel to manage the difficulty between Sylvie and Mark, to soften Sylvie's arrogance for Mark, to filter Mark's antagonism for Sylvie. There is nothing new about the pressure of bearing Mark's anger, regulating it for him, or of listening to my husband's impatience with this role I play in Mark's life.

"He's a grown man, Shelley. He can't be your responsibility any more," Steven would say time and again.

Right at this moment, standing at the still open grave, I think of hearing the news of Jack's death in my classroom. I think of my student's father, I think of Ian hugging me as I cried for my dead father. I was crying but I had felt calm. I had been comforted rather than doing the comforting. Comforted and calm and safe and yes, of course, sad, but also completely worry-free.

I think of this moment, savor it for its novelty and for the protected way it made me feel, if only briefly, and put it out of my mind. I have no time now to be anything but strong.

The service comes to a close. Under his breath Mark repeats to himself, "Wife Number Two, Number Two, Number Two," as a sort of mantra to block out the eulogy given by my father's good friend, his last words about Jack and Jack's character, white noise to muddy Sylvie's soft sobs. Mark's warm breath and the cold air meet and mingle, and small misty clouds issue with the words from his lips. Before we leave the cemetery workers to shovel the damp earth, Sylvie places a flower on Jack's coffin as she says a private goodbye. Her lips move in a silent prayer or a message of love. I would say a final goodbye too; given the chance I like to do what's right, what's respectful and seemly. But Mark holds my hand tighter, readjusting his grip until our arms are entwined and I am held firmly at his side. I can't leave him, and maybe that's his plan.

Sylvie allows herself to be led away from the grave by some friends. As she passes, other people in the crowd hug her or clutch her hands or wish her well and move on to their cars. Behind his owlish glasses, Steven's eyes widen; he is appalled that Sylvie is left to fend with strangers rather than family. Steven, like me, prefers to do what's right. Before Sylvie and I had finalized the funeral plans, even before I telephoned my principal at the small private school where I teach, Steven had arranged for someone to take his classes and asked to reschedule an English Department meeting. I married Steven in large part because of his adherence to decorum. I took his measure years ago and realized that even if he came to loathe me, he would never leave me; with his belief in family, in duty and fidelity, he could never leave his children. Even now he makes the right overture. With a quick glance back at me pinned to Mark's side and unable to move, a moment during which I can only mouth, "Sorry," Steven shepherds Margaret and Libby to the car. Over my shoulder I watch as he stops to intercept Sylvie, as he gives her a hug, as he manages to lead her to our station wagon for the ride back to the house so she won't, for a short time anyway, be alone.

At my side Mark curses.

"C'mon, Mark." I nudge him.

"Let them get ahead of us. I'll drive you back, okay?" he proposes.

"Okay."

We stand in silence a moment longer as Mark worries the ground with his boot heel. Finally he speaks.

"Fuck," he says one more time. "This fucking death thing," he says. "Up to now I could pretend . . ." He seems to search a moment for the right words.

I urge him on. "Pretend what?" I ask.

"That Dad and Sylvie didn't exist. Together, separately. And I did a good job of it too." Mark takes my elbow and we start walking away from the gravesite. He gives a brief snort of laughter. "He dies, I suddenly have to pay attention."

"I needed you to be here," I remind him.

"Yeah, I knew there was a reason why I came," Mark answers. After a moment's pause, he stops walking. He asks, "Do you want it, Shell?"

"Do I want . . . what?" I ask, bewildered.

Mark speaks impatiently. "Dad's house. Do you want the house?"

Given his retreat from Sylvie last night and his total withdrawal from Dad, I had imagined Mark would avoid the subject of the house. "Oh, well, it's Dad's," I stammer, flustered and unsure how to answer. Truthfully, I would miss my father and the house might keep him present for me, but I couldn't hurt Mark with the blunt truth. I hedge. "It's something of his, and I suppose he thought we should have something."

"Right," he answers with a sarcastic laugh.

"You must be cold," I say to avoid a confrontation, and I rub his arm, feeling his sweater sleeve warm with the friction. "Let's walk to your car. Steven's waiting." I pull on Mark's arm, hoping to lead him away from this place and to distract him from these thoughts.

But Mark's train of thought is undeterred. "He could have given it to Wife Number Two." He motions with his chin at Sylvie's back as she disappears into my Volvo wagon.

"The house?" I ask.

He nods. "But she got everything else, didn't she? What would she need a fucking cottage for?"

"Mark—"

"For that matter," he continues, ignoring the caution in my tone, "*I* don't need a fucking cottage. Do you?" Mark turns his dark and challenging eyes on me. "*You* want it?" he asks, his voice rising. "Will you *use* it? *Could* you?"

"I don't know," I say, another stall. When Sylvie explained the presence of the key in my palm, I admit I had considered it. I had spent vacation days there with Dad and Sylvie, although Mark didn't know that, so I had allowed myself to imagine a vacation with my family in our second home, beach romps under a bright sunshine. And though our father wanted both of us to enjoy living there, Mark reminds me that this will be no easy idyll. My unspoken admission looms over us.

Standing outside the driver's side of the Volvo, Steven calls to me.

"Are you coming?" he asks, his hands cupped around his mouth like a bullhorn, his call breaking the awkward silence.

I wave him on. "You go on ahead," I reply with a dismissing wave. "I'll ride with Mark." For a minute Mark and I watch as Steven lifts his hand in return, then steps into the car. Soon he steers the station wagon out of the cemetery. I watch Sylvie's blonde head above the seat back receding into the distance. I sigh. "Maybe I won't be able to set foot inside the cottage. To tell you the truth, I'm so worn-out I can't think right now."

"Well, I don't want it. But I'm glad she doesn't have it either."

I don't want to argue with Mark or provoke him. "Let's not worry about houses," I urge. "Or funerals. Or stepmothers. Deal?" I tug at my brother's sleeve. "Drive me home, Mark. Come back with us and have something to eat."

"Something to eat," Mark echoes, but he doesn't move. Still staring off into the distance though the car is now gone, Mark says, "Why do people always need to be fed after a funeral?"

"I don't know," I admit, "but it certainly gives me something to do." I offer Mark my hand. "I love you, Mark, you know that, don't you? Why don't you come home with me?"

"I'll drop you off. I should get back to my own home," he says and he sounds far away. He does, though, accept my hand and we begin to walk to his car. "I have work to do. And Jen's expecting me," he adds.

"If it's seeing Sylvie that bothers you, I'll make sure to keep you apart. I'll keep her—"

Mark cuts me off. "Drop it."

"Okay," I say. "It's dropped." We reach his car hand in hand, although Mark's grip has become uncomfortably tight.

"Can we talk later then?" I ask as we come to a stop. "When we're both more relaxed? We have decisions to make."

"What decisions?" Mark asks. "As far as I'm concerned, there's no 'decision' to make. But hey, you want the house, you take it," he challenges. "It can rot for all I care."

"We could sell it," I suggest. "Rent it out. You could probably use the money," I remind him.

"I don't need a thing from the old man, not a house, and certainly not his money."

"You'd rather let the house go unused than—"

"Make money off it? Live in it?" he interrupts. "Damn straight."

Although he is short with me, I have to smile. "You hold a grudge better than anyone I know."

Unexpectedly, Mark smiles back. "Damn straight," he says again. For a minute I am encouraged, hopeful that his mood is changing. But not for long. Mark takes his hand from mine, leaves me, and walks the last few steps to his car alone. "Better than you, anyway," he calls back to me without breaking his forward stride.

Mark

With the windows tightly rolled up against the cold of an April day, my car quickly filled up with a haze of thick smoke. I cracked my window a couple of inches. No point in attracting the cops' attention. That would just about make my day: driving to a funeral and getting busted on drug possession charges. I was high enough just then to smile as I imagined explaining the extenuating circumstances to a cop. Or more likely a defense lawyer. *My father died; I'm on the way to his funeral; I hated the guy; therefore, I lit up. So I smoked an illegal substance and operated a motor vehicle under the influence; so what? Makes perfect sense to me.*

Reduced to those few statements, I made it all sound so simple that I laughed out loud in my car. But understand this: without the grass I wouldn't've even been smiling, because none of this is very funny.

My father, whom I hadn't spoken to in a number of years, died at the end of last week; today is his funeral and we're about to bury him. At the wake last night I watched my sister Shelley as she watched me back for signs of my flaring temper. For good reason. I never forgave my father for walking out on us and leaving us for Sylvie.

My anger had eased up over the past three years, though. What happened was, I met my girlfriend, Jen. She's an art photographer who encouraged me to pay more attention to my own work as a mosaicist and sculptor. We started working together, then living together, and suddenly I had too many good things to think about. I had tons of new ideas and began working on a new series of mosaics and glass sculptures. A gallery agreed to sell my pieces. I had a taste of living without constantly hating, without the object of my hatred in my sight, and I liked it. I felt better than I had in years. It was as if there was a shelf life for anger, or a half-life, like with radioactive elements, and from one day to the next I thought about Dad one half as much as the day before, until eventually I completely ignored his existence. I mean, he's been as good as dead for me for the past couple of years.

Then Jack had to go and die for real. Fuck.

I stuck with Shelley at the wake last night, or she latched herself on to me. Both, probably. And from my safe place, I looked over at Sylvie first, then beyond her at my father stretched out in his coffin. Seeing them together for the last time made me think of how it felt when I was twelve and seeing them as a couple for the first time. Then, when Sylvie spoke to me and Shell like she had some place in our lives, as if we should pay attention to her, my anger came pyramiding back. Forget gone, forget even diluted; the anger had only been sleeping, waiting for the right moment to wake up: the moment when I saw Sylvie again and she tried to press a key on me to a house that Jack, after years of giving us nothing but checks to cover his absence, felt his kids should have. His present to us, she said.

There's nothing quite as touching as a deathbed guilty conscience.

"Keep the fucking house," I felt like shouting at Sylvie as she did Jack's dirty work. "If you tried forever you couldn't give me anything I need." Shelley kept a close eye on me. With a look, with her hand on mine, she reined me in, and in the end I said nothing.

Instead I thought, "Jack Manoli? Fuck him," and I walked away, leaving Shelley to deal with Sylvie and the problem of the key.

I share my anger with Shelley because she has always let me. I know she understands that with any mention of Jack and Sylvie a kind of static buzzes in my ears and bile churns up from my gut. Shelley understands that their names in my mouth feel like the spew of a bad case of food poisoning. Like she did when we were younger, Shelley will bear some of the weight of my anger so that I don't have to carry it alone.

Of course the grass helps too.

High, I can stand here at the gravesite and detach myself from thoughts of my dead father and my stepmother. Instead I let my mind go to work, deconstructing Sylvie down to pieces of brittle black and yellow glass until she no longer exists as a flesh and blood person with soft edges. I like this project.

As I said, I am an artist, a mosaicist. I work with glass and ceramic and porcelain and china, anything breakable. Since the age of twenty-two I have earned decent money through my art, mostly with the design and sale of anything from mosaic tabletops to tiles for garden paths. I have also designed and completed wall murals and mosaic entryway floors for well-off couples renovating old two-family homes in Cambridge and Somerville and East Arlington. It bugs me that these people are more concerned about whether the color and design of a mosaic will match their home decor, but for the right money I am usually only too happy to oblige. And I have sold these pieces for ridiculous amounts of money.

Design mosaics — working with uniformly cut tiles to make uniform patterns emerge, mathematical in their precision — that's artisan work, often beautiful, but so predictable. Sometimes I lay small square ceramic mosaic tiles. Sometimes I cut large sheets of pre-fab glass into geometric shapes with my glass nippers and get the same effect. All it takes is a pattern: a cross, knotted rings, a compass rose. Even when I cut glass into life shapes like leaves or fruit for decorative borders on table tops or floors, I'm still doing design work, a no-brainer for anyone with an eye for pattern and color.

Up until a few years ago I was also selling these same rich types top-of-the-line stereo components. That retail job was my steady and reliable source of income, and I was struggling to balance work I wanted to do with work I had to do. I wasn't rich. I'm still not, but since moving in with Jen, I haven't worked anywhere but the studio. I still hustle a lot of home design projects but I can be choosy, and most recently I've even made money by placing my art mosaics in group shows and galleries and selling them. Later this spring I've got a show coming up, my first really big show where I share the spotlight with only one other artist, a glassblower.

Fitting together pieces that vary widely in size and shape is the biggest challenge in art mosaics. It's something like putting together a jigsaw puzzle, because you have to find the one right piece among all the broken glass to fit in a particular space. And also like a jigsaw puzzle, when my pieces fit the space they complete a picture, one that comes close to the picture I've carried around in my mind. The comparison ends there, though. The example of a puzzle won't properly express the art of mosaic work, not when a puzzle's cardboard is preprinted and die-cut, and my glass or ceramic is scavenged and broken by hand. I must make the image appear out of nowhere, from nothing but unrelated shards and an idea.

For my projects I need more ceramic and glass than anyone can possibly imagine. There are stores where I could buy tiles or sheets of all colors of glass. But where's the challenge in buying my materials? What I do instead is, I pick trash to find the materials I use in assembling my mosaics and sculptures.

In a homeowner's weekly trash barrel in a crowded urban place like Somerville, I'm likely to see halfway decent furniture, children's outgrown toys, ten-year-old stereo systems, books. Mostly, though, what I go out in search of now is glass and discarded ceramic or porcelain or china. To find glass I raid recycling bins on alternate trash weeks. I end up with brown glass, green glass, clear glass, and occasionally a kind of cloudy, milky white. Dishware and stuff, anything with color or patterns, I usually find by picking through trash barrels or cardboard boxes set out next to the barrels. Willow ware, blue delft knock-offs, colorful and highly decorated mugs and plates from Italy or Portugal: it's amazing what people throw away, and astounding how much of their trash I can use in my work.

Someday I'd like to create an entire home from building materials and furnishings that I reclaim from the trash.

Jen and I met on a trash day late in the summer of 1996, and we found we had two things in common right from the start: we both were artists, and we both picked through the weekly trash for items we could use in our art projects. She used the whole pieces she found — bowls, books, cast-off tools, whatever — as props in her photographs while I only scavenged breakables and then broke them.

A good part of my life has been spent smashing the things I collect, and I love it, the sound of breaking, the feel of taking a swing. Sometimes I wrap glass in a bath towel, gathering the towel corners up like a sack and beating the package against a hard surface. The danger is minimal: the glass is contained, and I can break large glass objects into more manageable pieces this way, pieces which will then be ready for more precise cutting with my glass nippers.

Here's another method I've tried, one I can't really recommend. Once, on the open floor of Jen's loft, I laid out a ton of ceramic and glass plates and dropped heavy things like bricks on them. I admit it was cool to watch the glass splinter, to hear the earsplitting crashes; and maybe it would be a great idea if you live alone and just don't give a shit, or if you have a passive-aggressive streak, or harbor a grudge against a roommate; but the down side was I had little control over breakage. Most of the broken pieces were so small, splinters really, they were unusable. Plus I thought Jen would kill me. For months we had to walk around that part of the loft wearing shoes because the glass slivers were incredibly tough to clean up, and next to impossible to see until they were embedded in our feet.

Somewhere between control and chaos is this, my favorite method, personally satisfying on a few levels. I take a yard waste bag, one of those heavy, layered brown bags made to hold grass clippings, leaves, twigs and shit. I've never had to buy my own bags. Because Jen and I have no yard to speak of I have, on occasion, liberated the bags from my sister when I visited her house. Once or twice I've taken bags from people further down the street, if they have been stupid enough to leave them lying around their yards. After a couple of weeks of seriously committed trash picking, I can get a bag about a third of the way full with breakables. Sometimes I presort everything by like color and material; other times it's a free-for-all. Next, I fold over the open tops a few times and seal the bags with strapping tape. The fibers in strapping tape are a bitch but the stuff works. And it has to, because then I whack the hell out of those bags with an old baseball bat until every object is broken into pieces.

When I've got enough prepped material, I upend the bags, I spread the breakage across my work table with the toughened underside of my arm and then I look at what I have. I look and look at my pieces, at color and shape and even texture, and if I look long and hard enough the pieces start to assemble themselves into a whole picture right in my mind, a picture of a building or person or landscape or machine. Then, and only then, do I know what I'll be making. Sometimes I make a few advance sketches of what I want my finished mosaics to look like, but for the most part the image stays locked in my head. My mind first dissects the whole into angles, joints, lines, curves, then matches each feature with a particular piece or group of pieces from my materials.

I tried to explain the process to Shelley once. "It's like a puzzle, Shell. But instead of a whole picture that's been cut into pieces, I have the pieces first, then the picture. The glass, the ceramic, whatever, has its own idea, its own plan."

The concept eluded her. That, and the concept of perspective. I remember when she asked, "How are you able to make that tower so obviously existing in the distance? How come it doesn't end up looking like it's floating in the sky?"

And I laughed at her. "Perspective, Shell, is what it is. The smaller something is, the higher up you place it, give it depth, the further away it looks." When I saw the confusion on her face I gave up. "Hell, I don't know why it doesn't look like it's in the sky or on top of the trees, except that it doesn't. I just do it. But that's why I'm the artist . . ."

"And I'm not. Right," she agreed.

My workbench is a cheap plywood closet door, one of a pair of sliders I reclaimed from a house renovation, slung across a couple of file cabinets. The door has no detail, which makes it an exceptionally ugly door but a great work surface. I am not neat or particularly orderly about my work. Glass and ceramic are sorted in the morning into piles according to color and approximate size, but the piles litter the floor under my worktable. Over the course of a day my feet in their heavy shoes kick the piles back into one big heap.

Once I am caught up in the activity I hardly notice what I do or what goes on around me. I could be alone or working in the middle of marching band rehearsals and never know the difference. The work is good training for my concentration and the only thing I do in life that exhibits patience or perseverance. Otherwise my mind and energy are all over the place. Usually I don't sit still. I prefer to eat in refrigerator raid forages. I am uncomfortable sitting at a table, especially a formal table, when I feel nailed to my seat. I am the guest who offers to get bottles and forgotten silverware from the kitchen. When we have company, I'm the guy who jumps up to entertain the guests. After an especially long time sitting I will stand to tell a complicated story. I will use my hands and whole body in an accompanying pantomime. Sometimes Jen looks at me out of the corner of her eye, a signal, and then I know my antics border on manic. She has more than once suggested we get a dog so that I would have an excuse to leave the table for long stretches of physical activity.

My time with Jen is the longest I have ever stayed with one woman. There was a period when I changed girlfriends almost as often as I changed clothes. I try to be different now, more mature, less restless. Restlessness seems like a childish activity, a kind of foot-tapping or knee-bouncing that others yell at you to give up. Come to think of it, I always got those kinds of corrections. My report cards read: *Has trouble transitioning in tasks. Has difficulty settling down. Has trouble concentrating.* Those qualities have never left me.

Except when I work. Nothing bounces, taps, wanders, or strays then. I'm not bored in the act of work, only when I finish. Clever Jen keeps the work flowing in our studio and urges me to work at project after project.

Mostly I love what I do. I'm good at the spatial stuff. Above all, I love that I can have so much control over my work. If I'm careful, I create something; when I'm too rough, I destroy. Whack, whack, whack, I'm in charge. The work suits me perfectly, all of it: the glass, the ceramic, the breaking. Shortly after we first met, Jen asked me how I had gotten into mosaics. Back then I was still tongue-tied and awkward around her, her more sophisticated studio, her real shows, her seriousness. And I never really gave her an answer. But today, as I stand here trying to keep my mind off my father, I finally come up with an answer for Jen.

Because sometimes, Jen, I feel the need to administer a socially acceptable beating on inanimate objects.

Shelley

Mark parks at the curb in front of my house and idles the engine, anxious to go or anxious to be rid of me. He stares straight ahead but I move to kiss his tightly clenched cheek anyway before opening the passenger side door and sliding out of the car. Before I have a second to turn or move toward the house, Mark pulls about a foot away from the curb, stops short, throws the car into reverse and backs up again. He plants his right rear tire up on the curb. He leans across the front seat and rolls down the passenger side window. "Hey," he calls, and I step closer to the door.

"Hay is for horses," I say with a smile, hoping to make him laugh at the silly phrase our mother used when we were kids to correct our manners. If he has heard or recognized the words I can't tell.

"On second thought," Mark says.

"Yes?" I say, now placing my hands on the car door. I wonder if he has changed his mind about coming inside with me.

"Where is the key?" he asks.

"The key? The *cottage* key?"

Mark nods and holds out his hand. "Give it to me," he says and he wiggles his fingertips impatiently.

"*Give* it to you?" My voice rises.

"That's what I said."

"What—"

"Shell," he says firmly, his tone forbidding me to ask what he intends. Mark keeps his hand stretched out flat in front of me.

I stick my hands inside my coat pockets, and as I do I find last week's "To Do" list. Planning the funeral, I had felt very efficient, purposefully moving ahead, my usual briskly organized self. I had made a long and detailed list of things to do, beginning with Order Food and ending with Attend Funeral. I gave my friend, Emma Noble, a colleague at the school where I teach and perhaps my closest friend, a spare copy of my own house key. She had made, and I accepted, an offer to let herself in while we were at the chapel and take delivery of the cold cuts, salads, rolls, and desserts from a local delicatessen. One by one, as each task was addressed, I scratched the corresponding word or phrase from my list. I had folded the piece of paper in half this morning when I thought that all my tasks had been carried out.

The second pocket holds my hefty key ring, something I am never without. Steven and the girls like to tease me about its weight, especially when I fumble through each individual key as they wait for me to open a door. Margaret compares me to a school custodian or a prison warden in a way that makes me know I embarrass her.

I've always been secretly proud of all that I am able to manage and maintain. House, car, second car, school, classroom, four different bike locks, file cabinets, even a copy of my husband's university office key; a ridiculous total of thirteen keys.

Now fourteen. I take the ring out, hold the cumbersome thing in my gloved hand. Yes, fourteen, I count, for it is newly augmented with my father's cottage key, an old tarnished brass key still with its hardware store paper label attached.

I toss the ring up a few inches in the air and catch it. While it doesn't feel too much heavier with the addition, my heart suddenly does. The cottage only means one more thing to worry about, one more argument to have or avoid having with Mark. Mark: one more worry to add to my constantly evolving list of problems, chores, and projects. Will he toss the key down the sewer grate or drop it somewhere public for an erstwhile thief to find; will he drive up north right now, let himself in, and torch the place? This additional worry makes my usually helpful list feel less like a rundown of tasks to conquer and more like something to drown in. Like something that may, for the first time in my life, conquer me.

"You won't do anything . . . "

"Stupid?" he sneers. "How old do you think I am anyway? *Twelve?*" The scar along Mark's chin looks tight and angry. "For Christ's sake, Shelley, just give me the key." Then, perhaps sensing he has gone too far, Mark's voice lowers to a mumble. "Ah, forget it. It'll take you all day to get the damn thing off your key ring, and I've gotta go."

"You're sure you won't— " I start to repeat my offer of a respite and a meal, but Mark doesn't wait. He takes his foot off the brake and the old Chrysler lumbers forward. The chassis bounces as the tire comes off the curb. Mark lifts a hand and calls through the window, "See you around, Shell."

"I'll call you," I shout after him, acting normal, carefree. I add under my breath more urgently, "Or you can call me," because of course nothing feels normal. Mark and that house have history, and as he drives away, the memories that flood me have nothing in common with carefree.

We drive to the Rockport house to spend a weekend with Dad and Sylvie, our first extended visit with them as a couple following my parents' bitter separation. I am sixteen and Mark is twelve. The weather is perfect, sunny, and warm without being humid, a clear blue sky. Mark and I are supposed to be "eager for a weekend at the beach" – Dad's pronouncement. Instead, Mark sits sullenly in the back seat with me, and I feel nothing but anxiety that I vent by biting the cuticle around my thumbnail. With each laugh Dad and Sylvie share up front, Mark's scowl deepens. At one point he points his finger down his throat to show me that their conversation is making him gag.

The day gets worse when, once we stop at the house, Mark refuses to carry his suitcase up to the bedroom simply because Sylvie has issued the command. Knowing Mark's temper, I try to intervene. I offer to carry the case. I guess Sylvie feels she needs to assert herself or she will lose ground with us, Jack's children. She is young, and instead of yielding she teases. With a hand on Mark's forehead, she traces his frown lines.

"Don't ever touch me!" Mark yells, and he runs back out the door.

I follow, stopping on the porch. From there, I watch Mark on the front lawn, gouging a divot into the grass with first his sandal heel and then, when that doesn't make quick enough progress, with the toe end of his shoe, twisting his toe like a screw, mercilessly grinding up grass and earth. We are both still close enough to the house to hear laughter. Sylvie's laughter. "Just a boy," we hear Sylvie say. "A pre-adolescent boy," she adds with a kiss. We are close enough to hear the sound of kissing, of tender pecks and wetted lips. I look from Mark to the house and back.

We stare at each other for a minute and then Mark calls my name. "Shelley."

"Yes," I answer as I go slowly down the four steps and onto the front walk. "I'm here." I continue walking until I reach his side.

"That's quite a hole you've dug there, kiddo," I say. I can see that the tips of his toes have turned brown.

"I hate this grass," he says. "Feel it, it's like needles, worse than needles."

"Sea grass. Dry and reedy," I answer in my teacher's voice, present as early as sixteen.

"Can't you just hate something? Can't you just let *me* hate it without telling me about it?" Mark asks. "I hate the water too, the water and the grass and this house. I hate Dad. Jack," he simpers, mocking Sylvie's girlish, flirtatious voice. "And I really hate Sylvie."

"It's just a weekend," I say. "Two days. If we spend all our time at the beach, or walking downtown, we don't have to see them. Much. And then we go home."

"Oh, yeah. Home. I hate Mom too," Mark adds. But by now he has little anger left in his voice or in his words. "A weekend," he snorts. "*You* probably never have to come back here," he reminds me. "And when you're eighteen? You can go wherever you want then. You'll be out of here. Not me, not for years. Like I even care about visits," he mutters. Mark scuffs his foot over the pile of earth he has dug, flattening it. "Crappy weekends in their crappy apartment listening to them talking that lovey-dovey shit when they think I'm not listening." He stares off into the wooded area surrounding the house.

"Your mouth," I scold. I put my hand on his shoulder. "Even when I'm eighteen, when I'm away at college, I'll come home on weekends, as often as I can. Promise."

"Mom's crazy, you know." Mark offers me this information as if I am a stranger and wouldn't know, haven't witnessed for myself our mother's decline since Dad left.

"She's not crazy. She's– "

" –fucking nuts."

" –still upset," I finish.

"She hasn't left the house in months. I hate it. I'll run away. I'm never coming here again, I'm never staying with Dad again. No way." He looks directly at me for the first time since I reached his side, defying me to order him to be nice to Jack and Sylvie.

I opt to make no answer at all. Instead I take my hand from his shoulder and reach down for his hand. It is sweaty and hot from being balled into a tight fist. Mark's face also looks hot, beet red and twisted in an ugly scowl, yet I can't help smiling at him.

"I'm glad you didn't put me on the list," I joke. "'I hate Shelley.'"

"You're on the list," he says. "You are. I hate you too," he adds with a lopsided smile suddenly breaking out on his sweaty, red face. "Because you want all of this to be nice and I don't. Because you get to leave and I don't. Maybe I hate you most of all."

"Gotcha," Mark says after a second.

"I knew you didn't mean that," I say, relieved.

Mark's grin fades. "You don't how I feel, *or* what I mean." He looks at me, squints at me as if through the scope of a rifle, drawing a bead; then he lifts his face to the sky. A sound gurgles up in his throat, and it builds to a growl. Mark opens his mouth and roars. "Fuck you! Fuck all of you!" he shouts into the sky, scaring a few birds out of a nearby tree. I hear the frightened flap of their wings and see the frenzied streaks of red against black as if in flight they take the echoing end of Mark's scream with them. Turning tail, heading away from the house into the darker woods, Mark starts running.

I stand for a moment on the sidewalk in front of my house, shivering inside my wool coat as I watch Mark's rusty old Chrysler New Yorker peel out of my neighborhood.

About this one particular thing my brother is correct. I don't hold grudges. I see no point. Whether it was simply because I was the older child, or at heart a more practical child, I adapted to our family's situation because I had to; because when Dad left I had to become another parent to Mark, oftentimes the adult in the relationship with my mother, and the mature and reasonable liaison between both of them and Dad.

During freshman and sophomore years at college, I spent every weekend at home with my mother and Mark. Every Friday I stepped off the bus and without fail Mark was at the stop, waiting to give me his usual greeting: "You're here, and I am saved once again from Tuna Helper!" Every Friday he made a dramatic fall to his knees and hugged me so close I could feel my kneecaps buckle backward as he drew me into him. And every Friday, after the stretch of a week I was struck by how thin and pale, how neglected, he looked. During the week, he existed on noodles or boxed macaroni with brilliant orange powdered cheese or peanut butter sandwiches. Forget school lunches; Mark, I knew, spent his lunch money on cigarettes or marijuana. I never saw fresh meat or vegetables in the house unless I bought them, so I began each weekend at home by roasting a chicken.

On Saturday mornings, I would write the checks for household expenses and balance my mother's checkbook before organizing Mark's study timetable and assisting him with the actual work. Mom would sit at one end of the dining table, smoking the cigarettes she paid Mark to buy for her, while I would sit at the other end, checkbook before me and calculator within reach of my right hand. Having me as a captive audience, my mother often berated Jack or ripped into Sylvie in between puffs on her Marlboro Lights.

I got so good at balancing the checkbook that I could converse and work at the same time, but when the conversation turned to

Dad, I often tried to change the subject. I told my mother that I believed Mark had too much unsupervised time on his hands, and also too much opportunity to slack off from his work if he was constantly asked to do the shopping. Plus, I added, their diet left a great deal to be desired when Mark made the purchasing decisions. Breakfasts consisted of Sugar Pops, Captain Crunch, or Pop Tarts, and I found myself in constant need of a tooth brushing, a deep scaling, after a weekend in that house.

And speaking of tooth brushing, I continued, I reminded Mom that Mark needed a dental appointment. I realized that there was little chance that she would follow through on getting Mark to the dentist; my mother never agreed to anything I suggested if it meant leaving the house. Still, I aimed to push her back out into the world.

In my junior year, my workload heated up. I required a weekend, one weekend to myself to be spent between the dorms and the library in order to finish a large research project and to study for an exam. Although dreading the inevitable argument, I made the call to my mother on Thursday to explain that I wouldn't be home again until the following weekend.

"Your brother has homework too," my mother protested. "Tests, just like you. Papers to write."

"I know," I answered, "and I'll help him next weekend. This is important."

As if she hadn't heard a word I had said, Mom plowed on. "He's been goofing off. He doesn't listen to me." Her voice was shrill, rising nearly an octave. "And your father is useless. When I call there, that woman puts the phone back down and cuts me off."

"Why, Mom? Why would Sylvie do that?"

"Because she's a witch, that's why!"

"Did you explain that the call is about Mark? Dad would want to know if you were calling about Mark." Even as I spoke,

I knew the answer to my own question. I could practically hear my mother on the phone with Sylvie, launching into a harassment of my father's young wife rather than calmly expressing the reason for the phone call. If I were Sylvie I'd put the phone down too. I continued, "Maybe Dad can find a tutor for Mark. I mean, it keeps getting harder and harder for me to get away. Do you think if you explained–"

Mom cut me off with a frustrated growl. "No!" she insisted. "I don't need to explain anything to her. If I ask for Jack she should put him on the damn phone!"

"Maybe if I spoke to Dad," I suggested.

"Mark doesn't need your father's money for a tutor. He needs you to come home and help him."

I understood then that Mom's calls to Dad and Sylvie would never be for Mark's benefit but rather for spite, and for once, my mother's impossible demands nearly irked me into a rebellion. I was tempted to say no, to hang up and find some friends to go out with on a quest for underage beer served up by some careless bartender. But I also understood there was very little of my mother left in this woman. What had been set in motion even before the divorce had culminated in this new mother, more child than me or Mark, a bitter and irrational child.

Instead of hanging up, I asked, "Can you put Mark on the phone, Mom?"

"He's not here." Across the receiver, I heard the strike of a match and my mother's deep inhale.

"When will he be back?" I asked.

"I don't know."

I moved the receiver off my ear and rested the cool plastic on the side of my cheek. I took a moment to think. "Okay, Mom," I said when I returned, "here's what we're going to do. When Mark gets home, please tell him what's going on up here. Tell him I'll be home for the day on Sunday. If he needs help before then, you'll have to call his teachers at school tomorrow."

"I can't– " she started to interrupt.

"Call the school, Mom. *Tell* someone – one of his teachers, the guidance counselor, *anyone* – what Mark needs. Then you make him do his work. I'll be there in a couple of days."

"You don't understand."

"I do, I do understand. But I've got to go."

"You are so selfish. I can't believe I've raised anyone so selfish!"

"I'm hanging up now, Mom."

"Selfish. Thoughtless. Just like your father."

I hung up. I had too much to do before Sunday; I would have to suffer the sting of my mother's parting words and move on. After a minute I collected myself and took my books to the library.

Our lives had changed, and someone had to help make it work. By default, by necessity, that someone was me.

I turn and head for the house to check on our guests. With a full house, my guests' comfort should be my prime consideration. Three days ago, with Dad's death a reality, the guests *had* been my biggest concern. My list had been long and detailed. Now with no tasks facing me other than to relax and mingle, I find I cannot concentrate on anything or anyone but my worry. The rain that has threatened to return all day finally has. One fat drop hits my scalp and trickles through my hair and down my forehead. I swipe it off with the back of my hand. Pulling my coat around me I hasten my steps.

Just then, behind me on the street, I hear the chugging sound of a dying muffler. A car approaches and I think immediately that it is Mark returning to begin round two of our argument, coming back to demand the cottage key once again. In an argument my brother is like a terrier, unwilling to let a rat drop from his teeth until he's shaken the life out of it. My hand strays to my pocket and I finger my key ring. I won't give it to him, I say to myself, and I prepare myself as I turn to face him. I draw a breath and put some steel in my spine so that I may be as stubborn as he always is.

But it is not Mark. A teal-green Civic, not anyone I know at all.

Still, the breath I had drawn seconds ago catches in my throat. I have to force myself to push the air back out of my lungs, in and out, both a struggle. My heart too refuses to cooperate; it beats fast, won't catch a rhythm.

I stand on my lawn, cold and sopping wet but unable to move into the house. Between the funeral and Mark's mood, I feel overwhelmed and I draw my arms around myself for comfort and warmth. A movement catches my eye and I look beyond my yard, my hedge, and across a spate of trees to see my neighbor, Mr. Jenkins, walking his big black Newfoundland, Scout. Poor Scout is neither cunning nor swift, Mr. J. tells me when we have occasion to speak, meeting as we sometimes do at our property lines as he walks his dog and I garden. The dog is, though, a good strong swimmer with a tendency to save anything or anyone who appears to be drowning.

While I'm watching, the skies open up and the drizzle turns to downpour. As I walk up the path to my house, Mr. Jenkins spots me and waves, and Scout barks a greeting. Maybe that's what I need in my life, I think, not a detailed To Do list to keep me afloat, but a strong swimmer to jump in and save me, drag me to safety by my sodden clothing with one strong clamp of dog jaws. Because coming up in the wake of the day, I can practically taste the salt of the sea.

As I walk through the front door and hang up my coat, Steven catches my eye. He and Sylvie are standing off to one side of the living room and he waves me over to them. The good daughter and wife, I take my place with them at the center of the gathering.

Mark

"You're high again," Jen says as I walk past her on my way to the kitchen after locking the front door behind me. "You reek."

She sits on one of the couches in the living area, knees drawn up to her chest, reading, and her eyes never leave the page.

"Hello to you too." I plant a kiss on the top of her head and breathe in her own special scent of green tea shampoo and developing chemicals. "Did you eat yet? I'm starving," I add as I open the refrigerator door.

"Of course you're starving. You've been smoking pot."

Her eyes never leave the page.

Yeah, I'd smoked more pot on the way home from Shelley's. I left my sister in front of her house and thought to myself, I'll smoke a little or maybe a lot more of this excellent grass and hope the high will take the edge off. Postpone feeling anything, avoid thinking of Jack Manoli at least until I got back to the studio where I would then have Jen and plenty of work to keep me busy.

But for a few seconds I had enjoyed my anger. I had really wanted that cottage key. Wanted to feel it in my hand and keep it in my sight. If asked I couldn't have said why, only that I saw myself in that instant as some kind of twisted gatekeeper. Make everyone come through me when decisions about the house had to be made, and maybe they'd think twice about asking. My temper can be forbidding when I need it to be.

I could practically see the questions forming in Shelley's mind, my sister is so transparent: *What's he gonna do, torch the place?* When she hesitated, I challenged. "What do you think I am, some kind of a fucking infant that I can't be responsible for a key?" Or something like that.

Then almost as quickly as I thought of asking for the key, I dropped the idea. After all, I was mad but I wasn't mad at Shelley for being her usual, sensible self after we buried our father. I know she's trying to do the right thing by persuading me to do something with Dad's house. Shelley won't be mad at me either. By sometime tomorrow morning, she'll have called to check up on me.

Jen's attitude toward me is a different story. Under the disinterest she's fuming, and that's not likely to go away any time soon. There are scores of possible reasons for Jen to feel this angry at me, but I'm sure she's mostly pissed because I asked her to stay home today rather than come to the funeral. She would like to share more of my life, not just the "Somerville part," as she puts it. I've told her it's the only part worth anything, but she simply shakes her head.

From the day I learned from Shelley that our father was terminally ill, Jen and I have been communicating in these terse but loaded conversations, she taking a disapproving tone while I respond with a kind of adolescent humor, a rejection of all seriousness. At first I did this purposely as a way to talk Jen out of a bad mood with a laugh at my expense, but the banter's gotten way out of hand until my juvenile, my "bad" behavior only justifies her disapproval.

Things weren't always this way between us. When we met, I had been living in a studio apartment in the basement of a landlady-occupied triple-decker close to Davis Square in Somerville, at thirty-two feeling like an old guy among all the Tufts students. The place was cheap but I wanted to move. The live-in landlady gave me dirty looks every time I ran into her. She had a pinched, disapproving face, no friends that I ever saw, and an unnatural attachment to the building's temperamental late-1920s plumbing. It was as if instead of a social life, she had to settle for a relationship with the sinks and toilets and pipes. In my case she had a lot to keep her occupied. My toilet ran constantly, the antique chain and ball broke inside the toilet tank, but Phyllis insisted she couldn't remove any fixture or pipe unless a period replacement could be found. I could have put up with waiting for the period replacements, but Phyllis also had a tough time getting around to arranging for the repair. I figured she was either the laziest person alive, or she had buried a husband somewhere, maybe in pieces under the plaster of the walls or the foundation of the house, and therefore couldn't risk any major upheaval of her precious plumbing.

I knew it was time to go, time to grow up and lead a grown-up's life rather than live at the whim of this nutcase, but where? I didn't want to move too far away from the art gallery scene or the excellent opportunities for trash picking. And I definitely couldn't afford to pay much more rent than I was already paying.

On the day I met Jen, I was up and out on the trash hunt earlier than usual. I always try to get out by five, long before homeowners or renters are awake enough to catch me in the act. You get that sometimes, people glaring from their windows or doorways, even though the physical act of bringing the trash to the sidewalk to be hauled away implies that ownership and interest ends at the curb. I figure I'm doing them as much of a favor as the trash guy – my own recycling operation if you will – but not everyone sees it that way.

This particular trash day it was a little before five. I was picking my way through castoffs, thinking about the answer to my question, *Where could I move?* Usually my work is solitary work, which is great for thinking about answers or ideas for new pieces. But on that morning, there was someone, a woman, squatting and peering intently into a black trash bag, wearing a pair of heavy gloves, long and tough PVC-coated things that looked appropriate for an embalmer, sturdy boots and worn jeans. I stopped two houses down and watched her as she rose. In her hands she held an old wooden bowl, a shallow oval bowl so dried out from neglect that it had a fairly deep split down its middle. When she finally looked up from her inspection of the piece she noticed me staring, and she gasped. "Oh. You startled me," she said, and then she relaxed a bit and smiled. "I've seen you around," she added, pointing a finger, placing me although I didn't recognize her.

With my own box of dubious treasures I suppose I didn't look all that threatening. I approached her, stopping about two feet from her stack of finds. "Glass," I said, making a point of holding my box out to show her what I'd collected. "I make mosaics so I'm looking for glass. And ceramic. Anything breakable really."

"It's amazing what people will throw away," Jen said and passed me the wooden bowl to look at.

"It's nice," I told her and handed the piece back. "So, you come here often?"

Jen just laughed, then she peeled off one of her strange gloves and offered me her hand. "Jennifer Duffy, but everyone calls me Jen."

I shook her hand and looked down at it as I held it in my own. Turning her hand over, I looked at her wrist, palms, and the fingers in mine. Our hands were like a matched set: both large-knuckled, chapped, red, and run with the faint scars of nicks and scratches, our badges of carelessness. She watched me with a puzzled smile as I inspected her hand, but she didn't pull her hand away. It was as if she trusted me instantly, trusted that I wasn't a rapist or a murderer or a hand fetishist. Finally I looked up into her eyes. Jen was nice-looking, not the prettiest woman I'd ever met, and she had about the ugliest hands I'd ever seen – next to mine, that is – but her eyes were kind and soft, a golden toast brown, and they sparkled when she smiled. The longer I knew her, I learned that her eyes were usually bright with interest and sometimes mischief. All I knew at that moment was how much I liked those eyes smiling at me at five o'clock on a summer morning. I smiled back. I said, "Mark Manoli. After we're finished here, can I buy you breakfast?"

The direct approach was a risk, but it paid off; about an hour later we were dividing our take for the day between the back seat and trunk of Jen's car and walking a few blocks to a diner on Mass Ave. Over eggs and coffee, Jen told me about her photography. She ransacked trash for mostly wooden items, small pieces of furniture, boxes, crates, decorative things, although occasionally old metal tools and implements made it into her cull, which she then took back to her studio. She had a car and her own loft space in a converted factory off Magoun Square, which, trust me, is not one of the up and coming squares, and living there is still reasonably cheap. Her loft space, she told me, was for both living and working, large enough for her photographic equipment, a darkroom, and space to arrange what she called her still lifes. "Black and whites," she explained. "Sometimes I dress in black and put myself in the compositions, other times the stills are just different groupings of the stuff I find, playing with light and shadow." She named a gallery that was at that moment hanging her work for a group show, and she told me too that a piece of hers had recently won a prize and would be included in a modern photography exhibit at a small contemporary art museum this winter.

I was impressed: by the car, the loft, how seriously she took her work, the prize. But I don't think she told me to impress me. It was more that right from the beginning we felt comfortable with each other, with talking about our work and the odd pleasure we both took in finding stuff in the trash, seeing possibilities in old discards.

Over breakfast we fell easily into talk of trash. "Why do you look through trash?" Jen asked. "I know, I know. Making mosaics. Don't give me the easy answer," she warned me. "You can buy glass. Why get your materials from the trash?"

I thought about what she was asking. I thought about how I fell into the habit of sifting through trash back when I was in art school. I wasn't taking money from my father, so I never had enough money for the quantities of expensive paints or paper or sculpting materials I needed from the art supply stores. Should I say just that, that I picked trash out of necessity?

"Why do you?" I asked instead of answering.

Jen smiled and let me take a pass. She said, "I could buy props for my photography. Maybe no one would know the difference. But I think there is a difference between a bowl like the one I found today and one I might find at, say, Pottery Barn. One bowl has a history. Other people's hands on it. At one time, someone needed that bowl, bought it, used it, but then tired of it and threw it away. Why did they do that? And can those facts make a difference to my final photo?" She shrugged. "I like the history. I like reusing rejects."

I looked at Jen after she finished speaking. She now waited for me to say something in return, but the only answer I had ready felt lame. I changed the subject.

"What's the weirdest thing you've ever found in someone's barrels?" I asked Jen.

She barely hesitated before answering, "Sex toys. Definitely sex toys. Thank God for the gloves," she added with a shudder. "For that reason, and because of rotten food too."

"Rotten food is gross," I agreed and I wolfed down my omelet. "Chicken bones, moldy vegetables. I've found pictures of a naked person before, but sex toys are weird," I said through a mouthful of food.

Finished, Jen pushed her plate aside and sat forward in the booth. "I've had a couple of really sad finds," she confided. "One was love letters, shoe boxes full. I really wanted to know why they'd been thrown away. A break-up? Death? Apathy? I brought those home and took pictures of them." She paused for a moment, as if remembering something, and then she said, "But I think the saddest was a couple of photo albums full of somebody's baby pictures. I still can't figure out why anyone would throw their kid's baby pictures away. Even if a child died, even if it was too painful to look at the pictures, you think you'd want to hold onto them as a reminder."

"Maybe it was an accident," I suggested. "I swear some people put out boxes that have been cluttering their attics or basements and don't know half of what's inside them.

"Or maybe the kid himself threw them out," I added. "Maybe he always thought he was an ugly baby and didn't want them around.

"Or," I said, "maybe he turned out so bad, like an ax murderer or something, and he was executed in some western state like Nebraska or Wyoming, and his parents couldn't bring themselves to say his name again, never mind have pictures around to remind them of their devil spawn."

Jen looked at me a moment as she twirled her coffee in its cup. She shook her head. "You have some twisted imagination, you know that?" But she smiled when she said it.

"I've been told," I said, and smiled right back at her.

"You never answered my question," Jen reminded me. "And I asked because I wanted to know. Why trash?"

My smile faded. I looked over Jen's shoulder and out the front plate glass window of the diner. Out on Mass Ave cars were stopped at an intersection, the convex glass of the traffic light glowing red. "Your answer was way more interesting," I admitted. "I worked my way through art school — well, my sister helped, but I still didn't have much money. Finding supplies in the trash was cheap. Then I suppose," I added, taking my eyes off the road and focusing them back on Jen, "finding cheap and usable stuff became a challenge."

"Never underestimate a challenge," Jen said as encouragement.

I continued. "I also liked that practically no one was doing the kind of work I was doing. When someone learned just what I made a sculpture or mosaic out of, what I did to get the materials, it usually freaked them out. Especially if they had some idea of what was respectable and what wasn't. Diving into trash cans wasn't."

"The artistic equivalent of giving someone the finger?"

I thought of my father, how he might have felt if he knew I spent some of my mornings carefully looking through strangers' garbage barrels. "Maybe," I answered, as honestly as I could. Jen narrowed her eyes at me. "Hey," I said, "if you wanted an interesting answer, you should have asked, 'Why glass?' Or 'Why ceramic?'"

"All right. Why glass? Why ceramic?"

At that moment the waitress walked by and I stopped her for our check. "Let's get out of here," I said to Jen as I left some money on the table.

"Where are we going?" she asked.

I rose. "I'm gonna help you unload your car when we get to your place, in return for which you'll invite me in and show me your work."

Jen took a final swallow of coffee and wiped her mouth on her napkin. "Is that right?" she asked. She tucked the napkin underneath the rim of her plate. "You're a rebel. You live on the fringes of respectability. You don't answer my questions. *You* could be an ax murderer. I don't really know you," she added but with a twinkle in her eye. I knew then she wanted to add my story to her collection.

"You will," I assured her, and I reached for her hand.

So how did Jen and I get from there to here, to where we barely speak and when we do it's usually in these sarcastic, loaded conversations? About six months ago, Shelley had broken the news of Jack's lung cancer to me during a visit to our loft. Since then, Jen has cooled toward my sister, and has been passively pissed off with me. My relationship, or lack of one, with my father has been a point of conflict between us since the day I told her about our family history: Jack's infidelity, Jack's split, Jack's request for a divorce, Jack's remarriage. From a busted family herself, Jen can't understand my attitude. "It can't all have been his fault, you know. My parents' getting a divorce was better than listening to their screaming matches," she said. She has always thought I should move beyond anger.

"To what?" I asked more than once.

"To forgiveness," she said on one occasion. "To acceptance," was another stock reply. "Acceptance at the very least."

We had a variation of this same discussion shortly after Shelley brought news of Jack and then left.

"So you're saying I should be more like you were?" I taunted. "Or more like my sister, forgiving everyone and having them all over to dinner?"

Jen barked out a laugh. "Your *sister*," she snorted.

I took the bait. "What about my *sister*?" I asked, copying her mocking tone.

"Never mind." She waved away my question as if she knew she would regret bringing up the subject if she went any further. She started to walk away.

"No really," I pressed, and grabbing her arm I said, "I want to know. What about Shelley?"

We faced off. I felt we were about to walk into a very dark place. We knew it, we should've stopped, but we couldn't. Left alone, momentum is a very strong force. Jen shook off my hand.

"Shelley," Jen began slowly. "You're right that Shelley goes out of her way to get along with everyone, and she practically weeps over your 'estrangement' as she calls it." She emphasizes this with her fingers making quotation marks in the air. "Shelley could insist that you and your dad get together, that you make some kind of peace with him, especially now that he's ill. *She* could make you see a shrink. She knows you'd listen to *her*.

"But does she?" Jen asks after a pause to let her words sink in. "No. Every time she pushes, you get angry and she drops the subject, because heaven forbid if Mark gets angry. She babies you, Manoli, and it's time you grew up enough to see that."

"I don't even know what the hell you're talking about."

Jen was happy to explain it to me. "First she comes over here, wringing her hands over giving you the news, after she's known for how long? Almost six months herself? And she only tells you when she's sure he's dying? Come on, Mark. Get with it. She shoulders what she thinks you can't handle. She doesn't even give you a *chance* to handle anything. Mark doesn't want to confront something, Shelley makes sure he doesn't have to." She mimicked a big sister's defensive tone with alarming accuracy.

I said the only thing I could think of in the circumstances. "Go fuck yourself," I replied.

"Oh, that's very mature, Mark," Jen answered. She watched my face, gauging my temper. "Now I suppose you're trying to frighten me off, the way you do with your sister. I swear she's like the blindly loving, slightly stupid family dog that gets kicked and keeps coming back for more."

I scrounge around the fridge and find the last plain bagel way in the back – I am reminded that it is time to go shopping – in a plastic bag, so it's mine. There's cream cheese, and cheddar cheese too, both of which I take out and place on the counter. Along with a jar of zesty dills. Hot salsa. Sliced pepperoni. Milk.

Jen sits and tries hard to ignore me. From her nest of pillows and cushions, she sighs exaggeratedly. I smile at her and shake my head as I first split the bagel then spread cream cheese on it, press the halves together, and bite it like a sandwich. Stale, but it will do. On a plate I pile my bagel sandwich, three pickles, a handful of pepperoni circles, and a few thick slices of cheddar cheese over which I spoon chunky, southwest-style hot salsa.

"Do we have chocolate syrup for the milk?" I ask Jen. She grunts in reply, which I take for a no. Grabbing a stack of napkins along with my plate and glass, I join Jen on the couch. She continues to avoid looking at me.

"Why didn't you eat at your sister's?" she asks as she pretends to read.

"What makes you think I didn't?" I ask in return.

For this I finally get a response, a look, a raised eyebrow, before she returns to her book.

"Please close that," I say through a bite of bagel.

"I will if I don't have to watch you eat salsa on cheese," she negotiates.

"Okay," I agree with a shrug and she looks up. I dip a pepperoni slice into the salsa and stuff it into my mouth quickly, before the salsa drips on my lap. In spite of herself, Jen smiles.

"You are disgusting," she says and wrinkles her nose. "Plus you smell like all the roadies and half the audience at a Grateful Dead concert."

"It was good grass," I tell her.

"I wish you wouldn't smoke."

"Yeah, well," I answer. "I wish you wouldn't tell me what you wish I wouldn't do." We sit quietly a minute as we both try to decode what I've just said. I lick salsa from my fingers and finish what's on my plate, following it all down with a full glass of milk.

"Truce," Jen says, and I agree, putting up my free hand in surrender.

"How was today?" she asks.

"Today? Today was," I begin, "today was a good day to get high."

Jack

I don't want sympathy. I really don't. After all, I'm the only one in the room. I'm talking to myself and not trying to justify my actions to the judge and jury who is God or to my children. I don't believe in deathbed redemption; trying to put myself in the best light before my day of reckoning seems disingenuous to say the least. Nor do I expect points for honesty at this stage.

This stage is dangerously close to death. I lie on my back, tired but unwilling to sleep for when I do give in, I am uneasy knowing that this could be the day I might not wake up. My end is that close. And when a man faces Death eyeball to eyeball, when he can't get up and go for a walk or do the simplest things like dress himself, the most he can do with the hours he has left is to remember and to think. He shouldn't sleep his time away. What matters to me most is what's left to do here on this earth, and all I want to do with the time I have left is to think about Sylvie and the life we've had and what I did – and didn't do – to get it.

It seems Sylvie and I have known each other forever, but really it's been twenty-seven years, and only twenty-three of those years married. We met in 1972 when I was in the midst of losing my longtime secretary to retirement. Before becoming my personal secretary, Matilda had put in twenty years with the agency that employed me. For the last ten years of her employment she had greeted my clients, typed my letters flawlessly, and corrected my grammar while maintaining the best posture I had ever seen, and I was faced with breaking in someone new. Headhunters and placement counselors at area business schools sent promising candidate after promising candidate. Many were as old as Matilda, or nearly; most had impeccable credentials and work history. The one different candidate was Sylvie.

She had been sent over as a recent graduate of Katherine Gibbs. She arrived wearing a pale orange-yellow suit, a color and cut that I will remember until the day I die. The skirt was extremely short. During the interview with me, at the time a seasoned account executive and her potential employer, she appeared at ease and unflustered. She told me that she typed ninety words per minute, and that she loved greeting people, making people feel comfortable. She was twenty years old. Sitting across from her, mesmerized by the confident appraisal of her own skills, I, Jack Manoli, knew I couldn't let her go.

This girl, I think, could charm snakes, or at least tame overbearing clients. Her pretty smile shows off the end result of superb orthodontia. She might have been a model for one of my firm's own toothpaste ads, and I imagine standing behind a camera, filming her as she ran her tongue over her dazzling and straight teeth.

"Do you have any other questions for me?" Sylvie asks. "Any typing or shorthand tests you'd like me to take?"

Startled out of my daydream, I clear my throat and shift in my seat. I shuffle the sheaf of papers lying in front of me on the desktop. "No," I answer, bringing my mind back to the interview from my not so professional thoughts about her mouth. I slip my reading glasses on. "No, that's not necessary. Everything seems to be documented here – typing speed, office skills, and letters of recommendation. Excellent recommendations, by the way," I add, looking up, my eyes peering over the rim of my glasses.

"Thank you." Sylvie smiles.

"If we offered you the job, when could you start?" I ask.

"Oh, right away. I'm anxious to start working."

"I see. Good. Well, Sylvia– "

"It's Sylvie," she corrects.

I look down again at my paperwork. "Oh, right. Sylvie. I'm sorry," I apologize.

"Accepted," Sylvie says with a slight nod of her head. "It happens all the time."

I continue, though my stride is somewhat broken. I decide to bring the interview to a quick close. "I have a few other interviews scheduled today," I tell Sylvie, "after which I'll review all the candidates. I should have my decision within a week."

"Thank you, Mr. Manoli. I look forward to hearing from you." Sylvie stands and reaches across the desk to shake my hand. She picks up her briefcase and makes to leave my office. At the door, Sylvie hesitates and turns. "I should tell you," she begins, "that I had an interview yesterday. At a law firm," she adds. "I think it went well, and I may have a job offer from them as soon as tomorrow morning. At the risk of sounding forward, I believe I'd prefer to work in advertising. Could I maybe call you, let you know if I get another offer before I give the law firm my final answer?"

"Could you call me? You mean to see if I've made my decision?" Sylvie nods. "Well, sure," I agree. "I've only got two more candidates this afternoon. I don't imagine it'll be very long before I know whom I plan to hire."

"Great! Thanks again, Mr. Manoli." She lifts her hand in a wave and leaves the office.

I move to the door and watch her walk down the hallway into the front lobby, watching the slight natural sway of her hips, the lift of her slender ankles. Compared to the old battle-axes in the ad agency, the secretaries in their pleated wool skirts that fall below their knees, their support hose, the endless gray cardigans, compared to these other women – to any other woman – Sylvie is a stunner. I think of Matilda who walks as if she has books balanced on her head and a metal rod for a spine, Matilda who wears orthopedic shoes.

A girl like Sylvie represented the future of this business, the modern employee in a world anxious to purge its dinosaurs, the relics of the past. I picture myself walking through the glass front doors every morning and being greeted by Sylvie as she brings me my typed work and morning coffee.

"Um, Sylvie?" I call before she gets too far away, and she turns at the sound of her name. "Could you . . ." I begin then pause, lifting my hand and curling my finger in a beckon. Sylvie walks back.

"Yes, Mr. Manoli?" Smiling, Sylvie stands in front of me. She barely reaches my shoulder and she has to look up at me when I speak. Oddly, though, I feel at a disadvantage.

"Actually, I've been thinking– "

"In the time it took me to walk down the hall?" She glances over her shoulder to emphasize the brief distance.

"Actually, yes," I answer, "in that small amount of time. I was thinking I'd like to offer you the job." I smile back at her, confident that I have pleased her, impressed her with this quick and decisive action, confident that she will accept.

Sylvie fixes her eyes on me; I see shrewdness in there, something new that has crept in and replaced her youthful enthusiasm. "What were you thinking of offering for a salary?" she asks.

"Salary?" I repeat, flustered at this unexpected request.

"Yes. You know how it goes. I do a job, you pay me," Sylvie teases.

"Well, at her last review Matilda was increased to . . ." and without thinking I name a figure, then instantly regret speaking.

Sylvie smiles. "That sounds wonderful to me!" Maybe on this salary she imagines many more suits with short skirts. Shopping in Bonwit Teller instead of safe, moderately priced Jordan Marsh.

"But," I stammer, "of course she's been here for thirty years."

"It still sounds good to me."

"Your question caught me by surprise," I admit. "I was thinking out loud. You realize I can't pay you that much."

"I know," Sylvie says and she sighs, wistful. "But that much money would have been nice. Look," she continues, "the law firm is offering eleven-five; if you could afford the retiring Matilda's salary, I think you could afford, say, thirteen for my entry level position."

"Thirteen thou—" I whistle. "That's higher than . . ." I break off. "That's high."

"I believe I'm worth it," Sylvie tells me. I cross my arms in front of my chest and consider. "You can tell me you need some time to think about it, or to interview other girls," Sylvie continues, "and I won't be offended. But," she grins, "I think you'd be making a mistake."

I, by now no longer surprised by anything this young woman might say, don't blink. "You seem quite confident, so let's see how you work out."

"I *am* quite confident," she says, hand outstretched again.

Before I shake it I caution, "Three months' trial period, then a review."

"You won't regret your decision," she adds, looking straight into my eyes. I can only look down at the hand that waits to be shaken.

Sylvie has the naive attitude of invincibility that goes with being twenty, and it's heartening and heartbreaking at the same time. At thirty-four, I know life is full of mistakes and regrets. Despite what I know, I look up from her hand to meet her direct stare and say, "No, I probably won't," because somehow she makes me feel hopeful. I take her hand and hold it maybe a moment too long.

In this bed what I think about most is how, from the very first day I met her, Sylvie had been right: I never did regret hiring her. In fact, she worked out extremely well, took to the job and to advertising very quickly. A natural, as I used to tell her. And then I fell in love with her, which I didn't regret either. It sounds crazy now when I say I believed my kids would be happy for me, because of course ending my marriage, the way it ended, destroyed my children's foundation. My actions told them: people you trust will let you down, will lie to you, and will hurt you. Those failings I regret. I am sorry for everything I made happen.

And yet even now, with all this pain I've caused, to speak of my shortcomings in terms of regret seems a pointless, circular exercise because it takes me right back to the beginning, to the fact that I regret nothing I did because of or for Sylvie.

I remember the last time I made love to Sylvie, the last time *I* made love to *her*, and a tear falls from my left eye onto my pillow. It will be one year ago this June, in the summer house. We had opened the place for the season on Memorial Day weekend. Sylvie wanted to begin some long needed renovations in the kitchen and we planned to stay three weeks. She had an idea of doing some kind of stripping and over painting on the cabinets that would make them look distressed. I teased her all morning for choosing that project to begin with when there were others more pressing. I thought we should start outside first. The rotting soffits, the old roof, the crumbling mortar between the brickwork of the front walk. And if she felt compelled to start in the kitchen, I said, why not start with ripping up the linoleum floor, for example, which was worn and lifting and a hazard if one of us tripped on it. "What about the floor, Sylvie, when the cabinets are done over? Won't the floor feel distressed?" I asked. "Won't the rest of the cottage feel distressed? Or just stressed? Can a house be stressed out? Or will it be plain old depressed?"

Sylvie whipped out at my legs with a dishtowel. I dodged, only to circle around and grab her from behind, lifting her feet from the floor. Sylvie then laughed and shrieked and tried to wriggle free. In a dance-like move I set her feet to the floor and spun her to face me. I held her hands behind her back with one of mine, and she let me; with my free hand I smacked her bottom hard and she let me.

The moment after, we looked at each other, two pairs of intense eyes. We were both surprised. And aroused. After so many years I still desired my wife. She still desired me. Sylvie took a step toward me, pressed her pelvis to mine. This time I gently caressed the curve of her ass, soothing the sting of my slap. Within minutes we were up the stairs and in our bed. The sunlight came in through partially open blinds and lit the room, slatted the length of Sylvie's naked body with light and shadow. By the end of the second week we were back in Brookline, the job on the cabinets begun but not finished, because after making love with her I had complained of a tightness in my chest which I put down to inhaling the burning fumes of paint stripper or an allergy to the spring pollens, and which Sylvie thought might be a heart attack.

Once the doctor shot down my layman's diagnosis of mild asthma or an overexposure to the chemicals, the short-lived cancer treatments began, and that day went down in our history as the last time I was inside her beautiful body that way, reaching in and touching the very center of Sylvie, really knowing her.

Since then, my illness and the constant fatigue make erections impossible. Now all I can do is ask, "Let me see you," and she obliges, standing beautiful and naked before me, touching her own hands to places I would like to touch if only I were stronger. Sylvie says she still loves me, desires me. Sometimes she lies next to me and she spreads her legs and helps me slip a weakening finger in her. She says in a whisper at my ear that she imagines the finger is my cock and she is under me again or above me. I know it's not the same for her, but when she says those words she looks into my eyes and does not let me look away. I know I smell of death, that when I open my mouth the smell of rot and decay rises from my insides, that despite the humiliating sponge baths the nurse gives me, my body reeks of death, but Sylvie does all that for me without embarrassment or self-consciousness or disgust. She does all that with love, even for a dying man.

The death room is the truth room and here's the truth: although I feel a great deal of sorrow over hurting my first wife and my children, I would do it again.

And again and again.

It wasn't as if the instant I laid eyes on pretty, young Sylvie my married life with Kay went from wonderful to awful. What Sylvie's presence did from the start was make me question where my life was going.

On the warm days of late spring and early summer, I began to watch out my office window as Sylvie took her lunch break in the park across from the office building, alone on a bench, preferring her own company to the company of the older women she worked with. Before she ate, she smoked a cigarette, making it last.

Her one vice, she had confided in me, these two or three cigarettes a day: one in the morning at the bus stop out of sight of her parents' house; one before lunch here in the park; and sometimes a third during an afternoon break if it had been a stressful day at work. I knew these few things about her. I knew this too: I wanted to know more.

I watch from across the street as Sylvie removes the companion jacket to her sleeveless dress to get some sun on her shoulders and upper arms. As she smokes, she watches the cars, the people, the pigeons. She looks up when a shadow falls across her lap. Mine.

"You shouldn't, you know." This line is not one of the many upbeat openings I had practiced on the way over to her. I have wanted to join Sylvie for weeks, longed for our conversations to continue in the social realm outside the office, and today I screwed up my courage.

Sylvie looks up when she hears my voice, she shades her eyes from the sun. "It's bad for you," I add. Although I wanted our meeting to seem a coincidence, I had planned this lunch down to the extra sandwich I bought for sharing, but I wish I had done a better job planning what I would say. I'm more nervous than I expected.

Sylvie, though, takes my comments in stride. "I know," she agrees. "A bad habit. The only one I was allowed to pick up at Katie Gibbs, and then only because I never got caught."

"May I?" I point to the empty space next to her on the bench.

"Of course." Sylvie drops the cigarette to the concrete beneath the bench and stamps it out with her foot. She reaches into her paper lunch bag and pulls out an apple and a banana and a napkin.

"Only fruit?" I ask.

She nods, flattening the bag over her lap and laying the fruit on top. "Otherwise my mother tries to pack my lunch. I'd need a nap after one of her lunches! My mother is German," she explains, "and she believes in hearty meals. Pieces of baked chicken, slices of heavy meat pies." Sylvie clutches her stomach, but smiles. "If she sees me leave the house with a lunch bag, she's satisfied that I'm eating, and I get to eat what I want."

I reach into my own paper sack for the two sandwiches that I had bought on impulse from the deli down the street. "When I can't decide, I buy two," I say, as if this is my routine. I hold one out to Sylvie. "D'you like chicken salad?"

"Love it."

"Or black forest ham?" I pull out the second.

"Both I guess."

"Why don't you have one? Have half. It's only a sandwich, it shouldn't put you to sleep. Try the chicken." With the waxed paper-wrapped sandwich, I point to the steaming teakettle hanging above the sandwich shop down the street. "They make a mean chicken salad."

Sylvie reaches for the offered sandwich and takes a bite. "It *is* good."

"Yes it is."

We eat for a few minutes without talking while I try to think of different lines of conversation. I swallow the last of my sandwich and say, "You have an unusual name. Sylvie."

"It's French. German mother, French father. I was named for my great-grandmother Sylvie from Alsace. My parents left Europe in 1950, and in 1952 I came along. New American, old name.

"Everyone's always mistaking it for Sylvia," she adds, "which makes me think of an old lady with silver-blue hair and eyeglasses hanging by a chain and resting on an ample bosom."

I look down at the sandwich wrappings on my lap to keep my eyes from straying to Sylvie's anything-but-dowdy figure. "I'm sorry I made the same mistake," I mumble.

"Don't be. Like I said, it happens all the time." Sylvie wipes her mouth with her napkin. "You don't usually have lunch here in the park," she says.

"Not usually," I admit. "But I haven't been outside in days, and it's a corker of a day. So I thought, why not have lunch outside?"

"I knew I hadn't seen you here before. There are regulars, you know."

"Like you?" Sylvie shrugs in answer. I tell her, bending the truth only a bit, "I spotted you when I went into the sandwich shop. Sunning. And smoking." I mime the smoking motion with my hand. "I hoped you wouldn't mind if I joined you."

"Thank you, Mr. Manoli, for buying me lunch."

"It's not really buying lunch . . ." I stammer.

"Then what *do* you call buying someone a sandwich at noontime?" Sylvie asks with a smile at my obvious discomfort. "Or were you really going to eat both yourself?"

So much for passing this lunch off as a coincidence. "What I meant to say was," I say quietly, "you're welcome."

I pause, flustered again. I sound to my own ears like a stammering idiot, but sitting here with her, looking for excuses to go on sitting with her, I'm unable to stop rambling. After a moment I add, "You're doing very well. I realize it's hard to know what we're thinking if you don't get feedback. As I said, we're all very happy with your work— "

"We?" Sylvie prompts.

"I mean me. *I'm* happy."

"Oh, good. I like my job. I like working with you," she emphasizes. "I think we work well together."

"My clients are happy too," I add quickly. "Your typing, it goes without saying, is great, but I'm especially grateful for the way you handle my clients."

"I like talking to your clients. May I tell you something?" Sylvie asks. She wraps the second half of the sandwich back in its paper.

"Of course," I say. "Anything."

"It's just that, well, with you being my boss I don't want to sound—"

"Shoot."

"Okay. It's this: Someday I hope . . . well, I hope to do more than secretarial work. I like parts of what you do."

"What parts?"

"Managing the accounts, handling the clients," Sylvie begins to list.

"Oh, *those* parts," I say, laughing. "You mean my whole job, don't you?"

Sylvie smiles with me, but she admits, "Sometimes I'm too direct."

"And sometimes I tease too much. Remember, I said you could tell me anything."

"That's it, really. I know I don't have four years of college, and I don't know about coming up with the advertising campaign ideas, but I'm good with people. And I'm organized."

"Yes, you are," I agree.

Sylvie looks down at her watch. "I need to get back," she tells me. "Thanks again for the sandwich." She drops her cigarettes and lighter into her handbag, and then collects her jacket and the remaining half sandwich.

"I'll be along in a bit," I tell her. "I think I'll enjoy the sunshine a little longer. I never take breaks like this."

"Then you should. And enjoy it while you can. Next thing you know," Sylvie jokes, "the doctors will tell us sunshine is bad for us. Like smoking."

She waves and leaves me, stopping at the corner to cross the street. I watch heads turn, as men walking down the sidewalks do double takes as they pass Sylvie. I too find myself captivated by the easy swing of her hips under her dress. Once across the street Sylvie stops and looks back. She doesn't acknowledge any of the other men passing her; she looks at me. She sees me watching and she waves, and in that instant I feel exposed, a burglar trapped in a spotlight.

During those first two years of Sylvie's employ, as I learned about her and became her friend, I began to feel uncomfortable with the life I had made together with Kay over the past twelve years. I felt as if I had been putting up with wearing an ill-fitting suit day in and day out; worse, one made of a cheap and scratchy wool. Sylvie was young and vibrant, while I had never had the chance. Immediately after college I married and took on huge responsibilities: a wife, a job, a child. From that moment on, we adopted the rituals that went along with such responsibilities. Kay and I got up each morning. I went to work and she stayed home with our two children. These acts by themselves shouldn't have been a problem. We could have tried to fit enjoyment in around the chores. The problem was we didn't try. The only parts of our lives that intersected were the most mundane and dull: early on we had diapers and poor sleep and keeping track of train schedules in common; as the children grew, home life was about supervising homework, doing weekend yard work, putting meals on the table, unwinding with a drink, watching television, going to bed to do it all over again the next day. Somewhere along the way both Kay and I forgot how to enjoy life and each other's company. When I looked around, though, I saw people like us living the same sorts of lives. Part of me figured, isn't this what happens to everyone, this kind of blind devotion to routine?

Sylvie proved me wrong. In the face of her enthusiasm, it became clear that I was living the wrong life, one that fit me poorly, but I didn't have to. From Sylvie I learned that routines *and* lives could be shaken up.

My personal education was gradual and began at work, began ironically because Sylvie was eager to be taught the routines of the advertising business. Right from the start she devoured all the job instruction that I gave her then asked for more. She probed for my practices and opinions: *How do you pitch to clients? Don't you agree there's a lot of psychology involved in advertising?* Then she questioned the existing business standards: *Do you target new business or wait until the new client finds you? Do you ever try anything new?* The line between teacher and student blurred; was I teaching her about work, or was she teaching me about life? I only know that because of her questions, I began to see new possibilities, to see how my business and my life could change.

"New?" I asked her, overwhelmed with the rapid-fire questions but impressed by her ability to discuss all this with me. "New like how?"

"Example. On TV we have all these commercials for laundry detergent. In every single one, we see a woman who's upset about the whiteness of her family's whites."

"That's what laundry detergent is for," I pointed out.

"But then your target market is the same as the next person selling laundry detergent. Every company sells to the same consumer: the woman at home who spends every minute of her day doing household chores and feels mortified when her husband has ring around the collar. The world is changing, Mr. Manoli. What about," she asked me, "the women who work and want convenience?"

"Most women— " I began but she cut me off.

"Most women will be like me," she predicted. "Working and trying to maintain a home. Some will want the best products. Some will want the safest. Or the most convenient. Think about it. Environmentalists do laundry. Energy conservationists do laundry. Working women. Maybe someday," she added with a twinkle in her eye, "even men."

Sylvie was like that, she questioned and she pushed until she got an answer. She never settled for easy answers or the pap of applying old solutions to new situations, and because she didn't, I realized just how staid and set in my ways I had become, pitiful at thirty-four then thirty-five then approaching thirty-six, an unexciting, status quo, company man.

Around the same time as that unsettling conversation with Sylvie, I found myself having a few after hours drinks with a longtime, very loyal client. This client was a man about fifteen years older than I was, and he had been divorced for the past two years. Divorce – the idea a marriage could end – was completely foreign in my everyday suburban Boston Roman Catholic world. Even my cocktail-hour interest felt wrong, never mind the act of divorce itself, but I listened anyway in the dark of the Oak Bar, swirling my scotch and looking into my glass, as my client talked about the emptiness that brought his marriage to an end.

"It's about freedom, Jack, and I don't mean just the freedom to screw around. Freedom," he said as he leaned into the table, "to live in a way that makes me happy."

I wondered if the workplace was a mirror of the world at large for at the time that Sylvie came to work at my office, there were rumblings of discontent all over the country, even the world. It seemed to me that when the president had been shot in 1963, the world changed. Before that life had been predictable. You married the girl who was expecting your child and you made it work. Easy: acquire the home, the lawn, the job, more children, and soon you had the structure you needed in order to roll on each and every day. Almost ten years later, any terrible thing seemed possible. Looking back I wonder if we marched into 1972. More assassinations, a war that dragged, protesters, angry women, an energy crisis, and a liar of a president left most people upset, questioning, and dissatisfied.

I hadn't acknowledged any of this longing and dissatisfaction in myself until Sylvie walked in wearing a neat short skirt, until we began looking to spend hours and hours together, debating and discussing. Soon, everything at work that once seemed reliable and logical was suddenly not reliable and logical enough; soon nothing I had – children, wife, work – compared to the hours spent in Sylvie's company. If others could look for more, why not me too? *Don't you* ever *try* anything *new?* The question nagged in my mind. With that itch, and encouraged by the fact that Sylvie sought out my company too, I looked for something new. I looked right in front of me.

Sylvie slips through my partially open office door and stands watching me work, bent over a pad of paper at my drafting table, tearing paper, balling it up, tossing it to the floor. If I keep this up, I will be wading in paper.

"Knock, knock," Sylvie says softly.

I turn. I wear the heavy rimmed glasses I need for close work; throughout the morning I've raked my hand through my hair in frustration, making spiky tufts at my crown. Not the impression I want to make. The best I can hope for is that Sylvie thinks I look scholarly. I smooth my hair. A distracted scholar.

"Your wife called," she tells me. "About lunch. I wanted to put the call through but– "

"What about lunch? We're having lunch at eleven-thirty." I look at my watch. I look up. "It *is* eleven-thirty. I lost track of time. Is she waiting for me at the restaurant?" I begin to rise from my seat.

Sylvie shakes her head. "She asked me to give you a message. She said she's sorry, but she can't make it."

"Can't– I see." I drop back into my chair. "And she didn't ask to speak to me herself?"

Sylvie says, "Just the message."

I remove my glasses and rub my eyes. Looking down at the blank drawing pad in front of me and the pile of false starts at my feet I say, "Probably for the best. I'm getting nowhere with these sketches. Have you had lunch yet?" I ask Sylvie.

"No. I have some letters to finish. I have to take my lunch break late, maybe around two?"

"The park?"

She nods. "Same bench."

"May I join you?" I ask. "If I finish some work by two, could you save me a seat on your bench? By then I think I'll need to get out of here." I slide my glasses back on and turn back to my work.

"Sure. Of course. Two o'clock. I'll see you," Sylvie says as I settle back into sketching. She closes the door quietly behind her.

The air is noticeably cooler now that it's late September, less crowded with people although the pigeon population remains constant. Same birds fighting for fewer crumbs. Since sitting down twenty minutes ago, I have eaten a sandwich and watched the pigeons in silence. Sylvie must wonder why I asked to join her for lunch if I'm not going to talk, because this is the second time she has looked at me and sighed.

"Sylvie," I say, turning to her, acknowledging my rude behavior. "I'm sorry, I know I'm not much company," I admit.

"No, it's not that. I was thinking about . . . never mind." Sylvie waves her hand, shoos away the end of her sentence.

"You'll take my mind off work." She shakes her head, but I persist. "C'mon, what's worrying you? What were you thinking?"

"I'm not worried, exactly. I was thinking about Dan."

"Dan?"

"My boyfriend. His latest marriage proposal."

"You're engaged?"

"Oh no, God no, not yet." Sylvie shivers, wraps her sweater tight around her. "See, I'm beginning to feel . . . not so sure about Dan, and I'm *definitely* not sure about getting married. I mean, I've known him forever but we're both so young. Anyway," she says, again waving her hand, "I don't really want to think about it."

"I don't mind listening," I assure her, and I mean it. Especially if she asks for advice about getting married. *Should I or shouldn't I?* "Don't," I would say. "Please don't do it. Not if you have questions. And doubts."

"I know you would listen," she says, "but can we change the subject? We could talk about work?" I groan with her suggestion. "Okay, not work. Why don't you tell me about your children," Sylvie prompts.

"Better," I agree. "There's Michelle. Shelley. She's bookish, always reading. Mark, our son, is artistic, like his mother. My wife used to paint," I add as an aside.

"A painter! Portraits or landscapes?"

"I said she *used* to paint. We met in college," I explain. "Kay was two years behind me, an art student."

I think of all I long to tell Sylvie, things I've never told a soul. How I had been attracted by the bloom of cheerful freckles across a younger Kay's face. She was very pretty in college, in 1960. An artist. When she walked across the campus with her portfolio tucked under her arm, a secretive smile on her face, she was in her own world. I thought sleeping with her might give me a clue to the secrets behind the smile and a glimpse into her world. I wondered if sleeping with me would make Kay feel part of my more immediate, less cerebral one. Instead, sex brought us a child and no closer. We did the right thing and, both stuck, we ruined each other's lives. I tell Sylvie none of this.

"Kay left school after her sophomore year and eventually gave up painting altogether. I think maybe she felt her work wasn't good enough, or maybe she didn't want to paint badly enough. So she quit school and we got married."

"I see," Sylvie says, adding, "So she doesn't paint at all?"

"She's painted the kids' rooms, you know, murals. And she does art projects with them. Once Shelley wrote a story, and Kay and Mark illustrated it."

"But that still sounds so creative. It must be such a fun household!" Sylvie exclaims.

"Well . . ." I begin.

Sylvie interrupts, "Is your wife talented?"

"I'm not a good judge, but I liked her work. She was best at life drawing, you know, sketching nude models." Sylvie smiles a little when I can't look into her eyes at the mention of nudity. "But then she tried more modern work," I continue, "kind of colorful and chaotic." I shrug. "There was a lot of competition; her heart wasn't in that."

"Does she miss it?"

"I don't know."

"Does she ever talk about trying again?"

"Trying?" I ask, suddenly dry mouthed. I wonder if Sylvie has read my mind about us trying to make the marriage work. But no, her face as she asks shows only innocent interest. I frown deeply and feel creases form between my eyes and at the sides of my mouth. "You mean painting? No, she doesn't talk about it. Not to me anyway, Sylvie." I twist up the sandwich wrapper and stuff the trash into the paper bag. I look across the street. "Should we go?" I ask abruptly.

"I'm sorry," Sylvie apologizes. "I don't know you well enough to be asking such personal– "

I hold up my hand. "You know what?" I say. "It was just my turn to change the subject." I try to smile but it's not wholehearted. "And I think you may know me well enough," I look at her, "especially after all these lunches.

"I'll be right back," I say, standing. I collect our trash and walk it over to the nearest trashcan. Returning, I take my seat next to Sylvie, my eyes on a line of cars stopped at a traffic light.

"The thing is, I don't want to go back to work just yet," I say. "Do you mind sitting here a little longer?"

"I don't mind."

I stare into the traffic. After a couple of moments, I speak. "Kay doesn't have much to say to me these days," I begin. "When you said 'trying' a minute ago, it reminded me . . . well, like today, for example, we were supposed to meet in town for lunch. We're trying to make more of an effort, to do things together." I backtrack to explain, and look over at Sylvie. "It's pretty typical, I guess, after twelve or so years of marriage. After you talk about the kids – 'How's Mark?' 'Fine.' 'How's Shelley?' 'Fine.' – What's left to say? I figure we've got to work at it, so I suggest these lunches. But she has a habit of canceling."

"I'm sorry," Sylvie tells me.

"Anyway, what am I saying?" I give a short, wry laugh. "*I* should apologize. It was inappropriate for me to even bring it up. *I'm sorry.*"

"Is she sad, do you think?" Sylvie asks.

"Sad?"

"Or disappointed, about not painting, I mean. You said her heart wasn't in the competition. I think it must be difficult to give up something you're good at because you're afraid of failing."

"No, but you're different. You're ambitious, which is . . . different. And now I really think it's time to change the subject." I slap my knees. "We can talk about this ambition of yours." I pause a moment to consider an idea. "In fact," I say, "I have a meeting out of town tomorrow. This project I'm struggling with? It's a piece of business I really want; it's huge. I could use someone there to help me make the presentation, maybe take notes."

"Me?" Sylvie asks.

"Yes, you. Clear your desk when we get back to the office. If you could stay a little later tonight, we could get organized. You said yourself you've got a knack for putting this stuff together; why don't you come with me?"

At home with a bourbon on ice in hand, I sit down to a late dinner. Mark and Shelley wolf down the meal; it's a favorite and they are starving, although Mark picks out the celery and collects the slices along the rim of his plate. I take another look down at the ground beef, the tomatoes, the celery and elbow macaroni. Elbows aren't a pasta shape for grownups, I decide, but too often my meals are dictated by the children's tastes. Instead of eating, I fiddle with my silverware, aligning it just so, and as I do I brush with my left hand my salad bowl. The wedge of iceberg lettuce is drizzled with a vivid orange bottled French dressing; the color kills my appetite. I push the plate a few inches away and pull my glass of bourbon in closer.

"Don't you like your dinner?" asks Kay.

"I'm sure it's fine. I had kind of a late lunch, though." I sip my drink and watch the children eat. "When you canceled our lunch I worked right through. By the time I remembered to eat, it was two o'clock." I speak only a few sentences, but each sentence is infused with a second meaning, and in the hidden meaning lurks my reproach, my reminder of her failure. Well, of course it's her fault, I insist to myself. I would be enjoying dinner with them . . . if she'd had lunch with me today as planned . . . if she'd met me in the city at eleven-thirty as arranged . . . if she could make herself leave the house . . . I could go on and on. If I lose interest it *is* all her fault.

"Ah," she says, a world of nuance, a depth of understanding conveyed by the one syllable. Kay has always been quieter, far more economical with words than I am. After all these years I know how to interpret her few words. I know Kay smiles only to keep from wailing; I see it in the way her eyes dart around the table looking to light on something safe. I realize too what it is I am doing, what I have set in motion, but like perversely probing a sore tooth with my tongue, I do it anyway.

Kay sets down her fork and reaches for her ice water, looking to her left at Mark and to her right at Shelley, anywhere to avoid looking at me. She takes a good swallow. I don't trust her grip, the stranglehold she has on the glass. "So you what, grabbed a sandwich?" Kay asks, picking up any thread, struggling to make conversation.

"Exactly." I upend my glass and drink down the last of the harsh liquor. I savor both the burn and the dullness it brings to my brain. Shelley looks up at me. It's obvious my brevity alarms her, but I motion with a nod of my head for her to finish dinner. My children eat on, clean their plates, gulp their glasses of milk, the glugging noises in their throats an odd, almost musical accompaniment to this subdued dinner.

Kay rises. "Seconds, children?" she asks.

"Sure," they answer, nodding, smiling. Kay smiles back, at last pleased, pleased that she's made their favorite meal, pleased at this one thing she has managed to do right today.

"Back in a minute," she says. Along with the kids' plates, Kay collects her own plate, silverware, and glass, and she passes into the kitchen. From my seat at the dining room table, I can see directly into the kitchen. I fiddle with my empty glass and watch as she begins to put her dishes in the sink and then pauses. Maybe she sees, as I do, the setting sun through the window above the sink and the colors catch her eye. For a moment she stands, clutching the dirty plates closer, transfixed I believe by the changing color of the sky, by the bands of orange, pink, and gold. No longer painting but always an artist. As I watch my wife, the sun sinks a bit and the sky changes again, the pink and orange yield to a bright and vivid red.

I turn my attention back to the children with force. I joke with Shelley, and make Mark laugh. Out of the corner of my eye I see Kay's spine straighten and she stands rigid, still holding the dishes. I am still angry at her for today, and I hope the sound of our laughter in her absence rings in her ears like the thrumming noise of traffic, builds in her ears until she can practically taste it in the back of her throat.

And she does, she must, for as I watch, Kay winds up and, like a discus thrower, sends her armful of plates, silver, and glass hurtling into the kitchen window.

"Mom?"

"Mommy?"

Chairs scrape back on the hardwood floor of the dining room and we scramble to the kitchen doorway in time to see Kay standing still, empty arms hanging at her sides. The children and I, stunned, look past her to the window and, below, at the sink. I am appalled at myself, at what I have willed to happen. The children are shaken; the sink is a mess of porcelain shards and soft, swollen macaroni and silverware and Mark's cast-off celery; tomato and ground beef dot the back splash. And the kitchen window, broken wide open now into the darkening, purpling evening, reminds me of the outlines of mountain peaks, jagged and slicing into the sky.

Kay says one word. "Vermilion."

"Kay," I whisper to myself. "Oh, Christ."

In the morning, Sylvie finds herself balancing my notes on her lap as she sits beside me in my Town Car driving west of the city to pitch an ad campaign. In the back seat, she has buffeted the graphics and slide carousels. Earlier, preparing for the meeting, she took charge of organizing the slides of past successful campaigns; confirmed the setup of the company's conference room; and secured display easels, a projector, and a screen. And finally, taking initiative, Sylvie arranged for coffee service and pastries, carafes of ice water and drinking glasses to be waiting for us in the conference room.

"More windows came down early this morning," Sylvie says to me, pointing up as we drive by the new John Hancock skyscraper to pick up the Mass Pike heading west.

I shake my head. "That's a hell of an engineering flaw," I say without looking long at the temporary plywood barriers fitted where windows used to be, high above the ground.

Sylvie wonders aloud, "How come the windows pop out, but you never hear of anyone on the sidewalk being knocked out or sliced up by the falling glass?"

"That's a nice thought," I mutter wryly. I have had my own problems with window glass this morning. "Imagine walking to work, wondering, is this the day I get impaled by glass?" Out of the corner of my eye, I see Sylvie shudder with the image. I continue. "And the rent in there, I hear, is unbelievably high. Now, after all that hype, the building is unsafe. Someone should sue the architect."

"Or make them rebuild. Reinforce it somehow. Make the windows safer."

"Something like that," I agree. I watch the road. "You know, I think in ten years, twenty years, the whole face of this city will change. More skyscrapers, new roads, heavier traffic. I'll bet you."

"Are you a betting man, Mr. Manoli?" Sylvie asks, smiling at me. She is unacquainted with this brusque manner, and maybe hopes that a smile from her will somehow alter my mood.

"No," I answer with a little frown, considering. "No, I suppose not. I suppose I'm a little too cautious to make bets with anyone. How about this, though? Wherever you are in ten or twenty years, call me up and see if I was right. Because I'll probably still be here, watching the change happen around me."

"And where will I be?" Sylvie asks.

"New York. Chicago. Someplace big, bigger than Boston." I take my eyes from the road and scrutinize Sylvie. She is so pretty. And so young, with a whole world of possibilities ahead of her. "Running your own company. Maybe your own public relations firm. I can see it now," I say.

Sylvie laughs. "My own company! You think?"

I nod. "I do," I say.

Sylvie gets caught up in dreams of the future, a young woman with her life in front of her. She blurts out happily, "Or perhaps I'll stay in Boston. And you and I will run our own advertising or P.R.

company together. Rocher and Manoli," she says. "Or Manoli and Rocher."

Although I brought up the whole topic, I now have nothing to say in response. Too tired from cleaning up, too tired from staying up late to cover the gaping hole with plastic sheeting. I turn on the car radio and fiddle with the dial, aimlessly listening to the static between AM stations.

Sylvie, next to me, stares out the front window, probably imagining herself the head of a successful independent public relations firm. Or maybe she imagines herself working alongside Jack Manoli, for of course once we are partners she will call me Jack. Sylvie, my partner instead of my secretary.

"God, that would be wonderful," she says under her breath. "Don't you think?" She turns to me and waits for an answer.

"It's an idea," I reply. "One of many impossible ideas."

"Impossible?"

"One piece of business at a time," I chide. "I can only think about today." I note that Sylvie looks down to see the skin over my knuckles stretching, whitening as I grip the steering wheel. I make an effort to relax. "I want this account, I *really* want it."

"Okay," Sylvie laughs, "no pressure."

I don't share the laugh; after last night's scene with Kay, I haven't got a laugh left in me. I speak very little for the next forty-five minutes. Sylvie steals looks, taking in the tight clench of my jaw and the wiry tendons in my neck as I drive, wondering no doubt what has put me – her usually even-tempered boss – on edge.

"Did I say– "

"No," I interrupt.

" –something wrong?" Sylvie finishes. "Mr. Manoli?"

"No. Nothing. Really," I assure her. "Bad night last night. I was up late, and I'm anxious about this piece of business. Do you mind if we don't talk for a while?" I ask her. "I'd like to think for a bit. Organize my thoughts."

"No, of course I don't mind. That's fine." Sylvie pauses. After a moment she says, "Could I ask one more thing though? Then I promise, not another word."

I think how much she sounds like one of my children begging for answers. *Just one more question, Dad, please?* "Sure," I answer.

"Those windows, in the Hancock building?"

"Back to that subject?" I find myself smiling in spite of my black mood.

"I wonder," Sylvie begins, "if you can hear the glass fall. If that's why no one gets killed, because they hear the glass popping and falling. Like the whistles of bombs being dropped."

"Maybe," I reply. "Maybe it's just like a bomb, and you hear the glass make its way down. Or maybe," I continue, "you never hear a thing."

Shelley

Between twenty and thirty people had followed us back to the house this afternoon, so it takes Sylvie and me until just past seven o'clock to personally thank then close the door on the last of the funeral guests. The stragglers — a business acquaintance and his wife — hung around to hug Sylvie over and over and offer the standard condolences.

"It's amazing," Sylvie observes as she watches out the window as the couple's car pulls away from the curb. "They all think they were Jack's best friends."

I look at her in profile, waiting for the roll of the eyes or the wry smile that will reveal the sarcasm beneath the remark. Neither appears. Sylvie glows, and I realize she expects nothing less from their acquaintances. She turns to me.

"I'm bushed," she says. "Do you think Steven would drive me home?"

After months of illness, Dad died at home last Thursday and we whisked Sylvie from their Brookline townhouse to our home. Now it is Tuesday and she has been with us since we received her call. From here we alerted the newspaper with the death notice; we finalized funeral arrangements from my kitchen.

With Sylvie's approval, I had arranged for a cleaning outfit to air out her condominium, strip the bed, and remove all hospital traces of the last days of Dad's life. The cleaning firm offered to clear closets and pack up all of my father's belongings, but Sylvie told me she preferred to take her own time with that. I can't help thinking that no matter how neat and tidied her home might be, she shouldn't face clothing and photos, watches and cufflinks, even the familiar well-worn bathrobes and slippers tonight when she is so obviously exhausted. Of course I am tired too and it would be wonderful to reclaim my home, but I can't bring myself to make anything but the polite and proper gesture.

"Stay one more night," I urge. "You can go home rested in the morning."

Sylvie cocks her head and looks at me quizzically, as if I'm speaking a foreign language. "Really, it makes sense," I tell her. "Steven is going in to work tomorrow. He can take you as early as you'd like."

After a moment of simply looking into my eyes, she shakes her head as if stirring herself into action. "Sure I'll stay, if Steven really can take me early. I miss my life." Sylvie presses her fingers to her temple. She looks spent now the crowds have gone, almost as if she has relied on the energy of a houseful of people to keep her going. "You'll forgive me," she says, "if I go on up to bed without helping you clean up?" Anticipating my encouragement, she takes a step up onto the first stair.

"Yes, go on," I say. "Emma has stayed specifically to help. Besides I have my own system. Go on."

At the foot of the stairs we stop to embrace, but between the heaviness of our weary bodies lurching together and the divide of a stair, it is an awkward hug. Or maybe the stairs have nothing to do with our awkwardness. Maybe, without Dad, we have no idea what we will be to each other. Sylvie soon pulls away from me and continues on up to bed.

Alone and sobered by my thoughts, I look around my living room at the clutter made by all these guests. I own a lot of furniture, having inherited most of the pieces from my childhood home following my mother's death, and every surface of every occasional table is covered with plates and cups and napkins and picked over platters of food. Sighing at the sight of a few cigarette butts snuffed out in someone's uneaten plate of shrimp and pasta salad, I wonder how the smoker escaped my notice. I would have sent the person outside if I had caught him. Perhaps I am more numb today than I have realized.

I don't regret vetoing the use of paper plates and plastic utensils, not even when I begin stacking the plates and carefully collecting the stainless. The clearing and cleaning up provide a productive focus for my nervous energy. The cups, however, are paper and plastic for hot and cold drinks through necessity; I barely have enough coffee cups for a family gathering. And although I feel a twinge of guilt about their effect on the environment, especially as I look around and see how freely they were used and discarded, I will toss every last one when I make my next pass through the room.

In the kitchen, Emma chats amiably with Steven as she loads the dishwasher. When I arrive with my armful of plates, they both smile indulgently at me instead of complaining about the extra work. Emma moves to take the stack from my arms and invites me to sit. I shake my head, preferring, I say, to keep busy.

"Did either of you notice who was smoking in the house?" I ask. Without waiting for an answer, I wedge myself between the dishwasher and the sink, displacing Steven who has been leaning up against the counter while talking to Emma, and I begin scraping and rinsing the plates before loading. "Not that I can do anything about it now," I add, babbling on as I continue to work, "but we'll probably smell the smoke in here for days."

To add my rinsed plates to the dishwasher I must reorganize some of the stacking Emma has already done, and without hesitation

I unload and then reload the entire bottom rack. When I finish and ask Emma to pass me the plates, I look up. Steven and Emma don't move or speak; they just stare at me.

"What?" I ask.

"What else did I do wrong?" Emma asks with a wry laugh, which breaks the uncomfortable silence. She looks pointedly at my reorganization.

"The dishes?" I ask, looking down at my handiwork. "You didn't do anything wrong," I explain, "but I can fit more in this way."

"What an eye-opener," Emma says. "And I thought you were like this only at school."

"So she's like this at school too?" Steven asks Emma with a smile.

Emma nods. "Taking charge."

True, I agree as I think of how I have to take charge of my students, their education, but still the teasing puts my back up. "It's called efficient," I protest, "and it's not the least bit funny."

"It's a little funny, Shelley," Steven admits. "Redoing someone's work."

"When you put it that way," I add, "you make me sound more pathetic than funny. I only meant to stay busy. Besides, Emma's done way too much today." I continue loading what I can into the dishwasher, placing the rest in the sink. "Plus we've got school tomorrow morning," I remind her as I slip the dishtowel from her shoulder. "You should go on home. Please," I add when I notice she is inclined to linger. "Your family will think I've kidnapped you."

"Okay, all right," she says, holding both hands up in surrender. "I'll go, if you promise me you'll think about taking a day off tomorrow. Or better yet, take the rest of the week," Emma suggests.

"You know I can't think about it," I say, shaking my head. I have my students, I have Asya tomorrow afternoon and a parent meeting with her father, and I can't let any of them down. This would be the perfect moment to tell both Steven and Emma about Asya, boast about the progress I've made with her and the effective team Ian and I had become to help her succeed. But since they clearly disagree with me about returning to work I decide to keep the story to myself.

Just the thought of work improves my mood, and I link my arm through Emma's and walk her to the door. At the hall closet I stop and reach in for her coat, a hard-to-miss peacock blue wool cape. Flamboyant yet somehow classy, like Emma. "Thank you for all you've done today," I whisper in her ear when she hugs me goodbye. "I hope you don't think I'm ungrateful."

"Of course I don't, but don't push yourself so hard," Emma says back. After a moment she pulls back from our embrace. "At least think about what I said about rushing back to work."

I can't do much more than nod, knowing that I won't change my mind. I watch from the door until she reaches her car, give one last wave, and then return to my chores.

Having sent Emma on her way I pass back through the living room, and this time I collect the disposable cups. I separate the plastic from the paper, as though it makes any difference, by nesting them into two wavering towers. In the kitchen, Steven is staring through the window out over the backyard, whistling over and over the uncomplicated tune of "Simple Gifts," which Sylvie had insisted upon for this morning's service.

"When I die," I say as I come into the kitchen balancing the two columns of dirty cups, "please give me the ceremony I want. Cremate me and plant my urn of ashes in the backyard. Say a few words. No mourners. Donations to any charity in lieu of flowers. And no food." I remove my foot from the trash can pedal and the lid crashes down.

Steven stops whistling and turns to me. "None?" he asks, one eyebrow arched.

"Well, take the girls out for an ice cream. That's what I'd like. I love ice cream."

"I know you do." Steven, smiling, reaches for me. "But don't talk about dying. Please," he says, "don't even joke.

"Besides," he adds as he takes me by the shoulders and holds me at arm's length, "you won't die. You can't. You're too important. You'll just stick around to plan everyone else's funeral."

I feel restless and step out of Steven's arms. Using the towel I took from Emma, I start drying the bowls and platters that have been stacked in the drying rack, avoiding Steven's watchful eyes.

"Did something happen with Mark?" he asks, either reading my mind or the worried look that so often crosses my face when I think of my brother. "Has Mark upset you in some way?"

"Why would you say that?" I reply as I reach into the upper cupboards to put the dishes away.

"He left in an awful hurry today. And you're always worried about Mark," Steven reminds me, "even though he's thirty-five."

The familiar barb. We've been over this so many times in the past six months. Steven's patience was growing thin when it came to Mark's volatile moods and my need to soothe him. My husband knew so many things about my family, our history, but for all that he knew, there was so much he didn't – and couldn't – understand. And we, who had never fought in all our years of marriage, had been bickering too much lately about my brother.

"I know he's thirty-five, Steven. Anyway, it's not Mark." Not Mark exclusively, I should say, but don't. I shrug and lean toward the counter, bumping my hip against a drawer pull. It stings and I will probably have a bruise in the morning, but the rawness of the nerve seems appropriate.

Steven is patient. He looks at me and waits for me to elaborate.

"I'm thinking, that's all. There's a lot to think about. One thing in particular," I add. "Dad left Mark and me the Rockport house. Jointly. Sylvie told me at the wake and I meant to tell you when things quieted down. Which I guess is now," I say with a shrug.

"But that's good news," Steven says. "The old place meant a lot to your dad, and he wants you to enjoy it too."

"Yes," I answer, "great news," although I know it will be anything but.

Steven picks up on the flat tone of my reply.

"Then why don't you sound like you think it's wonderful?" he asks. "I know. It *is* Mark, isn't it? Mark doesn't want a thing from your father and now you've got the house to deal with." Without waiting for an answer he continues.

"Shelley, you want my advice? Don't spend a minute trying to think how you can make this right for Mark. I know you." He wags a finger at me. "Right now you're probably trying to come up with a way to keep Mark from blowing up over this. Am I right? What you need to do instead is enjoy the house and let him do what he pleases."

"Dad left it to both of us, so we should reach a mutual decision. Except that Mark won't think about it. He's angry, Steven. Is it wrong for me to hope he wouldn't be angry all the time?"

Steven stands quietly at my side, listening. When I finish he says, "Shelley, Mark's had years to work on this. Instead, he's gone to lengths to avoid facing his problems. And because you keep trying to coax your brother into being happy, you've made it too easy for him to ignore what he should face."

Touché. Of course I help Mark. My brother took Dad's departure harder than I ever did. Steven wasn't there, hadn't grown up in that house, and only had my easier nature to judge the situation by. When I was younger, my visits with Dad had never been full of anger. Unlike Mark's. I had been deeply hurt and disappointed by my father's departure, but I had needed to hold onto whatever family I could. I needed a father. So I held on, making what I had for family work. When my role of running interference between Mark, Mom, and Dad ended with Mark's graduation from high school, Dad and I sort of drifted apart. I was busy starting my own family and Dad was occupied with Sylvie and a new business.

Dad and I spent nearly eight years in a sort of limbo, communicating but not really meaningfully – Dad living his life, I living mine – until one afternoon, heavily pregnant with Libby, I came home from a pre-Christmas dinner grocery store run. The store had been crazy and crowded and I had a huge stomach, many bags of food for the holiday in two days, and a stressed-out, crabby Margaret in tow. And then Jack's message on our answering machine on top of all else. "Sylvie and I would like to have you and the family over for dinner the day after Christmas," he had said, getting right to the point. We hadn't had one family holiday, not one, since Dad remarried, and now my family was being invited into the inner circle of Jack and Sylvie. My father's invitation was not offhand or routine; but neither was he sheepish or apologetic. He sounded kind and convincing, jovial even, and I found myself longing to call him back. I was unabashedly grateful that he had, after so many years, turned his attention back to me.

Over coffee and dessert on December twenty-sixth we all warmed to each other. That experience led to another dinner later that winter, showing off the new baby and accepting a beautiful silver rattle. It led to less uncomfortable, lovely actually, visits to Jack's and Sylvie's Rockport cottage; to something very near fondness for Sylvie, whom I found charming and a genuinely devoted wife; to long walks along the coastline with my arm linked through my father's.

"She loves you," I had remarked spontaneously on one of these walks, surprising not only my father with this sudden flash of understanding, but also myself. Jack reached his arm around my shoulders and drew me to him. We made no reference to anything that might be at the root of our drifting apart. Neither of us said another word as we rounded back to the cottage where our families waited. I wasn't completely blinded by the attention, but I was too happy to ruin the moment by bringing up all the difficulties. After years without, I had a father. What you don't have, you make. Or remake.

Was it wrong for me to have wanted that for Mark too, always?

"Shelley," Steven says softly, bringing me back to my kitchen and my present concerns. "Maybe you need to stop taking on all of Mark's problems."

Stop? I look at Steven incredulously. When I first told Mark that I was seeing Jack again, and that Jack wanted to see him too, Mark had sneered. "I don't care what you do, Shell," he had said in a tone that indicated he did, "but don't expect me to fall at Jack's feet." Like you, he added by way of a long, contemptuous look.

"He misses you."

"What you've never had, you can't possibly miss," Mark finished, weirdly echoing and inverting my own adage, and there it was, the fundamental difference between us: optimism. I had it, he didn't.

"But I love Mark," I tell Steven. "I can't help taking on his problems, especially when I know he needs help." I can hear my voice rising but I feel frustrated. Lately all of our conversations end here, at this stalemate. *You shouldn't; I have to.* "Steven, I wish you would listen and not criticize."

"I'm not criticizing," he says, and I see he believes this. Nevertheless, I always feel defensive, under attack lately.

"You're tired," Steven points out and he takes me by the shoulders once again. "The last few days have caught up with you. I wish you'd go to bed," he adds softly. "Finish the clean-up in the morning."

Pressure builds in my throat and behind my sinuses. I feel like crying with frustration. I don't know what bothers me more, Steven's censure of my relationship with Mark, or his need to diagnose and fix me, or that the smooth and orderly life we have grown used to has become so unrecognizably bumpy.

I don't mean to speak sharply but I do. "I think I'm capable of finishing what I started," I tell Steven, and he throws his hands up in the air at my dismissive tone. There is nothing left to say; the conversation about Mark never progresses past these misunderstandings and hurt feelings.

"Knock, knock," Sylvie says in a tentative voice from the doorway into the kitchen. Steven and I jump a little in surprise at the interruption.

"I came for a glass of water," Sylvie tells us, "but maybe I should come back."

"No, please. Let me get you some water." I begin to step in and wait on her, grateful for the diversion from the tension with Steven, but Sylvie stops me.

"I interrupted you two. I can help myself and get back to bed," she says, holding back my efforts with a raised hand. "Although, now that I'm up, I think I'll have a glass of whisky."

Steven stops us both. "Please. Sit down," he tells Sylvie as he draws out a chair for her, "and I'll bring your drink." Almost as an afterthought, he pulls out a second chair, inviting me to sit also.

"I don't need to be fussed over," Sylvie argues.

"Of course you don't, but I'm going to anyway. Shelley and I were just saying that it has been a long day."

Sylvie looks from me to my husband. "You're right. That's important to remember. A long day, a long week, an interminable year. Thank you," Sylvie says to Steven as he returns with two fingers of scotch whisky with a twist of lemon peel and one ice cube, just the way Sylvie likes it. She looks Steven straight in the eye and smiles. "Perfect," she says as she takes her first sip. Satisfied, Steven returns to his place at the counter.

Watching Sylvie smile at my husband, I am struck by how deftly she gets what she needs from people. How she elicits Steven's care rather than his advice, a skill I'm clearly lacking these days. Sylvie's allure doesn't surprise me – she is lovely even in fatigue, even wearing my spare terrycloth bathrobe. Her skin is clear and nearly smooth except for a few faint lines around her eyes. Her large tawny eyes are wide open and clear, exactly the color of the drink in her glass. And on anyone else, the dark circles underneath would look like illness; on Sylvie the smudges look like expertly applied makeup. She looks like an overwhelmed but securely loved young girl.

After Steven watches over us for a few moments, he yawns loudly and stretches. "Hon, I'm turning in," he tells me. "Remember what I said, don't be late. I know you're tired." He bends down to kiss the top of my head and gives me one last smile as he straightens up. I bristle instead of soften.

"As soon as I get the dishes done," I say, my parting shot. I can't let my anger at his criticism go. Once Steven has left the room I sigh heavily.

"You had words," Sylvie concludes. "Again, I'm sorry I interrupted."

"Like you say, long day, long week."

She lifts an eyebrow and I can tell she has a few questions for me.

"It's nothing," I tell her. "Really. And I'm glad you interrupted when you did, actually. We were getting nowhere."

"You didn't ask for a drink. Why don't you join me?" Sylvie asks, raising her glass.

"Maybe tea," I answer. I put my hands on the table's edge to push myself out of the seat.

"Please," Sylvie insists. "I don't want to drink alone."

"All right." I stand, and instead of running water in the kettle I fetch myself one of the same heavy highball glasses and pour only enough scotch to cover the bottom.

Sylvie raises her eyebrow at the meager amount. "It's not really my drink of choice," I explain.

"Then you are extra good to join me. You always were, Shelley. Good, I mean. It meant a lot to your father, you know. How hard you tried to accept us."

How hard I tried. *Please, Mark, make an effort. Guess what I'm doing in Bio, Dad, in Chem, in English. Guess what I'm getting for grades. Did you see Mark's painting, his sculpture? Show Dad your work, Mark, come on.* Covering up the heavy, awkward lapses in conversation with a can-do attitude. While Mark dropped further and further into one of his sulks, I whirled like a dervish to keep everyone entertained. Everyone had been so incredibly unhappy the year that Dad left and beyond, during that period of adjustment. Mom was humiliated; Mark felt abandoned; even Dad and Sylvie who, under different circumstances would have been enjoying the early stages of love and marriage, were thrust immediately into the realities of dealing with a stubborn son and vindictive ex-wife.

Sylvie picks up her glass and comments, "Mark left in a hurry today." Her voice interrupts my thoughts. How much of my argument with Steven had she overheard? Discussing Mark with Steven is bad enough lately; I really don't want to discuss him with Sylvie. I keep my answer brief.

"He did, indeed," I agree. "He said Jen expected him," I explain but even to my own sympathetic ears, Mark's excuse sounds lame.

"Ah yes, the girlfriend," Sylvie says. "Remind me. How long have they been together?"

The question is a sign of Sylvie's distraction. Although Dad hadn't heard a word directly from Mark in years, I had fed them information about Mark's successes and his personal life. I refresh her memory. "Going on three years," I answer.

"That's right. What is she like?" Sylvie asks. She sips her drink.

"Jen?" I say unnecessarily as I give myself time to think of a vague answer.

I think back to the night when Steven and I first met Jen. Mark had called, excited about this woman he had just started dating. An artist like himself, he had said. Mark had never before referred to himself as an artist, a person with a professional focus and goals, and that he told me about Jen at all surprised me. I had seen various girls on his arm at parties, beautiful girls in the passenger seat of his car as he drove out to my house to grab something and just as quickly leave without any sort of introduction. With Jen I heard the history, the plans, even saw the work. Steven and I got invited to dinner — *you'll never believe it,* I told my husband right after I got the invitation, *dinner at Mark's!* — and then we saw it all, the life they had started to make together. After years of worrying about Mark and where he lived and how he made his living, I felt the relief of seeing him settled, something I honestly thought I would never see.

I always sensed, though, that Jen was wary of me, resented perhaps my presence in Mark's life. Truthfully, I am grateful for the fact of her in Mark's life but I don't know her that well. "Jen is a talented photographer," I say, choosing to answer with a fact I do know.

"You don't like her," Sylvie says with a twinkle of mischief in her eyes.

"That's not it."

Sylvie smiles at me. "Then what is she *like?*" she persists.

With the disarming smile and persuasion I find myself, in spite of myself, giving serious thought to an answer. "She likes a lot of the same things Mark does," I begin, thinking of their mutual fondness for picking through trash to find materials for their artwork. "But she is more disciplined. Ambitious," I add. Then I wonder if I have gone too far, if I have chosen a word that might show disapproval of Jen. Or that I was passing judgment on Mark's work habits. I explain, "By 'ambitious' I mean she works hard and she's successful. There aren't many artists who can support themselves doing what they love to do."

"And Jen does?" Sylvie asks.

"She sells her photographs for a lot of money, she's won prizes."

Jen *was* productive, and she nudged on Mark's productivity too. I pause, thinking about the last visit I made to their loft. Creative energy oozed around me: Mark moving around his work table, dipping down and reaching for pieces of broken china, zooming in to place a piece, retreating for perspective; the flashing of Jen's giant flash bulbs, Jen running between camera tripod and the stacks of wooden objects she photographed then rearranged; music from a small radio blaring and fading with a weak signal. Watching Mark at work, my heart swelled. I had nearly forgotten why I was there.

The action had stopped abruptly when I uttered the two words, "Dad's dying."

"She motivates Mark, which is good. He has a show later this spring. Not solo, but still." I smile with pride, again for a moment forgetting death. I see myself attending the opening, bragging to everyone I know.

"Mmm." Sylvie lifts her glass as if to take a sip, but she stares off into space as if considering something, drawing conclusions.

After a few seconds Sylvie tips her head, looks at me quizzically. "So, she whips him into shape?" she asks.

I think of my discussion with Steven, of Steven's belief that I coddle Mark. And if I'm the caretaker, then Jen's the taskmaster? None of this makes Mark look like someone who can manage on his own, and I think I am not wrong to worry about my brother. I would never admit this to Sylvie so I say nothing in response, raise my glass to my lips, take a sip of my unpleasant drink, and grimace with the smell as much as the taste. In this way I let the moment pass.

"Why, then, didn't Jen come today? Or to the wake last night?" Sylvie asks.

"I think that was Mark's decision," I say, "wanting to keep Dad's death separate from his life with Jen. You know how Mark can be about Dad," I remind her.

Sylvie stands and walks to the counter for the Famous Grouse bottle. She pours us each another half-inch of scotch before sitting. I don't even bother declining this time. When she sets the bottle between us, it begins to feel like we're in for a long night of drinks and confessions.

"I know how he *was*," Sylvie continues. "Remember when you and Mark first visited us in Rockport, the summer after Jack and I married?"

Not Mark's finest hour. "I do," I say, and then I avert my eyes from her face. I don't tell her the same memory filled my own mind when I watched my brother drive away today. He's still running, I think.

"He was such a little shit," Sylvie says with a laugh and although her bluntness shocks me, I can't disagree. She continues, "He refused to do anything I asked from the minute he stepped out of the car, then he tried to run away." Sylvie stops speaking then, lost in thought. She looks down at her hands wrapped around her glass, fingers woven. I wonder if she is reliving that day in Rockport or if she is simply tiring, the stress of the day finally catching up to her. When she looks back up, though, I see her eyes are clear and lucid. She smiles. "You know, before Mark, I wasn't used to anyone not liking me. I was always . . . admired. I had worked for your father only six months when he realized his clients liked me so well that he needed to promote me. They *all* liked me."

Looking at Sylvie and recalling Steven's solicitousness earlier, I find it easy to believe her. By her looks alone she is someone people want to know; even people like my own doggedly faithful husband want to do nice things for her. And believe me, if she is handsome today at forty-seven, at twenty she was like a fashion model with her straight, center-parted blonde hair and fresh good looks. Sylvie smiles across the table at me, and when she does, I can easily see how everyone in her sphere would have been captivated.

"And then I met Mark," Sylvie finishes. Tonight she is in a truthful mood. "Mark's dislike was a . . . surprise."

Yes, I think, it would have been, although a few happy clients were a far remove from a boy losing his father. Wrapped up in each other, Dad and Sylvie were oblivious to Mark's volatile moods, while all I could see was Mark running, the stripes of his shirt a blur. "He was only a boy," I remind her.

"Yes, and now he's a grown man still carrying around all that anger," Sylvie pronounces.

"He was just a boy," I repeat, not wanting that to be forgotten.

"Well, he's not a boy now. Time, don't you think, for him to get over himself?"

"I often think," Sylvie continues without waiting for an answer, "that if the divorce happened now, or even ten years ago, we'd have known how to be one big extended stepfamily."

"So all of this family dysfunction can be put down to a case of bad timing?" I ask her. After the pressure of the day and this conversation, I aim for a little sharp humor, but the line comes out sharper and less humorous than I intend. I hang my head and look into my lap. "I'm sorry."

"Stop apologizing," Sylvie says with impatience. "I really don't mind the sarcasm, Shelley. At least it's real. It's more real than pretending everything was peachy back then. Or even now.

"Messy emotions, messy situations. If I've learned anything in the twenty-seven years since I met your father, it's that life is messy. People don't always do the right thing, we aren't always good. Lord knows I wasn't. I used to wonder where the hell being good was going to get me. Living everyone else's life but my own, that's exactly where. It wouldn't have gotten me Jack, that's for sure, and with your father, I was the best person I could be. What I did in order to be with him? Well, my actions were questionable at best. But that's what I mean. It's messy stuff.

"And Shelley," she says, and here she pauses to shift in her seat. Until now Sylvie has been sitting very straight and still in her chair, one hand resting on the kitchen table, the other holding her glass. Now she moves, sets down her drink and runs a hand through her hair. Her movement sends a waft of her signature scent, the hard-to-find Cabochard she loves so much, in my direction. I breathe it in. She's worn it all these years.

"Shelley," she repeats, "even with the mess, if I had to do it all again, I wouldn't do anything differently."

Sylvie rises and adjusts the belt of the bathrobe a bit tighter around her waist before I can comment on what she has just said. She brings her glass to the sink and, with her back to me, I notice how fragile she looks, thinner than I have ever seen her after caring for Jack for months at the expense of her own health. I had had several years to watch Dad with Sylvie, the way she doted on him, the way he worshipped her, and I understand what she means. In their union there was a sort of alchemy, success created out of disaster. The messy gray area of life where doing the right thing can be wrong and choosing the wrong solution can mean salvation. Understanding this and knowing that I accept it stirs up disquiet within me, reminds me uncomfortably of Mark. It pits me against his absolutes, the black and white of his hurt boy's world.

"It's still not easy."

"I know," Sylvie says and I watch her shoulders rise and sink with a heavy sigh. She turns. "It was difficult, a difficult time."

"Yes," I agree with a nod of acknowledgment. "Yes, it was."

"You know," Sylvie says from across the kitchen, and I find I must pull myself out of my own thoughts to follow what she is saying, "when Jack was dying and thinking about what to leave you, I told him, 'Money. Anything else, anything personal, even a watch or jewelry – the business – it'll be tainted. Mark will call it a bribe. He'll think the same thing about money, no doubt, but at least it's not something you have a personal attachment to.' Then Jack said, 'The cottage.'

"I told him not to. I told him I thought it was a bad idea, and I gave him that advice because I remembered the first visit you and Mark had made and, well, it was hardly a success. Jack said, 'That's why they should have it.'

"That makes no sense to me." Sylvie shakes her head. "In business matters, your father always listened to me. But about the house

I couldn't get him to change his mind. He insisted. The house, *that* was his gift to you.

"Anyway, the house." She leans back against the counter and puts her hands in the bathrobe's pockets. "I forgot this last night, so I brought it to the kitchen for you to find in the morning. Since you're here, well, this goes along with the key." Sylvie pulls from a pocket a folded piece of paper and hands it to me. "Jack's letter of intent. The letter formally amends the will. Read it when you're ready, but it doesn't say much more than I already told you about Jack's giving you the house. The only difference is, it's in his words."

I take the paper, open it, and give it a quick read. Yes, the intent is there: "The Rockport house . . . I bequeath to my two children . . . to do with as they wish."

Sylvie speaks again which takes my attention from Dad's letter. "I'm tired of worrying about Jack's plan. As far as we're all concerned, it's just a gift, this house. If neither of you wants it as a summer home, or year round for that matter, don't feel bad if you decide to sell it. Or rent it out. Do whatever you want."

What she says reminds me of my last conversation with Mark. Knowing his position, occupying the house seems impossible to imagine. For me, though, doing nothing seems equally impossible. My world is becoming murkier for me by the minute. I slip the letter into the side pocket of my black dress. "Mark wants no part of the house."

"Of course he doesn't," Sylvie says dismissively. Discussing Mark is finished and she changes topics. "But enough about the house. Whatever you decide, I know it will be the right thing. And now that's behind us," she says with a yawn, "I think I should try to get some sleep. Will Steven be able to get an early start in the morning?"

"I'm sure he'll be happy to do whatever you want, Sylvie." Steven genuinely likes Sylvie. They are of an age and he shares no complicated emotional history with her. "Good night," I say.

At the doorway, Sylvie pauses. "I've been thinking," she says, turning. "I think I'll take myself on vacation. Somewhere warm." She shivers. "Some thoroughly hedonistic spot like the Four Seasons on Nevis. Or maybe Italy. Either way, I think Jack would approve."

Before I can respond, Sylvie leaves the room. I sigh. I should go to bed too, I think, listening to the sound of Sylvie's feet on the stairs. I recall Steven urging me to rest, and then I look down into my glass. Frugal as well as efficient, I can't bring myself to rinse out the smallest bit of scotch, and I drink the remains in one gulp. I try to appreciate what I taste, I roll its oiliness around my mouth then swallow, hoping I will soon feel tired.

In my bedroom I let my dress drop to the floor, tired enough to consider letting the clothing stay there until morning. Then thinking better of this idea, I gather my dress over my arm, open the closet, reach for a hanger. As I do, the sharp edges of Dad's letter poke at my forearm and I remember to remove the paper from the dress's pocket. The last thing I do on my way to bed is drop the note into my handbag standing open on my night table.

Once in bed I begin to fall asleep quickly but fitfully, dropping hard into a falling sensation not once but twice. I can't stop the latest To Do list running through my mind: get Sylvie safely settled at home, call Mark, resolve the house issue. I'm sure Sylvie isn't tossing any more, worried as I am by loose ends and unfinished business, not now that she's spoken her mind. *I used to wonder where the hell being good was going to get me.* Her words run through my overtired mind. Being good – thinking how to please everyone, running my chore list over and over in my head like so many sheep – isn't going to get me to sleep, I think. Blaming the alcohol, I shift in bed and try to get comfortable curled on my side. I concentrate on settling my body, purposefully slowing my breathing. Just as I begin to feel myself fall into sleep once again, Mark pops into my head, a vivid color picture of his face as he looked at me before driving off, a face on which anger warred with despair. I wonder how he is tonight, and promise myself that calling him needs to be my priority in the morning. It is my last thought before sleep finally takes over.

I walk down a path I know leads to my house, but it looks unfamiliar. My girls, Margaret and Libby, are ahead of me by a few yards. It is unusual for me to let them wander away for, unrestricted, Libby likes to run. She sees expanse around her sometimes where there is none, imagining herself a filly in the country. "Take care of your sister," I call to Margaret, but I see instantly I needn't have worried because Margaret holds Libby by the hand, pulls her close, and keeps her from launching into a run.

We should be approaching a brick walkway. We would be if this truly were my house, but here the path is graveled with pea stones that crunch together under the pressure of my footsteps, and the noise makes me shiver. As I round a bend in the path, I look to my right and see Mr. Jenkins walking his dog Scout and I wave.

The diversion makes me lose sight of the girls. Walking to catch up to them, I thrust my hands in my jacket pockets and set a brisk pace. I hold my head up and I begin to see the outlines of my house. As it comes into better view with every advancing step I make, I feel even more confused. I understand it is my house but it, like the path, is unfamiliar: peeling yellow paint where my house is a tidy and crisp white; dead dark and unoccupied looking where mine rings with young girls' voices and doors slamming and too many lights on. If Libby and Margaret haven't already entered the house, where are they? Despite my concern, I walk on to the house and its unwelcoming windows that stare like vacant black eyes.

As I reach the front steps, a voice reaches my ear, a shout, and I stop. I turn to see Mr. Jenkins waving an arm, violently slicing the air to get my attention. I feel it must be me he is trying to call; there are only the two of us. And his dog. Scout the water rescue dog, the benign giant. Behind Mr. Jenkins the sky is dark red like a bloodstain, inkily spreading toward me. I wonder if he is warning me of an approaching storm. "I can't hear you," I call back but my cry doesn't carry through the thick atmosphere.

The dog barks, a big black dog against a red background. Scout curls back his lips showing me red gums, white teeth, a black and bottomless gullet so clear to me even at such a distance. He barks again, strains against his lead, and Mr. Jenkins stoops, reaches down for the collar, a studded, massive piece of leather circling a trunk of a throat. I watch as my neighbor runs his hand down the dog's muscled flank, still large but lean now where he was in the past bulky, sleek where once he was shaggy. Scout strains against his master's hand, a hand that must feel the power bunching under the animal's skin, the stored threat. Mr. Jenkins' hand goes to the spring hasp. With teeth bared, Scout's annoying but harmless drool turns into dripping gore. The dog's legs tense, poised for a leap; the chain seems to stretch then melt, steel becoming mercury.

I begin to back up, walking slowly backwards, my head bowed and body low, trying with every slow servile step not to enrage this beast as I make my way to the door of the house which is mine yet unfamiliar. I hit the steps with my heels first, and stumbling, I back into the front door. As I slam to a stop against the wooden barrier, a movement in the tree line just beyond the dog catches my eye. My heart stops. The girls? Not in the house after all? Branches rustle.

Stepping out from behind a tree is my brother Mark, not my daughters; Mark at age twelve, small and slight.

Scout's large head turns at the rustling of the branches. The boy who is my brother tips his head back as if looking at the sun streaming through the trees. His mouth opens and breaks into a large grin. His eyes close as if he welcomes the heat of the sun on his face. Scout starts to turn, legs stepping back, his body lumbering around to face Mark.

"Mark! No!" I yell.

Mark appears not to hear me but the dog does. Scout turns again to look at me, all indecision gone. I am his focus. In me, relief – that Mark is safe, that my girls are nowhere near – squelches my fear. The boy fades back into the woods; the dog and I lock eyes. Rooted to the spot with the dog advancing, I close my eyes; I feel them roll back into my head. Every muscle – in my face, throat, arms, stomach, legs – tenses. Against the red blanket of the world etched on the back of my eyelids I still see the dog's open mouth, baring, see him straining, escaping, and advancing.

Mark

I belch after my disgusting meal and Jen rolls her eyes at me. It also pisses her off that I get stoned. Not that she hasn't ever smoked grass or woken up with a hangover, but Jen is pretty straight, especially when it comes to work. Since I've known her, Jen has taught me many things about getting serious about my work. Top of the list, though, she warned me to forget about all the crap ever said or written about the relationship between drugs and art. "When you're high or drunk and you go into the studio," she said when I started to light up in front of her shortly after we first met, "you may feel like you're creating something unbelievably profound or moving. But look at the work the morning after, and you realize that what you did under the influence is shit. Correction: you either produce utter and complete shit, or you become lazy. Drugs are an escape, end of discussion, and not some portal into creativity."

Nothing, and this she emphasized, *nothing* would derail her from producing good work. Nothing, she added as she watched me the first time that I rolled a joint in her presence, should be allowed to derail me either.

Jen's single-mindedness about her work is what got under my skin and impressed me about her in the first place. She was unlike any woman I'd ever met or dated. Before when I went out with women, it was after meeting in bars or at the store where I used to work, and it hadn't seemed to matter if we barely knew each other. But from that moment when I stood outside Jen's door, I realized I cared about knowing her because of her passion for her photography, her interesting conversation, and the things we had in common. As I stood outside the large industrial door to the loft, holding the large box full of her bowl and other treasures and waiting for her to unlock three deadbolts, I had time to think about how this visit to her house meant I had an interest in starting some kind of relationship with her. I wasn't sure what relationship yet — friendship? sex? — but the desire to know her better was there.

I stepped back a bit from the door as Jen swung it open. She stepped in and turned. In her black tee shirt and jeans, with her silvery brown hair pulled off her face and twisted loosely at the back of her neck, she looked completely relaxed and welcoming. For a minute I couldn't move for staring.

"Don't just stand there," she said with impatience. "Come on in." She waved me in and closed the heavy door behind me.

I entered a large open living space. To my right was a 1950s aluminum-framed kitchen table and six vinyl-upholstered chairs, beyond that was an open kitchen. Directly across from the entry was a sitting area clustered around an open metal staircase spiraling up to a loft floor.

"Come on," Jen said and she took my arm and led me through a curtain on our left. Beyond the curtain was one large room divided two more times along its length with more curtains. We stopped in the middle of the floor and Jen pointed, indicating a place for me to drop her carton. "Straight ahead is where I keep all the junk that I collect. That over there," she motioned to the far wall, "is the door to the darkroom, which is really just a closet I built. And here, where we're standing, is where I take my pictures."

Back then I knew little about photography but I recognized cameras, lenses, tripods, lights, light reflectors, and a couple of screens, one a flat, dark gray, and the other marbled in pale and dark grays, like the shades of smoke. The place was straight out of an audiovisual geek's wet dream.

"I've been shooting some photos all week and I'm not really happy with the results. I thought some new props might help." She bent over the carton and removed the wooden bowl I saw her holding when she rose from the trash pile. She set it on top of a footstool grouped with a couple of empty fruit crates.

"All work and no play," I teased, but really I was amazed by her dedication.

Jen shrugged. "I'll be the first to tell you that I'm a boring person. Trash and work and shows. This particular arrangement, though, isn't working for me. I don't like the grouping of these wooden objects. Oh well." She sighed and picked up the bowl and a crate and began moving the things out of the way against the walls. "Come see my pictures. I want to know what you think."

What I thought was they were stark, haunting, memorable. One in particular, a black and white of stacks of hardbound books and bundled National Geographic magazines and tied newspapers. "I got all those from an elderly couple in Belmont. They had placed an ad in the paper. I think they were trying to sell their house. But the trouble was the house was so full of this kind of stuff you couldn't see the walls, let alone know where to begin clearing it out. Pack rats like you wouldn't believe," Jen said. "I made them an offer on all the reading material, and I hauled the stuff away. Here, look at this one."

The next photo held the same objects but this time Jen was in the composition wearing her black outfit, her body wound around books and magazines and papers, her face turned from the camera and partially obscured by a shadow cast by a four-foot stack of newspapers.

"I like it," I told her. "Better than the first."

"What do you like about it?"

"That you're in it," I said, "a live thing, curved around inanimate angular objects. I don't know. Let me think of something coherent to say."

Jen laughed. "That was coherent."

"You know," I explained, "people talking about art can sound..."

"Pretentious?" Jen finished.

"Or just plain stupid. As if they know what the piece is 'about,' what the artist is trying to 'say.' People who talk that kind of shit make my teeth itch, make me want to punch their lights out."

"Are you always this angry?"

"Only sometimes," I admitted. "Only when people act like assholes."

"Ah," Jen said as if she'd understood exactly what I meant. "This picture?" she said, pointing. "I didn't really think it was about anything when I took the photo. I basically liked the idea of a body among all that junk. Like what you said. It makes me think of those two old people, living with all their crap everyday, unable to throw any of it away. It was sad. Any sane person coming into that house would've said, 'Oh my God, what a mess.' But it was kind of touching in a way too, I mean, that junk lining the walls and hallways and rooms was the physical sum total of their life together in that house."

"You should have brought your camera with you. You could've taken a picture of the couple with their junk."

"I never could have gotten the equipment through the door and set up! There was literally no room to turn around anywhere. Anyway," Jen said, taking my arm, "come see the next piece."

I followed her lead until I stood in front of the next framed photographs, a pair. They were both horizontal hangs, but again the layout of the inanimate objects was all placed vertically. This time Jen had photographed gardening equipment, nothing out of the ordinary or unfamiliar even to an urban dweller like myself. Everyone would recognize these objects: a pitchfork, a hoe, a gardening rake, a leaf rake, a short-handled spade, and a wheelbarrow stored standing upright, all pieces resting against what had to be Jen's backdrop screen. The tools were in a play of shadow and light but even in the darkest shot I could see discolored patches on the metal parts of the tools, patches that had to be rust. Rust had eaten a fairly large hole in the spade itself, making it useless. Again, there was a person in each photo, but this time the person was naked and photographed from the back.

In the first of the pair, the woman stood tall and upright between two rakes, her arms held straight above her head. I could see the triangles of winging shoulder blades, the place where her ribcage joined her spine, light on each rib, and shadows in each hollow. Every knob on her spine, depressions like thumbprints at the top of her ass, its cleft a dark shadow. In the second, the woman was reclining on her side, resting on her left hip and elbow, her head and back again to the camera. This time, the curves of her horizontal body were like ocean waves and played against the vertical height of the tools. I reached a finger to touch the glass and traced the length of the woman's spine and over the curve of her ass. I looked at Jen.

"It's like that painting, the one with the naked woman having a picnic on the grass with men in suits. Naked woman in a place you wouldn't expect to see a naked woman. Who's the model?" I asked. "She's beautiful."

Jen smiled and then turned to the photo. "It felt right, this once, posing without my usual black."

"That's you?" I asked.

"All of me. These two," she said with a nod of her head, "are the ones that will hang in the show in January."

"With crowds of people all talking about how the feminine form contrasts with the maleness of the tools, which are undeniably phallic symbols of power and aggression against women," I joked.

Jen laughed. "The only people saying that will be women whose husbands leave them to do all the yard work. I'll make sure not to tell them I only liked the idea of seeing both sets of subjects – tools and a naked body – taken out of context. The audience can think whatever they damn well please once it's hung," she added. "Want to see the rest?"

"In a minute," I said. Truth was, I was feeling overwhelmed.

"Break then?" Jen asked. "We could sit in the front room and have a drink. Talk."

"Sure, sounds good," I agreed.

We walked back through the curtain and I sat on Jen's couch with my legs sprawled out in front of me. I put my head back and closed my eyes. "Tea?" Jen asked from the kitchen.

"Beer's good, if you have it," I answered. I listened as she ran water then pulled open a drawer and raked around inside, the sounds of metal hitting metal, metal sliding around the drawer. Still resting I heard a bottle cap flip off and hit the counter. My mouth watered at the sound.

"Beer before noon," Jen said, shaking her head. "Here you go." I opened my eyes to see her standing next to the couch with a beer in her outstretched hand and a mug of tea in her other. I sat up straighter and took the bottle, took a long cool drink.

Jen sat next to me on the couch. "What did you think?" she asked me.

"I think," I said after swallowing some more beer, "that I need to go home and take a sledgehammer to everything I've been working on and throw it away."

That was then, as they say, and this is now. Now, Jen's focus seems to be criticizing me. Mark screwing up again, unable to work well, unable to stay off the grass, unable to grow up and move past the anger he has for his father. Again Jen frowns, her face falling into well-worn grooves. I realized for the first time: those lines around her mouth and between her eyes? They hadn't been there when we first met. I'd put them there.

"And how's Shelley?" Jen asks, and I watch as she forces her face to go all slack and neutral, as if this is an innocent question. Which, of course, it is not. These days, nothing is.

Despite what Jen says or thinks, Shelley's not the dog I kick. I don't get angry at Shelley; I get angry and Shelley's there for me. And she's definitely not stupid. Blindly loving? Maybe, but she is the only person who ever has been. Man, I love my sister for that. I love her as strongly as I hate this kind of discussion.

"Shelley's fine," I answer in the same "who cares" tone, which is tough to manage because my high is wearing off and my head begins to ache and I don't really want to think about the reasons why my relationship with Jen is going downhill so fast.

At the beginning of our relationship the challenge to keep up with Jen was attractive and exciting, but even then I didn't know if I could. Or why she would want me to try. On that first day in her loft I kept drinking my beer, stifled a burp and said, "Fuck, you're good." I looked over at her.

"Thank you," she said. She looked straight ahead and blew on her tea. "Don't trash your work," she added, and looked straight at me.

"You haven't seen my work. C'mon," I said when she raised her eyebrow, "after seeing your stuff, I feel like I've only been screwing around. I *have* been screwing around; I'm a fucking amateur.

Listen, I do more stupid console table tops than I do my own projects. I take jobs where the colors have to match the sofa or the walls; I make garden stepping-stones. I don't do serious work. I have to sell stereo equipment to make my rent, for God's sake."

"Your job pays the bills," Jen reminded me. "That gives you the freedom to work on your other projects.

"For the longest time," she confided, "I had to take wedding photos. I still do on occasion." Jen waited for my reaction. "It's true. When I was looking to buy a loft, wedding photos became a great source of down payment money.

"I started out telling myself that I'd try to do the weddings differently. I offered black and white photos," she said, "and more candids. Once, at a reception at The Four Seasons of all places, I caught a father of the groom on film doing bourbon shots and smoking cigars in the kitchen with the waitstaff. He was in there so long he missed the introduction of the wedding party. The bride was so pissed at her new father-in-law." She laughed. "I took a great snap of her in the middle of a temper tantrum, which of course no one wanted to see.

"You want to know what I've learned after all that? That in the end, all these brides and their mothers want are the same old standard shots. Bride and groom, bridal party, family groups, blah, blah. Bo-ring. But the boring work helped me buy this place." Jen swept the hand holding the mug of tea in an arc in front of her. "So, pretty much it's been worth it."

"So far, my work helps me pay off my crazy landlady's mortgage," I replied.

"Now you're just feeling sorry for yourself. If it's so terrible, then move."

"That's what I was thinking when I ran into you this morning," I said.

"And what did you decide?" she asked after swallowing a sip of tea.

"That the landlady may be crazy, but the rent's cheap." Draining the last of the beer from the bottle, I set the empty down on Jen's coffee table.

"You want another?" Jen asked, and without waiting for an answer she stood and got me a second beer from the refrigerator. "Where do you do your mosaic work?" she called from the kitchen.

"On the floor. Or on a large folding table in the middle of the apartment. Depends," I answered. Jen came back with the beer and took her seat. I continued. "A while back, I asked to use my landlady's garage because she wasn't using it to park her car. I even offered to pay more rent. She accepted, and I worked between the garage floor and the workbench for about a week." I took a drink. "I must have made the garage look more attractive to her just by using it, because out of the blue she decided she 'simply had to garage her car.'" I tried hard to make my voice sound mean and nasal like Phyllis's, but only managed a nasty falsetto. Jen laughed anyway. "I cleared everything out," I told her. "Well, not everything," I said with a growing smirk. "I left a little glass behind. At least the flat tire gave her something new to bitch about."

Jen smiled again. "Like I said, leave."

Leave, I thought. Easy for her to say living in this space, even if it was only Magoun Square. At nine-fifty a month, I was lucky the 21x21 studio apartment wasn't roach-infested. This was considered a good deal. I *should* leave, I agreed. I should buy my own place but I never seemed to have that much money. Yeah, I admitted to myself as I polished off the second beer, Jen is right. I am feeling sorry for myself.

"How old are you?" I asked her.

She didn't hesitate. "Thirty. Next month," she added. "Why?"

"Comparing and coming up a bit short," I told her truthfully.

Jen looked at me over the rim of her mug. She didn't say a word.

"Come on," I said, "look at all your work. Your home. Your accomplishments. I'm thirty-two fucking years old, I live in a hole, and I realize I've never taken my work seriously."

"So take your work seriously," she challenged as she finished her tea.

I had thought my work was good, but it was untested, my commitment only lukewarm because of a million excuses. No time, no money – the list went on. I hadn't taken the risks Jen had, and I wasn't sure if I would or even wanted to. You do that, take those kinds of chances, and you open yourself up to ridicule and failure. So I straddled the line, one foot not quite in the art world, the other not exactly in the earning world. I dabbled in my ideas and prostituted my talents to people who had none, and I always figured I was better than the assholes who ended up designing greeting cards.

But next to Jen, *I* was the second-rate artist. I wasn't even an artist; I was a commissioned tradesperson and a stereo components sales associate. And all of a sudden, looking at her work, looking across at her in the studio, I understood that my life was a waste if I wasn't doing – or at the least trying to do – what I had trained to do. And who, I ask you, can hope to impress a woman with the realization that his life has been one long string of nothing staring him in the face?

I stood to go, knowing that I had blown it with her. "You're right," I agreed. "You're absolutely right. Thanks for the beer," I said, "and the tour. I meant it, you're good." Forgetting that my boxes of glass lay in the trunk of Jen's car, I opened the door to the loft and let myself out. Once down the stairs, I crossed the square and cut over side streets to reach Highland Avenue, which would take me home. By the time I remembered my glass, that nice opaque aqua-colored vase I'd earmarked for part of a mosaic ocean, I had more or less come to terms with the fact that I wouldn't see it – or Jen – again.

I was surprised when she called three days later using the number I had forgotten I'd written down on a napkin lifted from the diner at breakfast. I was even more surprised when she said she was calling to offer me a place to work. And, oh yeah, she was holding my box of glass for me, keeping it safe; did I want it? I had absolutely no reason to say no.

Yeah, Jen and I, we started out fine, but nothing's been the same since six months ago when Shelley walked into my loft with news. Or since the phone call she made four days ago to tell me he was dead and I'd better get my ass out there.

"Do we have any beer?" I ask Jen, and without waiting for an answer I rise and head back to the fridge, where I already know there are four bottles of IPA, all with my name on them.

"Could you take your plate?" Jen asks when I've gotten halfway to the kitchen. She picks up her book and returns to her reading.

I backtrack and collect my dirty dishes. "Fuck," I mutter under my breath as I try to balance my plate in the sink on top of Jen's dozen or so mugs, all holding the filmy dregs of cold tea. I can see it now: Jen alone last night and today, brewing tea and letting it go cold.

I pop the cap off a beer and drink about half before tackling the dishes. I watch Jen across the large open room as I suck down beer. She is disappointed. I can tell by her frown and the way she buries herself in her book that she has seen something in me she doesn't like.

I look across the open rooms and beyond Jen to the wall below the ladder stairs. Between steadily draining the beer and procrastinating with the cleanup, I stare at the two photos that hang there, examples of Jen's work, two pieces that I love best.

The larger of the two is what I've always called the newspaper photo. It makes me think about the day that I went back to pick up my cardboard box of glass and dishes. Jen had remembered my rant about my crappy working conditions, my crazy landlady, and again offered me space in her loft to work.

"I can't do that," I told her. "I can't pay you, plus pay the rent on my apartment."

"You don't have to pay me right away. There's the whole front half of the studio, right under the windows, that I never use. It's yours. The company would be good," she added. "It may even make us more productive."

I didn't miss the "us." Jen's smile was even broader when she said "us" although her arms were crossed in front of her as if she thought it would help to look tough and decisive.

"Why would you let me work here for free?" I asked.

"You idiot," she said, again with a smile.

Jen was still smiling when I took her up on the offer, when I moved my boxes of glass and tools over, when I spread everything out on the long folding table she had set aside for me and got to work.

Shortly after I started sharing Jen's workspace in the loft, she gave me the photo of the stacks of newspapers, the one I had fixed on when she first showed me her work, as a gift.

That day started off like any other, but I was determined to try and finish a large mosaic I had been struggling with for weeks. I decided I would stay longer than usual. I had found some glass I thought might finish the problem space. Jen came up behind me and looked over my shoulder at my work. I could smell on her warm breath the sweet fruit she had just eaten as a snack. Her hand snuck around my waist; I draped an arm over her shoulders; we stood together looking at the nearly-finished mosaic. I was pleased. I had made a large semi-circle, busy with many colors, where the small chips fitted together to look like a sea of humans engaged in many different activities.

"It's like a little world," Jen said.

"Half a world," I corrected, running my hand along the arc of the rim.

"Mark's world," she then said, and smiled up at me. "Chaotic but beautiful."

In that moment I felt conscious of the feel of her under my arm, whereas only a minute ago it had been like a million times before when we had stood this way, arms draped, something like buddies admiring each other's work. I felt understood. The chaos in my head. My brain's hardwiring. Mark's world.

Jen turned slightly to face me. I kissed her. She said, "I have something for you," and she pulled away to get a wrapped package from her closet of a darkroom.

When I finally tore back all the heavy brown paper layers to see the photo underneath and recognized the outlines of Jen's body curled around the objects in the photo, I wanted to run my hands along the lines of the flesh and blood body that stood across the table from me. I told her, "Thank you."

She smiled then, her eyes never leaving mine, so I asked, "Can we . . .?" and let the suggestion hang there between us too.

Suddenly cautious Jen asked, "Do you really want to?"

And I answered, "I *really* want to," and we went to her bed.

I can't explain what changed that day. Sure, from the first moment I laid eyes on her, and then on her work, I had been struck by the beautiful outlines of her body in her tight-fitting black clothes. But it was the story of the old married couple, the pack rats in Belmont, that had really gotten to me. They had been unwilling to toss anything they had accumulated over the years they spent together. Other than with my sister, I had never had a bond as strong as that couple's. From the start, Jen had impressed me by the depth of her compassion for them, as crazy as they seemed to outsiders. I was looking for understanding like that in my own life. I figured I was just as crazy as those two, and I wanted Jen's compassion turned in my direction. Jen, collector of stories and organizer of discards.

"It's silly for you to keep your apartment. Expensive and silly when you're over here all the time anyway," Jen said later as we lay on her mattress on the floor of her loft bedroom. She wore only a stretched-out tank top. My hand rested between her legs, her head fit neatly under my chin.

"Are you asking me to move in?" I said with a mock gasp. "But we hardly know each other."

"Well enough," Jen said as she reached down to touch my hand where it lay, and pressed. "It simply makes sense," she added. She sat up and smiled down at me.

The second and smaller picture is an unclaimed photo from one of Jen's wedding jobs, one she worked before we met, of the bride's Uncle Monty wearing a sombrero and banging a tambourine, the head of an enthusiastic conga line. Jen had told me that when he wasn't on the dance floor, he acted as if it was his wedding, noisily greeting friends and relatives with hearty laughs and slaps on the back. Jen had been partial to this man, even more so when neither bride nor groom chose to include the photo. Both had been mortified by him.

Claiming copyrights, Jen had held on to the image. In developing, she blew it up and changed the focus of the shot by cropping the edges right in to Monty's face.

That Jen would catch with her camera an instant of such energetic happiness was uncharacteristic of her work. The wedding photos, posed and candid alike, had previously been restrained and elegant, sometimes somber, occasionally darkly humorous like the bride having her tantrum. But they were never carefree.

So different from the picture of Monty. Monty was all joy, no trace of self-consciousness.

I put the rubber stopper in the sink and run hot water in there along with a healthy squeeze of the environmentally-friendly dish soap we bought together at the health food co-op back when shopping together was still fun. I watch the bubbles swell and fill in the spaces between the mugs, and I finish my beer. I used to say Jen was my bullshit detector. I used to like that about her, that she would listen to me piss and moan and then tell me to grow the fuck up.

"So take your work, your life, your relationships seriously," she would say and it felt like a good slap across the face. She made it all sound so easy. I used to tell her that she saved me, taught me about discipline and routine: get out of bed, put in hours at the studio before breakfast; back to the studio all night if necessary; make those contacts at galleries and continue to cultivate them. She has taught me a lot, and she made learning the routine easy by showing me the way.

"It simply makes sense." My efficient Jen likes things that make sense. If Shelley babies me, then Jen herself has managed me, made my life make sense by forcing a series of wise decisions. She was even smart enough to make each decision seem like my own. Now I only want her off my back.

I am poisoned, I think as I finish washing and rinsing the last mug, as I tip the mug upside down on the drying rack. I dry my hands on a towel. Poisoned. Jen is right when she says I'm infected with anger, an anger that's now infecting this relationship. Hate is my personal parasite and it lives in me and feeds off everything I do.

Jen likes to call the shit with my father my "emotional baggage." It makes no sense to her. It wears me down, she believes, taking up too much of my creative energy and spoiling my work. She might be right; after all, she is the one who had to watch me drop bricks on my glass, smashing it to unusable smithereens.

I could have told her all those years ago when she offered to first let me share her space – no, back in the diner, right after we'd met – wait, Jen, just you wait and see who I really am. Wait until you figure out that my rebellion isn't fiery and interesting. That my energy isn't creative energy at all; it's destructive. No, I'm not who she thinks I am, and I should have told her I would fail her. I am failing her now; I see it.

As if to verify, Jen sighs heavily and pointedly. "I'm going to bed. Did you rinse all the soap out of the dishes?" she asks. "Sometimes you don't and my tea tastes soapy.

"Good night," she adds as she turns her back to me and walks up the stairs.

I sniff the inside of the last mug and it does smell soapy, faintly flowery. I fill it with cold tap water and take a drink. Tastes of soap too. I wince, empty the mug, and move to return it to the drying rack with the rest, figuring I'll re-rinse them tomorrow. It's been a long day. Then I remember why it's been a long day.

I buried my father today. I should feel free but I don't. The hand holding the mug stops, hovers over the full drying rack. I watch it as if I have no connection to this hand, no control over its actions.

Forgiveness. Both Shelley and Jen are on a forgiveness crusade, Shelley by forgiving him herself, Jen through nagging me. *If you don't make your peace now, you'll never have the chance once he's dead. You will regret that for the rest of your life.*

Shelley, I knew, would never pressure me. After my disappearing act today, she'll want to stay connected rather than alienate me from her. But Jen? Once she gets hold of an idea, this time the idea of how to change me, she never lets go. I can see that tendency in everything she does with or for me. I've seen it over the past three years, as I became the subject of Jen's total makeover plan. I see it now in the two photos staring at me from across the room, hanging side by side, a diptych of Jen's hope, hope pinned on a reformed, new and improved Mark. Standing here tonight and looking at Monty's goofball smile, I even begin to question Jen's motives in hanging these photos. I wonder if her choice is a clue to her state of mind. I wonder if she is trying to tell me something like, *This is how happy I was at the start. This is how happy we can be.*

Get over it. Make your peace. You'll never have another chance. So many meaningless words thrown at me over the past few months, falling through my mind like cards falling into a deck. Words meant to make me change. "You'll never have the chance to make peace once he's dead."

"Never have the chance to . . . " I must have spoken aloud because halfway up the stairs Jen stops.

"Did you say something?" she asks as if I've spoken to her. When I make no answer she turns and continues on her way to bed.

A chance to what? To make peace? To curse him one last time? Which?

My hands reach for mugs, each hand gripping two handles at a time not even feeling the familiar cold stone smoothness of the pottery. As if I have stepped out of myself I see one pair of hands, red, chapped, nicked and ugly working hands, grabbing for ceramic mugs and pitching them across the room at the walls. One hits Jen's framed photo, my favorite, the one of the stacks of newspaper; it breaks the glass.

I reach for the entire dish rack. I weave my fingers through the wooden slats and lift.

I hear a voice as if from a great distance, like an ocean's roar in my ears, as I lift the dish rack with the remaining dishes high up over my head and wing it across the room, smashing it into the second picture so hard that the entire picture frame falls onto the concrete floor.

Only after that last loud crash am I aware that Jen is screaming, "Stop, Mark. Stop it! Stop!" at the top of her lungs. She stays on the stairs for her feet are bare and I've made a dangerous mess.

Shelley

I gasp, sit upright, open my eyes, and wake to black. Steven snores beside me in rhythmic, throaty gurgles. The panic of the nightmare lingers, although the longer I lie still the more I try to focus on the dream's cartoonish aspect, its unreal horror-movie quality. I blame the unfamiliar scotch for bringing it on, like I would blame late-night rich food if one of my girls had woken like this, but deep down I know the nightmare is a mirror of my worry.

Our joint ownership of this burdensome house.

To this day, my heart races as I remember my brother running from me during our childhood visit to the house, more so as I remember Scout in the dream putting Mark in his sights.

First came the squeal of the poorly-oiled door as it opened, then the sharp slam as a tight and rusted spring snapped the screen door back into place. Like an echo fading in Mark's wake, the door knocked two more times against its frame with all the residual force coiled in that spring.

Then there was me and Mark, talking in the yard.

Then Mark was a blur of feet, of elbows and knees pumping as he raced past me.

He ran from the house so fast that the outline of his body and the pattern of his shirt were indistinct. I was rooted to the spot beside the porch; inside the house Sylvie laughed and cajoled Jack with kisses. A vacation, laughter – so much promise on this beautiful day.

My brain told my feet to follow but they moved so slowly. Lifting each one was a Herculean effort, as if I was dragging my feet through hot, sticky tar. Even my warning to my brother struggled to find a voice. I tried to call his name but could not force a sound. God, he was going too fast over unfamiliar, uneven ground. Damp patches spread under my arms.

At first Mark hurtled over rocks and roots and the spiny tufts of reedy sea grass that passed for the cottage's lawn as if racing to reach the water. He was a distance from me but somehow I could hear his heavy breathing in my ear, the wheezy, gulping breaths he took as he drew in air. At first Mark was nimble and quick, as surefooted and confident as the rabbits and deer that lived in the nearby woods. But beyond the property line a stand of trees loomed, ugly, stunted pine with gnarled, grasping roots in a shifting sandy soil. *Mark, slow down.* My mouth mimed the words, silent and repetitive as a rosary. But it was the world around him that slowed instead, that shifted. In that slowing of time where a single moment lasted an eternity I could see everything below, behind, around, and in front of Mark. I saw the open toe of one loose sandal. I saw the place between toe and sole gape and catch a taproot.

Inside, oblivious to Mark's danger, Sylvie laughed and sparked a laugh from Jack until there was an echo of laughter building around the sun of the day, laughter which swelled as quickly, perhaps as ominously, as a storm front might on a summer afternoon. I watched as Mark flew, not high but absolutely parallel to the ground, and in that first instant he looked happy, nearing ecstasy. Stay there, stay, I willed him against all laws of gravity. Stay. Or fly. Just don't—

If only I could will myself out of this memory, but no, I am back there, back in time, back at the house watching Mark run headlong into danger. To relax myself I practice the breathing skills learned years ago when I had my babies. The deep breathing helps a bit, the vivid images of the snarling dog fade. Poor old Scout, a dog whose worst offense has only ever been drooling. Breathing deeply helps me rid myself of the memory of the dream, but I am left wide-awake.

I sit up to reach for a book. Steven wakes mid-snore with the sudden movement. "Is something wrong?" he sputters. "Did you hear something? The girls?"

"No, no, go back to sleep," I assure him.

"I woke up, that's all," I explain as Steven sits up with me instead of rolling over. "A dream. And I can't seem to get back to sleep."

"Bad?" he asks.

"Bad when I dreamt it, kind of lurid and silly now."

Steven settles onto his side and, facing me, he puts a hand on my hip.

I lie back down too, try resting on my side facing Steven, and I wait to see if sleep will come. I concentrate on the slow circular motion of his caressing hand, breathe in time with it, in and out.

"Better?" he asks.

The first time I went to bed with Steven in his studio apartment, I recognized a kindred spirit. His order made sense and comforted me. As he undressed, he carefully folded every piece of clothing into a neat pile that he then placed on an armchair. He had even folded his two socks together to make a neat bundle, and this went on top of the pile. His glasses he put on his nightstand. He was as careful with me that night. My clothing pile resting next to his was the same. Tidy, responsible, we were two of a kind then. And now too, I must remind myself. Even if we find ourselves disagreeing about where responsibility begins and ends.

"Yes," I answer.

"Do you think you'll be able to sleep?" he asks.

"If I read for awhile," I answer. "Will the light bother you?"

Steven yawns. "I'm practically back to sleep already."

"Lucky you," I whisper, adding, "sweet dreams," out of habit. By the time I kiss his cheek he has started snoring again.

I don't turn on my bedside light after all. Instead, I take my book across the bedroom to sit by my bedroom window, making myself comfortable in the large armchair I had recovered in a mauve silk damask. Steven loathes the pink of this chair, says it's too fussy, and so it is mine, reupholstered and placed at this window when I was nursing an infant Libby. Although lulled by Steven's low, rhythmic snores, I am unable to return to a peaceful state, let alone to sleep.

When Mark was born and my mother was in the hospital, my grandmother came to care for me. She was reading a book to me when my parents walked through the front door, home from the hospital with my new brother. To a four-year-old, the bundle my mother held looked more like a swaddled football than a baby.

Out of work early to pick up Mom and the baby, my father was still in his business suit and tie. He smiled broadly at me as he walked into the living room. His arm was around my mother's shoulders. My mother, usually so pretty, looked tired and washed out, a stranger to me. She wasn't smiling when she walked away from my father and met me at the sofa. She bent down, still holding her bundle, until her eyes were level with mine. She laid the baby on my lap, and I could feel his warmth. I saw my brother for the first time, his face peeking through the swaddling blanket. Mom looked me in the eyes as she deposited him on my lap and then withdrew her arms. "He's yours," she said, and I believed her.

"Mine," I whispered. From the start I took responsibility for Mark very seriously. "Can I name him?"

"His name is Mark," Dad said from across the room. "Mark and Michelle."

I looked to my mother to see if this was true, but by that time she was standing. She turned to my father.

"I think I'll lie down, Jack," she said. Then to me, she added, "Take care of him." She touched the top of my head and left.

And so I did. Over the next few years, whenever my mother couldn't rouse herself to do so much as change his diaper, I did it for her. After a while I could change a mean diaper, tidy and tight. Sometimes I fed him. I made his lunch, walked him to school, and played with him after. When I would head out into the neighborhood to find my pack of friends for bike riding or hopscotch or kickball in the street, my mother always said, "Don't forget your brother," and I never did.

It is difficult to change my habits, especially when I see how much he still needs me.

From across the room I squint to see the time on the illuminated clock face on Steven's nightstand. Nearly three o'clock and my mind is a tangle of painful memories and worries about Mark. I shiver despite the heavy quilt. I know I need to relax; I need to try another approach. When my daughters were young and had bad dreams, I told them to close their eyes and think pleasant thoughts. I sit and try to think of pleasant things.

From my chair, I look out the window into my yard. The backyard landscape just before dawn, gray and still, is a perfect blank backdrop for thought and memory. This morning there is a light, almost ghostly white spring frost. We moved to this house when Margaret was a little over four and Libby had just begun growing inside me, my belly still small but hardening, rounding, my waist thickening. We moved here because I fell in love with the backyard and wanted it to be mine. My yard, my home, something I could own and also sculpt. It is not a tremendously large yard, but it is pretty, private, full of flowering shrubs and trees. In all these years, we've only lost one tree, a mountain ash, and only last year when it became diseased. Four feet of decaying trunk still stands, a feeding ground for woodpeckers in their constant search for insects. I'll have to get Steven interested in taking the rest of the tree down later this spring and maybe we can plant something new in its place, a Japanese maple or another flowering cherry, something hardy. I smile thinking of my lanky academic husband donning protective goggles and wielding a borrowed chainsaw. He hates yard work but conceded on the house, with its one-third-acre lot, because I longed for it and he loved me.

It was during another April, ten years earlier, that we began looking at houses to buy. I was only five weeks into the pregnancy, and I hadn't told Steven yet. As I sit, staring out the window, I recall that I loved this house instantly and so intensely that, once out of earshot of the real estate agent, I began painting with words a vivid picture for Steven of Margaret galloping around the borders of the back lawn, hiding behind the massive trunk of an old ginkgo tree, playing with its unusual fan-shaped leaves. And then I told Steven I was pregnant, described how the new baby could grow up from an infant sleeping in her carriage beneath the gingko, to a toddler being warned away from the poisonous leaves in the patch of wild rhubarb.

I told him, and I watched the look of surprise grow on Steven's face at my news. Then I asked the realtor if she wouldn't mind giving us maybe a half hour on our own to wander the yard, to stroll around unhurried? *Please?* I had asked smiling, a smile that promised at the end of that half-hour a concrete offer on this home. *The house is empty*, I reasoned, *nothing to steal, and do we look like vandals?* Relenting, the realtor went out to her car and headed to her nearby office to check messages and return phone calls. Her gesture was, at its core, unprofessional, but so kind.

I too acted out of character. I was impulsive, led by emotion and desire instead of my usual reason. I blush at the memory, even now in the dim light of early morning so many years later. The real estate agent gave us enough time alone for me to lead Steven around the yard where I then placed his hands on my already painfully swollen breasts. I had just enough time to lead him back into the house, into the empty master bedroom where I hiked up the hem of my dress to arouse him with the feel of my small, hard, newly-rounding belly. And just enough time to let him make love to me standing at the shaded window of what would be our new bedroom. Exactly where the chair rests now. My monument.

I shift in my comfortable chair, pull my knees up to my chest and gather myself up. I feel chilled so I pull the quilt right up under my chin, re-drape it over me as I remember how I fell in love with Steven in that instant, with our second child inside me and the promise of a beautiful place to live together and raise our family. This morning as I listen to him snore and roll over in bed, I remember clearly that instant, how the realization of love hit me like an unanticipated shout of "Surprise!" at a birthday party, a happy shock.

Being in love hadn't entered into my decision to marry. I felt that almost any two people could decide to marry and make a go of the partnership if both were willing, and I don't feel in the least ashamed admitting that eighteen years ago, when we began dating, I felt for Steven a great deal of fondness and affinity, but not romantic love, not then. Not at first when we came to know each other over cups of sometimes burnt, sometimes watery student union coffee; and not when we walked away from the church on our wedding day. No, I didn't fall in love with him until I had my second child and my home. What I loved from the start was the idea of having – *creating* – a family, and then I loved the fact that I found a reliable, kind, and hardworking man to build one with.

When we met, Steven was the teaching assistant in one of my second-year English courses, a paper grader and stand-in for the professor during discussion seminars. A student himself, six years older and working toward his Ph.D., Steven read and graded most of my work. Steven's tough grading showed me a rigorous intelligence. I never at the time considered him sexually, never ever turned an image of him over in my mind as if inspecting him as a potential mate. In reality, during most of my college career, I had no time to think of steady boyfriends, sexual conquests, or husbands.

In his typical, responsible fashion, Steven asked me for coffee nearly two years after our student-teacher relationship had ended. No improprieties there. We had stumbled upon each other browsing the same section of the library, and Steven struck up the conversation. I wouldn't have been inclined to make small talk with anyone at that time. In class, I had found Steven a demanding grader of a period of American literature I hadn't particularly enjoyed, and I was sure my work reflected just how dull I found the Hemingway and Fitzgerald texts, all bleak lives and unspoken angst.

The conversation in the library surprised me. Outside the classroom, I found Steven both witty and charming. I suppose I had expected him to lecture me on the merits of *The Great Gatsby*, or present a vigorous defense of *The Old Man and The Sea*, but once we sat down to have coffee, we talked mostly of movies, and discovered a mutual love of the screwball comedies of the 1930s.

Steven was six years my senior and knew, as I also did, the direction his life and work would take. As the English department's rising star, he had a good career ahead of him. He would defend his thesis and remain at the college to teach; the offer had been made and accepted. With my dual major of English and Education, I saw a safe career as a secondary school teacher in front of me. As we finished up coffee and conversation, Steven told me he had enjoyed my company and would like very much to see me again; was I free to date?

Was I *free*? I had no quick and easy answer. Across the table in the student union, I could only smile vaguely at Steven's question.

A social life meant seeing my brother less often. He had needed my help throughout his high school education. Even from a distance, I had made all the phone calls my mother did not. I called the school to arrange for tutoring, and then my father to ask for money for the tutor. As I wound up my senior year, Mark also closed in on his graduation. Academically at least, I felt I had Mark squared away. But somehow I couldn't forgive myself for leaving him alone with our mother.

Steven waited patiently while I thought. Finally I told him, "I'm not dating anyone," and he was so obviously heartened by my answer that I didn't want to spoil his mood by giving him an account of my messy family life. "I study a lot. And I do like to get home on weekends." Steven, assuring me he was equally devoted to family and studies, had understood.

In the end we agreed to a study date once a week and to go out on Friday nights. The deal was made with such care and attention to detail it would have felt right to shake on it. I would go home from Saturday to Sunday; Steven would drive me in his car when he could. I left the student union happy with the compromise I was able to reach, the deft way I was able to accommodate the care of another person into my life.

While I haven't always been in love with Steven, his family was a different matter altogether. I fell in love with them instantly, a sloppy, schoolgirl kind of crush. Even before I met them, I pictured them all in my mind, asked Steven for photographs to see what they all looked like, and for information about what each family member liked to do. When I finally met them all, as Steven's date at his parents' thirtieth wedding anniversary celebration, I was neither surprised nor disappointed by the living, breathing people. I felt I had known them all my life.

Steven's was my model nuclear family, loving and supportive, healthy and whole. And they easily welcomed me. His mother, Joyce; his father, David Sr.; his older brother, David Jr. – they all became role models in family behavior for me. They communicated, they achieved, and they loved, supported, and listened. And today, in the balance of fifteen years of marriage to Steven, I have created a safe, respectful, well-run, unbroken home for our girls using Steven's family like a blueprint. As soon as I met Steven's family, I *knew* I wanted the same for myself. Every day spent with Steven was an affirmation that I could make it, could design the perfect, loving, close, happy family that I so strongly desired.

At twenty-two, my future was planned. I would attend graduate school, land a teaching job, and marry a fine man, in that order. After an unsettled adolescence and early adulthood, the life I would step into in two years looked promising, stable, and productive. As I grew up, left home, attended college, married, I intended that the remainder of my life would be founded on family. My ideal was a tight unit, a band much like Steven's close-knit tribe. While I studied or did my mother's household chores, I longed to be planning children's birthday parties, anniversaries, holidays. I collected people at each step and built my family. Brother, husband, in-laws, children – even Emma became a kind of surrogate mother, a softly maternal and sensible woman. I imagined that in our gathering we would be protected by a shield, one whose crest would read *Unity, Fidelity*, words clutched in the front claws of a protective lioness. Me.

I knew there would be rough spots. My mother's mental illness was ruthless, and I had her long-term care to consider. I assumed watch over Mark as he transitioned from high school to college. My father and Sylvie hovered on the fringes of all our lives. And I would always be called upon to mediate. But as I stepped into the life I wanted and crafted, I tried to focus only on the good things.

That was my special skill, I believed, the trick of focusing on the positive and pleasant things in my life. I practiced it then and I practice it now, right now as I bury the more upsetting moments of my life under the many layers of happiness. It would be nice, I think to myself as I sit in my chair, to stop reminiscing, to stop right here with the happy memories lodged in my consciousness, to fall asleep like a child, a believer in the calming effects of recalling a life's happiest moments. Instead, I am still awake and trying hard not to think of what nastiness lies under the layers of happiness. No one running from a hellhound should be so foolish to think she is in control.

My mother is dead, my father is dead, my marriage has stress fractures, and my brother left me today determined not to speak about the house we've inherited; running then, running now.

Mark

After a noise like I've just made there can be peace and quiet and stillness, such a long painful stretch of silence when all you can hear is the blood pounding in your ears and the heavy breathing dragged up from the depths of your chest. Jen, after her shrill screaming, seems to have lost her voice. I can't say a word. So I leave.

Once outside, with no destination in mind, I start walking. I walk in a kind of trance for what seems forever but is probably no more than thirty minutes, cutting across Somerville to Porter Square, then up Mass Ave toward Harvard Square. I wear no watch, have no idea of the time. Nine? Ten o'clock? I keep on walking until there is an emptiness inside me that I could pretend was hunger. And thirst. Definitely thirst. I need a beer, and maybe some food. After a few dives, I pass a nice-looking bar with a restaurant. The sound of a young crowd inside, along with the smell of grilling burgers, draws me in.

Taking a seat at the bar I order a beer, drink it down, and then order another. While I drink I watch the bartender, a tall skinny woman with a tangle of dark red hair. She looks to be at least ten years younger than me, a grad student working for the tips. She moves around the bar with agility; her thinness, I realize, is sinewy and strong rather than gangly. Her nose is too large for her face and her breasts too flat but she has beautiful hands that I can't help noticing each time she draws somebody's pint or when she passes me my own. Long fingers, painted nails, creamy young skin. "Screw Jen," I think at that moment. After the third beer I can pretend to feel the redhead's nails raking my back, running along the insides of my thighs as she goes down on me.

A few years ago, unattached, I would have made a move to get this girl into bed because I could. That's what I used to do in the days of bad jobs and bad apartments. It would have been easy to fall back into, a game, like the winning moves in chess when all the right pieces are in the right places. A good-looking girl, someone's private apartment, more drinks? Check and checkmate. Tonight, by my third beer, I feel loose. I should be able to shift the conversation around to the personal. *"How about...? You and me...?"*

After all, my social life up until I had met Jen had been lived as a series of sexual encounters with marginal women, young, unformed women in that nebulous place between girl and adult where there is no real character or definition or wisdom. Even their faces were ill-defined, pretty in an empty way, and pretty in the same ways, usually blonde, big bright eyes, straight teeth, full lips. Before Jen I had a type: long legs, slim hips, full breasts, set apart only by a navel ring or a tattoo or an oddly placed mole. And I liked them that way, with my age and experience and lack of commitment defining the relationship. Commitment meant inevitable disappointment. When I stopped being happy with a particular girl, before she could stop being happy with me, I moved on.

Until I met Jen. With Jen it had all been different, and I found myself wanting a permanence I had never wanted before. Because of what I saw in her work. Because of what she saw in me.

As I sit here drinking and considering going to bed with a redheaded bartender, I can picture Jen taking stock of the mess I had made. I can see her walking up the stairs to bed, changing her mind halfway up and returning downstairs, gathering the dust pan and brush, sweeping the glass, removing the photo from its frame, checking the paper carefully for tears or scratches in the print, sandwiching the photos and the one intact frame in cardboard, throwing the other away, wrapping the packages in brown paper, sealing them with heavy duty tape.

In a happy moment about a year or so ago, Jen and I worked side by side in the loft with the photo of Monty smiling down on us. I might have been sketching or cutting up some ceramic with my nippers or maybe thinking about making supper. Jen was reviewing proof sheets or reading or paying bills when she suddenly stopped her work, came over to me and hugged me spontaneously. She told me that when she met me she thought she saw in me the things she liked about Monty, what she called our noisy embrace of life. Sure, like Monty, nothing much about me is still. My work can be physical and noisy. There is an energy in the noise of my work that I both run on and try to capture in a finished piece. I try to use the noise of destruction as I work so that the mosaics and sculptures project fluency and movement even after the shards are anchored down with grout or epoxy.

Fast-forward one year. I can only imagine what she thinks now. She must know now what I know, that for a while the energy I used in my work fooled her. She mistook all the crashing around for life-affirming enthusiasm, when in fact it was simply life-sucking anger. The truth is, every time I wield a baseball bat I see my father, not glass, beneath it. The noise I make as I work is as personal as the deliberate snap of a bone, as catastrophic as a natural disaster. My noise has nothing to do with joy.

Poor Jen. A few years ago she went looking for someone who lived larger than she did, someone like Monty, and she found me instead. But remember, Jen is a great organizer. She saw what must have looked to her like good raw materials, and decided to remake me. She took me on, my sloppy work habits, my careless attitude toward work, and proceeded to change me. It almost worked. Almost. When I threw the dishes, I gave Jen a glimpse into my angry world, and what she saw she could not possibly like. I had not changed a bit.

Tonight, with the fight behind me and still sporting a "screw you" attitude, I might easily cheat on Jen; I think about it. I order a burger to help sop up the third beer, and then I order a fourth beer to wash down the burger. By now it is closing in on eleven and I am on the road to getting wasted. When I find myself wondering if the redhead's bush is the same color as her hair, I know it's time to go home. I pay the bill and leave, leaving my transgression to my imagination. I back off and I go home, right then.

Amazingly Jen hasn't thrown the chain lock. The walk back has sobered me up a bit and much as I expected, the loft has been cleaned up in my absence. I find Jen in bed, lights out, pretending to sleep. I should try to apologize, I should say I've been a shit about my father, I have a rotten temper, I'll get help; will she forgive me? Only I would have to know that just a couple hours ago I was thinking of fucking the redheaded bartender in that trendy bar. Only I would know. Instead of waking her up, I use the bathroom then strip off my clothes and get into bed. Jen sighs and turns so that her back faces me.

Since I was twelve I wanted to be nothing like my father, and yet in every step of my progress tonight, down the side streets of Cambridge and into that Porter Square bar, I felt myself following Jack's stroll into adultery. Part of me was dangerously close to understanding why he walked and that, more than the hate, scared me. I was afraid that – given time, given circumstance – I might turn out just like him. I knew that he had willed me more than a house; he had passed along to me in his DNA his tendency to faithlessness.

This fear of becoming someone like Jack Manoli, someone who could apologize then close his eyes and see nothing on the backs of his eyelids but masses of red hair, this fear wouldn't stop me from making the same destructive choices.

Shelley

The sky has lightened considerably. Awake and feeling restless, I resign myself to heading for the kitchen where I will have an early cup of coffee alone, do some grading of my students' work to a background of soft music, use the quiet time well to plan my day or plot my chores. I know I won't listen to Emma's advice about taking a few days off. I need to work; I need the routine of work. So I rise.

When I reach the kitchen it is quiet and empty, eerily lit by the overflow of the outdoor floodlight and the first hint of sun rising. The bottle of scotch remains within my reach on the counter, the two glasses, rinsed and inverted, stand dry in the dish rack.

I had kept the bottle for my father when he visited; the rest of the year the scotch remained untouched. Something about the look of the bottle, the caramel color of the liquor maybe, maybe the highly colored plumage of the game bird on the label, reminds me of my father, of dinners with my father that began for him with a cocktail hour.

I reach for the bottle and hold it up to the window above the sink. I tip it back and forth and watch the oily legs of whisky running down the insides of the clear glass bottle. I see in my mind Jack smiling over at me, swirling the drink in his glass; I hear the pretty clink of ice against glass. A longing for my father overwhelms me. I have to say he became more of a friend than an authority or security figure. Nonetheless, in these last few years he gave me what I needed, which was his presence. He became available for information and advice when consulted, part of the birthday and holiday celebration crew, and a doting grandfather. Jack, with age, had grown into the role of father, albeit on his own terms, and I decided I would accept them. Jack and Sylvie had been added to my house, and with my father restored, I finally felt finished. Every day I consider this irony, that if he had stayed with Mom, he might have spared us feelings of betrayal, but I might never have had his friendship.

I return the bottle to its cupboard shelf above the refrigerator and, thirsty, I reach instead for the tap. I turn the cold water on full blast to flush through the pipes, and I let it run until I can feel a chill rising off the stainless steel faucet. Filling one tall glass I drink it down, cold and refreshing and tasting of minerals with the tiniest bracing odor of bleach. I refill the glass.

Taking my water, I sit down at the kitchen table, briefcase at hand, prepared to grade some quizzes I grabbed on my way out of school on Friday. A soft yellow pine, this table is one of the first pieces of furniture, along with the six inexpensive beech chairs, that I bought with Steven after marrying. It used to be our dining room table until, years later, we bought a larger, finer table for the dining room and shifted this one to the kitchen.

As a family, we continue to eat most meals here; the girls still use it for art projects and also homework; I too work here – student evaluations, exam corrections, red ink notes jotted in the margins of essays. Engraved into the table's soft wood surface are columns of arithmetic problems and practiced cursive writing. As she perfected her penmanship, Libby bore down hard with a pencil onto paper as she tried over and over to link the "z" to the "a" in her name. The pressure carved her name into the wood through the layer of paper. *Elizabeth, Elizabeth, Elizabeth*, I trace with my finger. Writing impressions, dried paint smears, the oils from modeling clay – a lifetime is being played out right here.

Life, I understand, boils down to things like a table or a house, the gathering place for the people you allow in to help you live.

I lived my ideal around this table.

Growing up, our family of four ate together in the dining room every night exactly one-half hour after my father arrived home from work. We all had chores that never changed. Mom cooked, Mark set the table, I made the salad and poured milk, and Dad mixed two cocktails as soon as his jacket was hung up. With my own family, I'm not so formal. I never wanted any of that, only for us to enjoy each other.

In my childhood home there was a sense of duty and roles and sameness. At the table, Mark and I told Dad about school. Mom prompted us to tell him about grades and projects and upcoming events – another unchanging routine.

Only one night, Dad changed the script of our dinnertime.

He pushed his plate, dinner untouched, aside. Mark and I looked at him, alarmed, but Dad raised an eyebrow at me and gave a nod at Mark's plate, telling us with these looks to eat up. We did, in silence. It was perhaps the first time I noticed that, in the absence of our schoolday spiel, our parents had very little to say to each other.

On that night, Mom rose to clear Dad's untouched plate with an offer to bring us seconds. When she reached the kitchen, Dad sat back in his seat. He smiled at us for the first time since arriving home. He said, "Mark, listen to this one I heard at the office today," and he proceeded to tell us a corny joke, the punch line a pun so bad that I began groaning before he even finished speaking. Mark, though, laughed. He begged Dad, "Say that again," and Dad repeated the punch line, setting Mark off on another round of laughter. His laugh was infectious, so rare and so worth waiting for. Hearing Mark made me erupt into giggles. Dad joined in, and soon the three of us were hysterical over this silly, silly joke, and the moment felt like it might go on forever until, coming from the kitchen, we heard one earsplitting crash. It was the sound of our mother throwing all the dinner dishes through the kitchen window.

My father, my brother, and I ran for the doorway to the kitchen. Mark and I arrived first. I drew him close to my side. Dad lagged behind us but soon he stood with us, just as openmouthed and wide-eyed. As we stood gaping at our mother who looked out through the broken glass to the night sky, I felt Mark's hand slip into mine. A minute before, the noise hurt our ears; immediately after the kitchen was quiet except for my mother's whisper of "Vermilion."

Dad took care of Mom that night. He dressed her for bed then cleaned up the kitchen. I took care of Mark. First I read to him and then we talked. I said, "Don't be scared. She wanted a piece of the sky. The red. Maybe for a painting."

He said, "Vermilion."

"That's right. Maybe she meant to take the red and paint it onto your wall, to add to the sky over the ocean," and I pointed to the ocean mural on the wall behind the headboard.

Mark said, "I don't want a red sky."

His head on my shoulder was heavy and it strained my neck, but I did not ask him to move.

Soon I will need to wake my children for school, help my husband and Sylvie out of the house, and get myself to work. Without sleep, I'll need lots of strong coffee. I rise to make some and at the moment I do, Sylvie steps into the kitchen doorway. We startle each other.

"I came to start the coffee," Sylvie says as she releases her breath, placing a hand to her heart.

"I'm up to do that very thing," I tell her. "Why don't you sit?"

"No, I'll do it. I want to. You sit." Sylvie heads for the sink to start the water.

"Really, Sylvie, you shouldn't—"

Sylvie shuts off the water and faces me. "I can make coffee, Shelley," she says, a reproof despite the smile on her face.

I sit and ask her with a sigh, "Are we going to do this all the time now? Fight over who shouldn't be waiting on the other?"

Holding the coffeepot full of water, Sylvie offers another smile rather than an answer. She returns to making coffee, filling the water tank, filling a filter with ground coffee, switching on the machine. She asks over her shoulder, "Did you sleep last night?"

"A bit," I say, then admit, "not much."

She turns and leans back against the counter. "No. Me either."

Hooking my foot around a chair leg, I draw out the chair next to me. "Now you can sit."

She does.

"Tell me about your night," Sylvie says.

I take a pass. "You first."

"You're doing it again," Sylvie points out. We look at each other a moment. Sylvie's eyes crinkle up first, then mine. We giggle at ourselves, a small relief from the tension of the past few days.

When the giggles trail off I say, "I swear I wasn't trying to be overly polite. Nightmare," I explain. "It woke me and I've been awake ever since. I don't feel like talking about it is all. You?"

"Thinking. All night long. I must look a wreck."

"You look beautiful," I tell her and she does. She is dressed, pulled together in a way I can only dream of this morning with earrings, scarf, and her hair twisted up in a sleek but complicated-looking knot. I look down over my flannel nightgown and scuffed leather slippers. I sigh.

"Do you want me to come with you today?" I ask. I cross my fingers that the cleaners I hired have made a thorough pass through the condo.

"You're sweet to offer," Sylvie says, "but no. I'll be living there by myself, and I should get used to going in on my own."

"Will you at least promise to call me if you change your mind?" I ask. "And I think it would be nice if you had dinner with us once a week," I add.

The coffee maker bursts into its final noisy round of chugs, clouds of steam rising from the filter basket.

"Coffee." Sylvie sighs contentedly.

"Delicious coffee," I agree. This time I rise to fetch the mugs and pour the coffee. "Get you anything else?" I offer as I set the mug in front of Sylvie.

"No, thank you," she answers, so I sit. We sip coffee in companionable silence for a few minutes.

"You are maybe the most thoughtful person I know. People," she amends, "you *and* Steven. Letting me stay here this past week, inviting me to dinner. I'm not," she adds, "thoughtful, that is. I can be, but not by nature. I remember clients' anniversaries, their birthdays, and their kids' birthdays. But I work at that, that kind of thoughtfulness is good business. Anyway, thank you for the generous offer."

"You shouldn't be alone," I say.

"No, you're probably right." Sylvie stands to pour herself another cup of coffee. She remains at the counter, holding the warm cup against her chest. "I shouldn't be alone, but I am."

"Then say you'll come to dinner next week," I urge.

Sylvie goes quiet for a few moments as she sips her coffee, and then she speaks. "I won't be around to have dinner, Shelley," Sylvie tells me. "When I was awake in bed last night I decided definitely to take that vacation I mentioned. A long one, maybe three or four weeks."

Sylvie's unexpected answer temporarily confuses me. "I don't—When?"

"As soon as I put someone else in charge at work. I thought somewhere warm."

"Well, then," I persist, upbeat once again, "dinner when you get back."

"Shelley," Sylvie says, her voice quiet yet commanding. She takes her seat again and I really look at her, beyond the impeccable grooming and the friendly smile. Her amber eyes hold mine. *Pay attention*, she wills through her bright gaze.

"Yes?" I say.

"I may sell the business when I return. The townhouse too. Settle in somewhere new and take my time to decide what to do next."

"Sell your house?" I whisper. "And Dad's business?"

"Ours," Sylvie reminds me. "Well, mine now. We've had a large firm nosing around us for the past couple of years. It might be a good time to consider their offer."

Her business, of course. Everywhere I look, reminders of our new reality: a defunct ad agency, an empty beach house, a lonely townhouse, and an unfinished bottle of scotch. What had I thought? I ask myself as I sit at my family's table, lovely, heavy pine all marked up with the various scars of a family's industry. That our lives would continue on as if uninterrupted?

I think of Mark saying, "What you've never had, you can't possibly miss." If he were here I would try to explain to him what I am feeling. I would say, "The inverse is also true. When you've had a taste of what you truly crave, you want more."

"That's a lot to change all at once," I say to Sylvie, beginning to see the path mourning might take, full of twists and forks. "Should you make so many sudden changes?" I ask.

Sylvie smiles as if she has anticipated this exact question and is happy to have an answer prepared. "It only seems sudden to you. You're forgetting that I had the past year to think. A whole year to talk over all my options with Jack. Everything I've decided has been well talked out and thought out." She sits forward in her chair, her eyes bright, almost challenging. "Besides," she adds, "death kind of forces big, sudden change, doesn't it?"

Steven walks into the kitchen still in his pajamas and looking for his morning coffee. He starts at the sight of Sylvie dressed and made up, the two of us with our heads together, me as sleep rumpled as she is pulled together. "Oh, morning," he quickly recovers. He walks to me and kisses my cheek. When I tip my face up to him, he runs a finger under my eyes where I know there must be deep dusky half-moons, a telltale sign of fatigue. "Didn't you get back to sleep?" he asks.

"I didn't," I answer. "I had to get up for a bit."

"You should head back to bed," he suggests, and then asks, "What were you girls talking about?"

Sylvie rolls her eyes at Steven. "*Girls?*" She feigns being peeved but I can tell she is happy for the diversion he provides.

"Sylvie's future plans," I tell my husband.

Steven, curious, looks to Sylvie for details. She shrugs. "A vacation. Nothing definite to tell you yet. The planning is still in progress."

"Well, whatever you decide," Steven says, "you deserve a good, long rest." He reaches out, takes her hand, and gives it a squeeze.

That support, of course, is the right thing to offer, just what Sylvie needs instead of my warning about making too many sudden changes.

"I thought so too," Sylvie says with a look in my direction.

But I can't meet her eyes. Instead, I rise from my seat at the table. "Steven, let me get your coffee," I offer, acknowledging as I do that the usual routines of home and school will help get me through these next days. Steven lets go of Sylvie's hand and follows me to the coffeepot.

After I pour, Steven reaches for his mug. "Thanks," he says with a tender smile. To Sylvie he says, "I can be ready to leave in about twenty minutes."

"Look, Steven," Sylvie says, rising, "you just got up. I'm all packed. If you'd rather not rush, I'll call a cab?" She lets her suggestion linger in the air.

"Don't be silly," Steven says. "You're not taking a cab. I'll shower and we'll go. Twenty minutes," he emphasizes. Steven kisses me again and heads for the bathroom. Within seconds both of us hear the burst of shower water and Steven's off key, exuberant humming. "Simple Gifts" again.

Sylvie says, "You chose well. He's a wonderful man."

"Yes," I agree, "he is."

In Steven's absence an awkwardness springs up between us, as solid and unavoidable as a piece of furniture. A cumbersome, heavy, wooden piece, the exact size and shape of all we haven't said to each other. Sylvie interrupts the uncomfortable silence first. "I think I've hurt your feelings," she observes.

"I was making so many plans for you," I say. "You had to tell me you need some time to yourself. I understand. It's fine."

"None of this is 'fine'," Sylvie says and then sighs. A look of sadness clouds her face and I have a quick glimpse of her entering an empty home later this morning. "You're sweet to want to include me in your family gatherings. I meant it when I said you and Steven are two genuinely thoughtful people."

"I sense a 'but' coming," I say, half-joking.

"You sense right," Sylvie answers with a brief smile. "But . . . it's not simply a matter of needing time to myself. Jack was my family, and now I don't have a family. I need to figure out for myself what my new life will look like."

"Maybe you and Mark need to do the same thing." She pauses to let me absorb her words, then adds, "And the first step is, worry about me less. Second, decide what you want to do about that house."

"Mark," I say with a heavy sigh, reminded that I need to call him today. "I told you he drove away still pretty angry about Dad and the house."

"A third thing. Stop worrying so much about Mark, Shelley," Sylvie says.

Worry less about Mark. This is Steven's advice, nearly word for word, and hearing it repeated by Sylvie distresses me. "I wish I could make you understand," I say in frustration, "how difficult this is for me. I care about you all, but Mark was my responsibility. The way he feels about things is too, somehow."

"You could let him own that," Sylvie advises. "It's a gift, letting someone own their feelings."

"A gift?" I ask, baffled. "Letting someone live like he does, always angry?" I shake my head.

"He needs to get over the anger," Sylvie replies. "He needs to get over the fact of me. I didn't cause any of your family's problems.

"Ask yourself this," she continues, her voice softening. "Or better yet, ask Mark. Who in your house was happy *before* I came along?" Sylvie looks at me with an eyebrow raised.

She reminds me of the looks, the silences of my childhood. We lived with a thick smog of tension long before Dad left, before my mother broke the kitchen window. From that day on, the tension was worse. Mark, always sensitive, became more anxious, Mom more withdrawn, Dad absent. I had had Mark to love and love me back, but our love for each other had been then and remains fierce and protective rather than joyful. No, not one of us had been happy. I can't find a voice to answer "I know" to Sylvie's question so I slowly shake my head.

"Your parents made each other miserable." Sylvie holds up a hand, anticipating my protests. "Yes, I know, your mother had problems. Well, she should have gotten help. After a certain point, Jack couldn't go on being responsible for her well-being.

"And frankly, he saw himself as part of the problem. He thought the bad marriage was making Kay miserable, that if he left her she would be freed from all their mistakes. Free to move on. Jack honestly thought you might all come to be as relieved as he was when he left. Maybe he was naive, but he never stopped being surprised by how miserable Kay and Mark continued to be."

After a moment Sylvie asks, "Remember I said I tried to tell Jack I thought giving you the house as a gift was a bad idea?" I nod. "While I was lying awake I thought about why he went ahead with the plan anyway." Sylvie pauses and stares off at some fixed point in the distance. I wonder if she sees herself in the house in happier times; or perhaps taking the key for the last time from Jack's bony, withered hand. She looks back at me as if only remembering I am here.

"And?" I prompt.

"And . . . nothing definite." She shakes her head. "My ideas are my ideas. Like me, you're on your own with this one."

Like Steven had earlier, I reach out for Sylvie's hand across the table. She grips it briefly then lets go. As we sit, the kitchen becomes so quiet that I notice the shower water is no longer running. "Steven will be down soon," I say. "When he says twenty minutes, he means it. He's very fast."

"Then I'll go and get my bag from the guest room," Sylvie says. Before standing, she rolls her shoulders back and holds her head higher as if to meet what's next head on.

"Listen," I add, not content to let her leave with the awkwardness between us. "At least call if you can before you go away. Call if you need *anything*." I smile and reach for her hand one more time. I squeeze.

Sylvie nods and rises, releasing herself from my grip. "I'll try to call," she says. "I'll send a postcard if I can.

"And if you don't mind, I think I'll walk my bag out to the car and spend some time in your yard for a few minutes while I wait. Get some fresh air." She walks to the kitchen doorway. "Kiss your girls for me," she adds. And then she is gone from my kitchen. Within five minutes I hear the front door open and close; soon she will be gone from the house, the post-burial period officially begun.

Maybe Sylvie is right, maybe we do need time. She needs a rest after watching my father die, and I need to reclaim my home life. Come to terms with all the changes then put my days back into a familiar shape, return us to our comfortable routines. Take control after death has defied me to muster any.

Steven passes through the kitchen jingling his keys. He looks questioningly at me when he sees no sign of Sylvie.

"She's waiting outside," I tell him and he lifts both eyebrows in surprise. "She's in a hurry to get into her own home, I guess," I add with a shrug.

"Then I'd better be in a hurry too." He kisses me full on the lips as he reaches me on his way to the back door. After the kiss, he looks at me intently. "Are you sure you won't stay home today?" he asks. "You could go back to bed."

I shake my head. "I'm *fine*. I'm actually looking forward to work. Go," I urge, "Sylvie's waiting."

After Steven walks out of the house and once I hear the car's engine start, I sit down again in one of the kitchen chairs. I look up at the wall clock. Seven a.m. In the upstairs hallway the bathroom door slams. Already the girls are up and the three of us need to be on the road in forty-five minutes. I'll have to scoot if I want to catch a quick shower.

As I try to rouse myself out of my seat, I hear the gurgling end of a flush as the bathroom door opens, then the rise and fall of bickering voices as the girls fight over equal time in front of the mirror. I sit and listen, and the sharp tone of their disagreement reminds me of the edge in Mark's voice yesterday afternoon. I need to call him.

It's much too early to phone now, and I make a mental note to call from school later in the morning. In the meantime, I rise and head up the stairs to help mediate the escalating argument between my girls.

Mark

I sit on the edge of the simple platform bed that Jen and I constructed together shortly after I moved in. All the time she lived alone, and up until I moved the last of my stuff in, Jen slept on a futon on the floor. The floor suited me just fine, but once I was there, Jen decided we should have a bed and so we built one.

Jen's desire to create a comfortable living space was a new concept to me, but she made the work fun, like a scavenger hunt. We used lumber we found in the trash and attached these boards together with nails retrieved from the ground around building sites, using tools both of us have collected over the years. The bed was easy. We assembled four boards to make a box-like frame and finished this with a large piece of plywood placed on top. Once we had the rudimentary bed, I painted it a deep shade of orange using semi-gloss enamel over primer and sealed with many shiny coats of polyurethane. The space stank for days but we slept there anyway after hoisting Jen's futon on top of the plywood platform, joking all the time that the worst that could happen was that the fumes would make us high or kill off whatever brain cells I had left.

I sit here waiting for Jen to come home from a job, and four partially packed duffel bags crowd my feet. I haven't seen her in close to twelve hours. We didn't speak when I returned from my walk last night, and Jen left the house today before I was awake. She called a while ago and left a message to tell me she was stopping for groceries after she finished this latest gig, a spring-themed Wiccan wedding, one of the few wedding shoots she had left on the books since she stopped advertising and aggressively looking for the work. When she first picked up the job about nine months ago, we wondered, what does a pagan theme look like? We joked that the green velvet bridesmaid dresses might look like elf outfits. It probably wasn't the last time we laughed together, but today it feels like it. I had known for months that Jen would be gone all day today, but it was only this morning that this fact became useful to me. I used this knowledge of Jen's schedule, and I planned my escape around it.

Earlier in the day I had cleared the studio space of my plastic storage boxes full of color-sorted glass and taped them securely shut. I wrapped the sharp edges of my tools in heavy brown paper, and gave the floor under my worktable a good sweep. Most of the completed mosaics earmarked for my June show have been packed for weeks. This show will be a big deal, my first really big deal, and I have been uncharacteristically careful; I have worked steadily and met personal deadlines; I haven't wanted to fuck anything up.

Today I boxed up the last few works in progress, using plenty of layers of bubble wrap for cushioning. There is no way, once I leave this apartment, that I could come back for them, so these were the first things to go, slid into the back of a U-Haul trailer I was lucky enough to find available at the lot down the street when I went out at lunchtime. These four bags are the last, holding all I've got to show for myself: my clothes, a few books and sketch pads, some junk, whatever else I managed to collect over the past three years. The rest, if I've left anything of importance, Jen can keep. Or put out on the curb for someone else to find.

Close to being finished I rise, shut all the dresser drawers, then sit back down on our bed – Jen's bed now – and wait.

This morning I woke, finding myself alone and sprawled out on this bed with no memory of how I got here. I turned onto my back. I lay and waited for my memory, any memory, to rush in. It felt like the blood had stopped circulating to my brain, like my brain had gone numb like a torqued or squashed limb, and I tried waiting for a pins and needles feeling, a sign of the blood rushing back, but nothing came.

I closed my eyes tight again, as if I could have squeezed an image, wrung some clue to what I did out of my spongy brain. There had been a funeral, that much I remembered. Then coming home high. And Jen's disapproval. But I remembered nothing past that, past walking in the door and being greeted with her disappointment.

Then as I became more awake and aware, a picture began to patch itself together, come together in pieces in my mind. Instead of myself I saw my mother, her arms hanging at her sides, her lips moving without uttering a sound. Shelley and my dad flanked me in the kitchen doorway. There was a broken window behind Mom, and beyond that a red and dusky sky. What else? Jagged glass everywhere, sharp shards on the floor and counter and sink, glittering under the fluorescent kitchen bulb. Ground beef, swollen macaroni, tomato splattered on cabinets and Formica and linoleum.

Mangled wood. Broken dishes. Scattered silver. A picture on the wall hanging askew. So much broken glass. Some remained in the picture frame, pointed like sharp daggers. The rest on the floor, reduced to pieces so small they were almost invisible in the dim light. Finally Jen, a statue, her mouth making a small sphere of disbelief, like a girl in a fairytale doomed to be frozen in eternal surprise.

My father died, and as much as it kills me to admit this, his death rocked me. When I think about the feelings I carry for Jack, I wonder why rage and apathy aren't opposites, why the two feelings don't just cancel each other out. If the world worked based on that theory I would be the mellowest guy around. I'm not. Turns out anger and apathy are a potent combination, leaving me feeling like I've been stunned by a blow between the eyes. The worst thing, the most frightening thing is that I feel a violent emptiness inside me, like I woke up with a hole torn in my chest. A black, gaping hole like a fist makes easily through drywall. Like I could make that same hole in someone else. I feel tired too, almost as if I haven't slept at all. Tired of everything.

Jen left before I had a chance to apologize, but it wouldn't have mattered. The minute I lifted the rack and fixed my target we were beyond apologies. There was nothing to say that would fix the debris of broken mugs and cracked picture glass; nothing new or workable could – or should – be fashioned out of the mess.

Shortly after I got myself out of bed, Shelley called. I listened as she left her message, but I didn't pick up the phone and I haven't returned the call. I can't, not yet, not when I keep seeing my mother standing limp and muttering to herself. I can't do anything but get ready to leave this house. And Jen.

Sitting on the edge of our orange platform bed, waiting with my hands clasped between my knees, I hear first the jingle of keys, then the scrape of Jen's key turning the deadbolt in the heavy fire door.

"Mark," she calls, her habit, only now her certainty that I will answer seems tinged with caution. Yeah, I'm doing the right thing.

"Up here," I answer and I hear the thud of heavy cases and paper bags dropping as she reaches to close the door behind her. I rise and head to the dresser where I remove the rest of my shirts and socks, making myself busy. If I'm busy I won't begin to question what I am about to.

"I'm putting the groceries away," she calls upstairs.

I should go help her, stow my bags and pretend nothing's going on, but I don't move from my own task. "Come up when you're done," I say. "We should talk."

Across the open loft I hear the rustle of paper and plastic as bags are emptied, then the refrigerator door and cabinets opening and closing as Jen quickly stores the food. The last few sounds I hear are water filling the aluminum teakettle and the click of the igniter under the stove's gas flame. I continue packing.

A few minutes pass while Jen makes tea. Finally I hear her feet on the stairs; I hear her voice before I see any of her. "You're right. We need to talk."

As Jen tops the ladder to our bedroom, she sees me placing a pile of my clothes inside the last open bag, sees me – hears me – draw the zipper closed. She has been eating on the way up. In one hand she holds a bowl, the other a spoon, and the spoon is halfway to her mouth when she realizes what I am doing. She stops, one step down from the top of the ladder, transfixed, as if she can't by any force of will make herself take that final step into our room. I train my eyes on the white bowl, on the white lumpy mass on the end of the spoon.

"What are you doing?" Jen asks.

I look at her. "How was the wedding?" I ask.

"What's going on?" she rephrases.

"The green velvet bridesmaid dresses," I remind her. "More like elves? Or Peter Pan suits?"

"Mark?" Her voice rises, now questioning, demanding that I answer.

Ignoring her, I squat and check all four bags. Finally I stand, close all the dresser drawers, and sit back down on our bed – Jen's bed now – and wait.

"Mark," she says again, this time firm, impatient. She drops the spoon into the bowl with a clatter. The spoon handle hits the rim just right and a chip of pottery flies onto the floor.

"Okay." I hold my hands up. "What's going on. I'm making some changes," I say matter-of-factly. "I was thinking about getting out of the city, working on finishing the pieces for my show somewhere quiet." I don't add that I've only just thought of this. "Sit," I say, and I start to rise to give the bed over to her.

Jen shakes her head, stopping me, and continues to stand. "You don't want *us* to talk at all, do you?" she asks, a hint of bitterness creeping into her voice. Jen holds up a hand, stopping herself as much as preventing me from answering. "Never mind. Where are you going?" she asks.

Ah, the big question. I hadn't thought this far. I guess I saw myself starting my car and pulling the U-Haul and making tracks and that's it. Like everything else I do, all impulse and little thought. I have very few options.

Except I do, as of yesterday, have my own place.

I don't need a fucking cottage, is what I had told Shelley. I thought of Shelley and what she might say if I told her I finally did it, set foot in Dad's house. She'd be pleased, the only one of us. *Good for you, Mark.* Yeah, hooray for me.

The only hitch is, I'd have to be willing to go there.

It's been years but I still remember the cottage well, standing at the end of a winding dead end road, off the busy, twisty main road wrapping around Cape Ann.

"Your summer treat," Jack had said over the phone when he called to plan the visit. "Our Rockport house. A weekend at the sea!"

The drive, with Jack and Sylvie up front, Michelle and me in the back seat with our suitcases between us, seemed long. When we passed the entrance to an abandoned quarry, Jack started the tour guide act.

"The quarry is practically at the edge of the sea," he pointed out in a hearty voice as if that alone would rouse us from our bad moods. "It's now a state park." He slowed the car as we passed the quarry's entry road. "And it's a great place for a picnic. Nice flat rocks." He exchanged a glance with Sylvie, gave her a wink, and she laughed. Jack joined in.

At twelve I knew enough to understand what nice flat rocks might be good for.

Our mother had gone on a rampage on the day of Jack's phone invitation, had left her bedroom in a fury, opening and slamming doors as if searching for something she couldn't, if asked, name. Mom cursed Wife Number Two using words I was happy to learn and add to my own collection. Every door slam got a different word: cunt, bitch, whore. "How did that bastard afford a second house, and why does that slut think she deserves one?"

Then Mom sat at the kitchen table and wept. She pulled at her hair until Michelle, afraid Mom would draw blood, held Mom's hands tightly in her own. By then, the novelty of the swear words had worn off. My mother, when she cried, had the knack of making a kid feel as if the world was tilting dangerously, and I watched from the doorway, helpless. Michelle, in spite of acting strong, returned my look with a helpless one of her own.

The truth was, I didn't want to leave Mom, fearing what I might find when I returned home on Sunday afternoon. I didn't want to stay home with her, either. I didn't want to be alone with Jack and Sylvie.

Shell and I had too many places to stay and no real place to belong.

Jack slowed the car again and swung widely into a graveled lane. Stones churned up and pinged off the undercarriage of the car all along the road until Jack stopped in front of a small house. "Here we are," he said as he looked over his shoulder to speak to us. He searched our faces for excitement, awe — any reaction at all — except perhaps the one he did catch: my fingers moving into my mouth as I threatened to gag myself. The hopeful smile on Jack's face froze then faded. "Everybody out," he ordered. He killed the engine, stepped out of the car, and moved around to open Sylvie's door.

Still seated, Michelle held out a curled pinkie finger for me to link mine onto; we gripped fingers for luck, pulled, and then separated. Michelle took her bag, and mine too when she noticed I left it behind. The four of us stood for a moment on the flagstone walk before Jack led the way to the front door. Sylvie broke the silence.

"Jack? The keys?" She held out a manicured hand and took the ring from him. She unlocked the door and Jack ushered us inside. Michelle set down the suitcases and we both looked around. The furnishings were pretty but sparse. Light streamed in through the windows.

"Let me show you two to your room," Sylvie said brightly. My sister hoisted the two bags and made to follow. "Mark," Sylvie said, pointing, "take your bag from your sister, will you?"

I fixated on one pale pink fingernail as Sylvie pointed. I thought of my mother at home, biting her nails and the skin around her nails, raking her ragged fingers through her hair. My forehead wrinkled, the wrinkles deepened as I brought my eyebrows together. My arms hung at my side, fists forming.

"It's okay," Michelle said, recognizing the particular storm moving through my entire body. "I've got them. They're not heavy." And she lifted.

"No," Sylvie said. "One is your responsibility, the other is not. Mark?" Sylvie nodded her head at the suitcase.

She was stupid to have chosen this moment to start acting like my stepmother. My eyes, directed at Sylvie, grew darker, narrower. Sylvie laughed.

"That furrow," she said, hoping to coax me out of my temper. "It's like a plow mark," and she raised a hand to trace the lines on my forehead, to smooth them away. I lifted a hand of my own and batted Sylvie's away before she got too near my face.

"Don't touch me," I said. "Don't ever touch me."

For a tense moment, no one spoke.

Sylvie recovered first. "Jack," she said quietly.

"I'll take the kids up," he told her. "Mark, get your suitcase from your sister and let's go."

I stared at the three faces staring back at me, waiting. I saw my sister mouth the word "Please" and I snapped.

"Leave me alone!" I yelled. "Just leave me alone!" And I ran back through the porch door, heard it creak and bang behind me. Once outside, I kept on going.

I probably wouldn't recognize the place after so many years, but if I closed my eyes I could see myself as I was then, running, falling, my head snapping back as my chin connected with the ground.

Like I'm gonna move in, change the house, make it mine?

"I'm going to Shelley's," I tell Jen.

"Shelley's," she repeats as if she should have known.

"Uh-huh," I answer. "For a couple of days. Or until I can think of something . . ." I almost say permanent and decide on, "else."

"So, did you arrange this with her yesterday and fail to tell me?"

"No."

Jen groans with frustration. "Mark, are you going to tell me what you mean, or do I keep asking these questions that make me feel stupid?"

I explain. "She's not really expecting me." Jen's mouth opens again but before she has a chance to ask I clarify, "I just decided."

"Okay," she says slowly, "while I was gone you decided to go live at your sister's."

"Looks like it."

"And this would be because . . .?" Jen prompts me to explain with a rapid roll of her hand.

"I need a quiet place to finish my work. You know," I remind her, "those changes I mentioned."

"So your idea of making changes is going to Shelley's to 'finish the pieces for your show?'" She puts a funny emphasis on those last few words.

Jen's not stupid; she doesn't buy any of my half-assed explanations. She knows exactly what I'm doing, and she deserves better. "To tell you the truth– " I begin.

"That would be a new one," Jen interrupts, and then she sighs, as if suddenly tired of her own sarcasm. "Sure, Mark, why don't you tell me the truth."

"I can't stay here," I say, scratching the back of my head. "Last night ... well, I can't stay."

"It's not that you can't stay, Mark. It's that you won't. You're leaving," Jen states and she stares at me, expecting maybe another denial. When it doesn't come, Jen drops to sit on the top step of the ladder. She sets her bowl on the bedroom floor, puts her hand to her forehead briefly, and then presses her temple as if overwhelmed by a sudden stabbing pain. She manages to force a question through the scowl. "Why don't you just say it?" she presses me.

"I mean, let me get this straight," Jen says with a wry laugh and begins to count off on the fingers of her left hand. "You go to a funeral, come home and have a fit, then announce you're leaving me to move into your sister's house? I do have that right?" Her voice climbs the scale and ends on this high shrill note.

I stand now, propped up against the empty dresser, taking the brunt of Jen's anger. "That just about sums it up." I shake my head and say quietly, "I have nowhere else to go."

"So you thought you'd let me walk in on you leaving. Or maybe you were hoping to leave before I got back? Or– " Jen stops mid tirade and says, "No, forget it." She holds both hands up, halting her fast traffic spew of words. "Why do I even bother trying to talk with him?" she asks herself. She's loud enough, though, for me to hear across the room.

"I don't know," I say. "I don't know why. I honestly don't know why you want me here in the first place.

"Look," I say. I take a breath then exhale. "I'm doing you a huge favor."

"Oh, please, don't even," Jen says, covering her ears to block out the dreaded cliché. "Don't be such a shit, Mark," she hisses.

With effort, Jen rises from her seat on the stairs and climbs the last step into the loft bedroom. She walks over to the bed, sits, and lowers her voice. "How the hell do you think I feel? Like I've been kicked, that's how."

"You're, what? Upset?" I ask.

"Oh, fuck you, Mark."

"I'm not being sarcastic," I tell her. "I really want to know." I'd love to know at this point why my leaving upsets her, how, knowing exactly what I am capable of, she'd want me to do anything but leave.

Jen glares at me. "What are you talking about?" Her eyes search my face. "Of course I'm *upset*. Haven't I been telling you all along that you need help? That you need to make some changes?

I just can't believe fucking up the only good thing in your life is the change you would choose!" she says.

As if she has surprised herself with her anger, Jen lowers her voice. "Last night was bad, I mean *really* frightening. I invested almost three years in this, in *us*, because I believed in you. All this time, you could've gotten serious about yourself and your work." She counts on the fingers of one hand. "Serious about us. Guess what I wanted to talk about today? You, seeing a shrink — we could have gone together — to help you get past that childish anger you have for your father. Those, Mark, *those* are changes you could have made any time. But do you? No. You get angry at me. You break my things— "

"You've been angry at me for the past six months," I remind her.

"Don't make *any* of this my fault, Mark. Don't even dare."

I let Jen's heated words hang around the atmosphere between us. I could have tried to explain. There were a lot of things I could have said if I wanted any hope of holding on to what Jen and I had made together. That I'm tired of waiting to fail, tired of her watching me like I was some living, breathing accident waiting to happen.

That I know what I did when I broke those things last night. I didn't just break glass, I ruined us too. My temper, my history, me. I know we are over; I'm simply moving things along before I do anything that would really hurt her. But I don't tell Jen any of this.

I do say, "Of course it's not your fault."

My admission softens Jen. She reaches out. From where she sits she can just barely touch my hand. Her voice drops in a reach for a tone that's close to gentle, a tone that comes so naturally to her when dealing with me. She says, "Do you even realize what you're doing when you leave? You can't come back here. I can't help you anymore."

Even with our bit of distance, on her breath I can smell the food she's eaten, her meal of apples and yogurt. I imagine the tartness in her mouth, sour yogurt, vinegary apples – a clean, crisp taste. I try to imagine running my tongue along hers, reaching beyond its sponginess, moving up to the harder ridged roof of her mouth to taste her, but I can't. Instead I speak.

"I know," I answer. "You've done a lot for me. And my career."

This more than anything else we have discussed frustrates her. I hear the edge in her voice. "You'll spend the rest of your life selling crappy little tiled . . . flowerpots," she says, sputtering as she searches for the most degrading object she can think of, "out of some crappy tourist gift shop in some crappy suburb! I thought you wanted more than that for yourself."

"No," I say, "you wanted more than that for me. I wanted– I want– "

"What?" Jen asks. "*What?*"

But I can't finish this sentence. What do I want? Peace? An end to the conflict inside me? To do something right for once, or at least to avoid doing something wrong? I don't know. When I don't answer Jen's usually open face closes. I see the retreat in her eyes without even a sparkle of anger left, as if she is resigned and has moved far away. Finally.

"Do one thing for me," she says holding up one finger.

"Sure." Suddenly tired, I sit down next to her.

"No more stories about making changes or doing me favors, okay? You tell me the truth. 'I screwed up, Jen. I'm leaving you. I've packed my stuff. I'm gone.'"

Jen needs the truth. The *truth?* I don't know what the truth is. I hunch forward with my elbows on my knees, I drop my head into my hands, I squeeze my eyes shut – actions that delay both acknowledging her demand and complying with it. The tone is such a contrast from earlier, when she walked in the house after her job, when she was still unaware of what was happening up here. Back when she sounded cautious about approaching me, but also hopeful that my request to talk meant I was ready to take her advice about getting help.

The truth. As we sit on the bed, I remember the night my father left home, how he came into my room before driving off. He softly called my name over and over until I stirred. He sat on my bed and waited, like I am now. It was late, past midnight, and I had been asleep for hours. He sat patiently on the edge of my bed while I rubbed my eyes into focus. I thought it was strange that in the middle of the night he was dressed for going outside. In his right hand he held a pair of leather driving gloves. Whack, went those gloves against his left hand as he waited for me to adjust to the light pouring into my room from the hallway. Whack, whack, whack. He played with his gloves, played for time to collect his thoughts and order his words. His truth. When I finally sat up he said, "Son, I came to say goodbye." No explanations, no apologies, just goodbye.

Jen hits me on the shoulder. "Be a fucking man, Mark," she says.

Throughout the past twenty plus years, whenever I have remembered that last night with my father, I have thought only one thing: asshole.

Be a fucking man, Mark.

I run my hand over my face and look up. "Jen, I screwed up," I say, "and I'm leaving you. I've packed my stuff. I'm gone."

After Jen retreats to her darkroom so she doesn't have to witness me moving my duffel bags out the door, I take a last look at the bed we made together. The boards, the plywood, and the nails – someone's trash, our bed. Once, Jen made me believe that together we would create an entire home from building materials and furnishings we reclaimed at dawn from the sidewalks of Somerville, Cambridge, Arlington, Medford. When she described her idea, I found myself believing that such a home could be made from the ground up, every room filled, walls and surfaces decorated with my own art work and Jen's. And that I would build it with her? Of that too I was certain. I still believe she'll make it happen, but with me? I just don't know.

Jack

Several weeks ago, when I could still sit upright and stay awake for decent stretches of time, Shelley came by for a visit. On previous visits she had read aloud to me, but during this one I said I preferred instead to talk. The two of us sat quietly for some time, not uncomfortable but more as if we both were using the quiet time to search for the things we wanted to say to each other. After a time, Shelley broke the silence. Reaching over to the arm of my chair to take my hand, she said, "I have to tell you, Dad, I'm going to miss you. I also need to say something else."

She paused and looked down at her hand on mine. "The decisions you made?" she began without looking up. "Leaving Mom? I didn't like any of it. I know I didn't act like Mark; I talked to you and visited with you. But still, I was hurt." She lifted my hand to her lips and kissed my knuckles. "I'm sorry," she said, finally meeting my eyes, "to bring this up. But lately . . . " she paused and I knew she meant since my diagnosis, "lately, I've wanted you to know that I haven't felt hurt in a long time."

"I've been thinking a lot lately too," I told my daughter, "about hurt. Mostly about Mark. I remembered his first art show. Do you remember?" I asked her.

"He was eleven," she said and smiled.

"I'm going to tell you something, though after you hear it you may wish I hadn't." Shelley looked at me with a puzzled smile on her face. My spine had begun to stiffen so I paused and shifted slightly onto my side. "That show was the last time I would leave Sylvie to race home for a family event. Remember I called home? And you told me the show was important to Mark so I had to go?"

I closed my eyes and continued to speak. "Up until that night, my life for close to two years was back and forth, back and forth. Birthdays, holidays, illnesses. Eventually I had to choose. I had to stop leaving someone." I looked at my daughter.

I kept looking at Shelley, but what I saw was my choice. I saw Sylvie. And how I walked straight toward her.

The morning after Kay broke the window, I am in the car driving Sylvie to our sales pitch in Worcester. Between my feelings of unease around Sylvie and the fact that I want this new business so badly I can taste it, I am uptight during the long drive. I haven't loosened up by the time I do my voice-over for the slide show, and the speech comes out in a clipped, no-nonsense tone to a roomful of flagging company officers. I watch them slip away, all eyes about to glaze over if I don't slow down and inject some personality soon. Sylvie, aware of my nerves after our tense drive, also sees my nerves reflected in the faces around the table. "Relax," she mouths to me two or three times over the course of the presentation in this darkened room, and, "Slow down."

But I don't. I bring my slide show to a close and shuffle my notes to begin addressing this potential client's current needs. Sylvie jumps up to switch on the lights. There are a few seconds of rustling in the room as everyone shifts in their seats and adjusts to the light, which gives Sylvie an opening to make her next move. Her words are like a quick foot catching a slamming door.

"Before Mr. Manoli continues, may I offer anyone coffee?" she asks.

At the sideboard she pours china cups of coffee and then passes them around the conference table. She brings over two services of cream and sugar, and two small trays of danish, and places them at either end of the table.

"Mr. Manoli? Some water before you continue?" she asks, moving behind me. I feel the pressure of her hand on my back. "Please sit down," she whispers in my ear, her soft words breathing a tickle, causing me to shiver. "Relax."

For Sylvie I try. I take a seat and she leans past me to pour my water. As her hair falls forward obscuring her face, I smell traces of balsam shampoo. I relive the sensation of her mouth at my ear, how the vibration had slithered down my spine. As she reaches to set the water pitcher back in the center of the table, Sylvie touches me again, this time a hand on my shoulder to steady herself. I look into my lap, staring at a bulge in the crotch of my pants, as reckless as the earlier attack of nerves. More so. I slide my chair in closer to the table hoping to block Sylvie's view. I take several small sips of cool water. *Should just pour it over my head,* I tell myself, *like a cold shower.*

Around me, I hear light conversation, some laughter, and the lilt of harmless flirtation as Sylvie makes her way around the table. She is pretty. And young. And no one else, including Sylvie herself, makes too much of the banter. The man sitting next to me taps my shoulder, and I lean my head in to listen. Sylvie looks up from pouring coffee, catches my eye, and winks. Everything fades – thoughts of Kay, my anger, and my tension. Only then do I truly begin to relax.

"Thanks for helping me today. We need this account, and I was more uptight than I've been in a long time. I don't know," I muse, "maybe I want to feel the business taking off. I'm a little anxious.

All right, a lot," I agree, seeing her raised eyebrow. "I put a lot of pressure on myself today."

"You did fine," she reassures me. "They liked you."

"Maybe. Eventually," I say. "But they liked you right away." Sylvie and I sit in a booth in a small coffee shop in downtown Worcester before driving back to Boston. The coffee is oily and old; I push my cup aside and fold my hands together. I smile, continuing, "I was smart in one way today, smart to take you along. You're a natural."

"I like people. It was easy making them, and even you, relax." Sylvie grins.

Staring down at my hands, I begin, "What would you say to . . . " I pause to consider my next words.

"To?" Sylvie prompts.

I look up, look across at her. "After today, it's clear to me that I could use more of a personal assistant. I need the sales help more than I need a full-time typist." I feel I'm going out of my way to prove how harmless I believe the situation is (I'm her boss, she's a great, a highly valued employee), to prove that I want Sylvie around for only the right reasons. "You've got a knack. You pulled everything together last night, and then today? You saved my ass in there, if you'll pardon my language. You did a fantastic job."

The waitress approaches with a coffee pot but I wave her away. "An assistant," I continue, "would have to do more than type and file. I mean, the clerical work still needs to get done but I think you're bright and ambitious, and, quite frankly, that your talents are underused."

Sylvie takes in all this praise; she seems pleased that I have recognized her skills, and yet she shows no surprise. She knows she's good, she saw the effect of her work in the smiles of the officers after the meeting wrapped.

"The job would be different, more like what we did today?" she asks, fiddling with her coffee cup, running a finger along its rim.

"Not entirely different, but you'd have more client contact, on the phone and on sales calls. The job description would change substantially."

Sylvie moves her cup to the far right of the table. She folds her hands together, leans in over the table, and looks directly at me. "Will I get that in writing? You know, a written job description? And what about my salary? I'd expect that to increase."

I meet her look, then roar with laughter, causing heads to turn. "You drive a hard bargain," I tell her when my laughter dies down. "But of course, all those things. In return, though, one promise," I add, holding up my index finger.

"If I can."

"I'd like at least a year's commitment. I realize that you may get engaged, and, if so, that your fiancé may have different plans when he gets out of school. If you think you may not be able to finish a full year—"

"I'll commit to a year."

I hold up a hand. "You don't need to decide on the spot. Take the offer home. Talk it over with . . . what's your boyfriend's name?"

"You mean Dan?"

"Dan, right. Talk it over with Dan. Make sure he doesn't plan on taking a job in, say, Cleveland, when he graduates."

"Cleveland?" Sylvie shudders.

"Or Topeka," I add. Sylvie's pretty laugh grabs me by the throat. "Topeka is funny?" I ask.

"Me in Topeka is funny," Sylvie replies. "And anyway," she continues, her smile fading, "Dan isn't an issue. I finally answered his question."

Again I feel a tightening in my throat, this time as if Sylvie's hands are on it, squeezing. I am so anxious to know her decision that I can barely speak or breathe. "And?" I manage to croak.

"I said no. I don't want to get married. I mean, I do someday, but he's too young." She sits back and puts her hands in her lap. "I'm too young."

I sit back, relieved. "You are young," I agree. "So tell me this, since you're so young, how do you know what you *do* want?"

"It's more like I know what I don't want, then I make choices to avoid those things. C'mon," she smiles and taps my arm, "you know how it is. Being young."

"You think I can remember back that far? The distant past." I shake my head. "You're assuming that my memory still functions. That was a long time ago, Sylvie."

"Not that long. And besides, you have kids, you see how we make choices. Impulse. What feels right."

Kids, I think. For the first time today, I think of my kids, I wonder how they are coping after last night. I sigh. "When I was your age, no one I knew made decisions based on what 'felt right' or made us feel good. Feelings rarely entered into any decision. Maybe," I conclude, "my generation missed out on youth." Funny, I think, how I feel younger now than I did in my twenties, and I remember the way my groin stirred when she rested her hand on my back and when she whispered. Looking away, I take one last sip of lukewarm coffee and wince. "This is probably the worst coffee I've ever tasted." I set the cup down and reach into the pocket inside my suit jacket for my wallet.

"You're not old," Sylvie says.

"No," I agree. I stop reaching and look up at her. "No, I'm just tired. It was more than nerves in that conference room today. I didn't sleep well last night," I admit.

"You were so worked up about the meeting that you couldn't sleep?"

"Bad night at home," I explain. "It was nothing, nothing I can't handle," I say seeing the questions in her eyes. "Now finish up," I instruct, discomfited by her eyes and the way her look makes me want to keep talking when I know I have no business telling her anything.

Sylvie slowly extends her right hand across the table. I see it reaching over the billfold that lies on the table between us. "I'd like the job," she tells me. "I like working. I have no problem making a year's commitment."

There's no turning back. I take the offered hand in mine and feel the contrast between her soft skin and her firm grip. "In that case," I say, "you've got a deal. New job description, new salary." Plump, unlined hands, dimpled beneath the lowest knuckles. Young hands. I picture my daughter seated here, drinking coffee with someone fourteen years older than she is, and I feel slightly queasy. I blink. "Let's get back to the office," I say as I release her hand and swing around in my seat to hide the flush creeping into my cheeks. I signal the waitress.

At home Kay's hair is unwashed, her skin dull and thick. Kay and I drink gin and tonics together, before dinner. A few months ago, when I had suggested drinks before dinner, or an occasional lunch together, I had hoped to get back into the habit of talking as individuals rather than as parents. Instead, with topics of children and child rearing off limits, we sit without speaking, separated by a length of couch. The ice in our drinks melts fast, the glasses sweat. I know this is not Kay's first drink of the day; I smelled a sour mix of gin and peppermints when I pecked the air by her cheek as I passed her on my way to change out of my suit. Kay's breath made me remember the spicy herbal smell of Sylvie, how fresh Sylvie had smelled compared to this fug of tangy breath and unwashed hair.

Mixing the drinks, I allowed myself one last thought of Sylvie. I wondered if my job offer was as much about Sylvie's hair and the feel of her hand on my back as it was about her skills? True, she is skilled, hardworking, creative and ambitious; she is also young, pretty, and dangerously easy to talk to. Would my impulsive offer have been longer in coming – would it have occurred to me at all – if she hadn't placed her hand on my back right beneath my shoulder blade?

That touch had started something else too. When I looked into my lap and saw everything else the touch had started – well, it was a miracle that Sylvie hadn't followed my gaze to catch the stirring of my prick beneath the fabric of my pants. At the conference table, it had taken several minutes' concentration and a few more deep breaths to get myself somewhat under control. Even now, sitting with Kay, both of us staring into our drinks rather than at each other, just remembering both the inopportune erection and my surprise, I feel my prick growing, hardening. Again, uncontrollably. I pass a deft hand over my crotch and tuck it safely between my legs.

I shift in my corner of the couch and look over at my wife. I cough. I promise her and myself to try one last time.

"The sales pitch went well today," I tell Kay.

"Sales pitch?"

"Yes, in Worcester. The new account, remember? I know I told you."

"No, I don't think so."

"I did. I told you yesterday," I insist.

Kay shakes her head then rises, a bit unsteadily. "Sorry, I'm drawing a blank. Get you another?" She tinkles the ice in her glass.

I look at my wife; I search her tired, lined face for some flicker of interest in my work or in me until, finding none, I look away. "No" I say, standing. "I think I'll shower before dinner."

I step in under the rushing hot water and begin soaping myself. I close my eyes. In my mind I see her, I picture Sylvie walking into the office, picture her at work listening to me and discussing ideas with me. I picture Sylvie stepping into the shower with me; I feel her hair wet and syrupy under my hands and the erection returns. Like an oversexed fourteen-, fifteen-, sixteen-year-old boy, I grip my erection and pump it. I hold my breath and by the time I come I am gasping for air. Braced with one hand on the wall, elbow locked, I lower my forehead to the tiled wall and feel the hot water run over my back and the rush of blood returning to my brain.

I will wake in the morning and conjure up her face. I will think of her in the middle of important business meetings when she pours cool drinking water and smells the way she does and gently rests her hand on my back. This, then, is what I feel for Sylvie, a potent combination of intellectual excitement and raw sexual desire. Wanting to work with her, wanting to sleep with her. All those sandwiches, working late, the sales trip, and our heart-to-heart personal talks – I made up a job for her, for Christ's sake. Maybe at the beginning I could fool myself that my interest was innocent, but not now.

Now, there's no turning back.

Stretching, her arms reaching into the air and her neck lengthening like a dancer's, Sylvie shifts in the wing chair in my office. She kicks off her shoes and tucks her feet and calves up into the deep seat. She and I have nearly completed a report and Sylvie's eyes burn with the strain of proofreading pages and pages of copy. She rubs at her eyes with the heels of her hands and then yawns.

I yawn looking at her but swallow it. She may be comfortable enough to kick off her shoes and yawn loudly but I'm not. I am too careful around her and don't want to gape my mouth, let her see my fillings or smell the stale breath of a long day at work and too many cups of coffee. My stomach rumbles and Sylvie, hearing it, looks up at me and smiles.

"Excuse me," I say.

"We've worked through dinner," she says, pointing to her watch.

"You must be hungry too. Maybe we should quit for the night?" I suggest.

"Why? We're almost done. You can get this messengered tomorrow if we stay."

"Is messengered a verb?"

"It is now," Sylvie says.

Sylvie stretches again and swings her feet back onto the floor. She lays paper in three piles on the floor in front of her chair; as she bends over to sort paper into the piles, I notice how indecently short her skirt is, how when she sits or bends the very short skirt hikes up her thighs. Her pretty legs in sheer stockings, her narrow feet, slender ankles, shapely muscles. Maybe her knees are too bony, her one flaw, the patella pressing up under her skin like a sharp stone. Sylvie flexes her feet, flexes then extends, and I hope the buzzing in my ears is only the hum of fluorescent bulbs inside the office.

The outer lobby and the other offices are all dark. We could quit now, right now, go home like every other person who works here has. Being here with Sylvie surrounded by this darkness should disturb me. Should make me question every decision: hiring her, promoting her, asking her to work late hours alone with me. If I were a better person I wouldn't put myself in an empty office with a young girl I am attracted to; I would be at home, playing Monopoly with my kids.

Over the years I've met other pretty women, especially when I've traveled, waitresses who flirt with me in restaurants when I'm alone on business trips, secretaries from the companies I represent. Once, back when Kay was in the hospital recuperating after Mark's premature delivery, I thought one of the nurses paid me special attention during visiting hours, bringing cups of fresh hot coffee, soft drinks, trays with hot meals, and a sympathetic ear. Another time I had run into a neighbor, a man I knew only well enough to borrow the occasional tool or ladder from, in a bar with a woman who the neighbor introduced to me as "my mistress." The word made me think of an apartment, a love nest, expensive gifts, wife and children at home, a secret double life. The mistress smiled, I recall, when my neighbor had used the word. I sat next to them and drank scotch while they had beer; I found myself liking the mistress, her openness, and her laugh.

But I never saw that life for myself.

With Sylvie though I have taken steps, maneuvered the time alone, cultivated a friendship. I have fantasies, and not just sexual ones. I can see myself living differently. I imagine a second life with Sylvie, coming home to her every night, sipping wine, discussing the day, a life that would take me away from Kay, from the quiet, frightening, dead life I have been living to a life rich with work and interesting conversation and love. A life rich with a future.

That is the trouble with Kay and with my marriage. I've been dissatisfied, or we've been ill at ease with each other. Just using the word "troubled" to describe my marriage is more telling than anything else. The marriage *is* troubled, deeply disturbed, and if I stay in it I have no future, only the promise of a living death. Every day at home feels like a dark drop into a ragged-edged abyss, another step forward into something frightening. Imagine: thirty-six years old; a staid and dull home life; wanting something, some*one* I don't have.

I look back at Sylvie. I see plump young lips, the shake of her lustrous honeyed hair coming out of its loose knot, her smiling golden brown eyes, the hollow of her throat where a small vein beats, a tic. I see the rise and fall of her breasts beneath her blouse as she draws breath then exhales, a right knee as it crosses the left leg, her high instep, her narrow feet, a pretty shoe lying on its side on the floor beneath her seat. My face colors as my thoughts travel back up her legs, as my mind parts them, as I picture what I might find if allowed beyond the shadows made by her skirt.

I get up and cross my office to the credenza where I keep the scotch. I pour myself a drink, a good three fingers of scotch in a glass, no ice, forget about the customary water. I stand, my back to Sylvie, and I tip my head to take in a good mouthful, let it trickle down the back of my throat.

"Mr. Manoli?"

I turn. Sylvie lets the last page of the report flutter down to the pile at her feet. "Finished," she says. "Could I have one?" she asks, nodding her head at my glass. Sylvie rises and steps into her shoes. She walks over to me where I stand motionless at the credenza.

"A drink? Water?" Setting down my own drink, I loosen a soda bottle cap, and the escaping gas hisses as water rises up the neck.

"No," she answers, stopping my hand with hers. "I'd hoped for scotch. I could use a drink. After all this." She looks back at the paper and poster board surrounding her chair.

"Do you drink?" I ask.

Sylvie smiles. "I'm kidding," she tells me. She removes her hand. "Water's fine. But to answer your question," she admits, "only wine, and then only on holidays. I'm old enough," she adds. "Oh boy, you should have seen your face when I asked for a drink."

"Yes, well," I say. I look down into the still empty glass I'm holding; I look down at Sylvie's knees. Little girl knees, that's what it is, like she's not much past spills from her bike and scabbing scrapes. They are the knobby knees of childhood on otherwise very grown-up legs. If anything could stop me from making a fool of myself, it would be her knees. I dismiss the image and finish pouring her water, adding a couple of ice cubes for good measure.

"I think we're in good shape for tomorrow," Sylvie says. I pick up my drink and we clink glasses in an informal toast to ourselves and our hard work. She lifts her drink to her mouth, sips, and then touches the glass to her cheek, her throat. "Oh, cool," she says, closing her eyes, draining the water. "I needed that."

I turn away. I set my drink down and walk over to the report as it lays spread out over the floor. I bend down and begin arranging the pages.

"Let me stack that," Sylvie says as she joins me. Squatting next to me, she takes the report from my hands. "I'll make the changes first thing in the morning and then call the messenger. Why don't you go home? Go on, you look tired. I'll tidy everything and lock up the office."

I'm not so much tired as I am worn out by my thoughts, these thoughts of Sylvie prompted first by the cool glass against her cheek, then by her nearness, now by the shadows I see underneath her riding up skirt.

I clear my throat. "How will you get home?" I ask.

"The trolley, same as always. It's not that late."

"It's pretty late. I could drive you."

"Brookline's out of your way. There's no need. Really."

"It's dark, it's late, I see the need." Even as I say it, even as I know a ride is the honorable, the *right* thing to do, I understand what my offer means to me. I acknowledge, looking at Sylvie, my desire, these adulterous thoughts that have been humming up, building in my mind over the past few weeks, gathering like thunderheads. But the thought of being with Sylvie no longer seems wrong. It seems instead right, perhaps the rightest thing I will ever do in my life.

"Well, then, I accept your offer," Sylvie says looking up from her work, and she smiles. Her smile makes me so happy that my heart hurts.

I watch her tap the stack of papers to neaten them, and then watch as she stands. "What would I do without you?" I ask.

"You'd manage," she answers, reaching her arms into the sleeves of her long sweater, wrapping it around her waist, cinching the belt.

"Somehow I doubt that," I tell her. "Come on, we should get you home."

Everything then becomes forward motion. Walking toward the door we collect our cases. At the desk I reach for my jacket and shrug it on as I continue walking. We step together to the door. I put a hand at the small of Sylvie's back and usher her out of my office. It's as if, right or wrong, I've put myself on a course, a path leading to Sylvie's front door. Knowing that, I turn out the light with my free hand, and lock the door behind us.

Sylvie speaks only driving directions during the twenty-minute ride to her apartment. "Brookline. I live just on the line." "Yes, it's practically in Brighton." "Here, take this right, it's the next block." "That's it, third house down." I speak little more, opening my mouth only to ask Sylvie for directions as I strain to see the street signs on the poorly-lit streets off Beacon Street. After I pull in at the curb and park, I begin to open my door. "Let me walk you up," I say, setting one foot out of the car.

"Wait," Sylvie says and she stops me with a hand on my arm.

"I want to get the door for you," I insist.

"I know, but wait. Please. Close your door," she says, and I obey. "What you said, back at the office. 'What would I do . . .'"

"'Without you.' I remember."

"Well, I'm glad," she says, "that you need me. I like our work. I like *you*. I thought you should know how I feel, that's all." Sylvie reaches for the door handle and starts to draw it back.

I don't wait for the pop of the door release. "Please," I say, "please. Let me walk you to your door." I step from the car and move around the front of the car to the passenger door. Taking Sylvie's elbow, I accompany her up the walk and front steps, stopping at the entryway of the apartment building. At the door, I ask for the keys. She obliges and I unlock the door. When I pass the key ring back our hands brush, and one of the sharp burrs on her house key rakes the knuckle of my index finger.

"I scratched you," she says, and we both look at the one inch long white line on my finger, the raised red skin around the scratch.

"Looks deadly," I say.

"May require stitches," Sylvie agrees.

"Except there's no blood."

"No."

"And it doesn't hurt at all." I smile.

"I'm glad. I'll be more careful next time." Sylvie returns the smile. "Well, thank you," she says, "for the ride. I'll see you in the morning." She steps in next to the bank of mailboxes, then turns. I make no move to leave. "It's okay, I'll be fine from here," she assures me. "Unless you want to check behind the door for intruders." Sylvie stands with one hand on the doorknob and her right shoulder against the frame. I linger on the top step. "Or under the bed for monsters? My father used to," she continues, "when I was very little. I'd make him check behind my closet door *and* under my bed. I was always so sure something scary was under there. Waiting."

"Don't," I said.
"Don't?"
"Don't joke."
"I'm not joking. I was terrified. Sometimes I still am."
"Of monsters?"
She shrugs.
"Sometimes I am too," I confess. "Of the way I feel about you. Sylvie," I begin, "Sylvie, I– Can you help me out here?" I ask.
"You'd like to come in?"
I nod.
"But you're scared because you know you should go home? Anyway, shouldn't you? Go home?" When I don't answer, Sylvie asks, "Or would you rather tell me how *you* feel?"
I tell her.
"I don't want to go home. In fact, it scares me how much I *don't* want to go home." I look away, close my eyes a moment and think. Yes, right or wrong, I've chosen Sylvie.

Sylvie takes a small breath, brushes her hand over her forehead, and rakes her fingers through her hair. "Well, then, won't you come in . . . Jack?" she asks, swinging the door wide open.

Sylvie sleeps on her stomach, uncovered. She's a kicker, a scrappy, restless sleeper. I left Sylvie for a while to wash before going home, and by the time I'm back she's asleep. Before I leave I stand by her bed, watch her sleep, whisper my goodbyes. Under the light shining from the bathroom, I can see the red imprints of my fingers still on her skin. I'd held her tightly the second time, when I moved beneath her, held her ass, pressed her body into mine because I knew if I didn't I might lose her. I've marked her; she is mine.

I take one more moment in the apartment to watch the rise and fall of her back as she breathes; I notice the fine golden hairs along her spine. Hair falls over her face in her sleep. Honey, caramel, butterscotch, Sylvie's hair is rich like thick sticky molecules flowing in a ribbon, thick hair falling like a curtain across eyes, cheekbones, jaw line.

When I leave, I close the door softly so she doesn't wake.

Sylvie

Shelley, determined that I shouldn't enter the house alone, sent me home with her husband, a surrogate for my own, a man to carry my bags and check for burglars. I wait in the foyer as Steven carries in my two pieces of luggage, and as I stand there I look around at all the usual objects. On the console table, the answering machine's message light flashes to let me know I have calls to return. Typical. On the wall to the left of the front door, a favorite painting hangs slightly askew, a victim of the door's tendency to stick when being opened. Predictable. A pile of mail rests in the basket beneath the mail slot. Same old reliable mailman. But nothing else is the same.

In the past, when I returned from the rare business trip I took alone, Jack would be at the door, insisting on taking my bags from me and whisking them down the hall to our bedroom. I used to stay behind in the entryway, a smile on my face, my heart racing because I knew he would return for me and carry me too, although with much greater care and interest, right into the bedroom. One of our many habits, rituals. Every time Jack and I reconnected after as little as one night apart, after he carried me to the bedroom, we made love.

I look at Steven, who hasn't yet set down my bags. Sorry, Steven. You are a great guy, steadfast and solid, good for Shelley but not my type, and definitely no substitute for my Jack. I want him to drop my bags and go. He looks back, eyebrows drawn together in worry. "Are you all right, Sylvie?" he asks.

"Yes, fine," I say and I force a smile.

"Let me," Steven says, and with a swing of my two suitcases he starts for the stairs.

"No, please," I tell him. My hand reaches for his arm. "Leave them here." I am sure Steven knows I want him to go from the tone of impatience in my voice. Still he persists.

"You're sure I can't—"

"Positive," I interrupt, firmer this time.

"Sylvie," he says and he reaches for me, envelops me in a hug. In this house these arms feel so unfamiliar, so wrong. He steps back and looks at me. "You'll need your family. Call if we can do anything. Anything," he repeats, almost word for word exactly what Shelley had said an hour earlier.

"Sure." I nod and reach around Steven for the doorknob. I stand aside so he may pass. I tell him, "Thank you for driving me home. And for welcoming me into your home these past few days. Thank Shelley too for all her hard work. Thank you both for everything," I add as he walks through the doorway.

"We are your family," Steven assures me. "That's what families do for each other."

Family again, this time from Steven, sounding like a parrot of his wife. Is this Steven's attraction for Shelley, these beliefs so closely aligned with her own? I look him over, a polite smile stuck on my face. I have never met two people so absorbed with family affection and expansion. I'm not being bitchy; I admire the spirit of generosity, I do. But in the way an average museumgoer might admire a Rembrandt as lovely but unattainable, I feel so detached from this concept of extended family. Myself, I never longed for one. I left my parents quickly enough. Then, when Jack and

I married, I hadn't longed to become a stepmother to his children. Neither one of us needed or wanted to create our own children as living symbols of our love; we had each other. Maybe that is what Shelley's family does for her, gives her that satisfied feeling of completion. Or perhaps it's the attraction of security. She will always have her daughters, her friends, and her in-laws should anything happen to Steven. I traded security for a life well lived. As I said to Shelley, Jack was my family; now I have none. I am alone. But he was worth it.

The most I can do in reply is nod. "Kiss the girls," I add. "Tell them I'll send a postcard."

With my abrupt change of topic, Steven looks momentarily confused, then he says, "Oh yes, your trip."

"My trip," I confirm.

"Well, if you're sure you don't need– "

"I'm sure," I say again.

"Then I'll be on my way to work. Take care, Sylvie," Steven says and he kisses me lightly on the cheek before walking down the front stairs to his waiting car.

Once the front door is closed and deadbolted, I walk down the hall to the stairs intending to go on up to my room. I reach the stairs, and am just about place my foot on the first step when I decide instead to continue to the end of the hall and enter the guest room. The last time I was in here was Thursday, five days ago. For the last time, I got into bed with the man I loved and I held him. I relished it all. The dryness of his skin. The acute sharpness of his bones underneath. Jack's brittle hair. The sink of his chest. His premature old man smell. I watched everything, the movement of his lips as he tried to speak and the unremarkable way he went from breathing to not breathing. I had this feeling that I would recognize death when it settled, and my experience with Jack would be profound, as deliberate and passionate as our life together had been. Tears, renting of clothes, dying professions of love – but I had been wrong. The nurse and I knew he grew so much worse every day, but last Thursday I couldn't have said, "This is it." Death day was like every other day of the last three months except that I came home in the middle of my workday, took a late lunch break to see Jack instead of waiting for the evening. Perhaps I sensed some urgency after all, I don't know. But as usual I sent the nurse out of the room and slid into bed with my husband.

Like every other day, on Thursday I simply slipped into that bed to whisper, "Hello" and "I love you" to my husband and to feel him under my hands. He tried to speak. His voice had been growing fainter and hard to hear so I put my ear nearer to his lips. "One thing," is what I believe I heard. "One more thing," then nothing, not a rasp of breath, only silence. Only then did I know.

I lay there without calling the nurse for close to half an hour. I kept Jack warm, imagined that the warmth was from his own heart pumping and not mine, imagined I had him alive for a little longer. The nurse returned of her own accord, concerned that I would be late to work, and found us, me clinging. A big, strong woman, she had trouble breaking my grip. It was she who sat me in the kitchen with a cup of strong coffee, she who brought me the phone when I felt ready so that I could call Shelley.

I haven't set foot in this room since.

I stand with one hand on the doorknob, one on the door. I think of my last moments in the room with Jack, and I expect to find the room much as I left it. I turn the knob, listen for the click of release, until the door cracks open.

Through the slit I smell the effects of the cleaning firm Shelley hired, the vigorous scent of industrial cleansing products. I had forgotten the cleaners had been here. Across the threshold and inside, the chemical smell is so much more potent that I feel lightheaded enough to go and sit on the bed. Once there, out of habit, I kick off my shoes and lie down. I run my hand over the length of the bed where I used to find Jack's body. I pull the spread down from the pillows, turn onto my side and nestle my head on a crisp pillowcase. Clean sheets, clean spread too. There's nothing left of Jack. When I was much younger, a young teen, I used to push pillows under my bed sheets in a long line and pretend they were a man's body to press the length of my own into. Pretend. After years of the real thing, I am back to pretend.

As I rest, my breathing becomes deeper, slower, but I don't sleep. I don't even look at the clock. As the sun moves around the building and the shadows grow in the room, I lose all track of time; I remain suspended somewhere between sleep and waking. The blank white of my mind turns yellow then orange then red. The brick red of a glass of Burgundy wine. The same red as the first glass of wine I ever had with Jack in the Oak Bar in Boston. Then the red turns black, as dark as the bar in flickering candlelight, as dark as the shadow falling on one half of Jack's face as he sat across the table from me. Against this shadowy background I remember everything – my first sight of Jack, our first conversation, the first cup of coffee, the first night we spent together – all our firsts; I remember nearly all of our days together.

I was the only child of post-World War Two, blue-collar immigrants, a first-generation American. My father worked for years as a mechanic, while my mother logged many hours as a clerk in department stores around Boston once I started school. Both worked hard so that I, their cherished daughter, would receive an education. They fantasized that their Sylvie would become a nurse and marry a doctor, then settle down to enjoy my days raising children in the suburbs. For them, that was achievement, and that achievement was *their* dream for me. For me, I had different ideas.

At the end of high school I held a transcript of good-to-very good grades, above average but not stellar. What could be said about me, what I might have said to describe myself was that I was clever rather than brilliant. I possessed good, canny instincts and a desire to work hard. I was also a realist, and I had learned an important lesson as I grew up. I learned that being pretty meant I held a certain kind of power. Most people were nicer to me because of my looks; or, like my high school boyfriend, Dan, protective of me; my parents indulged and overprotected me. Unasked, people would give me things like presents, extra attention, their secrets, good grades, even love.

I didn't take the courses my parents would have liked, however. No life sciences; I would never be a nurse. After that disappointment, my parents had some brief hope that I might become an elementary school teacher; after all, both professions were respected and respectable careers to my parents. If I had chosen either, had married Dan, who had his college courses and future career as an accountant mapped out, I would still make their dreams for me come true.

But what did Sylvie want? I wanted to go to work as soon as I possibly could. Earning money and moving out of my parents' home was my dream, and there were a few difficult months once I shattered my parents' illusion. Behind everyone's backs I chose a secretarial college, a tony one but a secretarial school nonetheless. If my mother hadn't been so robustly German, I might have been able to picture her fainting. Instead she ranted. But my mind was made up, and in the end they gave in, and off I went to Katherine Gibbs to learn very practical and marketable secretarial skills.

I was twenty when I completed my course in 1972, and I knew that women were entering the workforce in larger numbers. "Equal jobs for equal pay" was a common refrain, but it was not mine, not yet. Like all these other women I wanted a job. Badly. My boyfriend tried to convince me to work and save money for a down payment on our house, because once he graduated from college it was assumed we would marry. What I knew for certain was that a good job would carry me away from Medford under my own steam and not under Dan's. But unlike the equal-rights women, I didn't care much about group causes; I was on my own personal crusade for liberation. I braced myself for the day I had enough money to tell my parents I was moving away from home.

I dressed carefully for my job interviews, following the advice hammered into my head by the placement counselor at Gibbs. "Your skills are essential – and a Gibbs degree will set you apart – but your appearance is equally important. Gibbs girls look a certain way, and through dressing well present a certain competent, professional image." I had spent nearly all of my graduation gift money on one suit, a lightweight wool in a pretty shade of apricot that made my light brown eyes look golden, and I knew I looked good in it. Especially after I had the hemline raised. Whether I married Dan or not, finding work was important and I was shrewd enough to know that showing off my legs during interviews with decision-making men couldn't hurt. By the time I went out on my interviews, I was well aware of the way men looked at me. I felt eyes on me as I walked along Congress Street, Washington Street, Milk Street, between the train station and the office for my interview. Businessmen's appraising eyes traveled from my thick ash-blonde hair to my pretty ankles. I turned heads.

My first interview was for a receptionist position at a law firm; the second, at an advertising agency, combined reception with some secretarial work. Neither job presented me with any anxiety. During interviews I could truthfully report that I typed ninety words per minute, and that I loved greeting people and making them feel welcome. For me, salary was the important consideration, that and some potential for advancement, and on the surface, the law firm position and the ad agency job seemed interchangeable. Interchangeable, that is, until I walked through the ad agency's doors to be escorted by one formidable Matilda into Jack Manoli's office. Once I saw Mr. Manoli seated at his desk there was no comparison between the two workplaces. There was also no question in my mind about where I needed to work.

I knew I interested my future boss too, from that first day.

There was nothing improper about Mr. Manoli's greeting or his interview questions or his treatment of me during our hour together. I too was all business, touting my skills in a truthful, forthright way. But over the course of the interview I sensed a change in the air between us, a scent that made our noses twitch, alert. Or perhaps it was more of a buzz, an electrical current that sprang up between us, an invisible connecting line that vibrated with unspoken communication. Something was there. I felt it. He did too.

I liked the way the change in the air made me feel. Although from childhood I understood the power of pretty, this felt different. A pungent, addictive taste of sexual power. And it was delicious, something decadent and yet essential, like good, strong coffee or bitter dark chocolate, like the concentrated salt of roe or the blood of rare meat.

Our mutual interest starts out innocently enough, office and work concerns shared over brown bag lunches in the park. Soon, though, business talk yields to casual, get-to-know-you conversations. Then none of our talks feels casual to me. After the first six months of working together a strong desire develops within me, worse than my usual cigarette cravings. I now have a strong need to know more about Jack Manoli. I wonder what he thinks about me. I wonder about the butterflies I feel when I see him walk across the park to sit with me at lunch; wonder even more why I feel so strongly the disappointment of eating alone. I am not disappointed for long. Our lunches become a regular habit, greatly anticipated events, in that first summer and well into the fall. Often I let my boss do the talking, and little by little he opens up to me. Before long we are friends.

Maybe more.

New thoughts of my boss eclipse my old daydreams of Dan. Very soon these thoughts of Mr. Manoli overshadow Dan's persistent marriage proposals. I put him off for a few months, so much so that he hints the next proposal will hold an ultimatum. "It'll be time to decide, Syl," he says. I even begin to cringe at the way Dan takes to shortening my name.

The more I think of it, the more I realize my relationship with Dan has not been wonderful of late; its scope runs from his nagging marriage question to my evasions, with limited sexual contact in between. Our sex bores me. The last time we slept together I touched myself, and he moved my hand and scolded, "Aren't I enough?"

Well, isn't he?

In bed, Dan holds his body above mine with his arms locked at the elbows. Even after I assure him I won't break if he is a little rougher, he changes nothing. More often I wonder, will I want to make love with Dan for the next fifty years? Will I even make it through the next year, having sex with only the lengths of our legs and our mounds of pubic hair touching as Dan moves in and out of me slowly and painstakingly? Is he enough? Because I think he should be, I keep working and suggesting changes to our relationship, but nothing changes and I wonder why I bother. I know I am tiring of Dan.

Dan is young but the life he plans for us is old-fashioned. I could go this way, toward Daniel, toward the white house on a quarter-acre lot, the fruit trees bordering the property, the dark-haired son and blonde daughter, the PTA membership, full grocery bags in the back of a station wagon, and three weeks' vacation on the Cape.

But in the other direction there is work, independence . . . and Jack.

Often I wonder what he would be like in bed.

I had known all along what – and who – I would choose, had known ever since the interview day when Jack had walked me to the door of his office and started to send me on my way. He must have reconsidered; he spoke my name, an imperative "Sylvie." I stopped, and turned, and followed him when he crooked his finger all because I knew. In that instant I looked him over, head to toe. I noticed that his suit, a rumpled, boxy Brooks Brothers suit, needed pressing. I approved of his height, that my head just reached his shoulder; his warm smile, the laugh full of genuine delight when I negotiated myself into a stronger salary; the blue eyes; the dark hair. He was the handsomest man I had ever met. Dan hid a baby face under a heavy beard and tortoise-rimmed glasses.

As Jack described the work at the advertising agency, I imagined exciting workdays and clients and money. I imagined myself working with Jack Manoli. More than anything I wanted to hear him laugh again. So when the job was offered, I stepped forward not back, following the older man offering me a modern life, following the seductive curl of Jack's finger.

That Jack is married bothers me very little. I only know Jack's wife, Kay, as a voice on the other end of the telephone, an anxious, clipped voice asking me to take a message for her husband. She never asks to speak to him directly, though I do press her.

"Tell him I can't make lunch today," she tells me. Always him, not my husband, not even the more formal Mr. Manoli.

I counter with an upbeat reply. "Let me put you through, Mrs. Manoli, it's no trouble."

"Please tell him I'm canceling our lunch, and that I'll see him tonight when he gets home."

"All right. Bye now," the pleasantries unnecessary because Kay hangs up long before I get the "bye" out. I disconnect my line by pressing down the button with my finger, but I keep the receiver between my ear and shoulder. I check the clock: twenty after eleven. They have an eleven-thirty reservation. Do I call Mr. Manoli over the intercom, or bring him the news in person?

Kay's calls have become so routine, so predictable. Fifteen minutes to a half hour before they are due to have lunch, she calls to cancel. She never offers any excuse either. At first I assume her work schedule is as busy as Jack's, and then I learn she is a housewife with two children in school and no outside job. She has no pressing schedule. What, in the course of her unstructured day, could possibly stand in the way of lunch with her husband?

Because she never quite makes it into the office, we have never met. I haven't had the opportunity to size her up. Still, I find her non-presence telling. I think of her as a ghost, an angry poltergeist, the kind that destroys its surroundings in order to define itself.

Jack's door is slightly ajar. Phone still in hand, I look through. From my desk's angle all I can see is a sliver of Jack, his elbow, his forearm, occasionally his hand dropping a balled-up piece of paper.

"Bitch," I whisper to myself. "What a bitch."

I see how hard he works; does she? I know he goes home and works hard there too. Over brown bag lunches I have heard about his children, their homework, the outings; the upkeep of home and yard; the life he tries hard to maintain. Despite Kay's quirks, Mr. Manoli tries. He respects their marriage, respects his wife as he does everyone in his sphere, from his partners to the office cleaners. He has never once called me "hon" or "girl," as in the old "have your girl call my girl" that so many of his coworkers and clients do. He is the very first person, man or woman, young or old, to see past my looks into the workings of my mind. Does Kay understand what – who – she is throwing away with both hands? She might put in a little effort, put on a little lipstick maybe, and drive in to the city to have lunch with her husband.

I hold the receiver over my heart that by now is pounding, torn between buzzing Jack's desk and calling his wife back. How many times have I been in this position, the bearer of her bad news? "I won't do this one more time," I might say to Kay if I called her, and then add as a warning, "And if you don't take care, someone else will."

Soon I move out of my parents' home. I change more of my life, everything really, when I stop unpacking and outfitting my new apartment long enough to make a brief phone call. Daniel cries when I finally and completely break things off with him. I steel myself to his tears; I refuse to listen to his pleas. He insists that we talk, but I tell him there is really nothing left to say.

"It's over," I assure him. "I'm sorry, please know that I never meant to hurt you," I say and then hang up.

I sit on the edge of my twin bed that, with the addition of a few throw pillows, will double as a couch in my studio. The new apartment is small, but I can afford it on my own salary. My own *higher* salary.

When I got home the evening after Mr. Manoli offered, and I accepted, the promotion, I called a realtor who found me a tiny studio apartment. Then I made an appointment with my doctor, threw away my inconvenient diaphragm, and started on the Pill. This is the truth I had kept from my parents, from Dan. My move is about growing up.

I want more than anything to grow up. To work late without having to explain to anyone where I have been; to have friends over, a lover when I choose. Especially that. And to accomplish this I need to leave home, have to pack up my childhood bedroom and break up with my childhood boyfriend. As an over-watched only child, I had faced frequent restrictions, always prefaced by an emphatic "can't", "mustn't", or "won't." Now I have the opportunity to make my own rules, to counter my parents' restrictions with defiance: will, shall, see if I don't.

I go through the apartment that first night, placing all the books and framed photos and furniture exactly where I want them to go. I straighten the spread on my bed and hang my clothes in my new closet. I think about all the new clothes I can now afford as if I am seeing pages straight out of fashion magazines: the hip-huggers with bell bottoms; a long, belted sweater to wear on weekends; a pair of hand-tooled, brown leather Frye boots pulled on over my slim calves. Being able to make impulse buys. Paying my own rent.

In the Worcester coffee shop, I accepted the offer because I had just come out of a meeting where I felt on top of the world, fully responsible for the campaign's success and wonderfully appreciated. I accepted because during the presentation, while I was on top of the world and high on my success, I leaned over to whisper in my boss's ear. I touched his back – just once – and felt his body respond to my touch. He couldn't draw his chair into the table quickly enough to keep his desire for me a secret. But someone in that conference room *did* have a secret.

I wanted him too. Will, shall, see if I don't.

———

My enhanced job means relinquishing many of my old responsibilities, and after swiftly hiring a middle-aged working mother as a receptionist and light typist, I slide right into my new assignments with ease. I now research the companies Mr. Manoli targets as clients. I also organize his work. He and I meet and talk for hours to plan ad campaigns and strategy once my research is complete. More often than not in this first year of my new position, Mr. Manoli misses dinner with his family because of these meetings with me. Soon we are a true creative team.

One morning I go off to work, and it starts off a day like any other day with a big, anxious client and a frantic scramble to finish a slick proposal. Boss and assistant work very late – again, no surprises; these late nights are the rule.

We finish. We pick up the papers and sketches that have been laid out across the floor and we put them into some order. Mr. Manoli pours drinks, a toast to us and our hard work, and my glass of seltzer after a long day tastes so refreshing and cool. I drink to the end of a crazy day like any other crazy day at the office, but then everything changes with six well-placed words. After all the tidying and toasting is done Mr. Manoli says, "What would I do without you?" and our work, our relationship to each other, changes. I realize in that instant that I could ask the same question of him and come up with the same answer. It is not imaginable. I realize, and he does too, that neither one of us is whole without the other.

No more simple friendship or friendly flirting or cautiously circling each other, no more skirting the truth that exists between us. All that ends this night. The end. No, the beginning.

On that night Mr. Manoli insists on driving me home. He walks me to my door and lingers awkwardly at the threshold. He wants to come in, I feel it; I say, "Maybe you'd like to tell me how you feel."

It was about time. One of us had to speak.

"Help me out here, Sylvie," he pleads and I do.

"Come in, Jack," I say.

Inside the studio apartment, after I close the door behind us, Jack leans in to me slowly, gently; he touches his lips to mine. I feel him begin to relax, as if he has been holding his breath and can finally exhale. As if he has physically shed something, a straight jacket, armor. And as Jack yields, I assert; soon every push of his mouth is met by a push or a pull of my own. I feel safe and comfortable, like I am finally home. My tongue enters his mouth where he tastes of the peaty scotch he drank earlier in the office. He draws me closer. My heart swells, my mind sings: Jack!

If you don't take care, someone else will. See if she won't.

He is mine, he is mine, he is mine!

House

Jack

"I had to stop leaving Sylvie," I told Shelley during our frank conversation on that day several weeks ago.

After a moment of reflection Shelley said, "I know.

"I do love you, Dad," she added after a minute. She had a smile on her face. "And I'm glad we— Well, I'm just glad."

I thought back to years ago, to the forced visits and the forced jollity, and knew she meant we had reached a better place. "Me too," I said. "I'm glad too."

"But Mark—"

"Ah," I sighed. "Mark.

"Mark made a different choice," I told her.

"He did," she agreed, although she sounded exasperated. With Mark or my resignation or the futility of the situation, I couldn't tell. All, probably.

I said, "Choices. He made his, like I did with Sylvie," I reminded her. "Necessary choices."

And Sylvie was necessary to me. She was someone, I had come to realize quite quickly, with whom I could talk about anything. It was as satisfying to wrap a big business deal with her as it was to sit quietly reading together as it was to be in bed with her. And once I had a taste of what my life could be like, I kept asking myself this about marrying Kay fifteen years earlier: What the hell had I done? Except for the kids, Kay and I had nothing in common.

My kids. As Sylvie and I snuck hours here and there after work or on the weekend, very little of my time with her passed without some tug of responsibility from my children. A school event or simply homework assistance would crop up and return me to my everyday life. Sometimes I would find myself thinking that these duties brought me back to reality, the routines and responsibilities of fatherhood. And then I would look at Sylvie and understand that what I had with her was far more real than anything I'd experienced in my life.

One year of the affair passed. Sylvie's apartment, the scene of falling in love, became less of an escape and more of a hideout. On the rare occasions we went out of town together, hotel rooms, even the nicer ones, felt sleazy. Thinking back, all we wanted was to build a life together and not be connected only through a series of desperate fucks. I couldn't decide how or when to leave my family; Sylvie tried to project far less need than she felt. Around us was the sour air of desperation. Then, in the midst of this anxiety, we were given a gift.

My client reaches across my desk to shake my hand. Sylvie takes the opportunity to slip quietly out of my office with the amended proposals and contracts. We're standing alone in the office, the deal is done. The client, Herb, clasps my hand but instead of a simple shake he pulls me forward.

"You look like shit, Jack," he says inches from my face. Herb was a college friend before becoming a client, and by now I have worked with him for years.

"I'm working flat out," I answer and let go of his hand. I know I've looked terrible for weeks, and so far it's been easy enough to blame my fatigue on too much work. "You know how it is,"

I joke, "people like you knocking on my door, never leaving us alone."

"Everything all right at home? The kids? Kay?"

"They're fine," I answer, maybe too emphatically. Herb arches an eyebrow. He knows Kay from college too. "Really," I insist, "everything's fine. Nothing a little R & R wouldn't cure."

"Say no more," Herb answers, holding up a hand, halting the progress of my explanation. He reaches into his pocket, pulls out a small leather case, a much smaller version of the threefold wallet. Inside, a metal bar; hanging from the bar, clips; hanging from the clips, keys. He unhooks a key attached to a flimsy coiled ring. Also dangling from the ring is a string-tied paper tag. "Cottage" is written on the tag in cramped capitals.

"Here. Take a vacation. On me."

"What's this?" I ask, reading, "'Cottage?'"

"My summer house up in Rockport. No one's there this time of year. Bearskin Neck will be a ghost town, but that means you might just get some rest."

Right then there is a knock on the door. Herb turns as Sylvie re-enters. Smiling, Herb looks back at me. "Or not," he adds under his breath.

"Sorry to interrupt," Sylvie says, "but before you left I wanted you to know that someone's typing up your documents right now. I'll have them out to you in the afternoon mail."

"There's no hurry. Tomorrow's fine. I just finished telling your boss he's been working too hard. Which probably means he's been working you too hard as well, am I right?"

I clear my throat.

By now used to this kind of banter, Sylvie smiles and without missing beat says, "I absolutely love to work hard." She takes a few steps across the room and offers her hand to Herb. "It's been a pleasure working with you. And it's no trouble at all to get this package out to you this afternoon. Now if you two will excuse me."

This time when Sylvie closes the door behind her, Herb says appreciatively, "Wow."

I say, "I can't use your house," and start to hand back the key.

"What?" Herb says, turning back to me. "Why?"

"You're my client," I answer. "It wouldn't look right." My hand remains extended but Herb doesn't budge.

"I'm a friend first," he says, "so take my friendly advice. Get away, get some rest. Hey, it's a beautiful spot." My face must reveal some uncertainty because Herb says, "For God's sake, pay me some rent if it makes you feel any better. But the house is yours, any time between now and Memorial Day."

I look down at my hand, at the key in my hand, at the tag. *Cottage*. "I don't know what you think you know, but– "

"Know? Me? What would I know? Other than my old friend needs a break. Get out of town," Herb adds with a wink, and then he gathers up his briefcase and leaves.

Sylvie and I became the winter weekenders – occasional overnights from Sunday to Monday – whenever I could fake a last-minute, late, out of town business trip, driving roads that few dared travel when coated with ice and snow to a town that felt the harshest of winds off the water in February and March. Herb's wife had decorated the cottage like a country lodge or chalet, installing pine kitchen cabinets with rustic trunk hinges, a fussy panel of lace at each window, braided rugs, and wooden-armed and uncomfortable craftsman side chairs and sofa – but Sylvie and I paid little attention to any of it. Very little. There was Sylvie, me, a serviceable bed, our clothes that would come off quickly, and the barest essentials of food: bread, cheese, and apples. I remember bags and bags of wintered-over apples. And wine, lots of it. Less than twenty-four hours together and all of it spent talking, sharing food, making love.

"Try this," Sylvie would direct with a look over her shoulder, and I'd follow. Her hair, by workday smooth, would be wild, a tangle or thrown forward, obscuring her face, and I would reach for it from behind, lose my hands in the crazy mix of it.

Everything about our time together was crazy. Our affair was improbable from the start. It was a miracle that Sylvie wanted me. Me, who felt like an old and dull middle-aged man. At first I wondered if she was with me because she wished to learn something from me, or wanted to pursue me because I was a challenge. Then I decided I didn't care. For my part, I needed the attention Sylvie paid to me. At a time when my wife, lost in her own world of regrets, didn't or couldn't, Sylvie's interest was intoxicating.

How crazy was it that those initial attractions dropped root and grew into need?

And crazier still, even though we spent as little as twelve hours in that house, we were actually building a life together. The cottage felt like our house and our life there like our marriage. The cottage was so far removed from the realities of our lives that we felt completely together and uninhibited. There were no coworkers to mislead, and no wife or children to deceive. While there, it was Jack and Sylvie, Sylvie and Jack, and no one else's history but our own. Once I knew what my life could be like, rich with a loving home and a good marriage, I also knew the time was right to make some changes.

Well into our affair, it became our habit to end whatever evenings we had together with a drive, grabbing every last minute together before I had to head home, and during these drives we talked. About work, politics, the early parts of our lives, our dreams for the future. Even when it came time for me to leave Sylvie, and we became seriously quiet at the prospect of separating for the night, it was a companionable kind of quiet

Until one night when the atmosphere in my car was, instead, tense. Sylvie was irritable and I felt restless. I drove and drove in my restlessness, well past Sylvie's place, into Brighton and beyond, into an unfamiliar tangle of streets and run-down neighborhoods. I stopped at the first bar I came to, which was a mistake. The place was a dive.

Once inside, Sylvie, visibly annoyed with the surroundings, excused herself for the restroom. When I tried to order her a glass of wine, the bartender laughed until his gut shook above the spotted apron tied low on his hips. "Beer or liquor," he said after he recovered. I ordered a Budweiser then scanned the bottles behind the bar for a replacement drink for Sylvie. In the end I ordered a whiskey sour, a sweet drink I knew Kay favored. I realized my mistake the minute the squat cocktail glass arrived, complete with a plastic spear skewering a maraschino cherry. Maybe Kay would drink this but not Sylvie, not in a million years.

Sylvie had such good taste, taste that had seemed remarkable when I first met her as a twenty-year-old girl. At that age, I had been in college drinking beer from bottles, eating hamburgers, reading assigned books I never would have selected on my own. By twenty-two Kay and I were married and had Michelle. I had settled in to work and family life so young that it was only recently, as the children grew older, once I met Sylvie really, that I had discovered fine restaurants and good French wine.

I poured my beer into a glass. At least the glasses were clean; hell, the bar itself seemed clean enough. Clean but dark. And old. The only other patrons were a few older drinkers with beer bellies like the bartender's. Probably every last one of them, I imagined, thrown out of their homes by wives fed up with their belching and endless television viewing. Why had we come here, I wondered; why had I stopped here when I could have driven on a bit further, could have reached a better neighborhood and found a more pleasant bar and restaurant? At the very least I could have driven Sylvie home, bought a bottle of wine on Beacon Street then gone up to her apartment to drink it. Maybe then we would have made love. I could have perpetuated the usual routine.

Clearly, the place pissed Sylvie off; she hadn't said anything much more than "excuse me" and "wine, please" since we parked the car; and she was smoking again. Or had she been pissed off before she even got in the car? And if so, was it because of our long-planned trip I had to cancel at the last minute because it conflicted with my daughter's science fair, or the millionth phone call I had promised Sylvie but couldn't make? I think we both probably knew, going into the affair, how many lies there would be, how many disappointments. But knowing is different than experiencing. And no matter how many times you tell yourself you won't get caught in that trap, there it is, the trap of expectation and need. I needed Sylvie. And she, as young and modern as she was with her short skirts and her burgeoning career, was not quite as progressive as she'd like to think. I could tell she needed me too.

I looked up at the bottles stacked along the bar, the mirror behind making the selection look twice as deep as it truly was. I saw Sylvie at last coming through the restroom door, making her way back through the crowd to me. I took a swig of my beer, one last gassy gulp before she reached me. I turned and smiled, ready for her.

When Sylvie returns to me at the bar she finds, instead of the wine she requested, a short cocktail glass, a cloudy drink with a red cherry speared on a plastic pick. It reminds her of childhood, of a Shirley Temple, the child's golden drink with a sunken cherry. She challenges me with a raised eyebrow. "Do I look like a child?"

"We aren't at the bar at the Copley Plaza," I apologize. "They have beer or mixed drinks. I'm sorry."

Sylvie doesn't bother sitting. She clasps her handbag firmly under her left arm. "I can't do this, Jack. I can't go on like this."

Two years into our affair and lately we've spent a lot of our time together apologizing. *Sorry that I'm going home to my wife, that I can't see you this weekend, over Christmas, on your birthday. I'm sorry I brought you here to this place where they don't serve wine.*

Sylvie collects her cigarettes, her lighter, and her handbag. Next to her a middle-aged woman sitting with a gray-haired man turns her bleary eyes from the TV to watch Sylvie and Jack's real-life drama. "That could be me," Sylvie mutters under her breath, "in twenty years." Without taking time to put any of her belongings into her bag she leaves the barstool and the bar and me sitting with my beer. She couldn't care less about the scene she's causing or her disruption of the televised ball game; she leaves and a cheer rises from the television as she walks through the front door of this dark and illicit bar.

She is angry, she is weary, she too is so very sorry. I see all this in the set of her shoulders as she heads for the door and the parking lot. I should have seen this day coming, decision day. I drain my bottle of Bud in a swallow, slap some money on the counter, and follow Sylvie out into the night.

Once outside, Sylvie's hands shake and tears fall down her cheeks. She finally shoves her belongings into her purse, exchanging the lighter and cigarettes for the last wad of tissue balled up at the bottom of her bag. Behind her, as she stands under the sweep of the floodlights in the parking lot, she must hear the front door open and close. Her back is to me but she knows I am coming for her, knows it by the soft sound of my leather-soled loafers on the gravel walk and by the feel of my hands on her shoulders as I turn her, draw her to my chest, hold her, tell her, "Don't cry."

I plead, "I love you, don't leave. Marry me."

"Take me home," she says.

That night Sylvie had cried with the frustration of always being apart. She looked at me through her tears, her eyes shining, and I knew it was time to make the changes we needed to make. Before walking Sylvie to her front door, I had considered going into the apartment to make love to her. I wanted nothing more than to lose myself in her, the way I always could in the generous welcome of her warm body, but I knew if I went in, I'd never have the strength to go home and face Kay. Sylvie had understood, had sat next to me in the car holding my hand. I wound my fingers around hers, brought her hand to my mouth, and kissed the underside of her wrist where the skin was so thin and pale that I could see the blue veins beneath. I thought of her milky skin everywhere, the white skin of her breasts, the inside of her thighs, and the spread of throat below her ear where on occasion I had felt her rapid pulse under my tracing tongue. I kissed her wrist and saw her to the door.

That night after leaving Sylvie, I headed east, to the water, instead of heading directly home. I would take one more hour after many hours spent in my car traversing roads between work, Sylvie's home, and mine. There was a sense, though, of this being the last drive, the start of a new life, and I needed the time alone to think. When I finally stopped the car, I found myself at Revere Beach with my thoughts and the arcades and the smell of fried clams wafting from the beach parkway.

This is what I thought. Maybe twenty years ago, an earlier generation, I could have maintained two lives, two families, one legal and one illicit. Instead I was a product of my time, a man intended for dissatisfaction because such old-fashioned options were no longer open to me. Instead, I was willing to walk away from everything I had built over the past sixteen years – I was willing to walk away from the only life I knew – because of a gnawing, nagging emptiness at the core of myself. As I stood and kicked at the sand with my foot, I listened to loud voices rising from Kelly's Roast Beef and the blasts of car horns. Beyond the honky-tonk strip and the noise of cars peeling out from the sidewalks, the ocean roared in and out. The days would begin and end; my kids' lives would go on too. I saw my children waking up each day and going to bed each night no matter what I did or chose in the end. Anyway my choice had been made about an hour before when, already married, I proposed to another woman because I needed her more than I needed my wife and children.

All it would take was an imagination, a way to envision the future, this new world I would create. In my imagination, Michelle and Mark would have two homes to belong to, two mothers, a richer extended family, a parent and stepparent who loved each other, which must be better than two true parents who didn't. I even saw Kay, freed from her daily, heavy meal of disappointment, returning to school, getting her degree, painting again, or teaching art to young children. I thought I might even have a better relationship with all of them now that we were out of an unhappy situation. I saw it all clearly in front of myself. Life would go on.

I walk into the house, still calm from my solitary walk on the beach. As soon as I step across the threshold, I feel the warmth of my home, the heavy atmosphere of trapped humidity. From the front door, as I hang my suit jacket in the hall closet, I can see down the long hallway into the kitchen, can see Kay sitting at the kitchen table flipping through a magazine. Loosening my tie, I pause at the closet doors and take a moment to breathe and prepare myself before joining my wife.

Kay skims her magazine back to front, not really reading, and sips gin from a brandy glass, the wrong glass for neat gin. She clutches the glass by its bowl, the short stem rides between her first two fingers, an almost childlike grasp, tight and protective as if afraid her drink will be pried away from her. She looks up when I pass through the doorway, says "Hello," then returns to looking at the glossy advertisements spread out in front of her. Someday, I think, advertising revenue will be even more important to magazines. Standing here, pausing, I see advertising's future. There would be money to be made at the expense of lonely women like Kay poring over pages of slick, promising ads. An uncomfortable thought, Kay's loneliness, and in such stark contrast to my vision earlier in the evening, at the beach, of Kay being set free to live her life. I quickly push that thought out of my mind.

"Sorry I'm late, but we– " I begin, falling into the well-established habit of making excuses. But by now Kay is used to my late nights. She raises her glass to her lips and as she looks over the rim she is very nearly the pretty girl I met at a college party so many years ago. I see the same freckles across her nose and hands, the same delicate features and wide-set eyes. Much of her dark hair, though, is prematurely shot with white that is making advances on the brown. Her eyes glimmer, catching the kitchen light reflected off the surface of the glossy magazine pages.

"Kay," I say. I draw out a chair; the legs grate over the linoleum. I'll need to replace the felt pads on all the legs, I think, and then catch myself, reminded that I probably won't be doing too many more odd jobs around this house. "Look at me, Kay," I say, seated now. "Look, we've got to talk."

"Can I get you a drink?" Kay begins to slide her chair back, shifting her gaze over to the counter, to the comforting sight of the gin bottle. I can tell she finds it hard to sit with me, to sustain eye contact, to imagine that I need or want to talk.

"No, no drink. Just stay." I reach across the table and close the magazine, not bothering to mark her page. I slide it away. Kay moves her hands to her glass, one hand anchors the base and the other again grips the bowl. I watch as her knuckles whiten with tension. Nerves. Me too, I long to say. "Kay," I begin again. "There's no way to say this without coming right out and— What I want to tell you is that I'm not happy. I haven't been happy in a long time."

"Happy?" she asks.

"And I don't think you are either. We don't talk, we don't— " I lay my hands out on the table, palms up. "It's about living with someone you can't talk to. Even now you can't look at me, Kay. Life has to be about happiness."

"Oh, I see. *Hap*-pi-ness." She draws out the word by syllables. "Get with it, Jack. No one's happy these days. Look around you, it's an epidemic. Didn't you hear about the Taylors down the street? The McGraths on the next block? Everybody's deciding they're 'not happy.' And now you." Kay drums her glass with her fingertips, impatient. "You know what? Someone should tell you all that happiness isn't guaranteed. Do you think I've been wildly happy all these years?"

"Then you'll understand what I'm questioning. Why stay like this? I think we could both . . . move on. To find happiness." Kay turns from me as I speak, and I reach out with my right hand to turn her face back to mine. "*I'm* not happy, *you* aren't. You don't love me," I add after a beat.

"What do you want, a *divorce?*" She says the last word in a tone of mock disbelief and with a small laugh, as if everything I've said is absurd.

"*I* don't love *you*," I say.

Kay takes my hand and removes it from her cheek. She studies my palm as if some answer will be there, written in the folds and creases. Finding nothing, she drops my hand to the table. "And what am I supposed to do now? Hmm? I don't work, I didn't finish school, remember? I left to have your child. Look at this house, this kitchen." She sweeps her hand. "Like it or not, this is what I am. This is all I have. Life isn't perfect, Jack, it isn't 'happy' all the time, but this is what I have.

"Anyway," Kay snorts, "you're being ridiculous. You have a family, you can't simply decide—" She breaks off and lifts her drink, finishing off the dregs of gin in a single gulp. "For better or worse," she continues after she swallows. Pointing the bowl of the empty glass at me she says, "You took the vows, Jack, almost sixteen years ago."

"I know I did, and I meant them. I've worked hard at keeping those vows. But this isn't living. I'm tired, I'm almost forty years old and I'm tired of living like this. I never meant to hurt you. But Kay," I begin. I bow my head. "There's someone else. I'm in love with someone else."

When I look up I see that Kay looks stunned, that the hand that holds the glass, her right hand, is frozen in midair.

"Oh my God," Kay whispers. "Don't tell me I'm stupid too. Unnecessary *and* stupid?" she spits. "You must have had a good laugh behind my back. All those late nights when you said you were working. And I believed you."

"I was working. For a while. Then it just . . . happened."

"Nothing just happens. Not to you, anyway."

I say nothing. There is nothing to say. She is right. I knew all along what I was doing.

Kay stares at me, thinking. Finally she asks, "So who is it, Jack? Who are you 'in love' with?" Her voice rises. "Who has it been during all those late nights? Which cliché? My best friend? The neighbor? Your goddamned *secretary*?"

"Kay, I– " I look into my wife's eyes. In that one pained look, as my eyes meet hers, she sees the truth.

"She's a *girl*, she's practically a child, for God's sake!" Kay shrieks. Before I can answer, Kay raises her right hand, and then swiftly pulls it down. The bowl of the glass whacks the table's edge and glass shatters, splinters, falls to the table, the floor, Kay's lap. Kay's hand curls, contracts into a fist squeezing the glass's base; the stem points out from between her fingers, points at me like an accusing finger, like a weapon. "You son of a bitch. I don't *believe* you," she says.

"Put that down, Kay, before you hurt yourself," I warn. Instead, Kay squeezes tighter until I can see the tendons standing out on the back of her hand. "Put it down."

"Oh, I'll put it down," she challenges, and Kay draws back her right hand and hurls the fragment across the table. The jagged stem connects with a spot between my cheekbone and left eye. I bring my hand up, feel the wetness of blood but not much pain.

"Get out," Kay hisses. "Get the hell out of this house." As she rises from her seat, she brushes glass shards from her lap; wearing only her thin-soled bedroom slippers on her feet, she nevertheless steps and crunches through the glass and walks upstairs to the bathroom where she turns the lock.

I retreat to the small second bathroom off the kitchen, where I usually shave in the morning, where I will never shave again.

I inspect my wound in the mirror; no worse, really, than a shaving nick. I blot the blood away with tissue and use a styptic pencil to close the cut. The salts in the pencil sting. Then I throw all my shaving gear, my deodorant, my toothbrush, into my kit bag and zip it shut. Already in my mind I plan what I must pack, clothes I will need for the morning, or maybe for the next few days, at least until I can return for the rest. I see myself driving to Sylvie's, I imagine Sylvie a few miles away in Brookline waiting for me, dressed in her favorite emerald green slip and ready to start her new life. I leave the bathroom and head slowly down basement stairs to collect a small suitcase.

Once back in the kitchen, though, I look at the dangerous broken glass. I set down my case and reach into the broom closet for a dustpan and straw whiskbroom. I sweep up all the glittering, eye-catching shards on the table, chair, floor, then tip the debris into the trash bin under the sink. I walk to the stairwell; I look up the stairs. Soon I will make a quick sweep of underwear and dress shirts, a cursory packing, then I'll leave a note and arrange with Kay a day to come back for the bulk of my belongings. The children, of course, will stay here. There's barely enough room for two in Sylvie's apartment. But there will be visits, Sylvie and I will make a second home for them, it will work. I hesitate at the bottom of the stairs, preparing words for my children, my explanations and my goodbyes. Remember, I tell myself, the family won't be demolished but reconfigured. I wonder if up these stairs Kay, quiet in the bathroom, waits for the final scritch of my key in the lock. If upstairs my daughter finishes homework wearing headphones, oblivious to everything but the loud rock music blasting in her ears. If upstairs, in bed, in a darkened room, my boy drifts off to sleep while thinking of breaking glass.

I stop wondering. I put a foot on the first step.

Sylvie

Here, then, is the end of my life with Jack. Alone with a business I don't want to run by myself, and a townhouse redolent with death. I press my face into Jack's pillow and I finally find it, Jack's smell, the rank and sour odor of a dying man that not even Shelley's top-notch cleaning firm with their Lestoil could erase. How long should I lie so very still in this bed hoping to find some stray physical trace of Jack, something wonderful and not depressing? My desire for something of Jack's makes me think of my much younger self, sleeping with my boss, falling in love with him.

Back then I had so loved having Jack in my small, girlish apartment, having a man's height and breadth dwarf my collection of tea cups and saucers, the small vase of daisies, the wooden shoe shine bench that served as a lamp table, the narrow Harvard-framed bed, the unsteady milking-stool night table. In the nights we spent there, he embellished my flea-market decor; he furnished the place with his discarded suit jacket and size eleven wingtips, with his long legs stretched across the ottoman of the only comfortable chair, with traces of aftershave, with the beat of his heart in between our comfortable silences. Tucked away, exploring each other and delighting in each other, my small studio felt like a secret chamber holding a stolen piece of art, a place where only the thieves could appreciate the beautiful object they now held.

We knew the initial excited energy wouldn't last, that we couldn't go on forever at this feverish pace. We said it all the time, that something had to change. Jack would say over and over, "I have to leave her, but when? What time is the right time?"

A year into the affair, our time together started to have less of an aura of energy and something more like a feeling of desperation. Jack looked unwell, thin, and his eyes had dark circles from lack of good sleep. He felt the effects of too many demands on his time and too few hours in the day. At first he tried to please us all, squeezing in late weeknight hours with me, weekends with his kids.

And me? I developed a kind of mania. Every time Jack got ready to leave me, when he was in my bathroom washing away the scent of our sex before going home to his family, I searched pants, suit jacket, and coat pockets for something to take, some souvenir. By the time he stepped from the shower and opened the door to let the steam escape my small bathroom, naked and dripping in the doorway, I would have taken the most recent item. A stick of Wrigley Spearmint gum or a Sunoco gas station charge receipt or a light blue page from his pocket appointment calendar or movie ticket stubs from a night out with his son and daughter. I was not as independent as I thought. I needed him.

I clipped extra fabric from an inside seam of his trousers, had collected his hair from my comb into a plain envelope, I kept the handkerchief he lent me to wipe away his semen which snaked down my leg after we first made love. Stiff and rippled in places, the handkerchief rested in the top drawer of my tall, narrow dresser; I used it to cosset all these treasures stolen from him, mementos gathered against the future as if he was a trip which would end soon.

Of course everything begins and ends. Sneaking around had been thrilling at times, but inevitably it took its toll on us. After two years

I had my mania; Jack's tired face showed the strain; both of us were tense and, many times, unhappy.

Choosing to be together or apart was inevitable. That it happened on one of our drives, a stolen moment, felt inevitable too. Jack cut across the city to Commonwealth Avenue; within minutes we passed signs for Allston, Brighton, Newton, Chestnut Hill, weaving through streets neither one of us had ever seen with no idea of where we were. I sensed he wanted to talk but struggled to. That made me feel itchy, irked, and I said nothing as Jack drove.

Eventually he pulled to a stop in a small parking lot wedged between two brick buildings, a commercial block with a bakery and a bar.

"Can we stop for a bit?" Jack asked. I shrugged. He looked questioningly at me, I suppose confused by my lack of response, but I didn't explain.

Jack opened my door and I stepped out. I followed him into the dark bar. Still the wordless companion I took a seat facing the bartender's densely stacked liquor bottles and lit a cigarette. Jack had always disapproved of my smoking – for a time I even quit for him – but tonight I lit up anyway.

"Why, Sylvie? Why start smoking again?" he asked.

I answered with a narrow-eyed, disdainful look, and then turned my head. *Why?* I thought. *Because I know it bothers you. Because tonight I feel like bothering you.*

Why? I asked myself.

Because we had come to this, sitting together in a dim bar with the smoke wreathing us and silence filling the increasing space between our bodies. It had been two years since we were first enveloped by and swept along in a funnel cloud of desire and excitement, deceptions, and intrigue, our love affair like a tornado gathering dangerous but thrilling momentum. Drinks in romantic bars, intimate dinners out of town, fabricated business trips, stolen hours in a small apartment, sex in bland but costly hotel rooms along the Interstate. I looked around me through the smoke; I looked at my fellow drinkers, the shot glasses and highballs at their elbows and I knew. Here, then, was the end of the wild ride. We had been dropped in a dive bar surrounded by sad sacks and hard liquor, and in our wake we had left empty wine glasses and champagne bottles, lipsticked napkins dropped in haste on chairs after expensive meals, mussed rented beds with coverlets pushed to the floor.

And all this had left Jack with something to say but unable. For this reason I felt angry, unsettled, and I could not look at the man next to me. I smoked on for a few more moments, ignoring his plea, and kept my eyes peeled on whatever sports game was being broadcast on the television set above the bar. I gave a final blow of smoke from my mouth and nose, and then stubbed out my half-smoked cigarette.

Rising from the bar stool, I asked Jack to order me a glass of wine, then excused myself to use the ladies' room. The toilet stall was not quite filthy but it was unclean, as if someone thought a half-hearted swipe with a damp cloth now and then was sufficient. My mother would have called this kind of cleaning slapdash, the kind of cleaning that leaves behind just as much grime as it removes: a stray body hair, a couple of dried urine drops, slimy soap grunge, and the remnants of muddy shoe prints. The semi-squalor was another affront. I closed my eyes and squatted over the toilet, thankful my mother knew nothing of my affair. She had cried when, all those years ago, I had refused Dan's marriage proposal; my mother had ranted when I moved from her home into my own apartment. "You want to be a working woman?" my old-fashioned mother had demanded. "Working women become spinsters or the boss's whore. For this kind of future you're giving up a good man who loves you?"

No, not for that kind of future.

Once finished, I found there was no toilet paper. I wiped off using facial tissue from my handbag, and I flushed the toilet with the pointed toe of my navy blue pump. I opened the stall door then let it bang closed behind me. At the sink, to my surprise, I found powdered soap in the dispenser, operated by a hand crank which I turned five full times, and I began to wash well. The mirror above the sink was cheap, my reflection wavy. Through the distortion I saw the almost twenty-four year-old mistress of a much older man, a young woman who looked old, who looked from a certain angle both spinster and whore. My hair was dull under the single low watt bulb, my face pale; even my plump cheeks appeared hollow when I turned my face or lifted my chin. I looked back into the sink, rinsed off the last of the soap, and turned off the tap with my elbow.

When I walked into Jack's office looking for a job, I thought I had forever to decide what to do with my life. I gave one last look in the mirror, viewing my face from many different angles. With my chin dropped my eyes appeared large and questioning, but from all views I looked older and tired, time having finally caught up with me. Oh, I had grown up, all right. The idea of having unlimited time had faded. I had fallen in love and now I knew life's real limits. There was beginning and end. I reached for the door handle, ready to return to Jack.

I went back to him and I pushed, and I think I pushed because of the Rockport house. From the first, the house unleashed a determination within me, a determination to achieve a life that combined the bonds of work, friendship, cerebral love and physical passion in one intense relationship. Under one roof. I wanted a home with Jack; I found one; I could no longer compromise.

My first visit to that house was Jack's surprise gift to me.

He made me close my eyes as we turned off the main road. The pure sensation – bouncing along a rutted gravel road with my eyes closed as my heart beat with anticipation – nearly overwhelmed me. I felt I would pass out with longing. I was young, twenty-two, but part of me felt much younger, like a six-year-old child at the top of the stairs on Christmas morning. Another part of me felt experienced, a truly sexual being with an adult's desire to prolong the foreplay. Yes, the drive was like foreplay, all sensation: the heady disorientation of being blinded, my body vibrating with every jolt of the car along the road, the slow progress of the drive, the waiting. "I have a surprise for you," he told me only the day before. Even after Jack pulled to a stop at our surprise destination I remained still with my eyes shut tight. He understood what I was doing and why, and he encouraged with a whisper, "That's right, don't look, don't open your eyes until I tell you." I grew wet between my legs without needing his touch or the feel of his breath on my neck.

We sat and sat and sat some more, not touching, not moving, and my breathing became heavy, labored; I struggled to breathe through the longing. If I sat one more minute I felt sure I would come, harder and stronger than I ever had, out of anticipation alone. Jack knew. He brought me to that edge and just as I leaned over, ready to fall, he whispered, "Open your eyes," and I did.

Through car windows that were fogged with the steam of our breathing I could barely see where we were parked. Jack raised his hand and wiped away a circle of condensation with the back of his wrist. I looked through this porthole at a little cottage, unremarkable in its size, as pretty as a dozen others we had seen on the drive, less pretty than a dozen more. "But it is ours for the weekend," he told me, "a gift from a generous friend." The fact that it was ours alone made it more special than a palace and more exclusive than a luxury hotel.

We had been sleeping together in hotels for close to a year, hotels and my apartment, my one-room apartment with its tiny bathroom. By now I knew every inch of Jack's body: the crinkles at the corners of his eyes, his smooth chest, the freckles sprinkled across his shoulders, the heft of his penis, the weight of his balls, the gray-blue bumps of gravel that remained lodged under the skin of his left knee after a childhood fall, his ugly splayed toes. I had kissed all these places on him, loved each one. I would tell him as I kissed him, "No one has ever loved every part of you as I do," and he knew I was right. He gathered me up in his arms whether we were in my small bed or a larger hotel one and didn't let me go.

Sitting in the car I wondered what love would feel like in this house. Through the fog it looked unreal, unattainable, and tantalizing. Between my legs the feeling started again and it felt like cells dividing rapidly and mushrooming, like a flower blooming in rapid time, its petals multiplying. I said to Jack with great urgency, "Take me inside, quick."

He opened his door; he came around and opened mine. I could barely walk so he carried me, taking no time to close either of the car doors, to hell with the battery. He unlocked the front door of the house with some difficulty, clumsily maneuvering the key with the hand that held me under my knees. Once the doorknob clicked and turned, Jack kicked the door all the way open with his foot. Inside there were more closed doors, one ahead which we would discover later led to the kitchen; one to our left, closed, which most likely opened into the living room; and a double door on our right, all panes of glass through which we could see into a tiny dining room. I felt all of Jack's upper body muscles begin to shake as he held me tightly in his arms, unsure where to turn, thwarted for a moment by so many closed doors.

Then Jack said, "Up the stairs."

I whispered back, "What if there are more closed doors up there?"

"Here then?" he asked and he looked into my eyes.

"Right here," I nodded, and he laid me down on the braided runner on the floor in the hallway. Jack took his hands and moved my hair back from my face. My hands opened his belt, unbuttoned and unzipped his pants.

Afterwards, I whispered in Jack's ear, "I want to live here forever."

He answered, "Someday I'll buy us a house like this, near the ocean just like this." He was trying to catch his breath and it was hard for him to speak.

I said, "This one. It's ours now."

"It's not for sale," Jack told me.

"Maybe it will be, someday," I suggested.

"Maybe someday," Jack agreed.

We lay still a moment longer as Jack's breathing evened out. While we were quietly recovering he must have been thinking because he said, "If we do buy it," and here he lifted his head from my breast. He looked into my eyes and his eyes crinkled up with his smile. He said, "If we do manage to buy this very house, the first thing I will do . . . "

"Yes?" I asked, smiling back.

" . . . is take down all these goddamned doors."

"So that there will be nothing," he told me, "in our way."

Twenty-four hours is what we had on that first trip to Rockport. Twenty- four hours away from work, away from Kay, away from the pull of children. In the days before my surprise first vacation in the house, I found myself listing and examining all the potential pitfalls of being a mistress. Who, by then, hadn't seen a movie or read a book about naively faithful mistresses existing on promises of marriage? Unfulfilled promises. Although I was chronologically young and inexperienced, I wasn't about to be that duped woman.

I knew I wanted Jack right from the start but if I had had the least inkling that Jack was promising the world but delivering nothing, make no mistake, I would have walked. I have been called many things in my life – workaholic, vain, shrewd, a bitch – but believe me, sentimental has never made the list.

However, being unsentimental didn't keep me from falling in love. And how I wanted Jack! No one knew, but I would have traded business success just to marry him. Love, true love, changes everything. Fortunately, a large part of our mutual attraction was grounded in our working relationship. We respected each other; we were challenged by each other. I could imagine no better life than living and working together with Jack, our two lives entwined on every level.

My lack of sentimentality did help me recognize love when I saw it, and the turmoil an inconvenient love can cause. As if they were living and breathing beings in this affair with me, I looked love and turmoil squarely in the eyes.

I understood Jack Manoli almost as well as I understood myself. My talent in business arose not so much from an understanding of the marketplace, but from an understanding of people. What clients over the years have called charm is nothing more than my willingness to listen to people and understand them, and I understood Jack.

He was a man straddling two worlds, not content with the old rules of unquestioning fidelity to the home and office, and yet nervous about facing this new world, this place where you grabbed what you wanted rather than making do. Wanting me was tempered by the duty to stay with his children. Jack needed to know which he wanted more; he needed a push.

Love changes everything and I learned that looking into Jack's eyes. The balance shifted. No more would I be a diversion for Jack, by turns a sexual satisfaction, a burr of change under Jack's otherwise comfortable saddle, or merely a sane and rational conversation partner. I became then his equal, his acknowledged partner. He gathered me up, I welcomed him in, and together we moved into the future, our future. In the year that we were lovers in the Rockport house, Jack walked out of the web of his family and into the refuge of us.

Each moment together, finally together in that little house, was . . . well, intense would be the best word for it. Concentrated would be another, hours of love packed into each single minute. For years the air in that house was heavy with us. Sometimes a visit was brief, a day here or there; once or twice we had part of a week. But no matter. We crammed as much experience into each brief visit. That way of living, getting as much into each day as possible became the blueprint for all of our life together. We never took a day for granted. Walks, talks, meals, making love. Just looking at each other. Some of the best moments were passed in my summer home. I stop short when I think of ownership. The house isn't mine anymore, is it?

"It's hard to give that up," I whisper to myself, meaning both the love of my life and the house where that love was tended.

There was love here in this townhouse as well, of course there was. But in this home, the good memories are tempered by the lingering smell of death. Visiting the Rockport house might help; there are more happy memories there than miserable ones. But it no longer belongs to me.

"I want my children to have it, Sylvie," Jack had told me just a week before he died.

"But we've always been so happy there!" I protested, sounding to my own ears like a petulant child.

Even in illness, Jack was patient with me. "That's exactly why. Because we've been happy there. It's the only way I know how to give them back a piece of something I took away years ago."

"You feel guilty," I accused, possibly the only time in twenty-three years that I had spoken so sharply about Mark and Shelley. For the first time I was jealous of his children. It used to be "Forsaking all others," I thought to myself, and it seemed to me now the children were coming first.

I think Jack understood that it was his impending death that made me angriest of all. He gave me his crooked smile. "Not guilty," he said. "Never guilty. I can't explain, but I know it is the right thing to do."

The house that was no longer mine could never really belong to anyone else, least of all Jack's children. I knew that. Jack should have. As he told me his plans I could only wonder, *What is he thinking in the face of death? That he could share with them a piece of us? Make them understand what we had? The very thing that they rejected knowing and seeing back then?*

I said then in another sharp outburst, "They won't understand!"

But in the end I gave Jack my promise to see the plan through. At the wake, I pressed the key on Shelley and Mark. I gave up my home.

Once, I had clipped, lifted, and collected pieces of Jack and his belongings for my secret stash. Then once I had him for myself, I laughed at the raw need that made me hold onto those bits of him. But I never let go of those things. Somewhere I still had all those treasures, the hair, the fabric, the scraps of paper; they no longer lived in a dresser drawer but shared an archival box with my collection of love letters, also from my husband. And not just somewhere; my collection was in the house in Rockport.

I shift onto my back. I wonder about the cottage. There is no way that Shelley could have cleared it out yet. She would be back at work today and besides, she said to me that she wouldn't make any decisions until she had spoken to Mark. Mark! Left to him, it could take Shelley months to get into the house. I think of all the furnishings, the things I was fine with passing along, like secondhand sofas and beds and linens. I think about the more personal possessions I couldn't part with: whatever summer clothes and swimwear I stored there and might need if I do take my trip somewhere warm; boots, jackets, toiletries; the series of photographs that Jack took of me; my archival box. Of any place, that cottage would still retain some feeling or reminder of Jack's presence and better, of us together.

"And surely he didn't mean for me to give up everything in that house," I think to myself, "surely he would have expected me to clear out my personal items. The photographs especially won't mean anything to anyone but me." Mere hours ago I had walked back into the townhouse and I already know I am unable to tolerate one more day here. There is my trip, of course; the trip will get me away from here. "But I have to go pack up the house," I say aloud.

I sit up on Jack's bed, the guest bed. The death bed. Death bed reminds me of death room and I laugh wryly as I think of Jack sharing his misunderstanding with me. The laugh we shared at his mistake was our only relief in the entire awful last six months. Strange how laughter could spill out in the midst of death. As I remember, though, tears fill my eyes and my laugh turns into a strangled cry. No, I will not start crying, not now, I vow. When I close my eyes to pull myself together, I see Jack's face. Not as he was at the end, gaunt and cadaverous, but at some time further back in our life together. I see the happy, relaxed, and healthy face of a man totally satisfied with his life. In my vision he seems to nod to me as if approving my plan.

I wipe a lone tear from my cheekbone with the back of my hand. With my other hand I reach across the bed for the telephone and call my assistant, Marta, at the office. I tell her my decision to travel; will she help? She says of course she will make some calls for me to help set up any travel plans I decide on.

"Italy, I think," I tell her, choosing right then and there. "And lots of moving around. And please, near the ocean. None of those stuffy museum cities. I'd like to be outdoors as much as possible."

"Consider it done," Marta assures me. "Planes, cars, hotels, whatever. You won't have to worry about a thing. Ideally, when do you want to leave?"

"Ideally?" I repeat, pausing a moment to think. I pinch the bridge of my nose perhaps hoping to extract the perfect plan freshly formed from my mind. I give a quick look around the room. What a mistake it had been to keep the blinds shut. Already I feel the walls closing in on me. "I can't stay *here* too much longer," I say to myself.

"Then I can work on the earliest possible flight, and book you a hotel room in Boston while you wait," Marta suggests. "If you'd like."

Her voice jolts me and I realize I have spoken out loud. "Ignore that. I was talking to myself," I explain. Spending the next few days pacing a hotel room or wandering the streets of Boston sounds almost as unbearable to me as staying in this townhouse, and would only leave me longing for the days when I went into the office with

Jack. There is really only one place I could stand to wait, one place where Jack is still alive for me.

My mind churns with logistics. Even if Shelley works a miracle and manages to coerce Mark into a trip to Rockport so soon after Jack's death, the earliest they might arrive, given Shelley's job, would be the weekend. "Friday," I say to Marta, after quickly calculating that a Friday departure would give me a few days to myself in Rockport, if I could leave for the house right away. "I'm going to the summer house for a couple of days. Don't worry, I'll be back here in Brookline for whatever flight you book."

Marta knew of Jack's bequest. I had told her. "But the house—" Marta begins. Anticipating protests or warnings, I quickly cut her off.

"I know. Isn't mine," I finish for her. "I need my summer things for this trip and that's where they are. Besides, it will give me an opportunity to clear out anything else that's mine to take.

"Now," I continue, changing the subject, "if you can book an overnight flight, that would be perfect. I can take a taxi from the townhouse late Friday."

"Don't be silly. I'll drive you. But Sylvie, any guidance as to what you'd like to do on your trip? Any special requests?"

"Just the ocean. As for the details, surprise me." I can tell immediately by Marta's long pause that my sudden lack of attention to detail and passive surrender to another's plans take her by surprise. But she recovers quickly.

"All right, then. I'll get on it and call you when I have something to confirm."

That accomplished, I replace the receiver, and with great purpose I separate myself from Jack's death room. Up in the master bedroom I exchange one pair of suitcases and my dirty laundry for a new, small case from the same luggage set and fill it with a set of clean, casual clothes. I round up another empty suitcase and a few spare cardboard cartons from the storage room. I am going to Rockport, to the house Jack and I loved. After all, I have belongings to pack and remove. By the time Shelley gets Mark interested in making a decision about the cottage, I will be long gone. Meanwhile, for the next few days the house would still be mine.

As soon as Marta calls with a proposed itinerary ready for confirmation ("An exclusive yacht cruise through the Gulf of Salerno! You'll fly to Rome, pick up a hired car and driver, then head south. Leave from Amalfi. Sail the Gulf and make some stops in various ports. What could be better than that?" "Nothing," I assure her.) I am ready to leave.

I pack up my car, which has been idle for days in its parking space. When I leave, I lock the deadbolt behind me.

Shelley

This morning, Mark did not answer his phone at ten twenty-one when I called during a break between classes, but I left a message. He did not answer at twelve thirty-seven, the beginning of my lunch period, and this second time I waited through twelve rings; not even the answering machine was picking up. By one o'clock, I gave up my efforts and had to gobble down my sandwich before the students filed back into my classroom. Briefly I allowed myself to imagine where Mark might be, what he might be doing, but my imagination wasn't taking me to good places. With work ahead of me I had to resign myself to calling him from home later.

Throughout the day, fellow teachers and even some students had approached me to offer condolences on my father's death. Like so many others in my life, some colleagues found it hard to believe that I would return to school without taking a few more days' break. Even Emma can't let it go. She embraces me warmly when we meet outside the administration offices at the end of the school day, then chides me for rejecting her idea of taking more personal leave.

"I told you, I missed enough work as it is." I remind her that work is a perfect break from the funeral plans that began last Friday. For days all I have wanted was to throw myself back into work. I say simply, "It's wonderful to be here."

At that Emma looks at me, the sharp scrutiny in her eyes softening. "Of course it is. I shouldn't have badgered you. Your students missed you," she adds. "I think your last period students were particularly hard on the substitute."

I laugh. "I know. She left me a note. Not that I have too much sympathy for the sub. Those kids are hard on me every day. They're too smart," I conclude.

"They're a group of whippersnappers. And you wouldn't want it any other way," Emma says. *Whippersnappers.* Such an Emma word, it makes me smile. She reaches for me again and draws me to her for another hug. "I'm glad you're back too."

As she disappears around the corner that leads to her wing of the building, I remember that I need to get back to my classroom for my conference with Asya and Ian. Keeping the appointment with them had been another item on the list of reasons why I returned to work so quickly. If I don't pick up my own pace I will be late for our meeting.

I manage to get back to my class and settled at my desk, Asya's portfolio of work laid out in front of me, before student and father arrive. But not long before; as I am reviewing my notes and Asya's work, they walk through my door, Ian giving a few raps on the door's frame to announce their presence. Both are smiling, Asya happily, Ian a little self-consciously. They hover in the doorway as if apologetic for interrupting the quiet of my empty classroom. Ian carries a small brown paper shopping bag, handles gripped in both of his broad hands.

"Come in, come in," I urge, and I stand to greet them.

Next to her darker, ruddier father, Asya still looks very fair, but her grinning face has a healthy glow, a blush of color on her cheeks. She looks plumper too, and the robustness is new for her. This face proclaims: I am a happy and well-cared-for girl, a growing girl who is getting plenty of fresh air and exercise and wholesome food and attention. So different from the pale, almost bloodless, pinched and haunted face I first saw back in September. She has been getting better right in front of me, and yet it took the few days away from school for me to appreciate the changes.

I can't help but grin back at my student. "You," I say to Asya, "are a sight for sore eyes. I missed you."

The words fall from my mouth without hesitation, without anything glib or rote about them. I *had* missed Asya. I had missed all my students and my work, the support I give and the successes I reap in return.

Asya looks up at her father. "I told you so, Dad. I *told* you Mrs. Bennett would be glad to see me today."

I look at Ian, puzzled. "You didn't think I would be glad?" I ask him.

"In my defense," he replies, "that's not exactly what I said."

Asya interrupts. "Dad thought we shouldn't bother you today. He told me your father died last week. He told me your dad was old and very sick." She looks between her father and me as if for confirmation.

I smile again, but this time tenderly, at how Ian had tackled the issue of a parent's death. Age and illness had been the right explanation for her. I had been so reluctant to tell Asya myself, fearing that in the wake of her mother's flight she might worry about her remaining parent's mortality.

"Yes," I answer, "he was old and he was very sick. And I miss him. But you know what? I've told everyone today how much being back here at school helps. It really does," I add, looking at Ian.

"I knew it," Asya says, satisfied, and with that pronouncement she takes a seat at the student desk directly in front of my own.

"I feel like I'm getting beaten up here." Ian walks over to the desk next to Asya's and places the paper bag on the floor before hoisting himself onto the desktop.

"What I said to my very determined daughter was that we shouldn't take up too much of your time today, seeing as you had a lot on your plate. I told her we could do the progress report next week."

"I don't mind at all," I begin to protest, but Ian stops me.

"Hear me out," he says. "This was one thing Asya and I could agree on," he begins with a look over at his daughter. She nods her encouragement so he continues, "We agreed that instead of you doing something for us today, we wanted to do something for you."

"For me?" I ask.

He nods. "You've been great with Asya all year. You always know exactly what to do. Even when things were at their roughest, you knew.

"Anyway," he continues, "Asya wanted to give you something. We both did. To say thank you. And also to say we're sorry about you losing your father."

"And because we like you," Asya pipes in.

"That too," Ian says and smiles. He hops off the desktop and reaches for the bag on the floor.

"I picked it out myself," Asya says as Ian hands the package to me. "Dad made it, but I picked it out."

"You made it?" I ask Ian, looking up at him from the bag in my hands. "Then it's—"

"A piece of my pottery, yeah."

"It's his favorite piece," Asya adds.

Ian agrees. "She's right. It is, in fact, my favorite piece. Seems my daughter has really good taste in pottery. And teachers."

For a few seconds I am speechless, and a bit too overwhelmed to open my gift right away. Ian is the parent I have come to know best this year, and one of the things I know very well is that the pots he creates are beautiful. And highly regarded. And expensive.

Until now I had only seen examples of his work in pictures from a gallery catalog. He makes pots that look like vases and some that could be drinking vessels; they come long-necked and fragile, or short and sturdy; some are oddly whimsical, weirdly proportioned; others elegant, and finished with a traditional, almost Victorian explosion of slip trail detail. In that same catalog I had also registered the price quotes alongside the photos of each piece, and I know I can't accept anything so valuable.

"I can't—" I stammer, still dumbstruck.

"Open it," Ian says. "It's just clay."

"Art pottery," I protest, "is hardly 'just clay.' I really can't—"

Ian interrupts me again. "Please, Shelley, open the package."

I hold his gaze for a moment and then peek into the bag. Of course the colored tissue paper inside is tantalizing. So is the fact of a gift for me when it's not my birthday or Christmas — such a gift coming in the midst of mourning, aimed specifically at cheering me up, makes me feel giddy. The fact of the gift is almost all that matters; part of me feels no need to even unwrap it. Until curiosity gets the better of me and I do.

Inside the layers of yellow and hot pink and black tissue paper, I find a beautiful vase-style pot. The base is wide, a kind of flattened orb, and it curves inward and upward into a slender neck. At the join of the neck and the base, Ian has decorated the pot with a pinch and twist detail, giving something so simple and inert a feeling of fluid motion. The glaze enhances this effect. Although predominantly ocean-colored, cerulean blue with a blue-green lip, the pot has licks of pink above each pleated pinch. The patches of pink look like flames; the pot appears almost to be on fire, alive, a study in energy. I have no idea how this can be possible, but for the few moments when I turn it over and over in my hands, I am glad that it is.

"Asya. Ian." I look from student to father; both are beaming. "This is beautiful. Thank you."

"It's meant to be used," Ian reminds me. "So please promise me you'll use it."

"Flowers," I say. "I have a beautiful garden at home, and I like cut flowers in the spring and summer."

"You can buy flowers for your classroom until your own come in." Ian walks over to my side and reaches to take the pot from my hands. Our fingertips touch; his fingers cover mine, which makes it difficult for me to let go of the vase. Not that I want to. His hands are warm and reassuring. Ian has broad hands, large and strong, maybe because of throwing pots. Or perhaps he throws pots because he has the right hands for the job. I don't know for sure, but this could become a question to file away for another day when our conversation about Asya ends and turns instead to the minutiae of our lives. Which is happening more and more often lately.

Ian seems as lost in thought as I am and this touch goes on a few moments too long. Awkward, I realize, but not unpleasant. It feels, in fact, very pleasant to be touched by this man. Which is an entirely different realization, one that confuses me until I look away from Ian and down at our hands.

Ian follows my gaze. "Sorry," he says and he deftly slips his hands up the neck of the pot, gripping it tightly so that I may let go. It also feels as if something in the air between us has changed. I feel shy. Ian does too, if his scramble to find a spot on my desk to set down the vase is any indication. All of a sudden my desktop is extremely interesting to both of us.

"It looks fine right there," he says, setting the pot down on a clear patch among the piles of student work and various books on my desktop. To let the moment pass, we both give our attention to the landscape of my desk.

After a moment I shake my head. "I'd never forgive myself if it got broken here at school. Besides," I say as I look up into Ian's face. Part of me wants to say a simple and graceful thank you, but in light of our awkwardness, I feel it might be best to decline the gift. "Besides, there has to be some rule forbidding me from taking expensive gifts from parents."

Ian hears the regret in my tone and he smiles. "You know you want to say yes," he teases. "Anyway, it could only be an expensive gift if there were a price tag on it, and this pot," he nods his head in its direction, "was never for sale. I made it a long while ago, when I was still trying to figure out my own style and borrowing techniques from other potters.

"That one's a kind of tribute to George Ohr, the self-proclaimed 'Mad Potter of Biloxi.'"

"Mad Potter of Biloxi?" I shake my head. "I don't know much about pottery or potters, but I know this is a beautiful piece."

"Thanks," Ian says. He adds, "Seriously, though, it doesn't come close to Ohr's work. And there are some tiny blips in the glaze, so it might be kind of weak in places. But this was one of the first pots I made where I thought the color and the proportion and the execution all came together. It's got more sentimental value than anything.

"Oh," he says, his ruddy color deepening with chagrin. "That makes it sound as if I'm giving you a second. What I meant was, you shouldn't feel bad about accepting it."

"I understand," I say with a smile. "You're sure you want to give it away?"

"I'm sure. Besides," he adds and now his green eyes sparkle with mischief. He leans nearer to me and mock whispers, "I bet there's no such rule about accepting gifts. And even if there was, we could just agree to ignore it."

I laugh. "I can't tell you when I last broke a rule," I confide. "Maybe never."

"Then now is a good time to start." Ian turns to Asya, sitting quietly and taking everything in, and he points his finger at her. "Although I want you to pretend you didn't hear me say it's okay to pay no attention to rules," he says.

"I love it," I say. "I love it and when I look at it I will always think of you both."

Asya beams. " I wish you could come to our house for a visit," she blurts. I have never seen her so animated. "You could see all of my dad's pottery. Dad has a boat too, and we take it out on the lake in the summer. He likes to drive fast," she tells me.

"Fast-ish," Ian corrects. "I don't want Mrs. Bennett to get the idea that I'm some kind of daredevil boater."

Asya smiles slyly, a teasing sort of look, another look I've never seen cross her face before. "Sorry," she says to Ian, and then to me she clarifies, "Sometimes Dad likes to drive fast-*ish* out on the lake. And sometimes he likes to drive fast-*ish* on the lake . . . in the dark!"

Asya's spontaneous teasing is infectious and laughter bubbles up and out of me. "Oh, I think I have exactly the right idea now."

"Okay, that's enough," Ian says, his hands making a time out sign. "We've taken up too much of Mrs. Bennett's time for one day, and I also think I should quit while I'm ahead.

"Have you got everything you need for home?" he asks his daughter. "Books? Homework?"

Asya nods. "But can I use the girls' room before we go?" she asks.

"You can if you can hurry," Ian answers.

Once Asya is out of the room, Ian sighs exaggeratedly. "I guess I'm busted."

"I guess you are," I agree.

"What'll it take to keep my secret safe between us?" Ian jokes. "Is the promise of a nighttime ride this summer a fair trade?"

"Only if you also promise to speed," I joke right back, the words out of my mouth before I have a chance to think about how flirtatious the exchange sounds. I quickly change the topic. "No, really," I add, shaking my head. "It's fine. You're secret is safe with me. I'm just glad to see her so happy." I tip my head in the direction of the door. "She's like a different child. Relaxed, secure."

Ian nods, at once serious. "I'm trying to give her that security. I mean, we've always had our time together. The one thing Terry was good about was our sharing custody, and spending time with me was something Asya could always count on. But when Terry split . . ."

Ah, yes. Terry. The name I couldn't remember the other day.

"Well, it was like we had to start from scratch, me and Asya. Like I had to work for her trust. So it's been a lot of quiet routines and building on the things she can count on.

"And you helped so much. The routine of progress reports, paying attention to her. She knew someone else cared. Cares."

I consider demurring, telling Ian I'm only doing my job with his child, but I know my commitment is deeper than that. Asya is not simply another challenge for me to take on, another project, or one more person with a set of problems. Asya and Ian respond to my help and thrive with it in ways no one in my troubled family ever had. They make me feel useful. Along the way both had become my friends just as I had befriended them.

Before I say anything, though, Ian asks, "So, how are you, Shelley? How are you holding up?"

I look at him for a minute before answering. No one has asked me this question. I recall the end of last week when I had just learned about my father's death and Ian embraced me. The reversal of my usual role, the embrace had nonetheless felt natural and comforting, the offer of a friend. And now his question, his concern. Mark has been too occupied with his resentments to ask how I was holding up; Sylvie expected my concern for her situation and never once comforted me in return. Even my husband only recognized my strength during my father's final weeks, calling me a rock for Dad and Sylvie. Naturally. I had always put myself in that role.

But it was as if with one hug and one simple question, Ian had pushed past my strength and allowed me to admit what I couldn't when I was so busy being strong for others. I would greatly miss my father, as complicated, imperfect, and unconventional as he was.

Because of this understanding I am able to answer freely, without a trace of my usual stoicism. "I miss him. My parents divorced when we were kids, and my relationship with my father was difficult sometimes, and yet I miss him terribly."

Ian nods. "I can understand that. He's gone. And no matter what kind of parent your father was, no matter how old you are, gone is just rough on a kid. Look at Asya. Terry took off and left her, and still Asya misses her mother every day.

"Sometimes, Shelley, I still miss her, and she left me too."

I think for a moment. "Maybe Terry did the best she could as a wife and mother. After all, she gave you the opportunity to have a better life with someone else. And she left Asya with someone who is able to take really good care of her."

"You think?" Ian asks, and I nod. "Maybe she did," he says.

For the next few moments Ian and I are quiet, thinking about what we have just said, waiting for Asya to return. The only sound in the classroom is the ticking of the wall clock. Until Ian breaks into the silence.

"What do you think about– " He stops and considers. "About what Asya said? About coming out to the lake to visit us sometime?"

"A visit?" I repeat.

"Granted, it's not much. Our life on the lake is pretty quiet, riding my boat fast notwithstanding. And I can't do that until it gets warmer anyway." He smiles at me. "But we'd give you lunch and you heard Asya, she'd be excited to have you come over."

Even this briefest glimpse into their lives right now tempts me. Here, then, are two people in my life who should be there in limited context, as recipients of my teaching services. Our professional contact, the length of our relationship – these things would seem to establish certain boundaries. And yet there are none of these boundaries. It is as if all three of us have known and understood and accepted each other forever. And having the need to be understood and accepted met so readily and without asking is alluring.

"Quiet?" I say. "What's that? Seriously, my life in the past few weeks – months – has been anything but quiet," I admit. "I'm envious."

"Then maybe you will?"

I almost say yes without hesitation.

Almost.

Because as I think about what my friend Ian has just dangled in front of me – a lunch prepared just for me; a chance to look at his work and his studio; a walk around the lake with Asya; a brief quiet period full of the give and take of our very open and easy conversations – a picture forms in my mind. A picture of my father, of the part of my father's life that I, as a child and teen, never saw. But I could see it now, clearly. My father in his office, working side by side with an enthusiastic, beautiful young woman. Working at the same desk, perhaps, their chairs pulled close together. Perhaps as they work she smiles at him, or a strand of her blonde hair falls becomingly into her eyes before she brushes it away. Perhaps she listens to everything my father says with great interest, she understands him the way no one else does, can be quiet with him and still they feel somehow connected. Perhaps because of all this she becomes, inexplicably and against great odds, one of his closest friends.

Perhaps everything between them starts when Sylvie lays her hand on my father's and he finds her touch warm and comforting, a little awkward but not the least bit unpleasant, and they decide to have lunch. It is the moment when their budding relationship could go one way or another. And in that moment they make their choice.

For a minute, with this picture crowding my mind and my heart, I can't think or breathe, let alone come up with an answer for Ian.

Sensing my difficulty, Ian asks, "Did I cross a line?"

I shake my head no. If I could speak I would explain first that as my friend he did not, that he could *never* cross any lines.

I might then try to explain myself. I might say that I had spent a lifetime making up for my parents' shortcomings, being strong for Mark and my parents, then for Steven and my girls. Creating a well-run life but at the expense of allowing myself my own weakness with another person.

I might then say that there is a temptation toward that kind of understanding lurking in the ease of our communication, a temptation I could see myself succumbing to, given my history of setting aside what I need for the sake of holding everything together.

And finally I might also say I now fully understand my father's departure. I had forgiven my father's shortcomings, I had made up for my mother's, but I never really understood what might have seduced my father out of our family. I forgave his actions, but I never really understood why he acted in the first place. Until now. Until I realized how very easily it happens, that I myself might be tempted in the same ways for the very same – and also for my very own – reasons.

Ian begins to reach out to me, then thinks better of it and pulls his hand back. "Don't worry about it," he says. "It was just an idea."

I nod, still unable to speak.

Asya walks back into the classroom at that moment and it feels as if she brings with her some fresh air. I am able to take a deep breath.

"I'm ready, Dad," she says.

"Then let's get," Ian says. He takes his eyes from me and points to her backpack and jacket slung over the chair back.

"We'll reschedule the progress meeting, then. Same time next week?" I suggest, recovering into teaching mode. I follow behind the pair as they make their way to the door.

"Absolutely. We'll see you then?" Ian asks.

"Absolutely," I agree. Our eyes meet above Asya's head and Ian's question me; they hold mine with an intensity that is difficult to disregard. I give him a small nod as if to say, "It's okay," then I quickly look away.

After they leave and I am alone in my room, I lose myself in thought for a moment as I rewrap my ceramic pot in its tissue and place it carefully at the bottom of its carrying bag. Always so responsible and cautious, in control of creating the life I needed and wanted, I now find myself in a situation that could quickly slip out of my control.

I shake my head to dispel these thoughts. I have no more time for them now. The girls wait for me at their schools. Steven will be home soon and ready for my company and his dinner. I need to try again to reach Mark. I pick up my bag and my briefcase, find my keys, and make my way out of the school to head for home.

Once home and in the driveway, I barely have time to stop the car before Margaret has her seat belt off and her door open. She had sat slumped and quiet in the back seat on the ride home. Although lately an inward-looking teen contemplating so many changes – physical, emotional, and social – she seems moodier than usual. A trying day perhaps, an upcoming test she may be anxious about? Margaret doesn't love school. Like my brother she is a talented artist, and also like him she prefers her art classes to the core courses. Now free from the school day, she bounds from the car and sprints a few feet down the sidewalk away from our house. I too step out of the car and stand in its open door.

"Where are you going?" I call after her.

Margaret stops and turns to face me. "Court's house," she hollers back. Courtney, her best friend since second grade, lives only three doors down the street.

"You spent all day with Courtney in school," I say.

"I know," Margaret answers. Without waiting for my go ahead, she turns and continues on to her friend's house.

"You need to be back in the house at four-thirty to start your homework," I remind her.

"I *know*," Margaret calls even more emphatically, this time without a backward glance.

For a few seconds I stand and watch as Margaret disappears into Courtney's house. I count to ten. After a slow, deep breath and exhale, I feel a small hand slip into mine. Uncomplicated Libby. I look down at her and smile. "Would you like a snack?" I ask her, and she nods in reply.

We start to step away from the car but before I close the door, I remember my pot. I reach back into the car for it.

"Now we can go in." With Libby's hand in one of mine and the gift package in the other, we do.

Inside, I set down the paper bag and settle Libby with a snack of apple slices with peanut butter and honey before shooing her off to do her homework. Out of habit, I fill the kettle with a serving's worth of water and set it over a high gas flame to make a cup of tea. Once the water has reached boiling, I pour it into my mug. I watch the teabag puff up with air, float, flood with water, and then sink. I take the mug to the table and look around me at this favorite room in my house, at the familiar surroundings of my kitchen, the jumble of cookware, the cheery yellow curtains, the bright color of the walls, the table itself, its markings, its welcoming expanse. I'm home. I wait for the feelings of security those two words always trigger, but all I feel is restlessness.

Looking around the room, my eyes light on my gift. I remove the pottery from the bag and unwrap it. The vase is lovelier than I remembered, the gradations of blue in the glaze subtle, and the integration of color and design vigorous but also harmonious. Every design element works together to make something beautiful and complete. Amazing that this piece started out as dirt and water.

"Just clay," as Ian had said earlier as he convinced me to accept the pottery.

"Just clay," I repeat aloud and I lay my hand on the pot's rounded base. It feels cool, smooth, solid under my hand. The pot looks innocuous here at home. Without Ian's hand brushing mine, it means nothing more than a gift from a friend. "Just a gift," I add.

Those words recall something Sylvie said to me this morning. "As far as we're all concerned, it's just a gift," she had said about Dad's gesture, willing Mark and me the Rockport house.

Just clay, just a gift. It happens all the time that people bequeath gifts in death, and in difficult times friends often give tokens of thoughtfulness, I tell myself, and yet neither of these recent gifts is quite so uncomplicated. Behind the giving of these exists problems and pain, still there despite my efforts to disguise them with cozy meals and cheerful curtains, and keep them at bay with supportive pep talks and two available shoulders.

I leave my tea cooling and untouched at the table, and walk to the telephone. I dial the numbers that, after the several calls I've attempted today, my fingers find almost without looking. As I listen, the phone in Mark's house begins to ring. This time I am rewarded with the mechanical pick up of the answering machine after four rings. Still no luck reaching Mark, but at least I have confirmation that someone has been moving around the loft since my earlier calls. "Leave a message," says Jen in a terse recorded voice.

I record my second message of the day after the beep. "Mark, it's me. If you're in and working, I don't want to disturb you. But call me back when you can. Please." And then I hang up.

That the answering machine has been reactivated gives me confirmation of activity but not peace of mind. Feeling anxious, all I can do is fall back on meal preparation routines to keep busy.

I am mid-reach for the salad vegetables in the bottom bin of the fridge when the front doorbell rings. My first thought is that Margaret has chosen to come to the locked front door rather than walk the extra steps around to the side of the house where, of course, the door into the kitchen would be unlocked. Setting the head of lettuce on the counter I close the refrigerator door. As I wipe my hands on a kitchen towel, I look up above the doorway at the wall clock. Four-thirty. "At least she's right on time," I admit grudgingly.

Within seconds the doorbell rings again, this time with the impatience of someone leaning on the button. "Margaret, for heaven's sake, I'm coming!" I call from the kitchen as I begin to make my way to the front of the house. No sooner do the words leave my mouth than the bell sounds a third time.

"Mommy! Someone's at the door!" Libby calls from upstairs.

"I know," I call back, now taking long strides down the hall. Nearly there, I reach my hand out for the doorknob. "Ring this bell one more time, young lady, and I– " I begin. I grab the doorknob and give it a yank.

"And you'll what?" asks my brother, standing on the stoop.

Mark wears what I have always called his art school get up. Loads of cool black with a bit of flash. A maroon and gold paisley shirt untucked over tight black jeans that are short and slightly flared at the ankle. An open leather jacket, age-softened and a bit shiny in places with wear. Heavy black boots of pebbled leather with treads deep enough to pick up clots of mud from the front walk where I have been preparing the border for planting.

Mark's dark brown hair has been blown every which way in the blustery spring wind. Sections of his hair look like they have been nibbled at by mice rather than formally barbered. He holds two large duffel bags, one in each hand. I take in his entire presence in seconds as I stand in the open doorway, completely stunned. It is as if by merely thinking of him I have conjured him here. When I look back up into Mark's face, he grins; the scar on his chin stretches; I see the few places in his mouth where his teeth overlap. How he balked at the orthodontist appointments, how I worked so hard just to get him to school that I didn't nag in favor of better-aligned teeth.

"And you'll what?" Mark asks, shifting the bags in his hands for a better grip. "Ring that bell one more time and you'll . . ." he prompts.

"And I'll dock your allowance. And I'll make you answer that door for the rest of your life. And I'll make you write one hundred times, 'I will always use the back door.'" I explain, "I thought you were Margaret. Jesus!" I add in a release of my shock.

"Nah, not Jesus. Just me. By the way, I need a place to stay." He lifts his bags to show me in case I have missed them.

I nod dumbly, but I don't budge, feeling slow to process this latest surprise of the day.

"So, Sis," Mark asks, "you gonna let me in?"

"So you thought I was Margaret?" Mark asks with a smirk, pleased to know how much he has surprised me.

We sit in the living room. Mark lounges back into the plump cushions of the sofa, his legs outstretched. He holds a bottle of beer while I nurse a second cup of tea, this one receiving no more attention from me than the first did. Fetching the drinks gave me something to do while Mark brought his bags up to the second floor study that doubles as our guest bedroom.

"She's up the street at a friend's," I explain with a glance at my watch. "I expected her home about twenty minutes ago."

"Just when I arrived."

"Just exactly when you arrived," I agree.

"And surprised you," Mark adds. He drains his Sam Adams.

More than surprise, I admit to myself. Mark's unannounced visit shakes me. As he sits across from me, I cannot read his mood. He alternates between periods of wisecracking and intense quiet, and that makes me more anxious. I try to regain my footing. I take a sip of now tepid tea, and then set the mug down for good. Recalling a childhood attempt to read each other's minds, I say, "Maybe I shouldn't have been so surprised to see you," and I force a smile. There had been a summer many, many years ago when we spent hot, lazy days trying to transmit to each other all sorts of telepathic messages. We were wrong as often as we were right but both of us loved the game. It was a carefree time I think he will remember.

But he doesn't. "Why?" Mark asks, the look on his face souring. "Because I always end up here for help?"

"No." I am quick to remind him, "I meant our telepathy experiments, remember?" and I am relieved when he visibly relaxes. "Lately I've been thinking a lot about us back then, and all the things we used to do together."

Mark sits quietly for a moment, his eyes trained on the empty beer bottle in his hands. Soon he begins to peel the label from the glass, letting the shreds of paper flutter to the carpet.

The next moment, though, he makes an abrupt shift. He leans forward to set the beer bottle on the table then sits straight up. "Can I have another?" he asks.

"Sure." I start to get to my feet, happy to have a chore to focus on, but Mark waves me down.

"Sit," he says and I do. "I'll go."

The living room is quiet enough for me to hear him rummaging around the refrigerator. Beer bottles clank together as he lays his hands on them; the heavy refrigerator door closes with a thump; a discarded bottle cap clatters to the counter, then a second.

I sit up straighter when Mark reenters the living room carrying the bottles by their necks in one hand and my vase in his other. He takes his seat then reaches across the coffee table to set down the bottles of beer and the vase.

"Is that new?" Mark asks after he takes a long drink from his beer. He motions at the pot with his chin.

"Yes," I answer. "Brand new, a gift. It's from a student."

"No kid made this," Mark says with certainty.

"No, my student didn't make it. She picked it out."

"It's kind of nice," Mark says. "Nice colors. It'd make a nice ocean in one of my mosaics," he adds.

"I hope that's a joke," I reply, "because you can't have it. Don't even ask. I like it whole, thank you very much."

"It was worth a try," Mark says with a shrug and abruptly he loses interest in my pot. "This one's yours," he says as slides the second beer across the coffee table.

Rather than pick up the bottle right away, I look at it. "These are Steven's," I say.

"Meaning Steven'll be mad that we're drinking them? Or that he's the beer drinker in the family?" Mark asks.

"Meaning," I reply, "that I rarely drink beer."

"Well, you looked bored with your tea," he says with a nod at my second abandoned cup of the afternoon. "Anyway," he says, "I don't feel like drinking alone."

I think again of Sylvie, only last night saying something eerily similar and similarly roping me in, and I shake my head.

"What?" Mark asks.

"Nothing," I reply, knowing better than to introduce Sylvie's name into the conversation.

"Here." He sits forward and pushes the bottle even closer to me until I accept it.

I take a sip and, unlike last night's scotch with Sylvie, the beer tastes surprisingly good, cold and refreshing. I look over at Mark, again sprawled back on the plump cushions of my sofa and steadily pulling on his beer.

"Not bad, huh?" he asks.

"No, not bad," I agree. I tell him, "I've been calling you all day. I told you I would, remember?"

"Mmm," Mark concedes. "I was home this morning when you called, but I was kinda busy, packing and everything."

"'Packing and everything?' What do you mean?"

Instead of answering Mark says, "Drink up."

"Are you going somewhere?" I press. "Or have you moved out?"

His silence is my answer. Mark begins fiddling with the second beer label, all the while looking at me out of the corner of his eye. He waits for the "Oh, Mark" of disappointment and despair he is sure must be coming. *A "D" because you skipped school on the day of a final exam? In court because you're behind on your rent? Why didn't you come to me sooner? Oh, Mark.*

It is my first instinct to utter those very words. At this point in Mark's life, I had hoped he was settled with Jen. They were on the path of productivity and domesticity, I was sure, however different it was from my brand of the same. And now, *leaving* her?

I sip steadily at my beer without really tasting it, my mind going a mile a minute as I wonder what to say next. I look over at him as he upends the last of his beer, as he sets the bottle down, as he then reclines again in the overstuffed couch and closes his eyes. In this moment I love him so much that I ache for him. Talk about telepathy. I feel the pain of every mistake he makes and the open wound of every relationship he severs. I want to help; how easy it is for me to jump in.

I feel guilty that I could always mine veins of optimism and self-reliance, mother lodes that Mark never had. Mark never figured out how to navigate the obstacles in his path. Maybe he wasn't born with the capability; he certainly never worked at developing it. What he does have in abundance is sensitivity; he feels, hears, and sees too acutely. The random, cruel fact of our lives is our roles might just as easily have been reversed, but they weren't. And to make up for my luck and his deficit, one night long ago I appointed myself Mark's buffer to the world.

It had been an otherwise unremarkable night. As usual our father had been working late, our mother reading and drinking in the kitchen. I was in my room where I listened to music while I did my homework. I wore headphones, two large, padded vinyl cushions attached to a plastic headband. With those on I was cut off from everything but the music.

My school textbook lay open next to me on my bed. My knees were drawn up, my notebook open on them, and I worked diligently answering science questions while Elton John sang "Elderberry Wine." Sensing movement in my doorway, I looked up to see my father hovering there, home finally from the office. He lifted his hand off the doorknob and gave me an open palm wave. His presence this late was unremarkable, the wave too. He had said goodnight to me in ways similar to this so many times over the last three of my fifteen years. On that night he lingered a bit, he wore an anxious look on his face as if he wanted to say something, but I didn't remove my headphones to give him the chance. I had my homework; I pointed to the textbook at my side. Dad made the okay sign, and then raised the same fingers to his lips to blow me a kiss. I wiggled my fingers back in a dismissive wave and without sparing another thought for him, I returned to my homework.

I thought nothing more of the odd look on my father's face, or of the entire encounter in fact, until Mark entered my room maybe half an hour later, his own face wet with tears. He said one word, which I lip-read – "Dad" – and I didn't need to ask why he was crying; I just knew.

I slid off the headphones and held out my arms. Mark fell into them. We held each other so tightly that Mark's tears ran down my face.

At four and then again at fifteen, I couldn't have articulated why I, no more than a child myself, was given such responsibility for my brother, but I accepted it, unquestioning. There had been looks passed in our house, ones my father shot my mother when she wasn't looking, and my mother's blank stares directed at my father when he attempted conversation. There were uncomfortable silences and the heavy crash of glass. Looks, feelings, moods, actions; it was as if the adults around us were participating in some complicated, incomprehensible dance. The steps followed no pattern, made no sense. All I knew was that Mark was safer with me.

And yet I haven't succeeded in protecting him from getting hurt or being angry as a result. I have only postponed him dealing with those circumstances. "It's a gift, letting someone own his feelings," Sylvie had said. Is it now time for me to take a step back? Anyway, how does one change the habits of a lifetime?

As I sit and think and come up with nothing, I hear the back door open and close with a bang. Then cries of, "Uncle Mark!" from a joyful Margaret, who has spotted his car in the driveway. My brother and my oldest child have a special bond.

Margaret inherited the talent that seems to pinball around my family, hitting some of us – my great-grandmother, my mother, Mark, Margaret – while missing others – my grandfather, me, Libby. Margaret draws miniatures, tiny indoor scenes of places she knows well, like homes, schools, and stores. She began drawing with fine-tipped pens on squares of paper only slightly bigger than postage stamps. The detail of her work astonishes everyone. She recently completed a library scene in ink finished with colored pencil on a two-inch by three-inch piece of card stock. Despite the size, she fit in rows of books, and each book's spine holds a legible title. Beyond this technical proficiency and precision, Margaret's work has energy and vitality; the rooms teem with life.

Completely ignoring me, Margaret flops down next to Mark and begins talking rapidly. Her voice rises and dips in a singsong of excitement. I catch all the highlights. " . . . project I'd like to show you . . . art class . . . it's okay but not a real challenge . . . so glad you're here . . . are you staying long?"

Mark smiles at Margaret, the first genuinely happy smile I've seen since he arrived, and then he throws an arm over her shoulder and pulls her close. "I'd love to see your work," he tells her.

Margaret, her head tucked under Mark's chin, begins to pepper us with questions. "Are you staying for dinner? He's staying, right Mom?" she asks, acknowledging my presence for the first time since walking in the door. She turns back to Mark. "Can you stay longer? Is Jen with you?"

Mark and I make eye contact. "Whoa, Margaret. One thing at a time. You know what? I think Uncle Mark will be here for a couple of days, which means he's definitely staying for dinner. Why don't you go tackle your homework, and when you're done, come down and help us with dinner?" I suggest.

"I wanted Mark to see my art class project," Margaret pleads, looking between the two of us.

Mark answers. "We'll have more time with your homework out of the way," and he winks at her, sealing the deal.

I smile at both of them. "See? I say to Margaret. "All taken care of. Now, scoot. And Margaret?" I add as she bounds up the stairs, taking two at a time. "Before you get to work, could you check on your sister for me?" She nods without stopping and is upstairs in a flash.

Mark shakes his head at her speed. I tell him, "I think she's thrilled at having a real artist look at her work. I haven't seen her this excited in months. She's been so moody lately."

"She'll be all right," Mark says. "She's got a lot of people pulling for her."

"Yes," I agree, "and thanks for being one of them."

I look down at my watch. "Steven will be home soon, and I need to start moving on dinner. You can rest before we eat, or you can help me in the kitchen if you feel like it," I suggest with a smile. "Setting the table might make you feel right at home here."

Without Margaret as a distraction, Mark is once again quiet. He looks over my shoulder at some point across the room. I wonder if he is considering the options I have proposed or daydreaming.

"Earth to Mark," I joke gently.

"Thanks, Shell," Mark says. "Don't worry. It'll only be for a week. Maybe two. Once my pieces for the show are finished, I'll have time to look for an apartment. Or whatever."

"It's fine. You're always welcome here."

"Right at home," Mark says. His eyes focus on me but even so he seems not to see me. We sit in silence for a couple of minutes until Mark sits up and asks tentatively, "Could I maybe move some work stuff into the garage? I've got an idea for a new piece of work. I'd like to start tonight, before dinner, maybe after, and I need some space . . . " His request hangs there waiting for my response.

"Sure," I say. "Unpack. Use the garage, the guest room, whatever. I'll bring up the bedding for the futon later." I stand up and Mark does too.

Finally Mark graces me with a smile that is full of love tinged with relief. As he passes me on his way out the front door to begin unloading the U-Haul, he brushes my cheek with his lips. No surprise, my eyes fill with tears.

Mark

I still have the first piece of art I ever made and entered in an art show, my first show, a children's regional art exhibit held in Town Hall. At that show, there would be awards presented within categories: cheesy Honorable Mention and High Honorable Mention ribbons; and the coveted First, Second and Third Place plaques, more cheese. It's not fair for me to ridicule the prizes now because the chance to win something was actually a big deal for me back then. To me, just the chance to show my work was cool. What can I say? I was eleven, a kid, and excited. A trophy would be awarded for Best of Show, with the top pieces in each category competing for Grand Prize. I wanted to win my category and I wanted to win that Grand Prize but I didn't think I had a shot, not at all.

The piece gave me problems from the very start of the process. When I brought it in to my school's art teacher to register it for the show, she gave me some shit about it not exactly fitting into any category. Admittedly it defied categorization, and if I had known then what I know now as an adult I would have argued for a mixed media classification. But I didn't, and in the end she labeled it a painting. Still, her misgivings didn't exactly fill me with confidence.

The painting, or whatever the hell anyone wants to call it, is packed away somewhere among all the stuff I brought with me, but I don't need to see it to remember what it looks like. The title of the piece is "Where I Go." It's composed of large swaths of paint, blacks and reds and greens. At a closer look the patches reveal themselves as different landscapes. A terrifying dark. The fiery surface of the sun. A cool, vernal forest. I embedded chicken wire and dried grass and even some pin feathers collected from a dismantled bird's nest in the thick paint. I made maze-like trails leading in and out of each landscape using small chips of mirrored glass. Perhaps my first work in mosaic, these reflectors led into all the places, from bucolic to energetic to frightening, where the eleven-year-old me went in my mind.

Where I went. Where I still go. The manic places, the angry and frightening places. Today I'm running from them, down one of these mirror-tiled pathways straight into the cool green place that I have always thought of as Shelley's refuge, calm and safe.

She was that for me too when I was eleven. During the late afternoon of show day, my dad called home to say he was probably going to miss dinner. Meaning we would all miss the show too, for at the time we only had the one car. I had answered the phone because Mom was lying down.

"I'm delayed at work," he told me. "It's important."

When I told Shelley what he had said, she called him right back at the office. I stood at her side while she calmly reminded our dad that this was the night of my first art show, my competition. "You can't miss it," she added, and the only hint I had that Shelley was nervous about Dad's reaction was the way her voice rose at the end of that last sentence, both plea and question. There was a long pause while Shelley waited for a response. She smiled at me while she waited but all I could imagine was my father weighing me against all the other demands in his life and me coming up short.

Shelley, though, didn't let up and she didn't let me down. She got him to come home. Within the hour, Dad tore into the driveway, he honked the horn, hurried us all into the car, and we drove to the Town Hall.

Forever, I was pretty much convinced that Shelley could make things happen magically. And as far as I was concerned, the rest of the night only confirmed her magic.

My name was not called during the roll call of honorable mention and high honorable mention ribbons. My mother turned to me and said, "They must have forgotten to put your name on the list. Or maybe your painting is too dark for the judges' tastes." I looked up, looked at my parents. I looked at my father, checking his watch, and at my mother, shrugging her shoulders and making her mouth form a consolation smile. "That's life," she said.

So I turned to my sister, my rock, with eyes that were large and brown and wet, and she squeezed my hand. She said, "They didn't call your name for runner-up prizes because you won your category. Silly," she added, projecting more confidence than I felt. But then I realized Shelley was right. There was no other explanation; I had won.

"Forget it," she whispered to me. "Forget them. Listen." And I did. And I won.

I won First Prize in the painting category. I won Best of Show.

I looked at my sister with awe. "You know everything," I said.

Shelley pushed me up to the stage. I was eleven and she was fifteen, and she knew everything.

Except that in two months our father would be gone.

I knew, though. I saw our father slipping from our lives, a man with purpose and presence, all distinct edges and outlines morphing into a silhouette, then a shadow, then finally a phantom.

For the first time in my life I knew something before Shelley did, but not because I possessed magic.

No. I knew he was going because I had plain old bad luck.

My bad luck is something I don't want to think about, not now when I need to work.

I connect with a solid kick and the plastic storage buckets full of my supplies slide easily across the concrete garage floor. Unloading boxes from my U-Haul I shove aside most of the materials until I find what I have been looking for, a collection of ceramic I had broken and packed away almost a year ago. The ideas are churning now and these ceramics are just what I need. I lift off the blue snap-on lid and reacquaint myself with the contents of the storage container.

I had found boxes of this dishware outside a split-level teardown in Arlington. Some folks had bought the Arlington property for the prime piece of land and not the characterless 1970s-era house. Everything left behind by the previous owners and still salvageable was being cleared out before the demolition, left up for grabs on the curb. Each box I took with me that day had the odd remains of at least four separate sets of dishes, stuff the new homeowners had not wanted at all. There were a few glossy, oversized red dinner plates; shallow bowls painted sky blue with a sort of lusterware glaze; more plates, large and small, of green Fiestaware knock-offs; wide yellow coffee cups with matching saucers. They may not have wanted any of this stuff, but I knew that someday I could make something with these items. I took everything home.

I rake my hand through the bucket and pull out one of the cup handles, then three more. Here in the garage I lay all four out on my left palm. Right after I lifted the pieces and brought them home, I had snapped these handles from the cups and saved them intact before I broke the rest of the mug into smaller pieces. The handles are what I've been looking for specifically, what I remembered while sitting with Shelley shortly after I arrived. I wasn't talking details of why I had turned up at her doorstep, Shelley wasn't asking, and once Margaret left the room we were officially out of safe topics of conversation. This left plenty of quiet time, time that I used to avoid eye contact with my sister by alternately closing mine or training them on the objects on the table. Like the beer bottles. Like the strips of paper I peeled from the bottles. Like Shelley's new piece of pottery.

It caught my eye in the kitchen, and I could see why my sister liked it, my sister who likes everything nice and neat and all of a piece. I also knew why I liked it. In those quiet moments in the living room my hands ached to pick up Shelley's new vase by the neck and slam its body back down on the edge of the coffee table. Turn seamless beauty into chaos, a different kind of beauty altogether.

But I didn't do it.

Instead, Shelley broke the silence. The good hostess, she said something about starting dinner. She suggested I might help in the kitchen, unpack, rest, or whatever I wanted, just like one of the family. "You'll always have a home here," she added, the closest she came to referring to my uncertain living situation. Looking across at Shelley as she made these suggestions, I tuned out, and in those tuned-out seconds that followed when I was supposed to be considering all my options, I thought instead about homes. The difference between having one and not having one; the home Shelley offered, the one always available to me; then all the other kinds of homes people make for themselves, from mobile homes to perches in trees to places underwater. Even parasites and bacteria, lucky mindless bastards, found homes while I had none of my own. Okay, not lucky exactly, but there was definitely something ingrained, something programmed in the simplest of organisms that got left out of me. And still zoned out, with Shelley's words about families and homes buzzing in my head like swarms of annoying insects, I remembered all this broken ceramic from the Arlington teardown, the colors, the luster, the textures, the few unusual shapes like the mug handles.

The handles, I remembered, had been painted with a ladder of brick-brown brushstrokes along the outer curve. Often it is one piece or shape such as this that suggests a finished mosaic. This time it was the handles with their perfect arc shape and their painted lines that, when laid out horizontally, suggested bars or grates. The braces of a window box. Right then I could see window boxes and, above them, glass windows reflecting the blue of an early summer sky. The other pieces began assembling in my mind. Windows framed in a small yellow structure, the yellow itself framed by pitchy pines and blowing sea grass in a green that looked black in certain light and a sky blue with its luster that wasn't altogether pretty. Color took definite shape, filled expanses. Almost as suddenly as I imagined the scene, I snapped out of my imagination. I looked up at my sister. She had a smile on her face, like she'd been waiting patiently at a corner for me to catch up and was happy to see me on the horizon.

I asked, "Can I unpack my work stuff in your garage?"

Now I rest the mug handles on the neatly organized bench on the back wall of the garage and go back to the boxes of color sorted ceramic. I tip each color pile onto a piece of cardboard I laid out on the floor, one of my packing boxes easily flattened. I spread the pieces of plates, bowls, and mugs with the palm of my hand. I no longer see the wholes they came from; instead I see how each color suggests a very specific image. I can work with the slight curve and pearlized finish in each chunk of blue to make a rough sky, the stormy, cloudy blue of a gathering wind. The uneven pieces of green will be grass, tufted and textural and darker in places due to overhead clouds.

I load a CD into my shitty Sony boom box. Tinny speakers, limited projection, and two tape decks that eat tapes like ravenous mechanical twin animals. I miss my Bose. That stereo system was the only nice thing I ever bought for myself before I quit my job at the Sound Connection. In my generous period with Jen I stopped referring to it as "mine"; it became "ours." It wasn't exactly generosity that made me leave it behind with her. With the speakers wired all over the loft, between work and living space, what was I supposed to do? Dismantle it with Jen glaring at me? The boom box is Jen's, bought secondhand long before I moved in. Seemed like a reasonable trade at the time. I did, however, take my own CDs: Neil Young's *Decade*, the Stones, Dylan up to *Blood on the Tracks*, a collection of Elvis Costello through *Imperial Bedroom*, Springsteen's first four, *London Calling*. Nothing past the early 80s, nothing Jen wanted. Music up loud, I'm ready to work.

For workspace, I assemble a makeshift table from an old door and two stacked sawhorses that I find at the back of the garage. The only other things I need are my tile cutters, glass nippers, the square foot and a half of board I plan to build on, and of course my ceramic and a few bits of glass. I have my music. Everything else is set aside, the bucket of adhesive, my wide spackle knife, the grout. All I'm doing now is playing with a composition, its fit and texture, making a loose arrangement that I'll anchor down another time if I like what I've got. I no longer think about where I am or why, I don't think about Jen forty miles away. I only think about where I'm going in this piece and how I'm gonna get there. And then I go.

I work until I'm happy with the large areas of composition that give the piece its bones, until I've come as close as possible at this early stage to putting down the picture that is in my head. A yellow house with a red cedar roof on a green field surrounded by trees and an ominous blue sky. Smaller empty patches, and there are tons at this stage, get filled in as detail work. Blue sheet glass gets cut into windows that are reflectors of the sky. Slivers of brown bottle glass make a kind of balustrade surrounding a small, useless terrace outside an upstairs window. The horizontally placed cup handles become window boxes for the windows in the front of the house. Small chips of brightly colored ceramic, at first glance too small to be usable, I plant as flowers into some gaps above the window boxes. I also place some in the grass, making a winding flower-lined path to the front door. In the distance, above the tree line, I make a turret-like structure, a widow's walk on a neighboring home, to break up the expanses of green and blue. This building in the distance has the hint of a gingerbread roof, which lends a fairytale and slightly sinister aspect to the finished work. A pleasant day? Maybe, but with something lurking.

I step back from the bench and squint. Do I like it? Like would be the wrong word. It pleases me. The assembled work looks as close to my original idea as I've ever come, and I like that. The mosaic style is different, bolder and also more rough-edged and crude than my other work, but this change in texture is important; it describes the weather and atmosphere, and I like that too. I want my sister to see this piece. I have a feeling that both the technique and subject will affect her and I like knowing that my work will get a reaction. But do I like the finished work? Does it make me feel warm and fuzzy about houses and homes? Is it lighthearted, humorous like the Airstream mobile home I'm already planning will be? Or charming, like the tree house? Or baffling, like the underwater pod?

Or do I look at this piece, Yellow House, at the peaks and valleys of wind tossed grass or swirls of sky and think only of danger? Dangerous weather. The dangerous terrain of the family living within.

Shelley

Steven walks into the house through the kitchen door to find me brushing a less-than-fresh half loaf of bread with olive oil and garlic. The bread is ready to be wrapped in foil and warmed up. The large halibut fillet has already been transferred from its marinade to the grill. The salad is made. And Steven is home. A good meal with my family gathered to share it. My ideal.

I have had the past hour while preparing dinner to think about this ideal, a life that took its shape from all the agreeable events I had hand-selected from my history and strung together like a determinedly plotted story. There was the moment in college when I first looked at Steven with a new and appraising eye, when I took his measure and made my choice. I thought of the family dinners where, within the four walls of my dining room, glasses would clink in toasts and candles would flicker, guests would smile and good feelings would flow out into the room and envelop us all.

I thought also of Margaret's birth, and Libby's, how happy I had been to become a mother, how I had thrown myself into the role, knowing instinctively what kind of mother I wanted to be, but carrying out those instincts in a very deliberate way. I would create fantastic birthday cakes, sew Halloween costumes, organize art projects, and show up for every important milestone and also for every mundane task. I thought of the moment when I walked into this house for the first time all those years ago and fell in love with my husband as I looked out the window onto a garden and saw the way my life could unfurl well into the future.

Somewhere along the way I had come to believe that I had attained perfection. Of course I hadn't. Everything I created rode in on the back of my imperfect past. The divorce, my ill mother, my brother's moods, my own disillusionment – these are the underpinnings of my life. I believed these events wouldn't have a bearing on my future, or on Mark's life if I worked hard enough to keep him sheltered. But of course the past matters. The past is our weak spot, defining and sometimes breaking us.

An hour isn't much time at all but I felt an urgency to think and comprehend all that has happened in the past two days, indeed over the course of several lives. I anticipated Steven's arrival, his displeasure over Mark's disruptive presence; I even anticipated our disagreement. But I was ready for him. I would no longer try and divert Steven's attention and gloss over potential problems. I know I can no longer protect Mark from himself and his own feelings, not because I have given up wanting to, but because I know it is not possible. The damage within him is beyond the scope of my attempts to patch it up.

But there are other ways to be Mark's sister. There is a place somewhere in between perfection and devastation, I am sure of it, a place where all the many pieces of us – the pleasant and the painful – can be reconfigured into an imperfect but solid-enough life. Mark has to find his way there, that's all, and if I can't fix him or protect him, maybe I can at least start him on the path.

"Looks like my house," Steven says from the back doorway with a glance around at the familiar bustle of dinner preparation in the kitchen. "Looks like my wife." He steps all the way into the room, sets his briefcase down on a kitchen chair, and walks over to where I am working at the counter. "But there's a car that looks like your brother's in the driveway, and what's with the U-Haul?" His forehead is etched with worry lines.

Even as I prepare to tell Steven about Mark's appearance, even as I anticipate how Steven's worry lines will deepen at first, how his lips will stretch to a thin white line over his teeth, I am ready for whatever our discussion brings. "We need to talk," I say to Steven, and I start to talk.

I tell him everything from my unanswered phone calls to finding Mark on our front doorstep to learning about his breakup with Jen.

"He packed up the U-Haul, drove out here, and now he's in the garage working."

"Moved out?" Steven asks, frowning deeply. "Working? Wait. Back up. He drove out here . . . No." Steven stops himself and pinches the bridge of his nose. "Never mind," he says after a moment. "I'm not going to repeat everything you say. Go ahead, finish the story."

"Thank you," I say and I stand on tiptoes to kiss Steven on the cheek. "Come and sit." I take my husband by the hand and sit down with him at our kitchen table.

"This is all I know," I say. "So far. Maybe Mark and Jen had a fight. Maybe they've been bickering, like we have been." Steven begins to protest but I stop him. I am firm when I acknowledge what is true. "Like we have been, or maybe worse. I do know he's here because he needs somewhere to stay. He has to have a place to work. Remember he's in the middle of finishing work for his show? I told him he could stay as long as he needs."

"I told you last night how I feel about you jumping in to help Mark all the time," Steven reminds me. "I think you've reached a point with him where you can't make a difference in his life until he starts helping himself. And yet you made a decision to help him – again – by letting him stay here, letting him run away from his problems, and you didn't even talk to me about it first."

"I know," I agree with a smile, calm in the face of his displeasure.

Steven rolls on as if he hasn't heard me. "And not to split hairs, Shelley, but you're *telling* me about it now, not talking to me about it."

"I know," I say again. "Yes, I am telling you about it now. And I'm also telling you that I was wrong. You were right." Steven's eyes widen in surprise at my admission.

"You were right about me helping Mark too much. Mark needs me, Steven. He may always need me. Or Jen. Or *someone* to help him get along. That's who Mark is. But I'm not letting him escape his problems, not this time.

"This time, the only way I can help him is to let him confront his problems himself, head on."

"But doesn't that that put you right in there with him? You'll still be part of the solution."

I reach out to grip the lapels of my husband's blazer. "Of course I am right there with him. You may not understand why, or how that came to be, but you know who I am. You know who you married. Jack and Kay's daughter. Mark's sister. Me. Your wife.

"I just have to learn to be there in the right ways. I have to learn to let go. Which is only what you've been telling me all along," I remind him.

Neither of us speaks for a moment and then Steven reaches up for my hands and removes them from his jacket. He holds on to my hands tightly and looks me squarely in the eyes. "I still don't think this is a perfect situation, Shelley."

"I know it isn't perfect," I answer, "but it's the situation I have. It's a situation I've always had, only this time I don't expect perfection. The situation won't ever be perfect. Better, maybe? Or just okay? I'll settle for either one."

Steven still seems skeptical, although coming around, when he heads upstairs to exchange tweed blazer and tie for a casual shirt and sweater. On his way, he sends Libby down to help in the kitchen. When Margaret joins us, and Mark wanders in from the garage, they find me and Libby collecting dinnerware to set around the table. Mark is quiet but willing to join in, and soon enough he and Margaret take over the task and lay out both plates and silver. Mark even coaxes a few smiles out of Margaret in the middle of a chore she finds especially boring, by reminding her that after dinner they will look over her portfolio of work. The mood in the kitchen turns close to jolly when Libby recounts the mishaps of a storytelling puppet troupe that passed through the elementary school earlier today. Buoyed by this lively spirit after the past few days of bad news and mourning, I decide the time is right to open the bottle of chilled sauvignon blanc and pour two glasses. I hand the second glass to Steven once he returns. After a few sips of wine and all the laughter in the kitchen, my cheeks feel pleasantly flushed. I look around the room at my family, at everyone I need and love under this roof, and I feel good. I reach for Libby, who is closest, and draw her to my side for a hug.

At dinner, Mark is ravenous and it does my heart good to see him eat. He eats two pieces of grilled halibut, a mound of salad, four slices of garlic bread and drinks another bottle of beer. When he pushes back from the table finally full, he looks more comfortable than he did a few hours ago when I opened the door. Finished with my own meal, I too feel better. I sip my wine and make small talk. I ask Mark, "Were you working on a piece in the garage, or only unpacking?"

"Both. Working mostly," he answers. "Laying out some pieces for a mosaic. If I decide I like the basic layout I can start filling it in, then I'll epoxy it down. Grout it when it's dry."

"What's grout?" Libby asks.

"You're able to put something together so fast?" I ask.

Mark answers my question first. "Sometimes. Roughly, anyway. The picture finished itself up here first." Mark points to his temple. "I already knew what ceramic pieces I wanted to use. After that, fitting the pieces together was pretty easy. The grouting's the tedious part but I think the picture'll be okay."

"Will it be ready for your opening?" I say.

"I don't know if I'll put it in this show. I think it's the beginning of a new series, so . . ." He leaves the thought unfinished.

"What's an opening?" Libby asks. And before anyone has a chance to speak, she repeats, "And what's grout?"

Mark laughs, deep and throaty, at Libby's eagerness. He lifts the wine bottle to top off my glass, but I put my hand above the rim.

"Sure?" he asks.

I nod.

"Steven?" Mark offers, but Steven also declines. "Mind if I get myself another beer?" Mark asks. Without waiting for an answer, he rises and heads to the fridge.

"An opening," Mark tells Libby as he crosses the kitchen to his seat, "is the party given for an artist at or near the beginning of his exhibit. The artist's friends and family," he adds, with a look around the table, "show up so he can fool himself into thinking he has a ton of fans."

"Then I want to go," Libby states. "I'm your fan. And your family. But what's— "

"Grout," Mark says, anticipating her next question, "is a kind of cement. You know that a mosaic is a picture made up of small pieces of tile or glass, right? Well, grout fills the spaces between the individual pieces and helps hold them in place."

"Can we see your new mosaic?" Libby asks.

Margaret groans at her younger sister. "God, do you have to be so embarrassing?" she asks.

I start to open my mouth to caution the girls about their bickering, but Mark speaks first.

"Hey, Margaret, I can use all the fans I can get. How 'bout if I show you – both of you – tomorrow, if I start gluing?" He looks from one face to the other, and satisfied with the nods he receives, Mark slides his chair out from the table.

"But for now, let's get this show on the road," he says, rising. "Margaret, we're meeting out on the deck." He nods at the binders full of plastic sleeves that have been resting on Margaret's lap throughout dinner. "Bring your work."

Her books clutched to her, Margaret leads the way through the door and Mark follows. Steven starts to speak, reminding Margaret that she needs to do the dinner dishes.

"Let her go," I whisper with a hand on his arm. "It's fine," I add and I begin collecting dinner dishes and bringing them over to the sink.

Steven says, "It's fine for tonight. You bus, I'll rinse?"

"Deal," I reply as I bring two hands full of silver to the counter. As I pass Libby, I tap her on the shoulder and send her upstairs to shower.

"Can't I go outside with Uncle Mark?" she pleads.

"Shower." Steven echoes my command from his spot at the sink.

"But Uncle Mark– "

"Will be here tomorrow," I finish for her. "It's getting late and you need your shower. School in the morning."

Libby groans and drags her feet a bit until she reaches the foot of the stairs where she takes off like a shot. Libby is so predictable, never upset for more than a minute. Steven looks over his shoulder at me and smiles, and for the next few minutes we clear dishes and clean up the kitchen in a companionable rhythm.

Against the backdrop of this quiet, I can hear the shower water turn on with a blast. Together, Steven and I look out the window at our daughter and my brother, Margaret's body of work spread across the deck floor between them like a card game. They wear identical scowls of concentration. If I didn't know them, I might have thought they were miserable rather than passionately engrossed in something. Margaret bears a striking resemblance to my brother.

"Look at those two," I say to Steven. He nods. "Have you ever noticed how much they look alike?" I ask him.

"Sure," Steven answers, sounding surprised at my question. "Forever. Libby looks more like my side of the family."

"You know, I only noticed today," I tell him. "Driving home from school. I looked in the rearview mirror and Margaret was slumped in the back seat, sporting that identical frown." I motion out the window with my chin.

"Get used to it. She'll probably be frowning for the next two years," Steven adds.

"Fourteen," I say with a shudder, remembering Mark at fourteen, the year I went off to college. Fourteen, sixteen, eighteen — years when ordinary teenage dissatisfaction and loneliness can either begin to dissipate, then pass through a person, or under the wrong conditions stay, mix, harden into a tight nugget of pain.

Upstairs, Libby stops showering. All is quiet. I lift my head and turn a bit to look at the clock — seven-forty — time too for Margaret to begin the progress toward bed. I look out the window. On the deck, Margaret has moved to sit on the second step up from the lawn. Her fingers absently pluck at the grass. Mark now sits up on the deck railing. He is itching to smoke, that I can tell. He holds in his left hand his Zippo lighter, which he flicks open with his thumbnail and snaps closed with a flick of his wrist. In his rote activity I see the same small boy who waged war on a patch of beach grass with a rhythmic and incessant gouging of his heel. In one body I see the small boy and I see the grown man, and in that instant I know what I need to do. As I promised Steven earlier, I will not let Mark escape his problems, not this time. First, though, I need to get Margaret inside. Then I need to talk to Mark. And I know exactly what I need to say.

"Shelley?" Steven says. "You're very quiet all of a sudden. Everything okay?" he asks.

I look up at Steven as if only remembering he is so close, my frown still in place. He reaches for me and takes my face in his hands, brushes my lips with his thumbs as if trying to rub away the frown.

"No, everything is fine," I say, his words pulling me out of my thoughts. I smile, a striking change from the thoughtful frown. "Everything is okay.

"You know what, though? I need to go talk to Mark but it's getting late and I haven't checked Margaret's homework. Do you think you could do that if I send her in? That way, I can talk to Mark, and also get him set up for the night with some bedding."

"Sure," Steven agrees as he takes the dishtowel from his shoulder and sets it down. "Send her on in and tell her I'll meet her upstairs."

Once Steven is gone, I grab a jacket from a peg by the back door and I head outside. Margaret protests a bit when I tell her to go and review her homework with her father, but soon enough Mark and I are alone on the deck. He gazes up into the night sky and doesn't acknowledge me at first when I stop at the railing next to him and look up into the sky to see what he sees. The first stars have appeared, although the brightest is probably not a star at all but Venus. I feel the night breeze on my face; I hear it rustle through the branchy forsythia nearby. The breeze feels reassuring, steady, and I leave the deck rail to take a seat on the step that Margaret has abandoned.

"Everything's so quiet tonight," I say. "In the dead of summer all you can hear out here on a hot night are the crickets chirping." I tip my head to one side, look over my left shoulder at Mark on the railing.

"Want to hear something funny?" I ask.

He shrugs, still playing with the camouflage painted Zippo.

"When I was little, really little, like maybe even before you were born," I begin, "I thought that sound – the cricket sound? – was the sound stars made when they twinkled. It made sense to me. The noise started just after dark, a kind of humming, and I figured stars would hum, you know, like a refrigerator? I remember I told Dad. I was about four, and I was so sure of what I was hearing. He listened and didn't try to correct me.

"A couple of summers ago," I continue, "I was up at the Rockport house, and it was a hot night. The crickets were out in force. Dad reminded me of that story. He said at the time he thought my idea was so cute, and he didn't want to hurt my feelings by telling me the truth about the crickets."

"So you were, what? In your thirties when you learned the truth?" Mark cracks.

"No." I pick up a clump of torn grass from the pile Margaret had made while sitting and I throw it at him. Like confetti, it flutters but doesn't get too far. "I learned in first grade. My teacher asked the class one day if anyone knew anything about the solar system. One kid listed the planets in order, someone else said something about the sun being a star. I was naive enough to raise my hand and offer my twinkling star theory to the entire class. I thought I was pretty hot stuff, having figured out the universe." I smile at the memory.

"Well, one of my classmates – a particularly obnoxious boy – clued me in, in front of everyone! And I tell you, it was like learning the truth about Santa Claus and the Easter Bunny and the Tooth Fairy all at once. A few rotten kids had a good laugh at my expense. I was so devastated and embarrassed that I never told Dad I knew I was wrong."

Mark leaves the railing and joins me on the stair. "I like the thought of twinkling stars making noise better than crickets sawing their legs together, or whatever the hell it is that they do. So, once upon a time you had an imagination?"

"For a while," I agree. "Surprised?" I became a different child, more cautious, once my brother was born. How pivotal he was – is – in my life I think. "The thing is, everyone grows up," I say aloud, although whether to myself or to Mark I don't know. "We lose that innocence."

"Sure, everyone grows up," Mark agrees, "but a kid shouldn't be . . . forget it," he finishes. He stretches a leg out in front of him and slides his hand deep into his jeans pocket to produce a nice fat joint. "Mind if I smoke?" he asks as he starts to spark the flint on his lighter.

I put my hand over his. "You shouldn't smoke here," I say. "Not around the girls."

Mark looks to his left, then his right. "They're not here," he concludes with a grin.

I bump him with my shoulder. "I know that. And you know what I meant."

"If they come anywhere near here, I'll put it out. I swear," Mark pledges. I look away which he takes as assent. He lights up, takes a hit. When Mark exhales, he says, "Here, hold this," and he passes me the joint. The tips of my fingers burn with the intense heat radiating out through the rolling paper and I nearly drop it. "Ow!"

"Not there, you idiot," Mark warns me. "Hold it at the end. Have a drag if you want," he adds as he shoves his lighter deep into his pants pocket.

I shake my head and Mark takes the joint back from me quickly. "Thanks," he says.

"Don't mention it," I answer. "Where does a grown man buy dope, anyway?" I ask.

Mark snorts a laugh and inhales again. He says nothing for a few seconds as he holds in a lungful of the sweet-smelling smoke. "Around, I guess," he replies as he exhales, his words exiting in a cloud. "Why?" he asks with a squint that I hope is from the fast burn of the cigarette paper and not a suspicion of me.

"No reason," I say.

"I think this drove Jen insane," Mark tells me. "She couldn't stand me smoking pot. You, on the other hand– "

"Me?" I interrupt. "I'm an enabler."

"You are cool with it, is what I was going to say." Mark smokes on. "Sure you don't want some?" His hand holds the offered joint in front of my face.

I say, "No. Big square, remember?" For emphasis, I trace the figure in the air with my two index fingers.

Mark nods. "Yeah, I remember. Big, old, serious, square Shelley." He wets his fingertips on his tongue and pinches out the lit end. "Later," he says as he tucks this too back in his pocket.

"Not that I set out to be a square," I continue. "It sort of just happened. Like I said a few minutes ago, I had to grow up."

"You making a point here, Shell?" Mark asks.

"Not really," I answer slowly.

"C'mon." This time Mark nudges me with his shoulder. "I'm not that stoned," he teases.

"I told you earlier, having you here makes me think about being young, growing up, you and me. That's all."

"Because if I was one of those paranoid pot smokers, I might get the idea that you were trying to bring up things you know I don't want to talk about." Mark winks at me conspiratorially. "If you see what I mean."

"Poor, square, unimaginative me?" I ask in mock innocence, and then I smile. Mark lets loose with a roar of laughter.

"That's nice," I say once his laughter subsides.

"What is?" Mark asks.

"Hearing you laugh," I tell him.

"Mmm."

With Mark loosened up enough to laugh, I decide to leap at the opening he's given me. "You mentioned Jen's name," I point out.

"Meaning I must want to talk about her?" he scoffs.

"Do you?" I ask and Mark shrugs.

Not totally rebuffed, I interpret the shrug as a yes and I ask, "Want to tell me what happened?"

"I left," Mark says. For a minute I think that's all he intends to say, but then he adds, "She would've kicked me out anyway, so I figured I'd do her a favor. Save her the trouble."

"Why would Jen kick you out?" I wonder.

"We hadn't exactly been getting along for, I don't know, months? The leaving shouldn't've been, like, a huge surprise."

"But she *was* surprised?" I guess, and Mark snorts in answer.

"Maybe she – and you – need some time to cool off. This hasn't been the easiest week and– "

"It's not like that," Mark interrupts.

"Then what is it like?" I ask.

"No one's gonna cool off. I mean, there's no way I can go back. Jen made that pretty clear. I made that pretty clear."

"People say things when they're angry, things they don't necessarily mean."

"Trust me, Shell. She meant what she said. She was pretty pissed. Besides, maybe I don't want to go back anyway. She's been on my case all the time lately, mad at me about everything."

"Like what?" I prompt. When he doesn't immediately say anything in reply I press, "Nothing's that simple, Mark. Nothing ever is, not when you live with someone, not even when you're married. Steven and I, we've been kind of out of sync too, just like you and Jen were. The past six months, with Dad sick? They've been tough months for us too."

"Yeah, but you didn't— Forget it. It's nothing." Mark looks at me. "You know what? I don't feel like talking about Jennifer anymore, all right?"

"All right," I agree and I back off.

We sit side by side for a few minutes, Mark again looking into the sky, me looking at Mark's profile. Maybe he feels my eyes on him because after a few minutes he turns to me. "Shell," he says.

"Yes?"

"Wanna see the work I did this afternoon?" he asks, abruptly changing the subject. Mark then stands and jumps down to the lawn as if he can't stand sitting a moment longer. "You should."

"Do you want to show it to me?" I ask.

In answer, he stretches out his hand for me, his fingers beckon. I take them.

"All right," I say, and I allow myself to be pulled along to the garage.

Mark opens the door, flips the light switch, and I start to step into the garage. "Wait right there," Mark says, and he leaves me at the doorway. From here I can make out the outlines but not the details of his newest piece of work. Walking to the middle of the cement floor, Mark stops at his makeshift worktable, one he's made from an old closet door and Steven's two sawhorses. He walks slowly around the table in a kind of crossover side step, and he looks at the piece with such scrutiny that I wonder if he is having second thoughts about showing me. At the end of the table directly opposite me, Mark stops, squats, and looks across the top of the laid out ceramic. "Hey," he says, "c'mere," and I take a few steps. This little bit closer, my eyes are drawn to what Mark sees – the raised texture of the piece.

Forever, Mark has been a toucher, laying his hands on things as he looks and studies. He was one of those kids constantly in trouble for touching things: marble statues and carved picture frames in museums; fur coats in the upper floors of big department stores; the ruffled leaves of every last Savoy cabbage in the grocery store. His fingers flirted with the pinching metal hinges lying in open baskets in the hardware store, and with the honed edges of our father's flat razor blades, dangerously accessible in the bathroom medicine cabinet. He maintains that his hands, using them to discover the unknown through the feel of texture along the whorls of his palms and fingertips, help his eyes. I suspect that's only a part of the experience. It is also likely that he loves the danger stored in some objects.

And as I watch, sure enough, Mark runs his hands lightly over the surface of the ceramic, each finger pad brushing along the peaks and valleys of rough chunks of broken ceramic, reading it like a blind man would.

The work is small, only about a foot and a half square, but substantial looking. "You finished all this today?" I ask, awed again.

"Yeah. It's more or less roughed out the way I want it," Mark qualifies.

"And you don't mind me looking?" I ask.

"C'mon," Mark says without rising. He reaches out his hand.

I go. In a few strides I stand next to him.

"Get down," Mark instructs with a tug on my arm, and I squat too. "Close your eyes. Feel it first." Mark takes my hands under his larger ones and glides them over the surface, lightly, so that my hand doesn't disturb the design.

I enjoy soft textures like a pet's fur or a baby's delicate skin, even the smooth coolness of marble, but I don't rely primarily on the sense of touch when exploring the world. Unlike Mark, I have trouble forming a mental picture from the sharp sensations, the peaks and depressions under my palm, but his patient efforts with me almost make me believe I could. Already I can tell this piece is different from most of his work, more dimensional where his other mosaics are flatter.

"Can I look now?" I ask, and I realize I sound impatient.

"You are such a left-brainer," Mark mocks, but under the tease I hear affection. "Sure, go ahead."

I come to my feet slowly as squatting is no longer kind to my thirty-nine year-old knees. Doing so, I discover that slowly and from the varying perspectives of height is probably the best way to take in Mark's newest work. I can see that the raised surface at the bottom of the mosaic is grass, a bright lawn. The way Mark has placed the chunks of ceramic makes the grass look like windblown tufts. The sky too is made using the same technique; this time, a light blue ceramic has been broken and re-set into a choppy sky. From this sky I can feel the persistence of a wind capable of clumping and flattening grass. In the middle of the brilliant but somehow turbulent weather stands a yellow house.

I reach out to touch what I see now are mug handles laid horizontally beneath the house's windows like sills or planters, a placement so clever that for a second I smile. A bit of whimsy in an otherwise threatening picture. But as my fingers run along the smooth, bridge-like curve of the ceramic handle, I look closer at the stormy sky, the wind-tossed grass, the dark tree, the empty house and realize that it is almost exactly the house in my dream. Or nightmare, I should say. I realize also that both houses are almost exactly like Dad's – our – Rockport house. I pull my fingers back from the mosaic quickly, as if I have received a scratch or a sliver from its sharp surface.

I look over at Mark who has been watching me. "You see it, don't you?" he asks. "It's creepy."

"It's just that it reminds me of a dream I had last night. About a house very much like this one. And about you."

"Me?" Mark asks with a curious smile. "Was I creepy?"

"No. But the dream was creepy. Scary. Maybe I had the dream because I was worried about you when you left yesterday."

"You're always worried about me. What'd you dream?" Mark wonders. "That I crashed my car into a house like this on my way home? That the family who lived there dragged me to safety, but turned out to be sick fucks who chained me in the basement until I agreed to join their satanic cult?"

"No," and I laugh at Mark's imagination but mostly in relief for the interruption of my own disturbed thoughts. The relief is short-lived, though, for as I begin telling Mark about my dream I feel almost as unsettled as I did when I had it.

"I was walking home. No, I was walking to this house," I begin and I pause to touch the mosaic house, "a house *like* it, and my neighbor's dog began to chase me. You stepped out from behind some trees– " I point to the dark patch on the left side of his composition " –dense trees, like in the woods. You were a boy, though, only about twelve. The dog, Scout– "

"The dog has a name?"

"At the beginning of the dream, the dog really was my neighbor's dog," I explain, "but then he turned nasty. He turned into a beast." I shudder. "He spotted you and looked like he would change his mind about whom he would chase."

"And?" Mark prompts with a roll of his hand. "So get to the point. Did he get me?"

I shake my head. "There was no chase in the end. I yelled for you to run and you ran. I guess Scout decided I was closer, or less work, or something."

"So this Scout's a big dog?" Mark asks.

"Scout's a very big dog," I answer with a laugh, out of relief.

"Did he get you?"

"I'll never know," I answer. "I woke up."

"You saved me," Mark says. "The kid me, I mean. The twelve-year-old me," he adds for emphasis.

"I guess," I answer. "All in a day's work."

To break the silence I ask, "How will you glue the pieces down if you've got them laid out on the board you want to use?"

Mark shrugs. "I get another board? Or I might not keep the design. Who knows?"

As he says this I picture him sweeping his hands over the loose pieces; I picture everything bunching together before falling over the side of the worktable and onto the garage floor. "Why would you—" I begin, but Mark says, "Ssh," so I do.

He stands quietly for a moment, his eyes trained on his latest mosaic. He is lost in thought. His hand wanders into his pocket for his grass and his lighter. He then steps away from the work and hops up onto Steven's workbench. He lights up. I wait through the predictable ritual of him holding the smoke in his lungs.

"You know," Mark says eventually as he points to his mosaic a few feet in front of him, "Jen used to tell me I'd produce crap if I was high. But I thought this was pretty damn good. I thought the idea was a gift."

"A gift?" I ask. "How?"

"Well . . . like your dream, the idea popped into my head. We were talking in your living room, and I started thinking about unpacking all these pieces I found a few weeks ago, and the house came together in my mind. Right then. Once I had the idea, the piece practically finished itself. One of those rare times." He congratulates himself with a deep drag.

"Mostly," Mark says as he exhales. He motions with his chin to the opposite corner of the garage where the rest of his work stands, boxed, stacked, and neatly labeled. "Mostly, I'm tired of all this other stuff right now, the stuff for my show. The designs, the mosaic murals. I don't mind. It happens, it's supposed to happen that I get bored enough to come up with new ideas. Then the idea for this piece came to me, and working on it gave me ideas for an entire series. All places to live, one sort of traditional, and the rest unusual. A tree house, an Airstream, a bubble on the bottom of the ocean, microscope slides. Picture that one, little mosaic amoeba at home sandwiched between large sheets of clear glass.

"Pretty stupid, huh?" Mark asks. I shake my head. "Sure it is," he insists. "Anyway, this house isn't very original. You had the same idea."

"*You* thought of all different kinds of homes. And *my* house was a dream," I remind him.

"Whatever. The point is, I thought I was so fucking original."

"Did I ever say my dream house was the same as this one?" I ask. I walk over to the bench and hop up next to Mark, leaning my shoulder into his.

"You said 'this house' and 'these trees'," he reminds me.

"Is it really so strange that we'd sometimes have similar thoughts?" I ask Mark after a moment.

He looks at me, seated on his right. "That telepathy thing again?" he scoffs. "I used to tell you I believed in that telepathy stuff when we were kids, but that was just so you'd play with me."

"And I did," I remind Mark.

"Yeah, you did," he agrees.

Mark turns away from me, rubs a hand over his face. "Ideas and dreams. All the things you don't want to think about during the day come to haunt you when your mind shuts down.

"Lately, he was everywhere I turned," Mark continues after a moment, and although he doesn't say, I know he means our father. "For the past six months. When you came over to tell me about the cancer you might just as well've dragged Jack along with you, because he's been with me ever since." He shakes his head. "Now look at us. You're dreaming about Jack's house, and I'm making pictures of it."

Neither one of us says another word and Mark smokes on until his roach is little more than a twist of paper. He presses this out on the bench under the heel of his work-toughened hand.

"You knew what that was when you first saw it, right?" Mark lifts his chin to point out the mosaic. "Dad's house?"

I nod. "Were you hoping to surprise me? Shock me?" I ask.

"Shock you?" Mark shakes his head. "I only wanted to know if you saw what I did. Fuck," he says with a quiet resignation. "I didn't know I was building his house until after it was finished."

"I think we're both thinking a lot about the Rockport house," I answer, confident. His mosaic is proof after all. I see an opening to talk about the house, our looming decision, and I take advantage of it.

"Dad made us think about the house by giving it to us. Everyone thinks we should make a decision. Steven. Sylvie. But I don't know what to do. How about you?" I ask my brother. "Have you thought any more about what you'd like to do with the house since we talked yesterday?"

Mark responds to the pressure of my question with a question of his own. "Have *you* thought any more about what I'd like to do about the house since we talked yesterday?" His pupils are large and lazy but focused in my direction. His question seems half joke and half mockery of my own.

"What is this, Pot Semantics 101?" I ask, trying to inject some humor into the conversation.

"Very funny, Shell," Mark says, but his voice is still even, his mood contemplative.

I take a deep breath as I prepare to continue. I ask, "Did you want me to think about what you'd like to do? You could make some of your own suggestions if you'd like."

"Okay, like I said yesterday, I vote we do nothing. Or I do nothing, and you do whatever the hell you want with it."

"But it's ours now," I say finally.

"Oh, no, Shell, it's not *ours*. *Yours* maybe, but it'll never be mine," Mark vows.

"The way Dad left it, I can't make a decision about the property without you."

"Sure you can, Shell. I pick doing nothing, you pick doing something. Story of our lives."

After Mark spits out the last statement, he pats down his jeans pockets and then turns them out. Empty except for his Zippo, which clatters to the workbench. "Figures the rest of my grass is in your house." A growl of frustration builds in the back of Mark's throat.

I flinch at the volume of his voice so close to my ear, but I quickly recover. I resume speaking with calm determination, hoping to sway Mark with my idea to take control of the decision we must make so that he can take back some control of his life.

"What I think is, if we accept that the house is ours — not live there necessarily," I add hastily to head off another of Mark's outbursts. "Simply take ownership. We can rent it. Sell it— "

"Torch it," Mark adds.

I ignore his suggestion and continue, "Sell it. Make some decision. If you can do that, Dad, or the feelings you have for Dad, can't control you anymore."

Mark looks at me. After a moment he bursts into laughter. "You just don't get it, do you?" he says when his laughter dies down. "I don't want the decision, I don't want the house, I don't want a dime from the house."

"Then give the money away," I persist, although with each argument I make I can see that Mark becomes more agitated. I should stop, I know I should; the person I was yesterday would have. Instead, I am convinced that this is what Mark needs to do, that pushing him is what I need to do. *For* him. And for myself.

"Find someone who needs the money and give it to them."

"Basically, Shell, we have a difference of opinion and that's okay." I know it's not okay; Mark's voice drips sarcasm. "A difference of opinion. Just like I picked being angry at Jack and you picked denial. Whatever works. The important thing is we're true to ourselves, right?"

"Denial?" I repeat, curious. "What am I denying exactly?"

Mark holds up a hand and begins to count off on his fingers. "One, that Jack was fucking his secretary when he should have been home with his family. Two, that he left us with a woman who couldn't take care of herself, let alone two kids. Three, that he ruined childhood for both of us." He pauses only a moment to let these sink in and then starts listing again.

"Four and five? That our lives sucked back then. And that our lives ain't even close to shiny and bright now because of back then."

Mark jumps off the workbench and starts pacing the garage. "You want a decision from me? Here it is. I've decided that I can't live my life denying that Dad was nothing more than a selfish adulterer. If you don't want to be angry, fine. He busted up our family and you want to spend your life tidying up the mess he left behind him so everything looks great? Fine.

"Only don't buff him up for me, don't tell me he regretted what he did, that he changed and became this great guy who suddenly knew how to be a great father. I mean, that's terrific for you if you believe it but I don't buy it, Shell, I don't."

He stops in front of his mosaic and his hands reach for it, withdraw, then reach again as if some magnetic force within the mosaic itself simultaneously draws and repels him. Suddenly he pauses and turns to me. "Every time I think of Jack or that house, that's me," he says, pointing to a chunk of ceramic. "I'm like that piece there. Or there," he says, pointing to another. "Take your pick; it doesn't matter. Those pieces are just a bunch of broken edges and nothing on their own. Nothing," he repeats.

"Until you take them and make them into something." My voice grows softer as Mark's becomes angrier. "Which you do in your work. Why not with yourself?"

Mark stands quietly after I finish my question. But it's only a matter of seconds before his hands begin to hover again over the surface of his mosaic of Jack's house. I watch as he reaches for the edges of the plywood board base. Mark, whose hands produce art like this every single day, reaches for the mosaic as if he doesn't know and doesn't care what he's got, only that in about another second he'll be hurling the object through my garage window, and that maybe, *maybe* for a little bit after the satisfying crash the rage will be gone.

"Please don't do it," I urge.

"You can't keep destroying things– " and my voice, although quiet, grows more forceful as the muscles in Mark's arms twitch more, and then more again

" –because you're still angry, after all these years, at the person who, you think, destroyed your life.

"Survival, Mark, not denial," I tell him. "I only ever tried to survive and carry you along with me. It is survival – yours and mine – that keeps me going and has me pushing you now."

Something in what I have said seems to defuse Mark's rage. Within seconds, he turns to me, he lowers his arms and sets his work back down on the table in front of him. The room is quiet again, except for a heavy rasping that I recognize as Mark's breathing. In, out; gasping in air, forcing it back out.

"You can't keep doing this," I say, affecting cool, sounding calm in spite of Mark's wild behavior. "You can't." Calm, yet forceful.

Mark doesn't move; instead he lifts his head and howls, like some kind of animal, a wolf in pain or hungry or alone. Except that he's not alone. He never has been alone. I slide off Steven's workbench and in three long steps I am at his side, my arms around him, holding my brother tight until he is quiet.

"Hey," Mark says to me when he has pulled himself together, after he has wiped his eyes and face dry with the hem of his tee shirt, "don't take my tantrum personally." He cocks his head slightly in an attempt to look tough and adds, "The last person who suggested something remotely similar to that? I told her to go fuck herself."

"Her?" I ask with a raised eyebrow.

"I'm an equal opportunity asshole," Mark answers.

"Cursing at me won't scare me away from the subject of Dad. Or the house. Not any more," I add.

"Story of my life." Mark shakes his head. "It didn't make much difference to Jen, either," he says.

I flinch. "Jeez, Mark."

"I know," he answers. "Jeez." After a moment, Mark looks down at his feet. He says, sounding defensive, "It's not like I want to be like this, always wrecking things and pissing everyone off. Pissing every good thing in my life away."

Every little confidence he gives me is a small step, his way to show he wants to talk to me. I would be wise, I caution myself, to proceed slowly and listen uncritically.

"I know you don't," I tell him.

"But over the last six months I've felt like I was going crazy. Out of control, like I'm watching myself walk into trouble every single time and I'll think, 'You've really gone too far this time,' but I can't stop myself.

"Just like Mom," Mark says and he looks up from the floor, right into my eyes.

"And don't say she wasn't crazy," he adds quickly. "It's always, 'She wasn't crazy, it wasn't that bad,' like I'm incapable of knowing how I feel!"

I think of how often I do say or have said those very words to blunt the sharp edges of pain, hoping to make someone feel better. *It's all right*, meaning: *Don't hurt, please don't hurt; nothing is that bad, not while I'm here to help you.*

But there are some times when dulling pain with comfort isn't enough, times when life is rough, when it sucks as Mark might say, and a person has to take each soul scrape and then heal, scarred but stronger. I stay silent, give Mark his space to feel everything.

Eventually he continues. "No one else's mother was like ours. Someone in my class at school thought he had a crazy mom because she had a steady stream of one-night stands, but she was just a slut, okay? Our mom was *crazy*. You were more of a mom to me; hell, I was more of a mother to her. We were kids. That wasn't right."

Our mother died years ago. She was too young, but already I had been doing her shopping for years. Every two weeks I would bring the groceries that she wouldn't leave the house for. One day, I arrived at the house, the same house I grew up in, after the same two-week interval. In addition to her milk and bread, I came bearing small, frozen portions of my own family's weekly meals: a soup, a stew, a lasagna. At the last minute, I packed a bunch of the last mums from my garden. My mother's appearance when I opened the door was so startling that I nearly dropped the bag full of Corningware dishes.

"Don't try to bullshit me," Mark had said when I called him to discuss the doctor's prognosis. He also had said, "I always knew she would kill herself."

I had known when I saw all the untouched food in the freezer and the unopened – now undrinkable – milk purchased only two weeks earlier. She was starving herself.

"She's crazy."

"Don't," I had pleaded with Mark then. "She's ill."

Mark ignored me. "She has to want to die," he said. He stared off into the distance, back into his past. "When I was a kid, most days I dreaded coming home from school. I always thought I'd find her dead, like I'd find her bleeding out in the bathroom and I'd have to do something. I was maybe fifteen. Shit," he snorted, "fifteen." After another moment, Mark added, "You know what? Parents suck. You'd think they'd want to stick around for their kids."

And despite our efforts, the doctor's intervention and trips to the hospital, our mother did what she set out to do. I hadn't shed a tear at our mother's funeral. I hadn't made the smallest sob when Dad left and Mark was crying and I held him. Saddened, yes, but strong for everyone around me, so strong. But now, my eyes are wet, and stinging tears pool above my lower lid, ready to spill. I tip my head back like maybe the salt water will roll right back where it came from, but it's futile, so I go with it.

Mark goes on. "You know what, though? I still loved Mom. It wasn't until I was about sixteen that I thought, What if I turn out like her, a nut case? Or worse, what if I turn out like Dad? A loser who leaves his kids with their crazy mother because he'd rather live with some young, sane chick? And I'd go back and forth like that, one day figuring I'd turn out like Dad, you know, screwing around. Then the next deciding I'm just like Mom. At sixteen-fucking-years-old, instead of loving them and letting that kind of love kill me, I decided to hate them, both of them.

"See, I figured hating them would make me remember both the craziness *and* the leaving and keep me from turning into either one of our parents. Truth is, now I don't know who I am unless I have someone to resent for fucking up my life."

Yes, our father left us, our mother had wound up holding her disappointment before her like a shield that protected her from more hurt but repelled her children, leaving us in a different way. Mark, I could say, they left us with the people who could do best by us: each other. Not perfect, but not too bad either. Mark looks at me. Knowing me as he does, he expects me to offer something in return – an apology, an insight, a denial, *something* – but I stay silent. This time, instead of sympathy or soothing, I give him myself, listening. I reach for his arm, wind it through mine, and rest my head on his shoulder. His shoulder rises and falls as he sighs.

"I drove home from the funeral," Mark continues, quieter. "I got high in the car. Jen and I had been sniping at each other for months, I knew she'd be on my case because I made her stay home, and I had to get high to face that. The whole way home I thought: Jack's gone, maybe now I'll get some peace, but no. There he was in the car, and then at home, right between me and Jen, and I could tell that she was so angry with me that she'd love to kick me out.

"By then I was in the kitchen washing dishes and drinking beer. The high was wearing off and I was feeling ugly and I just . . . snapped. I reached down for the dishes in the dish rack and started throwing them. But that wasn't enough so I picked up the entire rack of dishes and threw it across the loft. I broke all the dishes I had washed *and* two of Jen's favorite framed pictures, even though she screamed at me to stop.

"I stormed out of the loft. I thought about picking up a strange woman. Going to her house. Fucking her. But I couldn't stand myself for thinking that. You probably can't either, now that you know. I felt like I was thinking and acting just like Dad.

"So the next day. Today," he corrects with a wry laugh, "I left."

We stand side by side in front of Mark's mosaic, my head still resting on Mark's shoulder, and the silence between us builds. I think of the urge Mark has just confessed, so similar to my own earlier today with Ian. A need, an ache. Or in Mark's case, an escape. Someday I may tell him how close I too came, and how that slip made me better understand our father. Someday, but not now when it is Mark's turn.

Mark reaches down to take my left hand. He lifts it to his chest and looks at our two clasped hands for some time, as if they may hold a message or an answer. Or as if they hold the strength he needs to speak. I squeeze and Mark nods, ready.

"'Forgive him, for God's sake,'" Mark whispers, "is what Jen kept saying. 'He's dying. You'll regret it,' like I was being stubborn and silly. But I couldn't, and everyday that I couldn't say 'Jack, I forgive you' and mean it, I let Jen down. She hated that, I knew she'd hate me too.

"But what happens when forgiveness isn't an option? What's left? I wish you could tell me, Shell, because I sure as hell don't know."

I lift my head from Mark's shoulder and look up at him. "I haven't got the answers."

"For once in your life?" Mark asks.

"That's right. Imagine that," I say.

"Hell of a time, Shell," Mark tells me.

I think for a minute. "I'm sorry I pushed so hard, but I do think making some decision about the house might help you take control. It's not the same as forgiving Dad, I'm really not suggesting that you forgive Dad for leaving," I say quietly, my voice barely above a whisper.

"You've never pushed me before," Mark answers. He senses my caution, holds his free hand up and says, "You don't have to worry that I'll flip out. I feel better. I won't go off again. Promise," and with the same hand, Mark crosses his heart.

"But Shell," Mark says, matching my whisper with one of his own. "There's something else. It's never been about forgiving Dad for leaving. Well, that was part of it. But I might've gotten over that, on its own."

I look at Mark, bewildered, my eyes full of questions that my mouth can't catch up to.

Mark asks, "Do you need to go back inside for the kids? You know, bedtime or anything?"

I shake my head. "Steven's got it all under control. I'm fine right here."

"Good," Mark says, his mouth set in a determined line. "But can we go back and sit on your deck?" he asks. "I think I'd like the air."

I let Mark lead the way before closing and locking the garage's side door. When I catch up to him, he is seated on the same stair we occupied earlier.

"You said there is more," I prompt. "More than hating Jack for leaving? I don't– "

"No, I know you don't understand," Mark finishes for me, and he puts a finger over my lips to make me stop talking. "But you will. Promise." This time, he crosses my heart.

"I'm gonna tell you a little story," Mark says. "Maybe it won't make sense at first, but stay with me, okay?"

"Okay," I promise.

"Last fall," Mark begins. "You called up, wanted to come over? You remember coming to dinner?"

Coming to break the news of Dad's cancer diagnosis. I do, and I nod.

"Usually Jen and I would do the shopping together, but she was busy developing so I told her I'd do it myself. Fine, she'd cook, fair deal. Anyway, the shopping was a quick job: drive to Alewife, grab a few things for dinner at Bread & Circus, beer and wine from the liquor store next door, then head home. I can't even remember what we ate, can you?" he asks, and without waiting for my answer Mark shakes his head and continues.

"I park in my usual place, go in the stores, do my thing. I come back out, ready to head home. But when I get to my car there's this couple standing between my car and the one parked next to it. They're, like, leaning up against their car and making out. But, no. I see when I get closer it's more like the woman's crying and the guy is holding her, talking to her. I want to get in my car but about the last thing I wanted was to squeeze by them to open the door."

"What did you do?" I ask.

"I made a lot of noise at the back end of my car, putting the bags in the trunk. Must've worked because they split up shortly after I got there. But get this. I watch as the guy walks the woman around to the driver's side, puts her in the car, and waits until she drives away. Then, he gets into the next car over and peels outta there. Two cars. Weird, right?"

As Mark had guaranteed, the story didn't yet mean anything to me. "That is a pretty weird story," I agree.

"Yeah, but which part of it is weird exactly? That's what I can't figure out." Mark looks at me with eyes desperate for an answer. "That they're probably a couple of cheating spouses leaving the Days Inn after a nooner? Or that I saw the whole sordid thing play out?"

"Both, I guess," I answer.

"Except that cheating's not so weird, is it? It's not that uncommon. We both know that, don't we?" Mark asks.

"Well, seeing that sort of scene in a grocery store parking lot? That's pretty weird. Or maybe what's weird is you seeing them up close and personal."

Mark nods. "That's what I thought."

I wait for him to say more, but he seems to be finished. I say, "You asked me to stay with the story, Mark, and I'm trying, but I don't understand what it means."

"I wasn't kidding when I said I need some more grass," Mark says, and he lets go of my hand. He runs a hand over his face, his fingers press into his eyes. When Mark takes his hand away, his face looks slack, haggard.

I'd like to tell him to go to bed, sleep it off, that everything will look much better in the morning. The old impulse. But I don't. I can't. "Take your time," I say.

Instead of losing his nerve, Mark takes a deep breath. "Here's the thing. The thing is, Shell," he begins and I slip my arm around his back. He puts an arm around my shoulders and pulls me close. He puts his mouth to my ear and whispers, "This all means something, this crazy story I just told you means something. Look at me." And I do. I turn my head so that I look into his eyes. His eyes fix on mine. Our faces would be a breath apart if I could breathe, but I can't for waiting.

"Means what?" I ask finally.

"I heard them," Mark says.

"You heard them?" I repeat, puzzled. "Heard . . . who? The couple in the parking lot?"

Mark shakes his head. "Not them. Dad. And Sylvie. I was a kid. I was eleven and I was unlucky enough to be on the phone extension just like I was unlucky enough to be in that parking lot last fall. Bad timing." He smiles, an incredulous smile, in awe of his own bad luck.

"I heard Dad and Sylvie making plans. He was taking her away. To Rockport. To fuck her in that house. I was eleven," Mark repeats softly. "A year later they tried to take me there, so I ran." Finished, he looks from my face to his lap. As he does, his forehead brushes mine.

I swallow Mark's information in one gulp and my chest aches as I take it down, sharp edges and all. Yes, he ran all right, until the tree root forced his fall. When I reached him, he lay face down, scrabbling with his hands across the dirt as if he meant to push himself up and continue running. Pine needles clumped in piles under his hands and poked through the spaces between his fingers. From his throat rose a creak, a horrible rasping wheeze: the sound of struggling for breath after having the wind knocked out of him.

The next few moments passed in a blur of frenzied action. Mark pushing me away, fighting my efforts to look at his wound; me trying to suppress horror at the amount of blood gushing from the cut which split Mark's chin along his jawline; the blood already soaking into the ground; my voice calling for towels; the screen door slamming behind Sylvie as she ran to get them; my hands at Mark's chin as if maybe I could somehow push the blood back into him. He ran and he has been running ever since, still hurting himself. Oh, Mark, I long to say one more time. Just that: Oh, Mark. For what else is there? There is nothing to say to make this better, this pain of Mark's. I reach up and touch the scar on his chin.

"I always thought it was my fault that you fell. That I could have stopped you but didn't.

"*Your* fault?" Mark lets out one big, "Ha!" and it echoes into the night.

"I had to run," Mark says when the air around us stops vibrating. "What else was I gonna do?"

"How did we ever get you in the car in the first place?" I wonder.

"You were going, and Mom said to go. Hell, it was just as bad at home with her. Ah," he snarls, "I was still just a kid. There was only so much protesting I could do." Mark stares into the blackness.

"Can you see why I didn't want anything to do with that house then, and I don't want it now?" Finally he turns to me, pleading, "Can you *please* see why I don't know what to do?"

Jack

I went back and forth, back and forth until I couldn't do it any longer. Day after day I left my wife and children and one home full of the false comforts of predictable routines to work by Sylvie's side, to look at her, talk to her, make love to her. Night after night I left Sylvie to go home to a wife and children until I knew whom I must choose. I could no longer leave Sylvie because the haven of her mind and body had become my real home.

With the best intentions, Sylvie and I planned to include the children in our new life together. Sylvie agreed to offer a second home to Michelle and Mark, although from the start she expressed doubts about her credibility as a stepparent when she could easily have been their older sister. Sylvie knew. She saw danger lurking where I didn't. Still, we made our plans. My children's new family life would begin where ours had. Bring them to the cottage, show them how happy we are, include them in that happiness and they'll come around. We made the post-wedding trip with the children and, well, look how that turned out.

Shelley screamed, and it was her scream, not Mark's fall, that Sylvie and I heard and responded to. We flew from the house, flew down the front steps, but Shelley reached Mark first. By the time I caught up to Shelley, I found Mark face down. He clawed at the ground, struggling to raise his face out of the dirt. Pine needles and dirt were plastered to his face with blood. I couldn't see how deep the cut was but there was so much blood. Sylvie stopped a few feet behind me. I held my arm out at my side, preventing her from coming any closer. I said evenly, "Towels. And quick." Without a word, Sylvie turned and ran back to the house.

I squatted alongside Shelley. Mark had also had the wind knocked from him, and he labored to draw a breath. Other than that and the cut, he appeared to be fine, arms and legs working and unbroken. I turned him to take the pressure off his chest. Mark resisted as I tried to roll him onto his back until halfway through I was able to grab his flailing hands and hold them still with my own. "Relax, relax," I whispered to my son, urging him and myself to remain calm.

Shelley brought the hem of Mark's tee shirt up to his chin to stanch the blood. "Good,' she encouraged as his breathing deepened and the gasping ceased, "that's good." I stood up, took a step back, and let the tension drain from my relieved muscles. As I did, I backed straight into Sylvie, returned with a white bath towel dangling from her hand. I rolled it into a tight cylinder and handed it to Shelley.

"I'll drive him to the emergency room," I told Sylvie. "You stay. And you too, Michelle," I said, looking down at her.

"I'm going," Shelley insisted firmly, meeting my gaze, projecting as always maturity greater than her sixteen years.

I sighed. "I need the keys," I told Sylvie after patting down my empty pockets.

"Here," she said as she pulled the ring from the pocket of her shorts. "I figured." She nudged me in Mark's direction.

Shelley whispered in Mark's ear. "We're going to get in the car now," she coached. "Can you stand?"

Mark nodded and, leaning into each other, they eased up off the ground. Sylvie moved to the front steps, I went to the car and started it. Shelley walked with Mark but at the car door he stopped his sister with a hand on her arm. Through the rolled down window I heard him croak, "Thanks," his voice still hoarse from the strain of breathing. Then Mark smiled. He removed the blotting towel, now red and white, from his face and showed us a broad smile that made the sliced skin stretch and separate into a bloody second grin.

Hours later, when the three of us returned to the cottage, Sylvie had the kids' suitcases waiting at the bottom of the front steps. She had packed a bag for us too, and then took a seat on the porch to wait. She knew as well as I did that the visit was over, over before it even began. We four left later that evening before the sun set, before spending one full night in the cottage, our weekend visit with the children, the "weekend treat at the beach" I had enthusiastically promised cut short by Mark's accident. Safe to say, none of us was looking forward to the ride home or to the eventual confrontation with Kay. We were still miles away and I could practically hear her scream, "How could you let this happen? Were you off with that . . . *girl?*" She would spit the word, froth building at the corners of her mouth as she continued. "Were you not paying *attention?* Aren't you supposed to be *watching* the children?" At the thought of Kay's likely reaction, I groaned.

"What?" Sylvie asked.

"His mother," I said simply and she nodded, understanding.

I looked in the rearview mirror, catching Mark's eye. He stared back, looking no happier than I felt, but I remembered his smile after the fall.

The scene replayed in my head. Mark runs away from us, Mark falls and splits open his chin. Shelley holds a towel under Mark's dripping wound. Mark smiles defiantly before getting in the car. Although hurt, he smiles once again through the pain. This smile shows no joy, no pleasure at being part of our idyllic life up here on

Cape Ann. It isn't even a smile of bravery under the circumstances. *I'm okay, Dad, really.* No, his smile is a victor's smile, beyond smug: superior. He set out to ruin the day and he has. Mark knows he has won.

I wondered then if a part of Mark greatly anticipated Kay's reaction to the neat row of black stitching that looked like a line of ants marching along his chin. And really, I thought, who could blame either one of them, Kay for her anger or Mark for his perverse delight?

Even at that earliest point in my second marriage, I knew Kay was a lost cause. When I told her I was leaving I expected that she would be angry, but I also expected that her initial anger might subside the way hot lava roils, then cools, then settles. But each time we spoke, her anger was hotter, more dangerous. She called and lashed out so frequently that I began negotiating every last child support detail — visits, purchases, money — through Shelley, the voice of reason and role model for patience.

But that didn't cause me to abandon hope that Mark would come around. We continued our bimonthly visits where Mark would reluctantly get in my car and ride to our condo and sleep one night in our guest bed. In the morning he walked his never-unpacked overnight bag to the front door and waited for the ride home. When he wasn't mute, he was loud and angry. After two years of subjecting ourselves to the horrible names he called Sylvie, to the painful silences and physical resistance to visits, I admitted what my wife had known all along: winning over Mark was too hard. He didn't try, so I stopped trying too. I'm not saying this was right, only that this is what happened. By the time Mark turned sixteen, my visits with him yielded to phone calls, which in time were replaced by my signature on a few important checks.

The next time I actually saw him was two years later, the day he turned and spotted me and Sylvie approaching him through a crowd of people. It was his high school graduation day. Sylvie and I had waited out a short downpour in our car, but with a break in the rain we crossed the football field to find our seats. I spotted Mark in the throng. Shelley was at his side, straightening his mortarboard, and I started to walk over to offer Mark my congratulations. There was no sign of Kay; I guessed she must have already taken her seat, which relieved me since I never knew what she might do or say. With Mark, I figured enough time had elapsed since our uncomfortable meetings, that time might have mellowed us both, and I walked toward him with a smile on my face. Although I could see the same lanky, dark-haired, handsome boy I had always known, there were hints in his demeanor that he was growing up. He rolled his eyes at his sister's fussing but tolerated it. He even looked happy for the attention. Happy . . . until he saw us. In front of half of his class and their families, a few administrators and teachers, Mark shook off Shelley's hands and took a step toward me. He raised his arm, extended it, pointed at us, and walked straight at us pointing all the time. "Fuck you!" he said. "Get the fuck off this field!"

All because I had left him.

The room I still like to think of as the death room is a kind of holding pen, a place to lie and think, and, ultimately, a place for the truth. At the time, I had believed everything I told myself. Include them in our happiness and they'll come around. I had been happy the day we drove out to Rockport, happy in my belief that everything would work out. The kids in the car, the sun shining, Sylvie smiling next to me. I was happy in the possibility that our new family would work. Within minutes I was faced with the reality that it never would, with Mark anyway. From that day on, Mark's ropy, sickle-like scar grinned on his face, a reminder of the day Shelley screamed and I learned with the scream that there was a huge gap between my naive beliefs and the harsh reality.

I take in a little breath and then sigh. There it is, not quite pain really but more of a heaviness, a kind of impeded breathing, a reminder of my diseased lungs. I go on thinking anyway, remembering in spite of my discomfort. When I left, I set in motion a chain of reactions that couldn't be reversed, and not the nice, neat reactions I imagined either. Instead of the richer life I imagined for us all, three people were damaged. My first wife had been bitter until her own death several years ago. My daughter had adult-sized burdens long before she was an adult in years. My son hates me.

Well before making the trip to Rockport with the kids, weeks before I left Kay, Sylvie called me at home on a Saturday, a day she knew I had set aside to take my children to see some popular movie, simply to hear my voice.

"Hi," she said. She tried to sound casual but her voice was husky with emotion.

"Where are you?" I asked in a lowered voice, immediately drawn in.

"Home. On my bed." I groaned at the thought of Sylvie's bed. "Alone," she added. "I miss you."

"God, I miss you too. The movie," I said, and my tone turned apologetic, "starts in half an hour. I have to head downstairs. We were just on the way out the door."

"Then go," Sylvie said. "I know I shouldn't have called you at home."

"No, no," I interrupted. "Stay. One more minute."

We said nothing more for a few seconds, both of us breathing, as if all we needed was confirmation of being alive. Finally I said, "I should go. Look," I added, "if we can swing it, we'll go to Rockport next Saturday, spend the day at the house. I promise, I won't let you out of that bed."

"I hate waiting."

"And I'll see you Monday."

Sylvie sighed. "Monday," she noted, "is only two days away."

"On Monday," I said, "I will drive to your apartment on the way to work. Early. I will ring the bell and hope you let me in. Will you let me in, Sylvie?"

"I will, Jack," she whispered.

"Daddy?" A high, reedy voice traveled through the wires, mixed with the echoes of our last words.

"Mark?" I asked, stunned. "Have you been on the phone . . ." I began but then abandoned the question; I already knew the answer. "Thank you, Sylvie, for bringing that problem to my attention. I'll take care of it first thing on Monday. Look, Mark, I have to settle something for work. Hang up, get your sister, and go wait in the car. I'll be right down.

"Christ," I exhaled when I heard the fumbling click of Mark disconnecting. "Shit, shit, shit."

"I'm sorry," Sylvie said.

"No. You didn't . . . it's fine. He won't . . . Sylvie, I've got to go."

"I know," she replied, and she put down the phone.

There were times when I prayed that Kay would pick up the extension or catch on to the bogus trips out of town, that I would be caught out and sent packing. Cowardly, true, but I knew my life would be so much easier if Kay could throw me out with the moral high ground of the wronged wife. To confront her with the selfish truth – that I didn't love her, that I loved my kids but not enough, that I wasn't being true to myself – seemed both difficult and cruel.

As I think about the decision I reached to leave Kay, I remember driving with Sylvie in my gas guzzling Lincoln Town Car on the way to our first meeting together, and what I said to her that day about windows falling from the Hancock building.

Maybe, I had speculated, there was some kind of whistle, like a bomb. "Or maybe you never hear a thing." No warning, I thought. Bad things happen without warning.

Bull*shit*. Impending death has a neat way of helping a person cut through all the crap. You *do* hear the bad things coming. Sometimes you help them along, you laugh with your children when you know your wife is miserable. You're not proud of yourself but sometimes you know this may taunt her into doing something irrational. Kay's act became the excuse I needed to start pulling away from her, the thing I could point to with my finger and say, "There, that's it, that's the moment." Sometimes you want the bad things to happen so you have a reason to leave.

In choosing Sylvie, was I being selfish? In trying to lessen the blow, selfish? To me the act of leaving had been so necessary, but yes and yes to both, absolutely selfish.

But I never wanted it to be Mark. Never. Still, I should have heard that particular window falling. With the risks we were taking, having someone as innocent as Mark find out was only a matter of time.

I didn't take any action then. I hung up the phone, got in my car, and drove my children to the movies. Beyond telling Mark I was finishing up a work call, we never discussed what he heard on the line. I spent a few anxious days wondering if Mark would tell his mother, or more likely his sister, what he'd overheard, ask what my words to Sylvie had meant, but he never did. I decided my phone conversation with Sylvie would have, at worst, confused rather than enlightened him, and decided further to leave the call unexplained. Children, I figured, spent a lot of their young lives being confused by the adult world; I know I had been at his age. I told Sylvie to forget the incident, put it right out of her mind, and I'm sure she did. I know she did. There was no fault. If anything, the incident was yet another expression of our need for each other, and the need to resolve the limbo in which we lived. I would make my choice for a new life, and the new life wouldn't be marked from the start by our one error in judgment. We would put it behind us and move forward.

I left my wife. I planned for a future as an expanded family. I took my kids to Rockport and ignored what the house might mean to my son because I wanted this life to work. I badly wanted it to work so I wouldn't feel guilty about my decision to leave, and I never looked back. Until now.

I haven't seen my son since his graduation, and there's so much you can't know about someone you haven't seen in seventeen years, no matter what Shelley tells me of the achievements and developments in his life. I don't know the man, what he thinks, what resentments he harbors. I only know the boy, the one who drew pictures and sculpted modeling clay for hours on end. The very little boy who would reach for his father's hand while walking whenever they reached an intersection. That very little boy's trust. Which I then betrayed.

Mark

In 1975, we were a couple of kids going to see *The Man Who Would Be King* with their dad. The movie was Shelley's pick; I'd wanted *Jaws*, but was happy enough to be doing anything with my dad. Since the day our mom went nuts in the kitchen, Dad had picked up some of the slack at home. Shelley and I came to count on a good amount of his time when he wasn't at work. Bedtime stories, homework help, and weekend outings – all so Mom could "have a break." You know, I would take a look around, see that my friends and other neighborhood kids had parents who were sort of weird so, okay, I said to myself. I can put up with my mother when she tunes out in front of the TV because I have my Dad for fun and he's around a whole lot, and because I have my sister who pretty much takes care of everything I need. Life was sometimes strange, but not so bad.

Until Dad started working more. The usual days, plus nights, plus weekends. At first he made an effort to take me with him to the office on Saturdays. I'd bring colored pencils, and Dad would give me paper to draw on while he worked. One Saturday morning, I met his assistant, Sylvie. She held out her hand to me, expecting me to shake it, I guess, like I was some kind of grown-up. Dad nudged me and I took her hand. She looked right at me with this weird half-smile on her face until I felt shy and had to look away. She was way too pretty, like someone on TV or in a movie. I snuck one more look at her out of the corner of my eye; no, definitely not like a real person at all. Soon after, Dad stopped taking me to the office.

He still wanted to do stuff with us, he said, and he came up with great ideas. Sometimes he even followed through on those great ideas, but more and more our time together dwindled to one bedtime story during the week, or, if we were really lucky, a couple of hours on Sunday for the zoo or a movie.

I had waited all week for the movie. We had five minutes before we had to leave the house, and I was ready. Then the phone rang. When the phone rang in our house nights or weekends, it was usually Dad's work. *My assistant*, he would mouth at us. *Work. I'll take it in the other room.* Then he would give me the receiver and tell me to hang up when I heard his voice on the other line.

On movie day, Dad picked up the phone in the bedroom. He didn't need me to hang up an extension, so I don't know what even possessed me to pick up the phone that day. I got tongue-tied when I heard Sylvie's voice, thinking about her and the way she had smiled at me that day at Dad's office like she was teasing me. So instead of speaking, I listened.

I know I shouldn't call you at home, but . . .

Where are you?

Home. On my bed. Alone. I miss you, Jack.

We'll go to Rockport next Saturday, spend the day at the house. I promise, I won't let you out of that bed.

I hate waiting.

And I'll see you Monday. Monday is only two days away.

"On Monday," my father said, "I will drive to your apartment on the way to work. Early. I will ring the bell and hope you let me in. Will you let me in, Sylvie?"

"I will, Jack," Sylvie whispered.

Then I spoke. One word. "Daddy?"

Dad tried to tell me it was work. He told me to hang up, get Shelley, and get in the car. He had to settle something for work and he'd be right down.

Work, my ass.

What does any kid know at age eleven? I mean, *really* know? If he goes to school and listens at recess to foul-mouthed classmates, he knows enough to make him worry when he hears his father talk about taking another woman to bed. Enough to know that adults' words and voices and moods can make his world tilt and lurch like the worst amusement park ride of his life.

Yeah, we made it to the movie on time. After putting some energy into convincing me I had been listening to a work discussion, my father never said another word to me about that phone call. He never again pulled me aside to tell me to forget it. The call was never, ever mentioned. And in the confusion and disappointments and, yes, even highlights of the next year, sure, I pushed it right out of my mind as another thing that grownups did that made absolutely no fucking sense to me. I didn't think about that call until Dad moved in with Sylvie and they invited us - me and Michelle - to go away with them for a weekend.

To Rockport.

Shelley says nothing when I finish my story. Evidently even my sister has a threshold and this story's way crossed it. While Shelley processes this, I think: I am thirty-five years old and the call I overheard was placed twenty-four years ago. I've gone twenty-four years without talking about what I knew. I probably would've gone another twenty-four, and another, if certain events hadn't been stacked up to fall on top of each other like so many rows of bowling pins. Pushed to the brink, I blew. Christ, I sound like I'm blaming everyone for their part in the chain of events that had such an effect on me, but I'm not thinking in terms of blame anymore, not really. Thinking of events this way, as a series of unpreventable reactions, is kind of soothing. I don't even feel so upset anymore. It's not me that's out of control; out of control is the way of the world.

Shelley takes her right hand from my forearm and brushes her knuckles across the scar on my chin. Lost as I have been in my thoughts, the touch startles me and I pull my face away from her fingers. Shelley's eyebrows knit together. "I always thought it was my fault you fell," she says, serious once again. "That I could have stopped you but didn't."

That made me laugh. "*Your* fault! It was never your fault."

But now, I think to myself, *now* maybe she can see why I can't deal with this house, and why I could never deal with Jack.

We sit for a little longer on the deck, our shoulders touching. Next to me I feel Shelley tense; she grabs my upper arm.

"Mark," she whispers as she reaches for me. "Listen."

I hear something, a rustle, the snap of a twig. Shelley points to the rear of her backyard. "Look."

I see two figures, illuminated by the strong floodlights hung high on the back of the house.

"Scout," she says.

"That's a dog?" I say quietly, awestruck. Shelley nods. "Looks like a fucking bear," I swear under my breath.

"Mr. Jenkins walks him very early and very late. I don't know why."

"Because he's afraid of scaring the neighbors?" I suggest as the dog disappears into the dark of the next yard.

"What would have happened, do you think," Shelley begins slowly, interrupting the quiet in the wake of the monster dog, "if I had stopped you from running? What if I had caught up to you, and stopped you, and you had told me exactly what was bothering you about being in Rockport? And about the phone call?"

"What if you had tried to stop me and I plowed right into you? Play that 'what if' game," I tell her, "and where do we stop? I shouldn't have thrown those dishes at Jen's photos? You shouldn't have brought up the Rockport house after the funeral? Dad shouldn't have given it to us? He shouldn't have left Mom? Mom shouldn't have checked out? Where does it stop?" I watch Shelley think about what I am saying, and then I continue.

"All those times Jack went to Rockport he should have been home with us, taking care of us, but he wanted to fuck Sylvie more than he wanted to be our father. Is that the place, the one place in time where someone should have chosen to do the right thing? Or before, when Mom and Dad decided, for God knows what reason, to get married? How far back do we have to go before we can find someone making a good decision?

"Even me," I add. "I got in the car. I got in because I was a kid. Because I didn't want to be home with Mom either. But what if I had stayed home? So what. The 'what if I'd done this, what if I'd done that' shit doesn't matter. It doesn't matter because we couldn't have stopped any of this from happening."

Shelley seems to consider every point I've made. "I've always felt guilty," she says eventually. "You fell and I didn't. I got away to college sooner than you could. Now this phone call." She shakes her head and then continues. "It shouldn't have been you on the phone. I could have handled it. I wish it had been me."

I look closely at my sister. "I know you do," I say. "And I wish none of this had ever happened. To either of us. But it did."

"It did," Shelley repeats. "I understand what you said about us as kids, being at the mercy of everyone's bad decisions. I think, though," she adds, "that Dad tried to make a good decision when he left Mom to marry Sylvie."

I snort. "A good decision? Leaving us with Mom? Yeah, that was some good decision."

"Actually," Shelley says and she smiles a little at me, "I think Dad left you with me. And that didn't turn out to be too awful, did it?"

"Leaving one of his kids in the care of his other kid is pretty effing stupid if you ask me," I say.

Shelley shrugs. "Dad knew I could do it, and he knew that I would. I could have refused but I didn't, and I own that. I never minded.

"And you know what else?" she asks. "I never told Dad how bad Mom was. That eventually she wouldn't leave the house. That she drank. That she stopped eating. He only came in contact with a small part of her when he got her on the phone or met her at the house when he picked us up. After a while, he didn't even have to face that because I became the go-between. But again, because I chose to. Doing it myself made life easier.

"So put that on your list of bad decisions. The thing is," Shelley adds, "it was a decision. I took charge and I did it for what I thought were the right reasons. I only wanted everything to run smoothly and everyone to be happy. That was my choice. It may all seem random and out of control to you, but we've all made our choices. And lived with the results."

I think about this for a few minutes. "That phone call? And Jack sticking me, a kid, in the middle of all his mess? What choice did I have back then?"

"You're not that boy in the middle any more. You can make choices now, right?" Shelley asks. "Or is it easier not to?"

"You think I should forgive him too?" I ask my sister. "Like Jen does? She's always after me to come to terms with the divorce and remarriage and how my life was fucked up by it. She wants me to get help instead of ignoring all that.

"*I* want *her* to accept that I can't let it go," I tell my sister. "But last night, standing in our kitchen, I looked across the room at the photograph of Jen's body among all the newspapers, you know the one I mean." Shelley nods. She knows the story of the hoarders from Belmont.

"As I stared at the photograph last night I remembered how sorry Jen felt for the couple, but also how she couldn't understand the clutter. And that's what I really saw, Jen surrounded by so many things she couldn't understand. Namely me. I started thinking, I'm like those freaking newspapers. Or I'm like the cast-off stuff she collects, the bowls and books and toys she photographs. She basically picked me up off the street to rescue me.

"I thought I made no sense to her the way I am. I thought that meant she wanted me to be different. I thought *you* wanted me to be different."

"I don't want you to be different. I want you to be happy. Maybe that's what Jen wants for you too. Because, like me, she loves you."

Shelley stares at me for a minute after she says this.

"What?" I prompt.

"Do you love Jen?"

"I think so," I say.

"You *think* so?" Shelley laughs a little at my answer.

"I don't love it that she's on my case about my pot-smoking. I mean, maybe I shouldn't smoke so much but she can be kind of intense about it. We're not perfect together."

Shelley raises an eyebrow. "That's it?"

I shake my head and try to explain. "It's not just about the pot. When we'd go out picking trash, Jen would find all this stuff, and everything she found had to have some meaning, some purpose. Her relentlessness can be annoying."

"Her relentlessness?" Shelley asks.

"Yeah," I say. "She'll work for hours grouping the things she's collected, and taking pictures of all the combinations. She'll do this over and over, until every single unrelated object is changed into a finished piece that means something to her."

"You mean exactly what you do with your work?" Shelley asks, and then she laughs again. "Maybe you two aren't as imperfect together as you think."

Are we both that much alike? I wonder. Are we both just trying to make sense of things, trying to make something whole and good out of whatever we can? As Shelley waits for me to say something, I recall how I loved Jen's work at first. And I loved the way she just got down to business and got things done. I loved that she saw something in me and in my work. I loved the way I felt when we were working side by side. Being thought highly of by Jen can make me feel so good about myself.

For a few more seconds I think about Jen's intensity, how everything I loved about her actually had everything to do with this intensity. I look over at my sister.

"No. I do love her," I answer. "What I'm not sure of is if that's enough between the two of us."

"You more than anyone know that nothing's perfect, Mark," she says. "But that doesn't mean it can't be pretty darn good."

True. I found Jen and for a while, our life together was pretty darn good.

And even though I really don't want to, I think about my father, also searching for something to make his life better. Which he eventually found with another woman, in his own new family, a family of two. Not perfect, not by a long shot, because by choosing one life he lost a lot of the other. But maybe at the end Jack felt the effect of his choice; maybe he knew what he had found and what he had lost in order to find it. Better, yes, but not perfect.

"I can see that," I tell Shelley. But can I see that with Jen?

Right now I honestly don't know if she looks at me like she looked at that Belmont couple and their junk, as something incomprehensible and in need of fixing. I could be getting Jen all wrong, though. Maybe when she looks at me she sees the real Mark, imperfect but hers. Maybe the only change she wants is for us to build a really good and productive life together. And maybe it's worth some of my time to find out.

Right now, it's up to me. My choice.

"This is me, Shell. I walk away from Jack and all of Jack's shit. These past couple of days I've had to deal with him but maybe I don't have to any more."

"Except there's the house," Shelley reminds me.

The house itself, the money from renting or selling it, the effort it will take to stay away or simply forget that the house is out there, that it exists. Fuck, I'm tired. The anger hasn't disappeared, but I am tired of it. And I have made my choice to walk away.

"All right," I say, resigned, "we'll do something with the house. Something that doesn't involve me owning it or living there or taking any money from it. I'll give it to you outright, if you want it.

"And, really," I say, anticipating the skeptical raise of an eyebrow, "I'm not being a wiseass again, like I'm pretending I don't give a shit. I mean that I'm open to doing something to put it behind me.

"You want the house? Take it. I won't ever want to hear about it, I don't want any money from it, but I swear I won't give you any grief, no matter what you do. It's yours." And here, I hold up my right hand, a pledge.

Shelley stares at me for a few seconds after I've finished speaking. I wonder if she's beginning to blank out, her fatigue getting the better of her. And then in front of my eyes, she shakes off the stupor, realigns her posture, and composes her face with a more engaged expression. She smiles. And when she does I'm so glad we're sitting under the floodlight by the back door because I can see her face clearly through the dark, and for me Shelley's smile will always be the light showing me my way. I'd follow her anywhere, the steadiest light I know. She looks, well, not happy, exactly, but decisive. Determined.

"But that's just it," she says to me.

"What's just what?" I ask, confused.

"What's been bothering me about why Dad gave us the house in the first place. It never made any sense, even if we looked at it as his way of sharing the happiest part of his life with us. He must have known you'd refuse the house, and that I'd be torn between you and a gift from him."

"So?" I ask. "Maybe dying makes you believe all sorts of crazy stuff is possible."

"Maybe," Shelley allows. "But why would Dad believe we'd react any differently than we always have?" She shakes her head. "No. I think he gave us the house knowing this is exactly how we'd react to it."

"Then why'd he give us the house in the first place?"

"So that we'd have to give it back," she says, the smile spreading across her face as the confusion grows on mine. "To the only person left who truly belongs there.

"Maybe, Mark, so that we could be free."

And with nothing any clearer for me yet, she takes my elbow and leads me out of the dark and into the kitchen.

Shelley

In the kitchen, the clock reads twenty-four minutes past ten. Out of the long-ingrained habit of delivering bedtime glasses of water, I go to the cabinet for a tall glass, then stand at the tap to fill it with cool water for Mark. The house is quiet but for the water running, and dark but for the light over the kitchen sink and two baseboard nightlights in the front hall to light the stairwell. I give Mark his water then we walk up the stairs together.

Once in the den I help Mark make up the futon for his bed, but before I leave him alone to go to sleep I do two things. First, I collect my purse from my bedroom doorknob and remove Jack's letter from it. Next I take some paper from Steven's desk. Sitting side by side with Mark on the futon, I begin to draft a letter and wait as Mark reads over my shoulder and his confusion clears. When the letter is finished and read over a few times, Mark nods his assent. Steven's old and clunky fax machine takes a couple of minutes to warm up but when it does, we use it. Someone will find our fax in the morning, perhaps a flat sheet of paper, perhaps curled up, a scroll on the fax tray or on the floor. No matter, I don't care, as long as the task is done.

And it is finished. We leave the room together, Mark stopping in front of the bathroom door to wash for bed. I hug him good night. We had spoken for over two hours and with such intensity that I feel a sense of relief when I let go. The only words I whisper are, "I love you. Sleep well."

I enter my room as stealthily as I can in the pitch dark. Coming in with the light of the bathroom still in my eyes, I need a moment to adjust to the blackness. Soon I see the outline of the room, my favorite chair, the bed, my husband's sleeping form, and the closet where my soft cotton nightgown hangs. I make my way to the closet, shed my clothes where I stand to be dealt with in the morning, and slip the cool cotton over my head. Tonight, instead of sitting down in my chair, I stand by the window with my arms wrapped across my chest. I look out over the dark yard, another late night for me. Tonight, after so many long days and nights, I look forward to sleep, and then waking to a new day when in the arc of the sun, its forward push, anything seems possible to accomplish.

I had visited my father often as he prepared to die. We tried to speak of happy things, of his granddaughters and their progress, of his memories of foreign places he had traveled to with Sylvie. Once he was confined to bed I took to describing the weather to him, the exact color of the sky, an unusual plant in my garden. I talked about my students, the funny way each class had its own distinct personality, how I was so fortunate to have a bumper crop of enthusiastic learners.

I confided in Dad that the book I chose to read aloud to my eighth graders, *David Copperfield*, was beneath them academically, but that I had chosen it because of the story's pure entertainment value. I explained that my last-period students were so often tired, restless. My reading aloud for the last fifteen minutes of class permitted them to put their heads down on their desks and simply listen to my voice, my accents, and follow the action. I told my father that one of the things I loved best about teaching was reading wonderful stories aloud to children. He asked, would I read it to him? I agreed with pleasure, and this became our routine. Jack's world was, by this time, very small – four rose-beige walls, a few familiar faces – and I hoped to make it larger for him. I began, "Chapter One: I am born."

David Copperfield's adventures, even his woes, seemed to give Jack such pleasure. And hope. Hope because there was between us a belief that death would wait for me to finish the book simply because my father needed to hear the end. Needless to say, I took my time.

One day I brought the book but it stayed on my lap, open but unread. Jack had had a poor night, a bad morning. Instead of reading, I held his hands. They were cold and wouldn't warm up. We sat quietly, and I felt very close to him. Our thoughts that day seemed to be running in the same direction. I was thankful for the closeness and I told him so.

The day that I left *David Copperfield* on my lap was the last good visit my father had with me. My father spoke of choices, specifically the choice he made to stop leaving Sylvie. I told him I forgave him, and that I would always be thankful for getting back together with him. We spoke of Mark. I tried to express my fears for Mark, my fear that Mark would never forgive Dad's choices. Dad said he understood why Mark couldn't. I may have been able to forgive but I didn't understand much then, and I remember being baffled by how resigned Dad was to Mark's rejection. He seemed calmly accepting, not bitter, certainly not bewildered by it.

Days later I visited and Dad was much weaker, unable to speak and taking oxygen from a tank. He could hear, he was alert, his eyes focused on my face and moved when I did, but only a few days later Sylvie called; Jack was dead. Dead and, in death, missed, but I was free to remember him any way I chose. I couldn't forget that the time I had with my father had always been doled out on his terms, his and Sylvie's. I had been fitted into their lives. Even so, I choose now to remember the man and all his imperfections because, despite his flaws, I found in him something I needed.

Even after hearing Mark's story, my feelings for my father are unchanged. I can't help feeling relieved that Dad became such an important part of my life. I will look back on that last meaningful day with my father, the spine of *David Copperfield* cracked but the book turned over on my lap, as a day we both felt at peace with each other, just two imperfect people accepting each other.

And as perfect as I have tried to make my world, I know I am as imperfect as he was. I have seen firsthand how chasms open up between two people. I know that even the smallest disagreements can lead to hurt feelings, which lead in turn to distance, resentment, fear of speaking, then finally brutal silence. Today I understood for myself how that space yawns and widens, how soon it may become unbridgeable. I have seen how the right person coming along at the right time can step into that space with a shiny and priceless gift in hand, a piece beautifully crafted from listening, understanding, total acceptance, and love.

As all this played out before me today I felt uncomfortable because I knew, given the right circumstances I might have taken the same chances that my father did, made the same choices. I might have even felt the same way, possessing some regret, but a regret that was far outweighed by much, much relief and happiness. I might still. The point is, who among us knows what chances lie in wait?

There was my father, and Sylvie walking through his office door for an interview one day by complete chance, and from that chance meeting Dad found a person who understood and cared for him, actions and emotions he reciprocated. Chances presented themselves but choices were made.

Mark has put himself at the mercy of this past. Early on he saw he had no power over the adults' decisions. Our mismatched parents found each other and came together and in doing so, set off something like a highway pileup, each successive crash adding to the destruction. Mark was the car that gets creamed and pushed along for yards.

I took control and left nothing to chance. When our world was broken up, I designed a new one for Mark and myself. I thought of this only a few hours ago when I held Mark as he wept. We might have been transported back in time to the night our father left us. At that moment, a little world sprang up around us. I held him back then and thought to myself: here we have four walls and a roof over our heads. We have a good meal in our stomachs and the clothes on our backs. *This close*, I thought, *I can feel every bone, every pulse of blood, every twitch of muscle between us. We have each other, we are safe.*

So tonight we reached a decision about the Rockport house. With this decision Mark can acknowledge, then walk away from the past. I know our decision has freed me from responsibility and the guilt I have always carried for being more resilient.

I sigh deep and loud. I have been so lost in thought that I have practically forgotten where I am and that I am not alone. Steven's voice from across the room reminds me.

"You shouldn't be up two nights in a row," he says in a voice full of concern. "Come to bed, Shelley."

And I do. I walk the few steps from my place at the window to my side of the bed, careful not to stub a toe on the heavy piece of furniture. Steven draws back the blankets for me and I slip in.

With Steven nestled against my back, I feel for the first time in days ready for a deep, peaceful rest.

Steven, it seems, is not. When he speaks his voice pulls me back from the brink of sleep. He says, "I just remembered something."

"Remembered what?" I ask.

"Something I wanted to tell you. Something I thought about tonight while you were outside with Mark."

The mention of Mark's name wakes me fully. "Something about Mark?" I ask, and I slip out of his arms and turn to face him.

"Something about Sylvie," Steven answers. "And dropping her off at the condo this morning."

The drive to Sylvie's condo. Another reminder of just how much has happened since seven o'clock this morning. Is it still the same day? *Only Wednesday?* I wonder, with a look across Steven's side of the bed to the digital clock.

Steven says it for me, "What a long day!"

"Yes," I agree, laughing a little in relief.

"Sylvie," he begins, "didn't want me to hang around to help her this morning. She turned down my offer to help with the suitcases. It felt weird, not helping her. I felt I couldn't just drop her at the door. But then again, I tried to see it from her point of view. You know, maybe she was testing herself to see if she could handle the empty house alone.

"In the end I said something like, 'Sure, fine, whatever you want, Sylvie. But don't hesitate to call if you need us. We're family.'"

In the dark I smile. "I said practically the same thing over coffee. I told her she shouldn't be alone."

"Of course you did," Steven says and he strokes my arm. "That's not so strange. That's what most people say in these situations. Offering support is part of the process, right? Otherwise we feel so helpless.

"But she refused my help, so I got in my car and drove to work. I was so early that I had time to think. About Sylvie. And your Dad." Steven pauses to bend his arm at the elbow and he props his head up on his hand.

"They were so wrapped up in each other," he says after a minute. "I have never met two people so meant for each other." Steven pauses. "Those words don't even express what I mean," he says. "What their marriage was like."

How did Mark put it? "He should have been home with us, taking care of us, but he wanted to fuck Sylvie more than he wanted to be our father." And Sylvie? "No, I shouldn't be alone. But I am." Even I had acknowledged the same. We were fitted into their lives, I had said, never the other way around.

Three or four summers ago, we had driven up to spend a weekend with Dad and Sylvie. Steven had taken the girls to the town beach for a swim, something they couldn't do from the rocks at closer by Halibut Point. I had stayed behind to start dinner, and was downstairs in the kitchen at the back of the house. I had been so focused on cooking that I didn't hear Dad and Sylvie leave their porch chairs to slip up the stairs. Thinking they were still on the porch, reading, I called out to them with some inane question about the timing of dinner. When I got no answer I dried my hands on a kitchen towel and walked down the hall to the front of the house where all I found was a pair of faded jeans carelessly dropped at the foot of the stairs. I blushed then as I'm blushing now, hurried back to the kitchen, and pretended not to notice when Sylvie came down later wearing a different outfit.

Steven is right, I agree silently. We would never find the exact words to express what Dad and Sylvie created.

"They were really selfish," I say.

"Incredibly selfish," Steven agrees. He lays his head back down on his pillow and turns onto his back to look at the ceiling. "Don't get me wrong, Shelley, I always liked your dad. I think Sylvie is charming. I keep remembering the times we were invited to Rockport, and how pleasant it was in the house with Jack and Sylvie."

Yes, I agree. Being inside that house, being welcomed in, it was very pleasant. Jack and Sylvie were at their happiest and therefore most relaxed in that house. A sight to behold. I remember my surprise – *She loves you!* – and how Jack laughed at my blurting. The way they loved each other exclusively was, at times, enviable.

"Maybe because they were only my in-laws, I have better perspective. I can't imagine what it would be like to be a child with such selfish parents.

"Children," he amends. "You and Mark.

"How is Mark anyway?" my husband asks with genuine caring. "Did you two have a good talk?"

I don't answer right away. There is so much to tell Steven. Right now he has no idea what we discussed and how my plan took its shape as we went along. No idea that we think we now understand Dad's reasons for giving us such a gift. Someday I'll tell Steven my hope that without the ownership of this house hanging over our heads, maybe Mark won't feel cornered into forgiving Dad. He might in fact wake up one day, no longer angry. Maybe he will begin to make good decisions, continue doing good work; he might even find someone who loves him just the way he is. That person might even be Jen. Maybe he will be fine.

And me? Maybe I won't have to worry about him quite so much. And wouldn't that be something?

Right now, though, I am tired, bone tired. I decide to save the whole story for the morning, start the conversation over a leisurely cup of coffee before work and perhaps continue it throughout the weekend. I picture a weekend of Steven and me talking, turning the details of so many lives over and over between us until, step-by-step, we make our way back to each other.

For now I simply say, "Thank you for asking. I think Mark is fine, Steven.

"I think he will be okay," I add with certainty.

"Do you really think so?" Steven asks without a trace of the skepticism of the past few months. This is a promising start.

"I am very optimistic," I answer.

Mark

The futon in Shelley's den is no softer or harder than the old mattress slung over Jen's sunspot orange platform bed. Shelley helped me lower the bed from its couch position, and now I sit on its edge, stripped down to my boxers and pitched forward as if I mean to get up in a hurry. I'm trying hard not to get up and pace, trying instead to sit with my thoughts and face them. In the half hour that I've been sitting like this in this small room, I think I've looked at every feature, every piece of furniture, every knickknack and book and throw pillow and office supply at least ten times. Some things, like a red celluloid fountain pen with hexagonal sides and a gold nib, have a lot of visual interest; others, like the tossed papers in the waste basket, all white, all balled up, have little.

The computer, the fax machine, the radio, the television – all these could bring in a little of the outside world. The telephone too. It sits on the end table at my right, within reach, just underneath a lamp that not only illuminates the telephone but also casts a circle of yellow light upwards on the ceiling. It's late for making a call, but still I reach for the phone. I wonder if the plastic receiver might be hot to the touch, might burn me in warning – *Don't do this!* – but it's not. Cool and smooth, I lift the receiver to my ear. My finger finds a familiar sequence of numbers without much thought from me. I know she'll be up working. I know her so well.

"Don't hang up," I say when she answers with a curt "Hello."

"I know you'll want to, but don't.

"It's me," I say, "but you know that. I'm sitting here, here being Shelley's guest room, and I'm thinking. Which, as we both know, is always dangerous."

I hear her breathing on the other end, waiting. Even breaths, in and out, waiting for me to continue.

"I have something I want to say to you but I speak better through my work. So I'll make you a picture. It's a picture of you. You're standing, your back facing the viewer, your face hidden. I'd have to find the right color porcelain for the skin of your back, your legs. Alabaster, something with a glow to it."

Across the lines I hear something more than just the breathing. A snort of disbelief.

"No, no," I say, "it's true. You have beautiful skin. Your hair would be down, over your shoulders, and it's the brown of bottle glass. And you're looking out over a universe at its stars, planets, spaceships, a comet, aliens. There's a planet directly opposite from you, but far away. On the second planet, there's a second figure. Both of you are there in that universe but in completely different places, unreachable to each other, but still you can't help looking.

"You think to yourself you wanna find this guy, and guess what? He wants to reach you. But right now? With the spaceships you've got to work with? It's impossible. So you guys tell yourselves, we're different species; it never would've worked anyway."

Here I am rewarded with a small laugh.

"Seriously," I say. I think of my mom and dad. "The two people staring at each other across outer space have to wonder, is it better to know all that and decide it won't work? Rather than try and fail? Or to try and keep trying? What do you think?"

For a few seconds I hear nothing and then, quietly, a sigh.

"I'm sorry. I'm sorry that I hurt you. That because of my problems, *mine*, I hurt you."

Jen says, "I'm sorry too.

"So you're at Shelley's?" she asks.

"For now," I answer. "She'll let me stay but it's a good idea if I move on soon. It's been great being here. The kids are great. Margaret . . . well, her art is incredible.

"She asks about you."

"Mark?"

"Yeah?"

"Why did you call?"

That question is all Jen, her directness, her intensity.

I think about Jen's question and many things cross my mind. Deaths, funerals, Sylvie. Dad's house. Rockport. I think about flying through the air, the ground stopping me. Scars. Dad. My mother. Of both of them, checking out of my life. I think of Shelley. How my family taught me what I'm capable of destroying, but also of making.

Only one thing's missing as I go down my list, as I sort through all the people and places and things that once defined me and possessed or obsessed me. Anger. Sure I can recall it, its rough feel, its uneven shape, as real to me as a piece of broken glass. The anger's still with me but it's no longer on the list of things I think about. I don't feel compelled to get rid of my anger by smashing it into smaller and smaller pieces. Which never made it go away anyway. The only thing I accomplished by making smaller and smaller pieces of anger was making more and more of them.

Why did I call, she asks?

To say I'm sorry, I might tell her.

To say that I wanted to hear her voice.

To tell her I remember she said I couldn't come home.

But that maybe I really want to. Soon.

To say that I need what she gives me.

Or that I wish I didn't.

To tell her Shelley and I have made a decision about the Rockport house.

Maybe ask her if my decision can be good enough for her.

To say, I love you.

To acknowledge that love isn't always perfect.

Or enough.

Or that this whole fucking thing is so complicated for me. The one way maybe I'm so very much like my father, for whom the choice and the answer were also not so very simple.

Or maybe just to say, I have no clue.

I take a deep breath. "Jen," I begin.

Sylvie

My eyes are closed behind my very dark sunglasses, but I am awake and my mind is active. I lean my head back on the passenger seat headrest to catch the heat of the sun streaming through the windshield. This New England spring follows a long and snowy winter and has been, for the most part, miserable, raw and wet. I had begun to think I would never feel warm again. I need this trip to the Amalfi coast, where I am promised a hedonist's dream come true: a luxurious sailing yacht, a small group of select guests, an attentive crew, gourmet meals made with market ingredients collected daily in each port of call, regional wines, day after day of sunshine sparkling on azure water, sails full of the warm winds, lazy stalls in the middle of the Gulf of Salerno. No one on board needs to do more than eat or nap, read or sunbathe.

I need the luxury of doing nothing. Today is Friday, travel day, and so much has happened since Wednesday. At this moment Marta is driving me to the airport where I am due to board the plane to Rome. When we pulled away from the curb outside my townhouse, Marta had congratulated me on my decision to travel. "Frankly, we were all worried. You seemed so withdrawn. I'm happy to see you reentering the world of the living. Taking a trip! Enjoying life!" she enthused.

Next Marta says, "You'll probably meet a handsome Italian doctor who will sweep you off your feet!"

After one week without Jack? After all the years we had together? What could I possibly say in reply? Fortunately Marta moves on without pause to some gossip overheard at the health club about a mutual acquaintance and one of the personal trainers. She continues to prattle on and on as we zip through the city, on and on as the interior of the tunnel whizzes by once we cut underground. And on and on. I half-listen and stare out the window as we approach the terminals.

As Marta chatters, I wonder about what she has suggested. Reentering the world of the living? Dating? Although I've made my plans, I can't rightly say that this is what my trip means. I think all I intend with the trip to Italy is to get warm, to perhaps enjoy some peace and quiet after the chaos of the past few weeks. Forget Italian doctors. I mean, what should I do? Allow myself to be swept off to a villa somewhere, never to do another lick of work again in my life? Let my hips grow broad on the pasta and wine of entertaining a doctor's colleagues?

And withdrawn? I look to my left at the woman driving and talking. Marta, I think, how little you understand.

Reentering the world of the living. Withdrawn. I repeat the words to myself as Marta talks, her voice as much a part of the background as the hum of our tires over pavement. I now know what people close to me have been thinking. Poor Sylvie. Nearly one year ago she closeted herself away with her ill husband. Sure, she came to work but her mind and her heart were elsewhere: in a sickroom, worrying at the kitchen table, on the phone with doctors cataloging each new symptom of a heartless disease. Poor, poor Sylvie.

So much pity.

I could tell Marta, tell them all, no pity for me, please. I have had everything I ever wanted. Love, companionship, meaningful work created from nothing, the complete engagement with another person. Take that back to your friends in the office, to those of you whispering in the hallways or gossiping behind closed doors about how sorry you feel for me, left, bereft, as thoroughly alone now as I was completely involved with Jack until only a few days ago. Take back your pity for, despite the absent physical form of my husband, nothing, really nothing, has changed.

Marta then would look at me, confused, brows knitted together in worried puzzlement, concerned that I had gone crazy in my grief. She and all our other employees, clients, friends, the very people I looked at after Jack's funeral and dismissed with amazement when I noted that they all thought they knew Jack so intimately. In fact, those people never knew us, individually or as a pair. Never knew or understood our rare bond. They saw the surface, a married couple like so many others, but never saw the private life lived behind the doors of either of our houses.

No one could be expected to understand Jack's absence from and yet continued presence in my life. How could they, when I didn't understand myself until just now that someone so close to me could be physically gone but never, ever really absent. And how could I blame them, those people like Marta with their generic, self-help book words of encouragement, for not knowing that a marriage such as ours could continue after death when, until yesterday, I hadn't been able to conceive of that myself?

On Wednesday I went to Rockport on a whim, with the intent of clearing out my personal possessions before Jack's children laid claim to the home. I left the townhouse in a hurry without any plans made beyond stopping at a liquor store on my way to pick up several sturdy boxes for packing and a bottle of wine to drink after I finished the work. In fact, I had been in such a hurry that I nearly forgot I no longer had keys to the house. But I left anyway, crossing my fingers for one unlocked first-floor window that I could climb through.

There was so much more I had absolutely forgotten though, all the same kinds of practical things, all of which I would remember much later when the sun began to set and waning light inside coaxed a headache, when the chill made me long to crawl into bed. In my hasty getaway, I had forgotten that there would be no sheets, clean or used, waiting for me here at the house. That the house in April near the coastline is freezing and the oil burner had been shut off for months, as had the electricity. That I had no cut wood for a fire. There was not so much as a flashlight to read by. Well, not quite true: there were plenty of flashlights. There was a time when Jack and I needed them on a regular basis, back when the town's electrical supply was sensitive to high winds and storms, and we bought loads. What I didn't have was batteries.

All I really needed was the corkscrew I found in the junk drawer because the wine, if I drank enough, would give the illusion of warmth.

My arrival was startling. All over, the house screamed neglect.

Something had died inside, a bird perhaps, up in the eaves, but it was not a particularly recent death. The musty, sweetish smell of decay permeated down through all the rooms on the lower floor of the house. I noticed the smell was strongest at the bottom of the stairs, as it wafted down from the second floor landing, cloying, not quite awful but not exactly pleasant either. I considered throwing open all the windows, or perhaps hiring yet another professional cleaning service. Or maybe a pest removal service. I smiled at myself. I fell so easily into listing projects as I walked through the house (crumbling asphalt shingles, peeling paint, lifting linoleum, dry and wet rot) and forming solutions (roofers, painters, floor refinishers, carpenters) that I knew part of me would never be cured of the desire to put my fingerprints on my home. I stopped at the bottom of the stairs, my progress through the house arrested by this thought: not my home, not any more.

And yet, there I was, looking around the house and listing the projects one by one. I took in all the dust and the cobwebs and the chips in the enamel paint on the moldings and the sun bleaching on the walls, and hoped that the good hard work of renovation and restoration would provide focus while I coped with my loss. Except, I reminded myself, it would not be me doing all this work. My job at hand was twofold. I would select only what personal items I wanted to take from the house, and start packing them.

So on Wednesday I packed. Jack's collections of shells and sea stars and sand dollars, smooth stones and beach glass and driftwood. A series of framed photos of myself, candid pictures that Jack had shot and enlarged, then hung in the stairwell leading up to the second floor in sequential order, mimicking the rise of the stairs. Photos of a woman from early adulthood to middle age, photos of this woman looking at the man she loved. I stopped at the twelfth photograph nearly at the top of the stairs and ran a fingertip across the top of its frame. My finger came up with a gray clump of dust, a hair, and a small dead fly. I blew the dust from my finger and waited as it floated then landed on a stair. When it came to a rest, I pulled this last photo from the wall and laid it on top of the others in their box.

Upstairs in the master bedroom I packed my clothes: swimsuits to take on my trip, sundresses, shorts, and lightweight shirts. Eventually I would decide whether to keep, toss, or donate, but for the moment the chore was done. I packed Jack's clothes next and that was difficult. In many ways Jack's summer wardrobe better reminded me of my husband than his more usual business dress and cold-weather gear. Here at the cottage Jack was a different man, freer and more relaxed. I loved both sides of my husband but a business suit can be a man's armor. In Rockport Jack was either dressed down or naked and in bed with me. I had a much more vulnerable man with me in this house. Here he was mine, without interruption, without reserve.

Finally I packed my treasure box, tucked far back on the high closet shelf under a spare woolen blanket. I packed it without even opening it and looking through it. I had a lifetime ahead of me to do that.

When I was done I brought all my filled boxes to the front hall, and not a moment too soon. Daylight was fading quickly.

Before night fell I rummaged closets and junk drawers and made a sort of sleeping bag for myself out of a spare down comforter and a couple of large safety pins. Folded in half lengthwise with a pin at the bottom corner and another midway up the open side, the blanket was too short and too ventilated to keep me very warm. But it would have to do. At seven o'clock I took the opened wine, a glass, and my sleeping bag up the stairs to my bedroom. I climbed into bed wearing the clothes I had worn all day since leaving Shelley's house, plus a cardigan and one of Jack's fleece pullovers, musty after months of storage. There had been no light left at that point to read by so I sat propped up in the dark with the sleep sack wrapped around me as high as it would go and I drank. And as I drank I thought, but no longer of Jack or the memories of our life together. Instead, I thought of sitting in Shelley's kitchen saying, "I shouldn't be alone, but I am." I drank wine until I comprehended that I would never again be in this house, and then I drank some more hoping to forget that detail. Finally I fell asleep.

There is no need to dwell on Thursday's wine-sour morning breath or the headache that pounded behind my eyes or the irony of feeling queasy and starving at the same time. I faced the work of loading up my car and driving back to Brookline. Had I not been hung over I would have folded up my blanket, rinsed my mouth at the bathroom tap, and done what I needed to do to leave. But I needed coffee and I needed something in my stomach for energy. After cleaning up as best I could, I drove to the local market. I paid for a loaf of French bread because the thought of its dry starchiness didn't make my stomach flip, a cup of brewed coffee from one of the store's urns, and a bag of apples out of habit. Jack and I used to feast on apples when we were here, passing one piece of fruit between us, our bite marks meshing until we stripped the fruit to its core.

By the time I returned to the cottage it was after nine o'clock. The coffee was warm rather than hot but I sipped it in between bites of a split length of dry baguette, and soon enough the caffeine began to kick in. I had just taken my feast to the dining room when I heard a car crunching on the gravel drive. My first thought was: police. Someone had noticed the activity after months of none and ratted me out as a squatter.

But then I heard my name being called in high, excited tones. A woman's voice. *Marta?* Carrying my coffee I approached the screen door to see.

It was Marta, indeed.

"Thank goodness I found you before you left!" she exclaimed, nearly breathless. "I wish you'd get a cell phone."

"Marta, what are you doing here?" I asked. "Is there an emergency at work? Did someone make an offer on the firm? Come in, come in," I said holding open the screen door. "I was just having some breakfast but I don't have much to offer you."

Marta made no move to enter. "I couldn't eat a thing anyway," she said. "This is way more exciting than a purchase offer. Why don't you come out? I need the air. We can sit right here, on the front porch."

More exciting? Curious, I took only my coffee and followed her.

Marta had already taken a seat on the porch steps and had started to reach into the large tote-like handbag sitting at her feet. I had never owned a bag like hers, so unwieldy, so full of things. Key ring, glasses case, telephone, wallet, checkbook, a notepad, pocket calendar, facial tissues, a large open pack of sugarless bubble gum. She took these out one at a time until everything was in a pile on her lap. I stood still, watching, and I might have been amused if I wasn't so impatient with Marta's uncharacteristic disorganization. Finally she pulled out a piece of white paper, folded in quarters, and she waved it at me.

"Sit," she suggested with a pat on the step. "Do you know what this is?" Marta was not smiling but she sounded excited.

I shook my head. "How would I?" I replied.

Here, Marta unfolded the sheet and held it closer to show me. As she reached with her arm, she knocked her glasses case off her lap and it landed on the lower step. I paid no attention, though, made no move to reach it for her. The copier paper itself might have been anything, but the writing on it could only be Jack's. It was a copy of the letter he had written to amend his will.

"Where did you get that?" I asked.

Marta proceeded to read. "The Rockport house and all its furnishings I bequeath to my two children, Michelle M. Bennett and Mark John Manoli, to own equally between them, and to do with as they—"

"I know what it says," I interrupted. "Where did you *get* it?"

"Fax," Marta answered. "It was in the fax machine tray when I got to the office this morning."

"From Shelley," I said, then wondered, "Did they find out I was here? Is this about me being here, removing some of my things?"

I thought of my pictures, the packing boxes filled with clothes and souvenirs of Jack. My head had started hurting again.

Marta, though, continued to look at me, then a wide smile broke across her face. She laughed. "No!"

"Then *what?*" I asked.

"Read this one," she said and she reached into her bag to pull out a second letter. This time she handed both to me.

"I still don't– " I began.

Marta reached across my lap and tapped her finger on the second letter. "Read it. This one is from Shelley."

I skimmed it then rubbed my eyes. I skimmed it again and had to take a few seconds to order my thoughts. "But Jack didn't intend that, Marta. He was sick and very tired when he wrote the amendment but he knew what he was doing. He wanted the house to go to his children."

Marta held up a hand, conceding the point. "Granted. But read Jack's letter again," she said and she pointed to the line that read: "To do with as they wish."

"And that's their wish," Marta said.

"Their wish?" I repeated, feeling slow. "I haven't had enough coffee, Marta, for this to make any sense."

Marta laughed. "Then read the second letter again, Sylvie."

"'I, Michelle Manoli Bennett, being of sound mind and acting with the consent of my brother, Mark John Manoli, hereby return this house to its only rightful owner.

"While we recognize the value of the property and the sentiment behind such a gift, we also understand the house is not ours.

"This is not a sale; no money will change hands. It is a gift outright to Sylvie Rocher Manoli, the woman whom our father loved more than anything or anyone.

"The above parties, Bennett and Manoli, will not change their minds, and will not at any time seek a return of the Rockport property to themselves. They consider Jack Manoli's transfer null and void.

"They only wish to be free.'"

With this small bit of ceremony, Shelley and Mark returned Jack's gift.

The coffee in my cup had long since gone cold but I couldn't set the cup down. I couldn't relinquish the letter either. I couldn't move. As I sat I remembered how I had disagreed with Jack's idea from the beginning. How when he told me the gift was the only way he knew to give them back a piece of something he took away years ago. I had accused him of feeling guilty. In the end, though, I agreed to carry out his wishes. The only unselfish gestures of my entire life had been promises made to Jack, and I had promised to give this gift.

"That leaves them nothing," I said finally.

Marta shook her head. Her smile was kindly. "Not nothing. Freedom. It's what they said they wanted."

Freedom. I repeated the word under my breath. I had thought Jack's intention with the house had been to share with Shelley and Mark some happiness he felt they had missed as children. In fact, Jack had never actually spelled out his reason. I had made my assumptions based on what the house had always meant to us, me and Jack. Happiness.

I let the letters fall back into my lap. "I got everything I wanted packed up last night," I said, as if it even mattered any more.

At that Marta had smiled. "Well," she said, ever the practical assistant, "you have a choice. We can stay here and unpack now.

"Or you can take your time. The house is yours, you can leave everything until you get back."

"Get back?" I asked.

"Sylvie. Your trip. You leave tomorrow."

Tomorrow. Friday. Italy. Today is Thursday. Meaning Jack has been dead one week. One week dead and yet he isn't really gone. Jack has done quite a job positioning us all, realigning us in his aftermath – an amazing feat for a dead man.

Finally I set my coffee cup down. I tuck it out of sight behind a porch rail. I hand the papers back to Marta who puts them back at the bottom of her purse. I think of the piece of French bread sitting on the dining room table, growing staler and harder by the second, and I realize how very hungry I am.

"Let's stop somewhere for breakfast and then head back into town," I say to Marta. "I have a trip to get ready for."

Traffic into the airport is heavy but moving. Our car glides on past the outer terminals, soon to stop at the final, international one. We've been quiet in the car for the past fifteen minutes as Marta concentrates on navigating the traffic and following the signs. Arrived, she pulls over to the curb. "Here we are!" she says brightly. I turn from looking out the window and meet Marta's gaze. She wears a cheerful smile that fades into concern upon seeing my face.

"You're crying," Marta says.

"No, I'm not," I answer with an indignant laugh.

Marta reaches her hand across the divide between us in the front seat and touches my cheek below my eye. She holds her wet fingertips in front of me. The sun through the windshield reflects off the tears and her fingers glisten.

"Yes," Marta nods, "you are."

I bring both of my hands up to my face and wipe, smearing the tears out across my cheekbones. "There," I pronounce, "gone. I didn't even know I was crying."

Marta takes my hands and squeezes. "You're tired. But you'll see, soon you'll feel like getting back into life. You go, have a good rest," she adds.

A rest. My purported reason for being here, curbside at Logan airport, preparing to board an Alitalia flight. Skycap is right outside and a porter appears at my window, taps it with his knuckles. Marta holds one finger up, telling him we'd be out of the car in one minute.

"Sylvie, are you ready?" she asks.

Ready? I realize that by this time on Monday I will be wearing nothing more than my bikini bathing suit and my tan because at my age I look fine. Since I never had children, I have a flat stomach and no stretch marks. I exercise, my upper arms have definition, and my thighs sport no saddlebags or cellulite. The only place my body shows its age is in the loose skin over my knees, my personal battle with gravity. My knees have always been bony but where the skin once stretched it now droops. None of the men on the boat, I know, will object to my body in a bathing suit based on this one flaw. I might even find I'm happy with the attention. Or content at least.

But ready?

"I'm not ready," Jack had said to me more than once over the last few weeks of his life.

"I know," I had answered.

I had hoped for more time. I had hoped that my life with Jack might continue. I had even hoped when I thought of this trip that I might meet Jack on it. Not as if meeting after an absence, not picking up where we left off, but meeting fresh at our present ages. I know if we were able to meet for the first time today, on this plane, on the yacht in Italy, in a grocery store checkout line or seated next to each other at a concert or at the party of a mutual friend, we would take notice of each other. We would eventually become lovers, I am sure of that; we were two souls destined to be together.

Oh, Marta, I don't need to feel better about getting back into a new life, I long to tell her. My adult life has always been about Jack, as his life was about me; why should anything change now? It won't. The house is mine, it is mine, it is mine! Not as a tomb or a prison, a place to stagnate, but as a vessel to take me further away than any airplane or sailing yacht, right into a very real past and into a just as vividly real future, past and future both with and about Jack. In the car I turn in Marta's direction and smile to myself at my fantasies.

Again, Marta misunderstands my gesture. She reads in my spontaneous smile gratefulness instead of the wistfulness I always aim at people who aren't as lucky as I. She reaches across the front seat to hold me in a tight embrace as the porter impatiently taps the window once again. "There you go. You'll see," she whispers into my ear.

Oh, but I already do.

Jack

I can see my fatigue now, and it's a black spot like a large floater in my field of vision. The spot grows, starts to cover what I can see around me in the death room and even inside my mind. Sylvie obscured, Shelley fading, Mark all blurred edges. As the black disk widens, I wonder if the dark field is sleep again, or death, my body finally succumbing to the fatigue of having lived my life over in light speed today.

The sun sneaking through the crack in the blinds tantalizes. I want to be out in the sun, to feel the sun on my face. I want to be outside: driving to work with my wife, then walking briskly with her down a city sidewalk, both of us in a hurry to make the meeting. I want more time with Sylvie, I want more time to experience everything: sight, touch, sound, taste, smell, thought; children and grandchildren, friends, work, the home I've made with Sylvie. I would like more beautiful days, more time outside walking in this sunshine. I would like to be healthy again. I would even take sleeping alone in this room forever if I could be healthy again.

It is spring and I would like one more healthy summer, at the very least to stay alive through August. I want the Rockport summers back. I want more time so that Sylvie and I can finish the work on the Rockport house. I want more of the sun over the ocean and the incessant wind off the water and the lobster boats and the quarry and our little house.

And there it is. I want more of the possibility that is life. Possibility coiled in one more day, hour, minute and, yes, second; possibility coiled and waiting to spring. Possibility was at the root of all my decisions – that a young woman might fall in love with me, that in choosing her I could live the way I wanted. There was always, I see now, potential in the mistakes I made, the potential to become a better person and a better father. There is also the possibility that a son may suddenly appear, kneeling next to a bed, extending his hand in peace. I want to be around to extend my own. I want more time to wait for Mark.

I said regret was pointless and circular because after all I wouldn't have changed a thing. But the truth is I do regret hurting Mark. I would change that, turn back time on that phone call if I could. But of course I cannot.

Death and possibility and Mark. I let the words swim around my mind; I see them as clearly as I saw my memories earlier. Thinking and concentrating make me tired, the words swim and they start to make no sense. They break apart and my sloppy mind becomes alphabet soup. I sigh and exhale a great amount of mental energy with my breath. All of a sudden there it is, the feeling as my diaphragm rises and lowers. This new tightness, is it the cancer or just a heaviness in my heart, the combined weight of my failure and Mark's rage? Christ, this is a low moment, acknowledging no other possibility exists but death.

I feel my body giving itself up to sleep against my will and it makes me angry. No, I'm not ready, I refuse to give in yet. When have I ever been ready to accept any predetermined course in my life? I think of all that Sylvie taught me those many years ago, in the first few weeks of coming to work with me: Think. Question. Challenge. Change. No, coming to terms with my mistakes is not enough for me, accepting my flaws and then dying is not enough.

Sylvie asked questions. What if? Why not? How come? So *think*, Jack.

All right then, all *right*. I'll think.

If there's no hope of seeing Mark again, then what about a different kind of possibility? The possibility of making things, if not exactly right with my son, better. Making reparation.

The Rockport house appears to me, not in its whole but in pieces, individual characteristics peeking out like a teasing imp from behind the black spot. I know that up north the sun shines on our empty house on its secluded lot at the end of a gravel road. Although empty of people, the house is not quiet. The strong wind off the ocean rattles wooden casements, and the house creaks and groans with settling. To me, it seems alive.

The house has pretty lines and classical proportions. Small and fronted with a porch, it is painted bright farmhouse yellow with an emerald green front door and window trim and shutters. Gingerbread trim runs the pitch of the peaked roof overhang, but by now, after this year of utter neglect, loose gutters and the resulting poor drainage must have caused rot. Perhaps the trim cracks, even crumbles in places.

Once inside, past the banging screen door with its too tight springs and after a few steps across an entry hall, I am always overwhelmed by the colors. When we first moved in, Sylvie had painted the pine kitchen cabinets with several coats of aqua semi-gloss. She had always hated the rustic look of the pine, so that was the first change she made. More recently, Sylvie, unhappy with the dated look of her chosen color, had decided we should partially strip the paint. Removing the top layers dulled the gloss finish to a nicer faded turquoise on the few cabinets we were able to finish. More work remains. Worn linoleum flooring covers a wide-plank pine floor, pumpkin pine, named for its rich pumpkin and spice hue.

This gem of a floor peeks out from a patch of lifting, curling linoleum, its rescue and refinishing yet one more project on a long list.

A steep staircase bisects the first floor, and the stairwell itself holds one of the home's most striking features: a succession of black and white portrait photos, twelve in all, of a woman taken at different stages of her life. The progression of photos follows the rise of the stairs and the aging of the subject. Softly pretty in youth; a certain plumpness around the cheeks recedes with age; finally, the older face with its more elegant bone structure, its beauty more evident in maturity.

Despite all the beauty inside and out, what I imagine most clearly is that the house shows its age and suffers from neglect: the rotting gingerbread, the worn and lifting linoleum, peeling paint, patches of gouged plaster. Gutters sag under the weight of waterlogged leaves and maple seedpods and wads of pine needles. Cobwebs fill the corners and a layer of dust dulls the glass and frames of the photos. I can imagine all this. The basic structure remains good, however. Miraculously no water drips in through the roof, no insects have invaded. Give the house a little love and care and who knows what beauty will be revealed. Even in its present state of disrepair, the house is not lost. Someone could fix it, could prime and repaint, replace and maintain the gutters, install copper flashing, lay a new roof, rip up the dated linoleum, sand and poly the floors, move in furniture, cool all the vibrant interior colors with neutral area rugs, hang gauzy curtains in all the windows to blow with the breezes . . . . Someone could love this house.

I can even imagine that in agreement, in satisfaction at the very idea, as if *alive*, the house groans and sighs once more.

By some sixth sense, Sylvie knew that the house would come to belong to us, in deed as it had in spirit, perhaps because we had claimed it in such an animal and territorial way, marked every inch of it with traces of ourselves. By virtue of the intensity of our stolen visits there within that one year, the house became more ours than my client's. His rentals dropped off; he too lost interest. When he offered it to us, he said the house finally felt dead to him, dark and joyless. Sylvie and I would swear the house was alive. We surely felt it urging us on. We married, we bought the house, we lightened and brightened it with paint, with the energetic reds and yellows we loved most. A soft chamois yellow entry and hallway and stairwell. The living room in a pale gold. The kitchen in the red of faded bricks, a surprisingly successful match with the scrubbed aqua. A burnt orange dining room, its vibrancy softened by lines from a favorite poem stenciled in gold around the uppermost perimeter of the walls: *My true love hath my heart, and I have his, By just exchange, one for the other given.* Unsentimental Sylvie surprised me with that. Between us and that house, anything was possible.

On the heels of these images – the colors, the house, me, Sylvie, Mark, *possibility* – comes a plan. It's a convoluted one, not an idea that makes a great deal of sense on its surface, but neither did many of the decisions I made throughout my life, and anyway, I stopped seeing only the surface of things a long time ago. Once past the surface of my decision, what do I expose?

I see the sun rising on a place I loved, one that I created, a place full of love.

I see a young girl with too many responsibilities for her age, biting her nails in the back seat of my car.

I see too an angry boy, his life stunted by anger, and I can't think of anything better to give that boy than an understanding of the healing possibilities of love. An understanding that he doesn't need to forgive me so much as he needs to let me go.

So tired, so much pain, but I can't give in to it now. I have to wait for Sylvie. I've said it before, awareness above all is very important to me. I need to stay awake and remember everything I've thought about so that I can tell Sylvie when she gets home. You want to know where Mark got his defiance? Fuck this fatigue, fuck the pain. How alike Mark and I are, I think, in refusing to do what's expected of us.

"It's okay that Mark isn't here," I said when Shelley told me she wished Mark would come to see me. I hoped that she understood what I meant then. I had paid no attention to duty and I shouldn't expect it from others. I hurt him; he shouldn't be with me if he doesn't want to be. I squeezed Shelley's hand as tight as I could so she would pay attention. I really did mean it. Of all the things I've learned over the course of my very full life, the thing I appreciate most is that a person can only control his own destiny. And even then . . . well, look at me. I made myself the happiest man alive and I'm still dying.

I believe I hear a door opening but it seems so far away. The nurse reporting for her shift, or perhaps only a noise from outside, a car door or a footstep or someone's mail slot slamming shut once relieved of the weight of another day's mail. I continue to think and hone my plan because it is all I have left to keep me connected to the world of the living. Maybe the noise I hear is Sylvie, home early, which would be a real gift because of all the ideas I need to share with her. I'm very sleepy, I'm in agony, but I need to wait for her. She has been a good, good wife.